THE LIST

A Novel

STEN SVEHN

HSJ Publishing

THE LIST

First edition, 2026.

Published by HSJ Publishing, Rancho Santa Margarita, CA, USA

For permission requests, contact: stensvehn@gmail.com

ISBN Paperback: 979-8-9951667-9-5

ISBN eBook: 979-8-9951667-4-0

LCCN: 2026911949

THE ORDER

THE LINE BETWEEN LIES

1973–1990

THE LIST

1990–1993

THE NEW FIRE

1993–2000

AUSPEX

2008

'There are six others. I do not know who runs them. The seventh is mine.'

—Margaret Howell, in eight pages retrieved from a Zurich safe deposit box, March 1990

INTERNAL MEMORANDUM

6 February 1990

RE: CALDER, James—FINAL DISPOSITION
DESTROY AFTER READING

The Vasilieva asset was terminated at Webber Street on the third of January. Two rounds. Makarov. Architectural signature.

Twenty-four hours later, the Greenwich substitution was compromised by an unregistered second party. The body that reached the Iowa channel weighed eleven stone. Calder's medical records place him at thirteen.

The two-stone margin is the ghost in the ledger.

Calder is active. Calder is carrying the FEUERWERK file. Calder has begun a list. The list is unfinished.

The Conclave is advised: reclassify from *subjecta extincta* to *subjecta sub vigilantia continua.*

The hunt is the appropriate watch.

Pax in tutela.—Peace through the watch.

PERSONS OF INTEREST

PRINCIPAL FIGURES

Calder's Network

JAMES CALDER. b. 1942. MI6 officer—officially dead since January 1990.

KLAUS MÖLLER. b. 1939. East German. James's friend since a Stasi cellar in 1969.

EDMUND (EDDIE) FREARS. b. 1932. Welsh. Lisbon armorer. Ex-22 SAS.

MARGARET HOWELL CALDER. b. 1935. James's ex-wife. Latinist.

HANNAH DOYLE. b. 1951. American. CIA officer. Brother killed by the institution, 1988.

The Custodians (Custodia Auspiciorum)

THE CUSTODIA AUSPICIORUM. Founded c. 391 CE, in the years Theodosius outlawed the old Roman augury. Its keepers moved their work underground. Continuous since.

THE CONCLAVE. Its governing body. Rome. Seven men.

THE SEVEN COORDINATORS. Its regional executives, operating under the Conclave.

Historical Anchors

ELENA VASILIEVA. Russian. KGB illegal. Killed January 1990.

EDWARD WALTER MASON CALDER. b. 1905. James's father. Trinity, 1945.

(The list is incomplete by design.)

ACT I

1990–1991

1

GREENWICH

January 1990

12:34. Thursday.

He took the long way back from Century House. He walked across Westminster Bridge and along the South Bank to Greenwich. He paid the bus fare in coins for the last leg because he wanted his hands to be doing something. He had eaten nothing since the previous night, when Andrew Ruskin had climbed the stairs to the Greenwich flat with a manila envelope and the message that the woman he had met at the Mayflower would be delayed getting to Greenwich and would arrive by ten. She did not arrive by ten. She did not arrive in the hours after it. Some hours before dawn he rose from the sofa and wrote, in four paragraphs, the resignation letter he had been planning for two weeks. He laid the photographs on the Chief's desk that morning and the resignation letter on top of them, and walked out of the building a little before ten with his face composed into the neutral arrangement of a man who had finished the only thing he ever needed to finish.

The arrangement had held across the bridge. It had held along the river. It had held on the bus. Calder did not know how much longer it would hold.

The arrangement had been built, in the hours since he had set the letter down, around a single face. The face was on six of the eleven photographs Calder had laid on the Chief's desk that morning. The face was a man's face: late fifties, clean-shaven, receding hairline. The man was on the curb outside the Mayflower on the evening of the third of January, his right hand at his side, the gold signet ring on the little finger of the right hand visible in two of the six frames. The photographs had come through the Greenwich letterbox at some hour after midnight. Calder had not heard the slot. He had found the manila envelope on the mat when he had got up to write the resignation. The man's name was Laurence Henry Thornley. The Chief had noted the face in the half-second before Calder set the resignation letter on top of the photographs, because the Chief had been a year behind Thornley at Trinity and had stood at Thornley's funeral in Kent a decade and a half before. Calder had stood at the same funeral. Thornley was a senior man whose Vienna and Beirut briefings Calder had taken as a young recruit. He had expected, then, to work for Thornley one day. The expectation had been ended by the small obituary in the Telegraph and the small Kentish service to which the Service had not sent flowers because the Service had not, by the institutional convention of the period, sent flowers to its own.

Calder had not thought of Thornley in fifteen years. The Chief, by his face at 09:30, had not either. The photographs had introduced a fact the Chief had spent the next forty-eight hours not yet finding the institutional language for. Calder had not waited for the language. He set the resignation on top of the photographs and walked out, because the walking-out was the only operational instruction the photographs had left him with.

He let himself in with the key the bookseller's widow had given him three years ago. The widow was in Devon, as she had been every first week of January.

The hall smelled of cigarettes.

He never smoked. He never permitted smoking in any flat he

kept. The smell registered. He knew it in the same instant. His face did not change. His hands did not move. He had been trained out of involuntary recognition in a room above a tailor's shop in Bonn.

He understood, in the same instant, that the thing he had been told at the Mayflower Hotel forty hours earlier was the true thing. Elena said her real name aloud—the first time she had said it to anyone since 1970. She had laid the dossier on the wooden table of room 14 with the considered precision of a woman setting down sixteen years of work. He told her, across the dossier and the unopened envelope and the small yellow lamp, that he had known about Lillehammer since 1977; that he had been keeping his colleagues from looking at her for thirteen years; and that the keeping was the only operation he had ever been proud of. Margaret was not in the room. She had been in Ealing, asleep or reading, entirely unaware that the woman whose name she had never learned was, at that hour, naming the silver key on her bracelet across a wooden table to him. The bracelet was four silver charms on a thin silver chain —a small open book, a sitting cat, a heart, the letter M. Her mother had clasped it onto her wrist at sixteen on a Saturday afternoon in 1951 in the kitchen of a Norfolk farmhouse. A fifth ring had been left empty at the clasp. Her mother had said, in the dry tone she kept for small dry truths, that the fifth ring was the one Margaret would fill herself when she found a thing worth filling it with. Margaret had worn the bracelet for twenty-six years without filling the ring. Calder had filled it in November of 1977 with a silver key. The bracelet had told him, last November, that Margaret was running her own operation. He did not ask. His silence was the thing they still had.

The watch on his left wrist—a military-issue face on a worn civilian strap—had been Margaret's Christmas gift. He had worn it for sixteen years. He had not, in all of them, looked at the case-back deliberately. He wore it the way a man wore a wedding ring he had stopped registering. The wearing did not change when the marriage ended.

Four weeks earlier he had taken the watch in to be cleaned by an East German friend named Klaus, who was between Hamburg jobs and performed the service over three days at his flat as a private favor. Klaus had returned the watch on the eleventh of December with the case-back resealed and a note in German on the workbench saying the movement had been cleaned and the wipes had been replaced and the action would now run smoother by approximately fourteen seconds a day. Calder had noted the precision of the note and the precision of the gift and the way Klaus did favors and had not asked. His silence had been the discipline of the year.

Calder took a quick breath.

He opened the door to the front room.

The two men were in the armchairs by the gas fire. Their coats were folded across the arms. Their hands were not.

The first man held a Walther PP, threaded barrel, Swiss aluminum can, eight-round single-stack magazine. .32 ACP. 90-grain hand-loaded subsonic. Klaus had chosen the round because .32 ACP did not have the energy to punch through the scapula into the lung. He chose the PP because the smaller frame sat flat against his ribs under the wool overcoat and did not print at the closing of the door. The second man held a Makarov PB. Soviet integral suppressor, two-piece, 9×18mm. The same instrument the Russian woman he had loved for sixteen years had owned. The same model another woman named Dina had used the previous evening at 18:14 to fire two rounds across a worktable on the second floor of a building on Webber Street—the first round into the chest, the second a quarter-second later and higher because the body was already folding forward. The Makarov was pointing at the floor.

The first man he had known since 1969.

The second man Calder did not know.

Klaus did not look at him directly. Klaus looked at a point about eighteen inches to the left of his head.

Calder smiled.

He had not, until two weeks ago, known the smile would be a smile. Klaus had come to the Chiswick study late one evening that week, let in by Margaret, who went upstairs and stayed there. They sat at the desk for the better part of an hour. Klaus told him, in the six concise sentences he used for things Calder needed to know in their irreducible form, that the institution had specified him and a second hire for the Greenwich kill. Margaret identified the specification through the channel she would not name, and Klaus agreed to be the first hire on the condition that the second hire would be the body that went to Iowa. The signal would be a smile. The smile would tell Klaus that Calder had reached the half-second beyond which there was no other operational room, and that he was choosing the half-second over the alternatives. The choosing would be Calder's. Klaus would not choose for him. Calder said yes before Klaus rose to go. Margaret came down a little later, set a cup of tea on the desk, said I am going to bed, and went back upstairs. She did not ask what he said. The unasked question was the thing they still had.

The smile was now the smile.

The second man—the one with the Makarov—saw it. He did not understand what he was seeing. He had been trained in many things; he was not trained to read a smile delivered at gunpoint.

Klaus fired.

The Walther coughed twice—the suppressor and the subsonic .32 ACP combining to put the report at the level of a heavy book closed too hard. The first round entered Calder's right shoulder at four feet, slightly above the clavicle, traversed the trapezius, glanced off the upper edge of the scapula without penetrating the chest cavity, and exited through the back of the shoulder into the wall behind him. Klaus had been a marksman with a sidearm for decades and had been instructed, in the same Bonn back room where his own Stasi runner had instructed him in the only reliable non-fatal shoulder shot, that the only reliable non-fatal shoulder shot was the shot that did not enter the chest cavity. The shot did not enter the chest cavity. The wound bled. The wound did not kill. Calder went down.

The second round, fired in the same instant by the same hand in a different direction, entered the second man's chest at four feet, slightly left of the sternum, through the left ventricle, severing the anterior descending coronary artery before lodging in the upholstery of the armchair behind him. The Makarov dropped. The second man slumped forward in the slow boneless way men slumped when their lungs stopped being lungs. The collar of his white shirt darkened to the second button in the sheeted absorption of a hundred-and-twenty-millimeter exit pattern at the back. He tried to speak. The trying produced a fine pink froth at the corner of his mouth—the air from the failing left lung passing the bubbling pool of arterial blood that had begun to collect in the trachea. His left hand opened and closed once on the upholstery, the fingers curling against the woven brocade in the specific reflex motor neurons fired in the last six seconds of cerebral oxygenation. His bowels released into the trousers. His pupils dilated to the limit of the iris. He looked at Klaus. He understood, in the second of the dilation, that he was the man the architecture had specified by weight and not by name and that the specification had been the form his death would take. The understanding did not save him. The closing of the left hand did not finish. The body settled into the armchair the way bodies settled when the body had been carrying a man for twenty-six years and was now no longer carrying him.

Klaus stepped past the body. He crouched beside Calder. The

Walther went into his coat pocket. His left hand went to Calder's shoulder, above the wound, in the inward curve at the base of the thumb that Calder had noted the first time he had felt it in 1969, in a basement in East Berlin, when Calder had come down the stairs at 03:42 and lifted Klaus from the concrete floor of a Stasi holding room where Klaus had been bleeding for six hours.

Klaus said, in the flat voice Calder had heard him use exactly once before, in the same basement, with the same hand on his shoulder: 'Stay down. The bleeding will be enough. The cleaners are nine minutes out.'

Calder stayed down.

The second man weighed eleven stone.

Calder weighed thirteen.

The two-stone margin was the margin of the morning. It was also the decision. Calder had decided, in the room above the Mayflower forty hours earlier when Elena had laid the dossier on the wooden table, that he was going to be dead to the architecture and alive to the work. The man in the chair with the Walther in his pocket was the form the decision had taken. The man on the floor with the unfired Makarov was the cost.

Klaus had calculated the margin three weeks earlier, when the architecture had specified the second hire by name and weight at a back-channel briefing in a hotel in Hanover. He noted, in the quiet clinical way he cataloged such things, that the man the architecture had paired him with was a man whose body could pass, in the rendering machinery beneath an Iowa hog barn, for the body of a thirteen-stone Englishman if no one looked closely. The architecture would not look closely. It had not looked closely at any of the bodies it had processed through the same machinery in the previous thirty-four years.

Klaus took the photograph of Margaret from inside Calder's

briefcase and laid it on the second man's chest, glass-side down. He took Calder's MI6 access card, expired the previous morning, and folded it into the second man's wallet behind a Boots receipt. He took the gold wedding ring from Calder's left hand and worked it onto the third finger of the second man's left hand. The finger was the right size. The finger was always going to be the right size. Klaus had specified the second hire's ring size in the same Hanover dossier. He had known Calder's ring size since the winter of 1977, when Calder had come to him in Bonn with the gold band catching on a Hoppe's tin and had asked for a set of fine tools to widen the shank. Not asking why had been the discipline of that year.

The body went into the plastic sheeting Klaus and the second man had brought up the back stairs that morning, intended for Calder.

Calder said, looking at it: 'He doesn't have my face.'

Klaus said: 'The body will not be in a state to have a face by the time it arrives in Iowa. There is a farm. There is machinery beneath a barn. They render it the way they render the hogs. There will not be a face. There will not be teeth. There will not be bone a pathologist could type. There will be a manifest weight and a wedding ring and the registration of the freighter and the ledger of the rendering and the slow patient discipline of an institution that has been not-looking at this kind of body for thirty-four years.'

Calder nodded once. He understood it then, in the wet warm pulse of his shoulder against the wall: he was now two men. The man on the floor in the plastic sheeting was the Calder who would arrive at the Royal Albert Dock that evening manifested as agricultural processing equipment. The man bleeding against the wall was the other one. The two would not converge again. The dead man would go to Iowa with Margaret's photograph and the wedding ring, and the private fact of his existence would dissolve into a fine bone-and-tissue meal across a continent and the inside of two thousand hogs. The living man would walk down a back staircase in fifteen minutes and become the work the dossier on a wooden table in Bermondsey had been preparing him for. The architecture would believe in the dead man. Margaret had constructed the believing. Klaus had constructed the believing. Elena, who had begun the constructing in November of the previous year by laying her real name across a wooden table beside a folded dossier, would not get to see the believing completed. The cost of the believing was the woman in a workroom at Webber Street whose body Dina had folded forward at 18:14 the day before. The cost of the believing was sitting in the plastic sheeting at his feet. The cost of the believing would be, in the months and years to come, things he had not yet identified.

He noted the arithmetic. He did not let it reach his face. The face was the only thing he had left to manage.

Klaus was looking at him. Klaus had seen the look pass.

Klaus said, quietly: 'Yes.'

Calder said: 'Yes.'

Klaus checked the room. The Makarov on the floor where the second man had dropped it. The Walther in his own coat. The wallpaper behind the armchair where the second man had slumped, with the spray of arterial mist on the brocade in a fine arc the cleaners would render to the wall in seventeen minutes with a bottle of bleach. The window. The kitchen door. The corridor.

They went down the back stairs. Klaus's cleaners—two men he had used twice before—would be in the flat. They would carry the second man, in his plastic sheeting, with the wallet and the wedding ring and the photograph of Margaret, down to the black panel van Klaus had parked in the alley behind the bookseller's shop at 11:30. The van would take the body east to the Royal Albert Dock for the freighter Atlantic Compass, manifested as agricultural processing equipment, sailing on the evening tide for Norfolk, Virginia. The cleaners would render the upholstery and the wallpaper to a state the metropolitan police would accept as a struggle that had ended badly for one party.

Klaus had the Land Rover on Crooms Hill, parked at a meter he had fed on the way in. They walked the two streets to it without hurrying. Klaus drove south through Greenwich, then east, then south again on the A2.

They were three blocks away when Calder said: 'There was someone.'

'Where.'

'I saw a Ford Sierra in the alley when I came in. There was a man at the boot.'

'Trevor Cooper. The widow's son. Drove down from Surbiton to pick up a Christmas package his mother had left for him.'

'He saw me.'

'He saw a building inspector with a Yorkshire accent and a clipboard and a fictional file number. I had three years on a Leeds cover in seventy-six. The accent will hold for thirty seconds against a man on a doorstep, which is what it had to hold for.'

'You did not kill him.'

'I did not.'

'Why.'

Klaus drove for another block.

'He was wearing a brown jumper. He had your ex-wife's shoulders. I could not do it. The jumper was also terrible. I could not kill a man in a terrible jumper.'

Calder did not say anything for the rest of the drive.

They drove south. Klaus took A roads, not motorways. The A roads took longer. The A roads were not photographed.

Calder lay in the back seat under a wool blanket. The blanket smelled of dog. Klaus had borrowed the Land Rover from a man in Whitstable.

It was a 1981 Series III in the long-wheelbase 109 chassis, the kind of working vehicle a Kentish dairy farmer kept for thirty years. The 2.25 diesel started on a glow plug after fourteen seconds. Klaus had counted. He counted to four in his head when they walked to it. He counted to fourteen when the engine took. The cabin smelled of dog and damp Wellington and the small farmyard residues that had been settling into the seat fabric for nineteen years.

Klaus did not comment on the count. The Land Rover had nearly not started. The Land Rover was the part of the morning that was outside the briefing dossier, outside the Hanover cell's expectation, outside Klaus's own three-year arrangement with the man in Whitstable. The cold front that had come up the Channel overnight had aged the diesel by three degrees in its pre-chamber. The glow plug had needed the extra ten seconds to do the work that four normally did. If the cold front had been one degree colder, Klaus and Calder would have been on the back stairs of the bookseller's flat with no transport, the second hire's body in the plastic sheeting in the front room, and the cleaners not yet arrived.

The work had margins like that, Klaus thought, and then did not think about it for the next four hours.

Late afternoon, he pulled into a service station near Maidstone. He had doubled back twice across the river through Bromley and Sevenoaks; the journey had taken three hours and forty minutes for what should have been ninety. He filled the tank himself, paid in cash, bought two Mars bars and a copy of The Times. He came back to the car. He got in. He passed one Mars bar over the back seat to Calder.

'Eat.'

Calder ate the Mars bar.

'The Times,' Klaus said, passing it back. 'Page nine. Three paragraphs.'

Calder turned to page nine.

There was a notice in the lower left. British civil servant dies in Greenwich incident. Police investigating. No further details available at time of going to press. The article gave no name. The article was three paragraphs long. The article's tone was the institutional tone newspapers used for civil servants who had died in incidents the police were investigating, which was to say neutral, brief, and not the tone newspapers used for civil servants who would have a name and a photograph in the morning edition.

Calder folded the paper. He put it on the seat beside him.

'They're confirming,' Klaus said, watching the road. 'They will not have a name until tomorrow. By tomorrow we are in the harbor. By the end of the week the obituary is in the paper. By Monday the obituary is the only thing the architecture has of you.'

Calder did not answer. The architecture would by Monday have decided to accept the eleven-stone body as Calder. The architecture would have decided this because the alternative—publicly hunting a man whose death the architecture had publicly confirmed—was the kind of operational humiliation institutions did not survive. The two-stone margin would be filed under the operational fictions institutions accepted in order to keep their internal record consistent. The architecture would record the substitution as Calder. The architecture would also, separately and quietly, begin a second internal accounting that would in time produce its own document. The two accountings would not contradict each other. They would simply not refer to each other.

He filed the registration.

They drove.

They reached the channel port after dark. Klaus paid the trawler captain in fifty-pound notes from a Marks and Spencer carrier bag.

The crossing was rough. Calder vomited over the rail twice, but only because of the sea, not the work. The bandage Klaus had put on the shoulder in the back of the Land Rover had soaked through twice in the same hour. Klaus had changed it once on the trawler and not commented on the bleed.

'This is the easy part,' Klaus said. 'You will look back on this crossing and miss it.'

They arrived at an Atlantic port before dawn the next morning.

The building was three stories. Stone below the second floor. Wooden beams above. Klaus had selected it for use in exactly this contingency. The window of Calder's room faced the harbor. The wooden beams creaked in the wind in a way that was something between a ship's hull and an old man turning over in his sleep. The bakery woman lit her oven before dawn. The smell of the oven reached the room within the half-hour. Klaus had decided on the room because of the bakery.

Klaus had laid in the provisions days before. A sack of coal, four blankets, a kettle, three tins of corned beef, half a bottle of Grouse—the scotch Klaus had been drinking since 1968—a tin of Lyons tea bags, a bunch of dried lavender from a market in Bayonne, a Welrod, a Walther PPK, four boxes of 7.65mm Browning, and the cleaning kit Eddie Frears had sent ahead from Lisbon.

There was, in addition, a folded note Klaus had left on the kitchen table under an enamel mug. The note was in German, in

Klaus's careful hand. It read:

James—the Welrod is your grandfather's pattern; the rounds are old Belgian manufacture from a batch I have been holding for you. The wipes inside the can are old. Five clean firings, perhaps six. Eddie is sourcing replacements. The kettle whistles before it boils. Count to three after the whistle. The harbor will be the harbor.—K.

The grandfather's pattern reference Calder understood. His paternal grandfather, Arthur Calder, had been a forty-two-year-old Cumbrian estate manager when the Special Operations Executive had identified him as a man whose Norwegian was good enough to be useful and whose discretion was good enough to be trusted. Arthur Calder had spent three weeks at Arisaig, had been issued a Welrod, and had used it on a single occasion against a German harbormaster in Trondheim. He had returned the Welrod to the SOE after the war. He had not spoken about the work to his son or to his grandson. Klaus had been given the file in Berlin years earlier by a Hungarian counterpart who had been carrying it since a parallel-service exchange Moscow had run on aging Norway operations. Klaus had been carrying the knowledge for years.

The five-firings note Calder also understood. The Welrod was nineteen years past its last service. The rubber wipes inside its can were old. Five rounds was the operational instrument the morning had given him. The morning had not yet asked him to fire any of them.

'Drink it. Then sleep. I will be in the chair.'

Calder drank the tea. He lay down on the bed in his coat. He did not sleep until morning.

He lay listening to the bakery oven warming below him in the dark. He thought, in the not-sleeping, about the Ronson lighter she took apart on her kitchen table in Kensington. The watchmaker's screwdriver in its felt roll. The roll she bought for four pounds at a shop on Portobello Road. The small mechanical care she gave to objects that did not need it because the giving was her way of being still alive in a flat that was not hers. He watched her once, from the doorway, with the lighter in pieces on the table and her hair fallen forward and the precise movements of her hands. She did not look up. The not-looking-up was the work she was doing on herself. He had not, in those years, known that the Ronson had not been a Ronson. He learned in the autumn that the lighter was a Soviet camera with a half-millimeter burr on the cable release housing that Elena had filed down at her kitchen table on a Tuesday evening with the watchmaker's tool kit because the institution that sent her did not build instruments to the tolerances she needed for her own hand. The mechanical care was, in the doing, the mechanical care of a woman fixing a thing the institution gave her wrong. It was also the other thing. The two things were not, in her hand on the screwdriver, distinguishable. They were the same hand.

He thought, also, about the Sunday afternoon in the autumn of 1985 when she had taken apart a Bakelite radio Margaret had given her—given to Alice Marsh, in the Kensington bookshop in December 1973, by a woman who had never learned the name beneath the cover. Elena was told it was thirty years old. She was certain, by the screws, by the wiring, by the arrangement of the speaker housing, that the radio was older—and she had asked him, with her hands on the back panel and her hair fallen forward, what year the radio was from. He said: 1956. She said: I would have said 1948. The silence afterward was the silence of a woman registering that she was wrong about a thing she had been certain of. The wrongness was a mercy. It meant the thing she had been certain of was a thing one could be wrong about, and that the wrongness was the small permission for everything else of which she had been certain for sixteen years.

She had laughed. The laugh was the only laugh he had heard

her give that had not had any operational shape inside it.

He filed it in the private file he had not yet given a name to.

2

THE HARBOR

An Atlantic port—winter and early spring 1990

On the morning after they arrived, Klaus said it.

'She is dead.'

'When.'

'The evening before last. Approximately eighteen-fifteen. A workroom on Webber Street.'

'Who.'

'I am not going to tell you today. In three days. You are going to sleep and eat what I cook and walk on the breakwater and on the third day, when you are not the man who walked into this room last night, I will tell you. I have known the answer since the morning I met you on the bus.'

'Who decides when the time is right.'

'I do.'

'Why you.'

'Because I have been waiting twenty-one years to be the man you owe a debt to. I am calling it in. Eat your soup.'

'There is no soup.'

'There will be soup. The bakery woman has potatoes.'

Klaus left.

Calder lay on the bed and looked at the ceiling. The ceiling had a water stain in the upper corner above the wardrobe. The water stain was the shape of a country he could not immediately identify.

He did not cry. He thought he would. He did not. The not-crying sat in him like a stone that had not yet found its weight.

That night, and on most nights of the first three weeks, he dreamed the same dream. The dream was a tight kitchen with a black-and-white tiled floor and a Russian woman across the table from him. The woman was talking. He could not hear what the woman was saying. The not-hearing was the dream. The dream ended when he reached across the table to ask her to repeat herself and she dissolved at the wrist into the photograph of the East Berlin apartment window at the Paxton Gallery in Fitzrovia—the curtains, the geranium on the sill, the Wall beyond—the gallery where he had met her. He did not tell Klaus about the dream. The silence was the work.

On other nights the dream was two rooms. In the first room Margaret was at the kitchen table in Chiswick, her hands folded on the wood, the bracelet catching the light from the window above the sink. In the second room Elena was at the Mayflower, the lamp low and yellow, the dossier between her hands and the empty chair where he was sitting. The two rooms were the only rooms the two women occupied in his sleeping mind. The dream moved between them without corridor or door. Margaret looked at the wall. Elena looked at the dossier. The two women had never shared a table. The dream did not require them to.

He remembered, in the second week, an evening in the Fitzrovia studio in the autumn of 1985 when Elena had been at the kitchen counter chopping a small dill cucumber with a paring knife, with the radio playing the World Service in low Russian-accented English, and she had said, without looking up from the cucumber, that the small word *prosto*—simply, plainly—

was the most dangerous word in her language. The architecture had been using it for forty years to mean its opposite. Any time a Russian official told her something was *prosto* she had been trained to assume the something was elaborate, classified, and not for her to ask about. She said, then: 'When I tell you a thing is simple, James, I will tell you in English. The English does not yet have the disease. It will, in time. The English always catches the diseases of empires. We have a few years before it does.' She finished the cucumber. She had laid the knife flat on the board the way her grandmother had taught her in a Leningrad kitchen years before. She had not looked at him while she had said it. The averted gaze had been her gift.

On the third day Klaus told him about Dina.

He confirmed it through three channels. The Makarov PB she had used was the weapon Werner Bruhn had placed in her hand before his death in 1983—the Stasi major who had handled Elena across the Berlin years—an instrument held unfired for seven years by the patient operational accumulation. The kill had been authorized by a board of three men in Vienna whose composition Klaus did not yet know. Two rounds. The first into the chest. The second a quarter-second later, higher.

Calder vomited into the porcelain washbasin.

Klaus stood at the window with an F6—the East German filter cigarette, the one from Leipzig—and lit it with the chrome Ronson Varaflame he had carried for years. He said nothing. There were three trawlers at the quay and a fourth coming in. One of the men was swearing at a winch. Klaus listened to the swearing.

'I told you the easy part was the crossing.'

That was all he said.

Calder did not vomit again at the harbor.

When he had rinsed his mouth and was sitting down again, he found a cup of tea on the desk. Klaus had set it there without comment. The tea was too hot to drink. Klaus was not a man who knew what to do when men cried. He was a man who knew what to do when men vomited. The tea was his gesture. Calder drank it slowly. It scalded his lower lip in a place that would heal.

He noted, in the small sip of scalding tea, that the man he had been on the morning of the fourth, laying photographs on the Chief's desk and walking out of Century House, was not the man drinking tea on the third day at the harbor. The man at the desk had been finishing a thing. The man at the harbor was beginning one. He had a name now. The name was delivered by Klaus across the porcelain washbasin and the cigarette and the chatter of the winches outside the window. He did not say the name aloud. He did not need to say it. The name was already the file he would carry on the walks on the breakwater. He would carry it on the runs along the cliff path in March. He would carry it on the morning in Marseilles when the breakfast tray would go up to the dressing-gown man at oh-six-fourteen, and the file would not close until the name had a body the way Elena had a body, and the body would not be found by the men who were paid to find such bodies. The body would be found by him. The finding had a date. The date was not yet on a calendar. The date would arrive when the work the harbor had been built for had built him into the man who could go and do the finding. The finding was the work. The work was now revenge. He marked the word. He did not retract it. The word was the right word. He let it stand.

The harbor had its own light in February.

The light came up at first light over the breakwater on the eastern side, low and wet and the color of old pewter, and worked its way along the wooden quay through the gap between the chandler's shop and the bonded warehouse before reaching the second-floor window of the room above the bakery half an hour after that. The water in the lee of the breakwater was the color of slate that had been wet for a long time and was not yet allowed to dry. Out past the breakwater the water was the color of slate against which someone had been striking another piece of slate and was doing it for forty thousand winters. The wind off the Atlantic at first light came in at the angle the channel had been built around in the seventeenth century. The bell-buoy on the eastern reef rang on a count of eleven seconds in calm weather and on a count of seven in bad. Calder learned the count in the second week. He learned the count without intending to. The count was the form the harbor took in his sleep on the nights he slept.

The quay machinery began at oh-five-fifty. The trawlers came in between dawn and full light depending on the haul. The winches were old British equipment from the early sixties and the larger one had a three-stroke chatter on the lift that was the sound he came to know first by the absence of which on the morning the smaller boats had stayed in. The chatter was the sound of the harbor working. The not-chatter was the sound of weather coming. The fishermen knew the absence of chatter twelve hours before the BBC shipping forecast did.

Klaus cooked badly.

He had been cooking badly for as long as he could cook. Corned beef stews. Kartoffelpuffer—German potato pancakes—with the potato shredded too coarsely and the egg insufficient.

The room had its own smell within a week. Coal smoke, corned beef, dried lavender, and underneath it all, cordite from the Welrod cleaning kit.

On a Wednesday morning a fish appeared on the doorstep, wrapped in three-day-old pages of the regional Bordeaux paper, the Sud-Ouest. The oldest fisherman in the harbor, a man with a face like an old saddle, had left it before dawn and gone back to his boat.

'You have made a friend.'

'I nodded at him.'

'In this part of the world that is the same as marrying him.'

The fish was terrible. They ate it.

The following Wednesday a different fish appeared, smaller, fresher, wrapped in the same three-day-old paper. Two Wednesdays later it was a pot of cockles in salt water. After that the saddle-faced fisherman returned to fish, but never the same fish twice in a season—mackerel one week, sole the next, once a small octopus that Klaus had refused to clean and that Calder had cleaned poorly and that they had eaten anyway. The fisherman was making a running argument with the doormat about variety. Klaus, who understood arguments of this kind, did not interrupt it.

In the second week the bandage on the right shoulder needed changing. Klaus did it. He laid in two surgical pads, a roll of cotton, a bottle of iodine, and a small jar of zinc oxide ointment from a pharmacy in Bayonne, all in a flat tin he had wrapped in oiled paper and brought up the stairs without comment. Calder sat on the edge of the bed without his shirt. Klaus knelt beside him. The pad came away. The wound was at the second stage, the flesh beginning to take the small purple-pink declaration of new tissue along the entry mouth and at the exit, the surrounding skin still yellow-green from the bruising. Klaus cleaned both openings with iodine on a folded square of cotton. The hand that did the cleaning was not the hand of a man who had not done this work before. The hand had, in the years Calder had been at his desk in Century House, cleaned a number of wounds in a number of small rooms in a number of cities, and the hand had developed the small economies of pressure and angle and timing that were the difference between cleaning and adding to the harm.

Calder did not speak.

Klaus did not speak.

Klaus laid the new pad. He cut three lengths of tape with the folding scissors he kept in the tin. He fixed the pad. He put the iodine and the cotton back in the tin. He took the tin away.

In 1969 Calder had cut Klaus loose from the cuffs of a Stasi holding chair at 03:42 with a knife borrowed from the man Calder had killed on the basement stairs. He pressed Klaus's left side closed with a folded section of his own jacket lining for the eleven minutes it had taken for the second extraction team to come down the stairs and take Klaus from him. The pressing was the first time he had touched Klaus. The cleaning, twenty-one years later, was Klaus pressing his way back along the same minute. Neither of them named it. The silence had been doing the work between them for twenty-one years.

The wound began to take, in the third week, the rounder and more disciplined shape a wound took when the body had decided it was not going to lose the man.

In the second week of February, on an operational walk Klaus had sent him on without explanation, Calder went south to the fishing port of Sète on the Mediterranean. The walk was the first walk. The walk was a route check for the journey he would make to Marseilles in March. He had been told to take the train down, walk the harbor for an hour, and come back. He had been told to be a man going for a walk in a port that was not the port he had been a man in for the previous month.

The man came at him in the cobbled alley behind the Criée aux Poissons at twenty-two-fourteen, with a small folding knife already open in his right hand and the urgency of a surveillance asset who had been sent without backup and had been told to make the closure look like a robbery. The man was about thirty. He was operational. The man had identified Calder by the photograph the institution had been carrying since the morning of the fifth of January. The man had decided, on the cobbles between the fish market and the chandler's wall, that the closing would be the work of the next eleven seconds.

Calder did not have a weapon. The Welrod was at the harbor. The Walther was at the harbor. The right shoulder, four weeks into healing, was not yet at the strength a fight would ask of it. The left arm was the arm.

The blade came forward at the angle a man trained for close work brought a blade forward. Calder stepped inside the angle. He took the man's right wrist with his left hand, turned the wrist outward against the joint, and brought the heel of his right hand up under the man's jaw on a short driving angle that did not require the shoulder to do more than report the work to the body. The jaw closed on the tongue. The man's head went back into the chandler's wall behind him with the wet sound a skull made when the bone met old stone. The knife dropped onto the cobbles between them. The blade had come off his left forearm in the turning, a line of heat through the wool of the sleeve that the body filed and did not yet rank as pain. Calder did not let the wrist go. He turned the wrist further. The radius cracked at the styloid. The man's face went white in the half-second the central blood pressure registered the break and the dark had not yet had time to come up. Calder picked the knife off the cobbles with his right hand, the right shoulder reporting the clean line of pain it would report from now on whenever the work asked the right side to do something the right side was not yet ready to do. He brought the blade up under the man's ribcage on the left, on a slight upward angle, into the hollow beneath the false ribs that was the angle a Bonn instructor had drawn on a chalkboard in 1968 with the dry notation: 'The pump is under here. The pump is the work.' The blade went into the pump. The pump stopped within the instant.

The man went down at Calder's feet on the cobbles. The blood came up in a slow heavy pulse for two beats and then stopped pulsing and began the slow patient seep that was the seep a body did when the heart had stopped doing its work. The cobbles around the body darkened. The blood ran along the cement seams of the cobbles in the way liquid ran along seams it had been built into the stone to follow. The slope of the alley was a quarter-degree toward the harbor. The blood found the slope. The blood ran toward the harbor on a private route an old port had been running such liquids on for four hundred years.

Calder went through the man's coat. He took the wallet. He took the small spare clip from the inside left pocket that the man had not had time to bring out. He took the folded sheet of paper with the photograph of Calder taken at Heathrow on a previous travel day. He took the brass key on a leather fob that would, by Klaus's reading the next day, be the key to the rented Peugeot the man had left at the train station with a Lyon plate. He left the knife. He wiped the stone where his right hand had braced against the wall with the inside of the man's coat. He walked to the end of the alley. He went down the harbor wall. He took the train back at oh-four-fourteen.

The shaking that had come up on the morning of his future Marseilles work was the shaking that did not come up that night. The body had found, in the alley, the argument with itself that the harbor would not have produced for him in a year. The argument was the work. It did not need the mind's permission. It had been waiting for the cobbles, and now it had them. Klaus, when Calder came in through the kitchen door before first light, looked at the small stiffness in the right shoulder, and at the dark stain on the cuff of the left coat-sleeve that the train lavatory had not entirely taken out, and at the careful half-inch the left arm was being held off the body, and said: 'You took the long route.' Calder said: 'I took the long route.' Klaus said: 'Sit. The arm first. I will get the iodine.' He cut the ruined sleeve away. The blade had opened the outer forearm along its length, shallow at the wrist and deeper toward the elbow, the lips of it clean the way a good edge left them. Klaus closed it with the butterfly strips from the flat tin and did not ask which of the two men in the alley the knife had been meant for, because the answer was in the wound and the wound did not need translating. They did not name the alley.

Late one night, at 03:14, a footstep in the hallway outside the door.

Calder was awake. He had not slept since 22:00. He was sitting on the bed with the Walther in his right hand and the FEUERWERK file—the operational dossier he had been compiling at Century House for years on hidden munitions beneath civilian buildings across Europe—face-down on the coverlet, doing the breathing exercises a Bonn instructor had taught him for nights when sleep did not come and would not come. The civil-defense inventories on page nineteen of the file were not inventories of canned food. His father had spent his working life at the other end of the process that had produced the things being inventoried. He had not yet, in those early weeks at the harbor, let himself name the connection that the file was beginning to ask him to name. Leaving it unnamed had been the discipline at Century House for six years. The discipline was now, on the bed in the second-floor room, beginning to move.

The footstep was in the hallway.

It was a single footstep. There was no second.

Calder set the file down. He moved off the bed without sound. He went to the door. He stood beside it, against the wall. He chambered a round in the Walther—the slow careful chambering, not the fast one—and held the gun at low ready against his thigh.

He listened.

There was no second footstep. There was no breathing. There was no key in the lock. There was, beneath the silence, the sound of the harbor—the bell-buoy, distant, and the wind in the wooden beams above the second floor.

He waited.

Forty minutes.

He heard a door open and close two floors below. The door was the front door of the building. He went to the window. He looked down. A man in a workman's coat was walking away from the building, carrying something draped over his shoulder. Calder watched him to the corner. The man turned right onto the rue de la Mer. He was gone.

Calder uncocked the Walther. He returned to the bed.

In the morning Klaus came in with the bakery bag and saw the file on the coverlet and Calder's face.

'What.'

'There was a footstep at 03:14. Forty minutes later a man left the building carrying something draped over his shoulder.'

Klaus thought about this.

'The landlord's widow's adult son. Came down from Bordeaux yesterday evening. He was retrieving his mother's winter coat. She had asked him to bring it to her in Spain. He let himself in with his mother's key. The widow's coat was hanging on a hook in the hallway.'

'You had this confirmed.'

'I have a man at the bakery counter. Old Henri. He sleeps in the back from midnight to dawn and watches the front door from the window beside his cot. He saw the son come in just after three and leave just before four. He is not the bakery woman. The bakery woman thinks I am a sad Norwegian and gives me potatoes. Henri thinks I am a German who pays him in cash on the second Sunday of every month. Both are correct.'

Calder considered this.

'I almost fired through the door.'

'I know.'

'You arranged the watch on the door because you knew I would.'

'Yes.'

'How long has the watch been arranged.'

'Since the second of January. The widow believes she rented to a Norwegian merchant whose business is sad and whose business does not concern her. Henri has a long memory and a short pension and is content with both.'

Calder ate the bread Klaus had brought.

'I would not have heard the door just after three,' he said. 'I would have heard the footstep at 03:14.'

'You did. You did the right thing. You did not fire. The work was holding it. The firing would have been a different work.'

They drank tea.

He thought about Margaret, on the third Sunday at the harbor, while watching Klaus chop onions at the kitchen counter with the small economy of a man who had been chopping onions for forty years. The watching produced, without his asking it to, a memory he had not opened in ten years.

A Sunday morning in the Chiswick kitchen, years before. He

came down early. Margaret had been at the kitchen table with a gray notebook and a fountain pen. She closed the notebook before he had reached the doorway. She closed it without looking up. She had, in the closing, registered him and not registered him in the same second. He noted the closing. He did not ask.

He registered, that morning, that they were two operatives in the same kitchen.

He had not, until now, retrieved it. He retrieved it on a Sunday in February in a harbor flat above a bakery, watching a Hamburg hydrologist chop onions at a counter, and registered for a second time, ten years late, that the marriage he was not allowed by his work to attend to had been attending to him without him.

One night Klaus drank too much.

He had been drinking by mid-afternoon. By late evening the Grouse was three-quarters gone and Klaus was sitting at the desk with both elbows on the wood and his head in his hands. He had been talking for an hour.

'I was married,' he said. 'Briefly. A woman named Inge who was not in the work. She left me because I would not tell her where I went on Tuesdays. I told her on a Sunday in October that I was a hydrologist who had been recruited by the Stasi and had been spying for British intelligence and that my Tuesdays were operational. She listened. She said nothing for fifty minutes. Then she said: I prefer the lie. The lie was a man I could marry. The truth is not. She left on the Tuesday following.'

Calder answered: 'I did not know.'

'No. I did not tell you. I told you about my mother. I told you about my hydrology degree. I did not tell you about Inge because Inge had been an operation of my own, and small operations of one's own are not for the ledger. I am telling you now because I am drunk and because we are in this room together and because the woman you loved is dead in a workroom on Webber Street and I have been thinking about Inge for the first time in years.'

'Is she alive.'

'I do not know. I have not looked. The looking would be a separate operation. I have not had time for the looking.'

Calder thought about this.

'I have three children,' Klaus said.

He set his glass down. He did not look at Calder.

'Two I have not seen in ten years. Ilse is eleven. Lukas is ten. Their mother lived in my building in Wiesbaden and was not married to anyone and had decided I was sufficient. I left before Lukas was born. The mother had not asked me to stay. The mother told them their father had died of cancer because the story was operationally easier than the story of a father who provided money but not himself. The story is also easier for them to live with than the story of a father who is alive and does not visit. I have decided in the last hour that the story may be wrong. I am not yet sure.'

Calder was quiet.

'And the third.'

Klaus did not answer for some seconds.

Then he said: 'The third is older. The third is from before. The third I do not speak of tonight. The not-speaking is the part of her I have been keeping. Some hour I will tell you. Tonight is not that hour.'

Calder did not press it.

'Names,' he said.

'Ilse. Lukas.'

'Ilse plays an instrument.'

Klaus looked at him. 'How did you know.'

'I am guessing. You said Ilse first. The first name is the one with the picture beside it.'

Klaus almost smiled.

'Recorder. Three years. Her Wiesbaden teacher gave her a recorder when Ilse was seven and she has been carrying it in her school bag since. The mother sent me a Christmas card a few years back with a photograph of the children on the front step of the building, and Ilse had the recorder visible in her left hand in the photograph. She did not want to put it down for the picture. The mother had not made her. The mother had let her hold it. The letting was the small kind thing the mother continued to do without me.'

'And Lukas.'

'Lukas catches with his left hand. The same Christmas card had him holding a small ball. The ball was in his left hand. I had been right-handed all my life and his mother had been right-handed and I had spent some weeks after the photograph thinking about what it meant that he was not. It meant nothing. It meant his hands were his own.'

He poured himself another measure.

He sat for some time with the glass in his hand and did not lift it.

Then he said: 'Tonight is permitted what an ordinary discipline would not permit. The evening has earned what an ordinary evening would not.'

He drank.

'The third child is Marianne. She is in Lyon. The mother is Renate, a woman I knew briefly in Lübeck on an early operation that did not appear in any service's register. Marianne is twenty-one. She teaches flute at the music conservatory. She has my mother's mouth. I have visited Lyon four times in the past eighteen months. I have seen her three times. I have not introduced myself. The not-introducing is the gift I am giving her until I have decided whether the giving is also a kindness.'

Calder was quiet. He understood that Klaus was telling him a thing Klaus had not told anyone in ten years, and that the telling had cost more than the drinking, and that the telling had not finished with the names.

'Three children,' Calder said.

'Three children.'

'Klaus.'

'Yes.'

'Thank you.'

Klaus did not respond for a moment. Then he produced a leather wallet from the inside pocket of his coat and took out a single black-and-white photograph of two children on a Wiesbaden front step—a girl with a recorder in her left hand, a boy with a small ball in his. The photograph had been creased in three places from the wallet. He set it on the desk beside the empty mug. He left it there for the rest of the evening. He did not put it back in the wallet that night. In the morning it was gone, returned to the inside pocket of his coat. Calder did not mention it.

Some weeks in, Calder opened the FEUERWERK file.

He had been carrying it since the day he had walked into the Chief's office with the photographs. The file was thirty-seven pages. He read through. He was looking for one thing—a note he half-remembered making.

He found it on page nineteen. His own handwriting, in the margin of a memorandum about Italian civil-defense inventories:

Karlsruhe is not where the file says Karlsruhe is.

He had no memory of writing it. The memorandum it was beside had nothing to do with Karlsruhe. The memorandum was about Aosta and Trento.

He closed the file. He went to the breakwater. He picked up a flat stone. He skipped it across the harbor water. It skipped three times and sank.

Three skips was not a record. It was not a failure. It was a fact.

He went back upstairs. He sat at the desk. He opened the FEUERWERK file again. This time he read it through.

What had been on page nineteen was the marginal note in his own handwriting that had pointed him at the pattern. The pattern itself had been on pages eleven and twenty-four and thirty-three. The same architectural irregularity in each: a basement whose published square footage did not match the Land Registry extracts. By fourteen square meters in the first building. By twenty-two in the second. By eighteen in the third. The mismatch was the pattern. Eight buildings across eight European cities. Eight basements with the specific volumetric discrepancy that meant something had been built into the basement that was not on the building's plans. Something approximately the size of a steamer trunk. Something the visa records of two-man inspection teams in a different section of the file had been visiting on an eighteen-month rotation for three decades.

Each of the eight buildings was, by the particular architectural fact of its postcode, within four kilometers of a civilian nuclear research facility, a power-station siting study, or a thorium-fuel laboratory whose funding had been quietly terminated between 1958 and 1965.

The buildings were apartment blocks. The apartment blocks were occupied. The Italian civil-defense inventories on page nineteen were not inventories of canned food and bottled water for civilian shelter use. They were inventories of munitions. The munitions were not on any official register and the buildings were not military installations. He had been compiling, for six years, a file on hidden weapons stored beneath residential buildings without saying the word weapons to himself. The silence was the work the file had asked of him from the morning he had opened the first folder.

He had not, on first reading, understood what the discipline was preserving. He understood now. The file's compiler—the version of himself who had been at Century House between 1983 and 1989—had been pointing, in his own neutral procedural prose, at twenty or twenty-one or twenty-three small architectures of catastrophe distributed across European cities the file's compiler had walked through in his university years and had loved without reservation.

He did not yet have the count. He had eight buildings, eight cities, eight basements. The basements were beneath buildings whose ground-floor residents currently had their shoes by the door and their kettles on the hob. The devices in the basements had been there since 1962. The residents had been there since whenever they had moved in. The residents had signed leases. The residents had paid their rent. The residents had lived, for thirty years, above a thing that their governments had placed beneath them and had not told them about, in the manner of an institution that had decided the not-telling was the keeping.

He set the file down on the desk.

He had not yet allowed himself the private grief the body had been carrying since the morning of the fourth of January. The grief was waiting in a folded place under the ribs. It would wait. The work was the keeping of the grief small enough that the work could continue.

He thought, also, about the inside of Elena's left wrist. The compass rose she had drawn there at eighteen in spring 1966 with the needle hot from the lamp—four directions, a dot at the center, shop-bought ink, the precise proof that some part of her was not going to fully consent to what was already being arranged. He had been the dot for sixteen years. He had not, in those years, asked her what the four directions were for. He was waiting for her to tell him. The waiting was now the silence the telling had left behind it.

He held the rose where it was.

He thought, also, about two women at two tables. Margaret at the Chiswick kitchen, pouring tea from the blue pot she had bought at Portobello market the week after the wedding into the blue mug she had used every morning of the marriage, the bracelet catching the light from the window above the sink. Elena at the wooden table of room 14, the dossier between her hands, the lamp low and yellow, not raising her eyes. The two women had never shared a room. The two women had shared him. The pouring and the choice not to raise it were the disciplines of two women who had each been doing the work without the other's knowledge, and whose work had converged, forty hours before the body swap, in a hotel room one of them had never entered.

He held the convergence beside the compass rose.

He thought of the geranium. The photograph at the Paxton Gallery in Fitzrovia in October 1973. An East Berlin apartment window. Domestic curtains, half-drawn. A potted plant on the sill. Past the plant the Wall, and past the Wall the death strip raked into parallel lines no foot was permitted to leave a mark on. He said, the curtains are the detail. Elena said, it's a geranium. They're almost impossible to kill. The first sentences they spoke to each other. The half-second after, when both their masks dropped at the same time and each looked at the other person under the cover and chose, in the same fraction of a second, not to say so. The masks went back on smoothly, the way two musicians returned to the score after an improvised bar. He did not understand on the evening what he had been looking at. He was looking at it for sixteen years.

He thought of the tie. The dark gray with the thin maroon stripe she had given him for his birthday in 1981. On the morning of the third of January at the Mayflower his hand had reached for it without choosing. She had reached across at the door and straightened the knot at his throat. Her face had been close enough to read the faded scar at the corner of his left eyebrow she had cataloged in October 1973 and had finally been close enough to ask about across the dossier the night before. She did not ask. The closeness was the answer. Her fingers were against the wool and the wool was against the artery and the artery had been louder than either of their breaths. Her hands had been shaking. Neither of them had said her hands were shaking. The Mercator knife was in her handbag. The Welrod was in the inner pocket of her coat. The shaking had been everything that would not fit in her hands.

He banked the geranium beside the tie, the tie beside the compass rose. The file was the ledger he was keeping without yet knowing what the ledger was for.

On the evening after Calder returned from Marseilles, when Klaus came back from the bakery with the loaves and the small twist of olives, Calder asked the question he had not, in twenty-one years, asked.

'What is it called.'

Klaus put the loaves on the desk. He sat down in the chair with the loose front leg. He took a black notebook from his coat pocket. He did not open it. He held it on his knee.

'It has six Latin syllables. Most people in the work who have noticed it do not say the syllables. The syllables are Custodia Auspiciorum. The Custody of the Auspices. The auspices are what the Romans took from the flight of birds at the threshold of a war or the founding of a city, and the custody is what an institution keeps when it has decided that the keeping is too important to be left to the elected. The Custodia keeps three things. It keeps the small atomic demolition munitions that the Italian and German services and the French and the Belgians and the British, in the years across the sixties, buried in the basements of civilian apartment buildings within four kilometers of every nuclear-research siting on this continent. It keeps the silence around them. And it keeps the patience to be slow about both. There is also a fourth thing it keeps that I have not yet been able to identify. The fourth thing is a Latin word that recurs in the dossiers without explanation: *auspex*—singular, neuter, the diviner who reads the auspices. The institution uses the word as if the word names a physical object. I do not yet know what the object is. I have been reading the dossiers for the object for some years. The object is not the bombs. The bombs the dossiers name plainly. The auspex they do not name. The absence of the name is the thing about the auspex I have been registering. We will find it in time.'

Klaus said: 'One more thing about the keeping. The Custodia did not invent itself. It inherited itself. Margaret has been working on the genealogy for some years and has, by the seventh page, traced it: from the College of Augurs at Rome, through the chanceries of Byzantium, through the Venetian Council of Ten in the fourteenth century, through the Habsburg court astrologers of the seventeenth, into the boards of the European clearing houses of the twentieth. The men who sat in those rooms had each, in their own century, considered themselves authorized to read the omens for the rest. The vehicle changed. The vehicle is now boardroom and a phone in a Brussels kiosk and a basement under a piazza in Rome. The authorization did not change. The men who claim it are the men who claim it. The Custodia is the long form of a habit two thousand years old and Margaret has been making the argument, in her notebook, that it is the same habit, in the same hands, with a different set of capital cities. She may be right. She may be making the kind of argument a Latinist who has been reading the same texts for thirty years makes when the texts begin to talk to her. We do not yet need to decide. The decision is not yet ours.'

He drew breath.

'The architecture has two tiers. The lower tier is operational: seven Coordinators across seven regions, each one running the cleaning in his own arc. Seven who execute. Above them, seven who govern. The upper tier is the Conclave—a separate body of seven men in Rome, distinct from the Coordinators, who do not run the cleaning but authorize it. They eat carbonara in a trattoria in Trastevere on the second Friday of every month and do not write anything down. Fourteen men, in two tiers, governing the architecture. They have not, in all the institution's long memory, been operationally activated as a Conclave. They are the institution's reserve. They will be activated when the architecture has been operationally threatened to a degree the seven Coordinators can no longer manage. The activation, when it comes, will be the institution's last instrument. The activation has not come. We may, in some year I cannot yet name, be the fact that brings the activation. Beneath the Coordinators there are operatives. The operatives clean. The cleaning is what was done to the engineer in Tadley last March and to the metallurgist who fell on a Sunday walk near Burghfield in May and to the journalist who was killed in Antwerp in 1971. The cleaning is what was done to the small woman in the workroom on Webber Street on the third of January. The Custodia is what we are working against. The Custodia is what your ex-wife has been working against for nine years. The Custodia is what the eight pages will tell you about, when we have them. We are not going to be able to dismantle it. We are going to be able to take seven names off it. The seven names will be the seven Coordinators. The seven Coordinators will take some years. We will not finish all seven. The taking will be the work.'

He set the black notebook on the desk. He had not opened it.

'That is what it is called.'

Calder did not respond for some seconds.

Then he said: 'The man on the curb outside the Mayflower.'

Klaus did not look up. He cut the bread instead, into the careful slabs his Bremen grandfather had cut bread in.

'Laurence Henry Thornley,' Klaus said. 'Born Vienna, the fourteenth of March 1931, to an English father and an Austrian mother. MI6 from 1953 to 1967. Vienna, Beirut, Nicosia, Geneva. Transferred in 1967 to a NATO counter-proliferation desk that does not appear on any published chart in any of the four services that maintain it. Officially dead in a motor accident on the A21 in September 1974. The car was empty. The man who drove it off the road died of a heart attack four months later. Your Chief attended the funeral. So did you.'

A pause. He laid the slabs in a careful row on the wooden board.

'Thornley is the administrator. The Conclave is the reserve. The seven Coordinators are the regions. Between the seven and the seven is one man. He keeps the books. He selects the weapons. He signed the order that put the Makarov in the workroom on Webber Street. He chose the Makarov because Lillehammer in 1973 had been a Makarov. The institution likes its work to rhyme. The hand on the order is left-leaning. The hand has been left-leaning since the man was a Trinity recruit.'

Klaus set the knife down beside the bread.

'There is a single sheet of carbon paper in a metal box at Highgate Cemetery, buried in November of 1986 by an English journalist whose work the architecture has been trying for fourteen years to silence. The sheet is titled, in pencil, *4-SVC P*. Beneath the title, in four columns, are the names of twelve senior officers across CIA, MI6, BND, and SDECE who agreed in writing, in early October 1974, to treat Thornley's existence as a classified asset whose operational activity would not be acknowledged by any of the four services individually or jointly. The agreement is forty years from running out. We are going to be running, you and I, before the agreement runs.'

Then Calder said: 'And the mark. The eight rays and the eye.'

'The mark is on the things the Custodia has touched in public. Banknotes. The corner of the Le Monde masthead. The lintel of a Geneva bank. The watermark of a Bundesbank twenty. The mark is the proof that the Custodia is not separate from the institutions. The Custodia is inside them. The mark is the vanity of an architecture that has decided, after thirty years of patience, that it can afford to sign its own work.'

'And the theta.'

Klaus looked at him.

'You have seen a theta.'

'In Marseilles. The back of the Hôtel du Vieux-Port. A doorframe at the rear stair. Inside, chest height, chalked.'

Klaus thought for some seconds.

'I have seen one theta. In a basement in 1969. I assumed it was graffiti. I am no longer assuming.'

'Two thetas.'

'Two thetas. We will come back to this. The eight-ray sun is the institution's mark. The theta is something else. Something that is on the underside of doorframes, in chalk, where the eye of a man going out the back of a hotel would catch it without intending to. I do not yet have a category for it. I will tell you the two things I am sure of. I have never once found it on anything the Custodia has touched. And both times it has been at the threshold of a room a man walked out of alive.'

He picked the black notebook back up. He put it back in his

coat. He cut the bread.

They ate.

Calder said, in the small voice he was keeping for the question he had been holding since the bridge: 'And Elena.'

Klaus did not put the bread down.

'Elena had been seeing the institution since the night she killed Petrov in Lillehammer in 1973. There was a Western nuclear journal on the man's writing table—Nucleonics Week, four months old, folded open to a column on the failure rate of British mixed-oxide fuel-handling, the column circled in pencil—and a folded Italian newspaper under a saltshaker on the kitchen counter, two years old, headlined Incidente nelle miniere. The headline was an Apennine mining accident the institution had produced as a fizzle from a warhead it had been moving through a sulfur-mine tunnel network in southern Sardinia. Petrov had been thirty-one minutes from being the second man in the Western intelligence community to identify the institution. Elena had walked past the table. Elena had filed the journal and the clipping in the same second she filed the slippers on the feet of the man she had just shot. The filing was the beginning of her own ledger. She had been carrying that ledger alone for the sixteen years between Lillehammer and the Mayflower. The dossier she laid on the wooden table for you at twenty-hundred hours on the second of January was the ledger's last entry.'

He cut another slab of bread.

'There were others. A Stefan Voss in 1977—an East German chip engineer at a Kombinat in Erfurt whose radiation-hardened logic was the brains of the small munitions the institution had been moving since 1968, and whom Elena walked east through Checkpoint Charlie under cover of being his BND contact. An Andrei Lebedev in 1983—an IAEA analyst in Vienna whose suitcase, when Elena opened it on the eleventh of August before she killed him at eighteen-forty-six, contained twelve sheets of typed paper predicting nine institutional radiological events to the month, each one identified in advance by between twelve and twenty-one months. The Voss chips are on page six of your ex-wife's eight pages. The Lebedev predictions are on page seven, in the column that crosses page six. I will tell you the rest of those two when we come to the pages. The pages will be the right place.'

Klaus set the bread knife down.

'Lillehammer in 1973. Geneva in 1976 with Hatch and the Italian inventory. The corridor at Checkpoint Charlie in 1977, which is the one she did not finish. Vienna in 1983 with Lebedev. Friedrichshain in 1987 with the child in 2B. The Spanish embassy in October 1989. The Mayflower in January 1990. The ledger is the trajectory. The trajectory is the work. We are completing the trajectory. The names on the page are the men whose elimination is the trajectory's arithmetic, save the one your ex-wife has been keeping.'

Calder did not respond for some seconds.

Then he said: 'She was alone with it.'

'She was alone with it for sixteen years,' Klaus said. 'She is not alone with it now.'

Klaus came back from Bayonne one afternoon with a black eye and a leather pouch of pencils.

'You will write three names.'

'I have only two.'

'Then you will write two and a question mark for the third.'

Calder wrote, in 2H pencil:

1. Vernet, Henri. Marseilles.

2. Brückner, Wolfgang. Berlin.

3. ?

He put it in the oxblood leather notebook he was keeping at the harbor since the second week, identical in maker and binding to the one Margaret had taken from his study desk at Chiswick a month before the Wall came down, the absence of which from his desk drawer he had registered the morning after she had taken it and had said nothing about. He bought the new notebook from a stationer in Bayonne. Klaus had paid for it. He had been writing in it without intending to write in it, the way a man wrote in a notebook he had been carrying for a reason he had not yet fully named.

'There is something I would like you to know.'

'Yes.'

'My ex-wife wrote a sentence in pages I do not understand. There are six others. I do not know who runs them. The seventh is mine.'

Klaus took down the Grouse. He poured them each a measure into the chipped enamel mug that had held the Bayonne lavender.

'I have been thinking about that sentence. I have understood that I do not understand it. That is a different thing.'

'Yes.'

'Your ex-wife was wasted on the geraniums.'

'Yes.'

They drank again.

On the last day of the sixth week, Calder walked to the breakwater at dusk.

The bell-buoy was making its small mournful noise, a higher note in the wind that had come up from the southwest at four o'clock and had been pulling the buoy harder against its line for the last hour. Three trawlers at the quay. The saddle-faced fisherman on a coil of rope mending a net. He nodded. Calder nodded back.

'Bonsoir.'

'Bonsoir.'

Calder stood at the end of the breakwater. He thought about Vernet, alive in Marseilles and weeks from his Tuesday morning. He thought of Brückner, alive in Prenzlauer Berg.

He went back upstairs.

Klaus made a soup that smelled of onions and a stock cube the bakery woman had given him out of pity.

'It is terrible.'

'I know.'

Calder did not lift the spoon for some seconds. The not-lifting was the private silence the body had been holding before meals for as long as the body could remember without ever having named the holding. Klaus, across the table, did not comment on the not-lifting. Klaus was watching Calder do it at tables in Bonn and West Berlin and Vienna for twenty-one years. Klaus had not asked.

They finished it.

Klaus came in one afternoon with a paper bag from the bakery and the smell of cigarettes on his coat. He sat in the chair with the loose front leg. He set the bag on the desk. The bag held two loaves, a packet of butter, and a paper twist of olives the bakery woman had pressed into his hand because she had decided he looked like a man who needed olives.

Klaus opened the twist. He ate an olive. He spat the pit into a saucer.

'Marseilles.'

Calder looked at him.

'Henri Vernet. Sixty-seven. Retired SDECE—France's Cold War foreign intelligence service. Hôtel du Vieux-Port for five months. Wife buys croissants on Tuesdays. He opens his door for the tray.'

'How long is the window.'

'Nine days. Three Tuesdays.'

Calder folded the page with the three names. He put it in the notebook.

'Tell me what he did.'

Klaus did not open his notebook. 'Last autumn. Vienna. He gave a deposition to a board of three men at oh-nine-fourteen on a Tuesday morning—the architecture has its preferred hour, and that is the hour. The board does not appear in any directory. He named her. Gave them the name and the timeline and the operational pattern. The deposition was the procedural authorization. Order issued in November. She was killed in January.'

Calder did not move.

'Confirmed her,' he said.

'Confirmed her. Lillehammer, the Mossad mistake of seventy-three—the wrong Norwegian waiter who bled out on a hotel pavement. The deposition cited the registration of an art historian on a hotel ledger four blocks from that pavement.

Vernet confirmed it. Vernet had been carrying it since November.'

Klaus ate another olive. 'The bakery woman has decided I am a sad Norwegian. The olives are her solution. She has produced them at increasing intervals. I will be a sad Norwegian for as long as we are in this harbor.'

Calder said: 'Are they good.'

'Adequate. The pits are too small. A small pit suggests a young tree. A young tree suggests an inexperienced grove. The olives are from a grove planted within the last ten years, which makes them not olives my mother would have served. My mother served only old olives. She believed the pit was the better part of the olive. She was wrong, of course. But she was my mother, and I am her son.'

'Yes.'

Calder went to the wardrobe. The leather case on the second shelf held the Welrod. The leather case on the third shelf held a Walther PPK in 7.65mm Browning, factory blued, with two spare magazines and 200 rounds of Geco-marked ball ammunition. Both cases had been laid in by the man in Lisbon. The man in Lisbon had also supplied the Welrod's most recent cleaning kit, two bottles of Hoppe's No. 9 solvent, and a tin of graphite for the Walther's slide rails. Eddie had never done a commission badly.

Calder took the Welrod out of its case. He held it.

'I have not killed a man this way.'

'I know.'

'I am about to kill someone.'

'I know.'

They looked at each other. The bell-buoy at the breakwater made the sound it made. Neither said anything else. There was nothing operationally necessary to say.

Calder put the Welrod back in the case. The case in his coat. The notebook against his ribs.

'Nine days.'

Klaus nodded. Once.

Calder left.

Klaus stayed in the chair. He tore the loaf in half. He held the half he had torn for some seconds in his right hand before eating it, the way a man held a thing he was deciding whether to put down. He ate it without butter. He had been taught to eat slowly in a Stasi training facility outside Potsdam. The instructor had told him a man who ate slowly was a man who would not vomit when the work began.

Klaus had not vomited yet.

He thought he would. Not today.

3

HÔTEL DU VIEUX-PORT

Marseilles—March 1990

Two nights earlier.

The rue Sainte ran from the Vieux-Port up the side of the Saint-Victor hill in three slight bends. By 22:00 on a Sunday in early March it had the smell Marseilles had at the start of every spring—diesel from the ferries, the brine of the port, French cigarette smoke, and the cold wet stone of streets that had been streets in this city since before the Greek colonization in the year six hundred BC. Calder walked it slowly, with his coat buttoned and his hands in his pockets, the way an English tourist who had been overcharged at a fish restaurant might walk back to his hotel.

The men in the doorways smoked and watched. There were three women in red doorlamp light at the upper end of the street. The forty-year-old at the upper bend looked at him. She tipped her chin a quarter inch in the universal gesture that asked the question.

Calder shook his head once. He walked on.

He noted, in the quarter-second between the chin and the shake, the angle of the collarbone above the red dress where the strap had slipped a half-inch on one side, and the smell of cheap apricot soap. The body was insisting on being alive in the presence of a woman, and the man inside the body was permitting the insistence.

He walked back down to the Vieux-Port. He stood at the rail and watched the fishing boats come in for the night. He went back to his pension on the rue Henri-Tasso.

He ate alone that night at the small restaurant beside the pension. The waiter brought the menu, and Calder set it aside without opening it and ordered the daube he had ordered from the kitchen the night before. The waiter wrote nothing down. The kitchen was the kind that did not need a ticket for a man who had ordered the same thing twice.

Calder did not pick up the fork at once.

He sat with his hands flat on the linen on either side of the plate. The grace was the small held second his father, Edward Calder, had observed at every meal since 1945, and that Calder had absorbed by observation since boyhood at the long oak table at Egremont, before he had been old enough to ask why his father did not raise the fork until the silence had passed. He had never named the holding. Tonight, with a Welrod in a leather case in his coat against the chair leg and a man sleeping six streets away whose chest he was going to open in thirty hours, the holding was the hardest he had ever asked his hands to perform.

He raised the fork.

The waiter brought a small dish of olives with the second glass of wine. The pits were small. The grove was young. He did not eat them.

The night before the kill, he dreamed about the saffron.

It was a Saturday in the autumn of 1981. Late afternoon light through the kitchen window of the Fitzrovia studio. She came back from the rue Mouffetard with a paper twist she had bought at a spice merchant in the fifth, and she had unwrapped it on the kitchen counter and held a single thread of it up to the light.

She said, in the dry tone she kept for small dry truths: This. This is the red work the world does for nothing.

He said: 'For what.'

'For nothing. The crocus does not know it is making it. The merchant does not know what it costs him to lose so few stigmas at the edge of the field. The cook does not know he is using a thing the field made for no one. The world is full of small red work like this. Most of it goes uncataloged.'

He said: 'Are you cataloguing it.'

She did not answer for a moment. She had set the thread down on the counter beside the white packet, and she had looked at him with an expression he had not, in all the years of looking at her, learned the name of.

She had said: 'Some of it.'

He did not ask what some of it meant. He crossed the kitchen and put his hand at the small of her back, and she had leaned into the hand without turning, and they had stood at the counter for some seconds in the autumn light with the saffron between them on the white packet. She had then made the dish she had been planning to make, which had been a Persian rice with chicken and barberries, and she had used the saffron for the rice, and the rice had been the best dish she had ever made for him, and he had said so, and she had said: I know. The crocus knew.

He had laughed.

He had been thirty-nine years old and he had not yet understood what the red work the world did for nothing was. He understood now. The small red work the world did was the work she was doing on her own dossier for nine years without telling him. He banked the saffron beside the geranium.

He woke before dawn with the taste of the wine still on the back of his tongue and the kitchen counter still in his hand,

and he understood that the dream had not been a dream. The dream was the memory the body had been keeping for the morning the body needed it. The morning did not yet need it.

He lay awake until 05:42.

At 05:42 he got up and dressed.

◆◆◆

06:14.

The man in the paisley dressing gown opened the door because room service had knocked.

The room was Calder's decision. He had walked the hotel three times in the previous seventy-two hours. He identified four entries, two exits, six staff routines, and one window the cleaners did not check. He had selected the morning, the breakfast tray, the dressing gown, the angle of the round. The man on the other side of the door had not yet become the man Calder was about to kill. He was the man Calder had been killing, in his head, for six weeks.

He was sixty-seven. He had been drinking the night before. His mouth tasted of red wine and the green pills the French doctor in Aix had been prescribing him. He saw the tray. He saw the uniform. He caught, four seconds late, that the cuffs were too crisp for a Marseilles hotel and the embroidered crest above the breast pocket was a fraction off-center.

Calder stepped in with the tray. He set it on the round table by the window. He turned.

The Welrod was in his right hand. The raising of it had cost him more than the work would have asked of a man whose right shoulder was not carrying a two-month-old gunshot wound through the trapezius. He had practiced the raising in the mirror at the harbor for four mornings. The body had learned to deliver the weapon to the line without telling the wound it was being asked to.

It was a 1942 design, Birmingham Small Arms, originally manufactured for the Special Operations Executive. Hand-cranked bolt action—the way a man wound a pocket watch. 7.65mm Browning. Subsonic at the muzzle, with no supersonic crack to give away the shooter's position. Eight rounds in the magazine. Integral suppressor running almost the full length of the weapon, twelve rubber wipes stacked in series behind a forward expansion chamber, the whole assembly rated at 73 decibels on the test bench at Aston House during the war, which was quieter than a typewriter being struck once. The bolt had been cleaned and oiled by Calder twice a year for nineteen years. The wipes inside the can were forty-eight years old. Five clean firings, perhaps six. The bolt had not been fired at a person. The wipes had not. This morning would consume one of the five.

He pulled the trigger.

The Welrod made a sound that was something between a magazine drawer closing and a man clearing his throat. The round entered the man's chest two inches below the suprasternal notch, traversed the aortic arch on a downward angle, severed the descending aorta cleanly between the third and fourth thoracic vertebrae, and exited through the left scapula at three feet, taking a fragment of pulverized rib with it. The aortic transection meant the central blood pressure dropped to zero in approximately a heartbeat and a half; the brain, denied perfusion, would shut down inside fourteen seconds. The man in the paisley dressing gown sat down in the way bodies sat when their legs stopped being legs. A small wet sound came up from his chest, the air from the failing lung passing the bubbling pool of blood that had begun to collect in the throat. His bowels released into the silk pajamas. His mouth opened. He looked at Calder. He understood, in that second, that the operation he had signed off on the previous autumn had been the operation that would end him. The understanding did not save him.

Calder worked the bolt. The action was stiffer than it had been when the bolt had been new and the weapon had been young and the man using it was not yet a man who used weapons. The casing ejected into his left palm. He pocketed it.

Around 06:18 his hands started to shake. He set them flat on the round table beside the tray. He waited. The shaking stopped at 06:21. He picked the Welrod back up and put it back in its case. The case went into the inside left pocket of his jacket, against his ribs.

He turned to the body.

The man on the floor was still bleeding into the carpet. Calder lifted him under the arms and arranged him in the armchair facing the window. He smoothed the front of the dressing gown over the entry wound. He poured coffee from the French press. Black. The man had ordered black. He set the cup beside the man's right hand. He put the croissant on the white plate.

He opened Le Monde to page three and folded the paper across the body's lap. The front page he placed across the chest. The blood would not show through the newsprint until his wife pulled the paper away.

When she pulled it away she would find a saturated patch the size of a child's hand. The wool of the dressing gown black-red and stiffening. The silk pajamas beneath darkened from the bowel release. Her husband's face composed in the half-surprised expression of a man who had not, in the final fourteenth of a second, been permitted to finish the thought he had begun.

She would close the eyes first.

On the round table beside the tray was a leather wallet of Vernet's. Calder had not opened it. The corner of a 500-franc note protruded from the wallet's fold. On the note—at the lower right of the engraving of Blaise Pascal, in the ornamental border below the Saint-Jacques tower—was a mark Calder had been seeing on European banknotes for months without understanding what he was seeing. The mark was a sun with eight rays surrounding a single eye at the center. It was approximately one millimeter across. It had been on banknotes he had handled across Europe for the better part of a year. He had not yet asked Klaus what it was. He banked the registration. The file was the private file he still had not given a name to.

He sat in the chair across from the body.

He drank his own coffee.

He drank his own coffee, on a different morning years earlier. A Russian woman whose name he had not yet learned had stood across a photograph of an East Berlin apartment window—curtains, a geranium, the Wall past the sill—at the Paxton Gallery in Fitzrovia and had told him, in the accent the voice would have for the next sixteen years, that she was Alice Marsh.

She had not been Alice Marsh. The name was a cover she had worn for sixteen years; the woman beneath the cover had been someone else, and Calder, on the afternoon she had told him she was Alice, had caught without speaking that she was not.

Sitting across from a dead Frenchman in a Marseilles hotel, he had not finished registering that the small woman who had not been Alice Marsh had been dead for two months in a workroom on Webber Street.

Calder studied the face.

Vernet had a small mole on the left side of his jaw that his MI6 photograph had not picked up. The hair at his temples was thinner than the file suggested. There were fine scars on the right side of the chin that were the kind of scars a man acquired in his fifties from shaving with a straight razor on the morning after a sleepless night. Vernet's small finger on his right hand was slightly bent in a way that suggested it had been broken once, badly, and not properly set. The bend was old.

On the little finger of Vernet's right hand was a gold signet ring with a worn intaglio that the photograph in his MI6 file had not picked up. The intaglio was a sun with an eye at its center—eight rays around a circle, the rays slightly uneven in the way old engravings showed wear from generations of pressure into wax. Calder noted the device. He did not yet know what it was.

Margaret would have removed the frayed thread on the dressing gown's lapel in the same way, in their kitchen on a Sunday morning, with a pair of nail scissors that had been her mother's. She had said to him once, without turning at the sink, that scissors were the small instrument by which a woman registered she had decided to keep a thing. The thread on the cuff of Calder's own jacket had been removed by Margaret on a Sunday years earlier with the same scissors.

Margaret had not spoken. She took the cuff between her fingers, snipped the thread, smoothed the wool flat. The scissors had gone back into the drawer. She did not ask him to look at her. He had not looked. The thread had been gone.

Calder was catching each detail without intending to.

The newspaper across Vernet's chest was that morning's Le Monde, which Calder had bought himself at the kiosk on the corner of the rue Sainte at 05:48 and folded into the inside pocket of the travel jacket. The crease lines were not in the right places to hide the dark stain that was beginning to spread on the front-page newsprint above the edge of the dressing gown's lapel. The MI6 file had given him 09:14. The file was wrong. By two hours, at least.

He registered, drinking it, that he was sitting across from a man whose chest he had opened with a single round at 06:14 and that he was drinking the man's coffee from the man's pot. The noting did not produce a feeling. The feeling would come later. The feeling that was now in the room was the feeling that he had been training himself, since the January morning he had walked out of Century House, to be present for. The feeling was that he was the man who had now done the thing he had decided to do, and that the doing was the thing he had thought it would be, and that the having-done was a different room than the about-to-do had been. He crossed the threshold. The threshold was a porcelain coffee cup at a round table in a hotel in Marseilles at seven in the morning, and the man across the table was not in the new room with him.

His father, Edward Calder, had been at Trinity, on the desert floor, three miles from the tower with the welding glass against his face and the count in his ears. He noted, in the seconds between the count and the shockwave, the fact that the desert three miles away from him had become brighter than the sun for a half-second and that the brightness had been the work of his hands. His father had returned to England in December 1945 and had not, until his death of stomach cancer, eaten a meal at his table that he had not first held a private silence over. The silence had been the private grace he had said for the dead at Hiroshima and Nagasaki. He had observed it three times a day for twenty-three years without explaining it to anyone. The explaining would have required naming Hiroshima and Nagasaki at his family's table—and the naming was the thing the silence was protecting them from.

Calder, sitting across from a dead Frenchman, understood what the silence had been for. He did his father's grace at his own table for thirty years without naming it—he had absorbed it by observation since boyhood, sitting opposite his father at the long oak table at Egremont, before he had been old enough to ask why his father did not raise the fork until the silence had passed. The grace had moved from one Calder to the next without instruction.

Calder Hall had been built in the valley his family had been in for nine hundred years; the valley had taken its name from the family, and the reactor from the valley—the world's first commercial nuclear power station. His father had been one of the men who commissioned it, and had walked its charge face for the rest of his working life, and had talked about it at the long oak table at Egremont the way other men talked about a regiment. Calder had grown up inside the talk and had not gone into the work. He read History at Cambridge, rowed crew for his college, and was recruited in his final year. The Foreign and Commonwealth Office gave him a junior analyst's title in its Research Department, which was the title the firm gave the men it did not want named. He served in Bonn, and then Washington, and had been at the Counter-Proliferation desk at Century House ever since—the small desk that tracked the missing fissile material and the inventory discrepancies the larger desks preferred not to acknowledge. He had spent his career reading, in the spacing of a column of figures, the absence of a thing that should have been there. He had done the work for more than twenty years without making the connection between the work and the name.

The name was a coincidence. The institution had not regarded it as a coincidence. The institution had regarded it as the kind of operational poetry it permitted itself in the long centuries of its work—a Counter-Proliferation officer named Calder, the son of the man who had walked the charge face at Calder Hall. He walked out of Century House on the fourth of January. The walking-out was the first room. Marseilles was the second.

What his father had been silent over at Trinity in 1945 was, he was beginning to register on the morning he sat across a small dead Frenchman in a Marseilles hotel, the same thing the architecture had been killing his peers' children for thirty years. The question was which fire the world would burn. The architecture had been burning one fire. There was another fire. He did not yet know its name. He registered what he did not know. He filed it. The filing was the second file the new man kept.

Some minutes later, a key in the door of the suite next door. Wrong room. The wife was back.

He stood. He took his cup and the casing. He left through the staff stairwell.

On the fifth-floor landing he stopped. He noted, in the half-second before he started down, that he had walked out of the moral room and was about to walk into the operational one. The body knew the difference. The body went on.

On the second-floor landing he passed a maid coming up with linens. She was fifty. She was carrying a stack of folded white sheets in both arms with the small competent posture of a woman who had carried such stacks up such staircases for many years. She glanced at him. The glance was the half-second professional registration of a woman whose work had been to acknowledge guests and not to remember them. She had been a maid for decades and had stopped looking at faces. He had been doing the work for the morning of his life and had stopped wearing one. They passed each other on the worn marble of the second-floor landing without speaking. The breakfast tray would arrive at the suite above her, by another maid, on the wife's standing order. Calder's right hand, in the pocket of the travel jacket, was on the spent casing. The casing was warmer than the pocket. He held it as he descended. The maid did not turn. The maid's linens were the linens that would, by oh-eight-fifteen, be on the bed of a dead man whose face she would also not look at when she came in to change them.

She was carrying a wet embroidered handkerchief in her left hand. She had been crying for some particular reason—a son's letter, a husband's silence, a niece's cancer—and was carrying clean linens up a staircase because the linens had been the next thing on her morning. Calder let the detail go. It was not for the ledger.

On the windowsill of the half-landing, beside a brass ashtray that had not been emptied, was a folded white paper object. It was the size of a thumbnail. Folded with the precision of a hand that had been folding the same shape many times. The shape, on the second look, resolved into a crane. The folding was clean. Calder did not pause. He registered it as he passed and did not stop. It went into the file with the eight-ray sun and the small unnamed objects he had been carrying.

On the ground-floor landing, at the back door that gave onto the alley, a thumbnail-sized mark had been chalked into the inside of the doorframe at chest height. The mark looked to Calder like a Greek letter of the kind a hotel maintenance crew might have used as a minor inventory notation. It was a theta. It was on the inside of the doorframe, at chest height, where the eye of a man going out the back of a hotel would catch it without intending to. The eight-ray sun he had been seeing was on banknotes and bank plaques and the corners of newspaper mastheads—the visible surfaces of the institutional world. The theta was on the underside of a doorframe, in chalk, a thumbnail across. He noted the difference. He did not yet have a category for it. He filed it beside the eight-ray sun and the small folded crane on the half-landing windowsill, in the file of unnamed objects the work had been pressing into his attention since the body in the chair upstairs, and went out into the alley.

The wife came back from the bakery before seven. She set her parcel of pain au chocolat on the entrance hall table. She called his name once. She walked into the front room. She found her husband. She called the gendarmerie. By the time the call connected, Calder was on the regional train to Avignon.

The coffee was the kill.

He sat by the window. Coat across his lap. Hands inside the coat. The casing was in the envelope in his inside pocket. He was not holding it.

The train cleared the dockyards. The dockyards were of the same order as the London dock from which the Atlantic Compass had departed on the fourth of January with a refrigerated container Calder had been told was full of agricultural processing equipment.

It had not been.

There was a London gallery years ago. Margaret had drawn, in pencil on the back of the catalog, a small circle the size of a wedding ring with nothing inside it. She had pushed the catalog across the table to him and gone back to her wine without speaking. He carried the catalog in his coat for sixteen years. He had not, in any of those years, asked her what the empty circle was. In November of 1977 he had answered the question without knowing he was answering it, by placing the silver key on the bracelet's empty ring while she was making tea. She had found the key the next morning. She looked at him. She had said nothing. The pact had been the silence. Sitting on the train out of Avignon he understood, for the first time, that the empty circle on a 1974 gallery catalog had been a Latinist's quaestio—a question put on the table without a verb, waiting for the answer that would come in its own time. The answer had been a key.

There was a locked drawer in a Chiswick study. Two files. ALICE. FEUERWERK. They had been the same investigation. He did not understand the same-ness for years.

He had named the ALICE file himself, on the afternoon he had walked back to Century House from the Public Records reading room with a photocopy of a Lillehammer hotel register in the inside pocket of his coat. The register had carried, on the line for the twenty-first, in the careful hand of a Norwegian night clerk, a name not Alice Marsh's and not English. The naming had been a joke with two halves. The first half was Lewis Carroll. FEUERWERK was the country at the bottom of the rabbit hole. ALICE was the going down—into a country that turned out to be inhabited by a woman who was not who she said she was, which was the kind of country he had been working in since 1968. The second half had been a woman who had stood across a photograph of curtains and a geranium and told him she was Alice Marsh. The second half he had not written down. He had carried it for sixteen years.

There had been a Tuesday in the autumn of 1984.

A junior analyst at Century House—a man named Arnott, recently transferred from the Far East desk, twenty-nine, married eleven months to a primary-school teacher from Sevenoaks who was, by the operational inattention that allowed Calder to know such things about junior officers, six months pregnant with their first—had assembled over the previous weeks an operational dossier on a Russian woman living in London under the cover identity Alice Marsh. The dossier was good. Arnott had cross-referenced four kinds of evidence: visa records; hotel registers; the inconsistencies in Alice Marsh's National Insurance contributions; and the physical anomalies of a woman who had not aged eleven years in the eleven years the file could account for. Arnott had brought the dossier to Calder's office on a Tuesday afternoon in October.

Calder had read it in twenty-three minutes.

He noted, in the reading, that Arnott was correct on every operational point. The cover was Alice Marsh. The woman was Russian. The Lillehammer register Calder had photocopied in November 1977 had been the same name. The dossier on his desk was the dossier that would, if escalated, produce the Tuesday-morning meeting at which the firm would be told one of its assets in London had been identified. A set of channels —channels Calder did not yet know existed but suspected the existence of—would then ensure the asset did not survive the Tuesday after.

He set the dossier down.

He had said: 'The cover is good but the inferences are not. The visa records can be explained by the Foreign Office's administrative inconsistencies. The Lillehammer register is a Norwegian clerk's bad transliteration of an English name. The aging is the natural aging of a woman who teaches at a primary school in Camden. You have done good work. It is not yet sufficient. Take it back. Run it for six more months. Bring it to me again in April if the additional six months produce evidence.'

Arnott had nodded. Arnott had taken the dossier back. Arnott had been transferred to the Latin America desk a few months later and had not returned. The dossier had gone into the archive. It had remained there until the fourth of January 1990, when Calder walked out of Century House for the last time. He had carried the Tuesday in October as a private annual accounting for six years.

He had been forty-two.

He had not told Margaret. He had not told Elena.

Elena had not asked. Her silence had been her discipline.

In the early weeks at the harbor, Calder was reading. The pencil page on the desk had begun, at the end of the second week, with two names and a question mark. Vernet from FEUERWERK. Brückner from the same file, cross-referenced against an obituary in the German daily Frankfurter Allgemeine he had read years earlier and not at the time understood he was reading. The third name was the question mark. The third name would come.

Two names was the start of a list.

The work was the list. The list was the two names and the question mark. The names were the operation.

It would not be the end of the list.

The train pulled in at Avignon mid-morning. He stood. He took his coat. He crossed the platform to the southbound train. He bought a coffee from the kiosk. He paid in francs. The kiosk also stocked Paris Match. Calder did not buy the magazine. He bought a paperback copy of La Peste—Camus's The Plague—because he had not read Camus in thirty years and because a man on a long train journey reading a book was a man who was not a recently-active operative.

As he was paying, a man in a brown raincoat brushed past him at the kiosk.

Calder did not register the man at the time.

He drank the coffee standing up.

He felt nothing about the man in the paisley dressing gown.

He set it aside.

The work had begun.

4

SÈTE / MARCH

Sète / Lyon-Perrache / An Atlantic port—March 1990

Eight hours past Marseilles.

The restaurant was on the rue Alsace-Lorraine, a place with seven tables and a window that gave onto the Canal Royal. The cat on the windowsill was asleep. It had been asleep since Calder had sat down.

The air inside was warm with rouille—the rust-red garlic paste of the coast—and saffron and the bitter undertone of a sea that had been cleaned of its fish for three hundred years.

At the next table a family of three was eating. The parents were arguing quietly in French about a grandmother's medical bills. The daughter, perhaps ten, was reading a book with a yellow cover.

The daughter did not look up. The daughter was the most disciplined operative in the room.

He was on his second glass of Picpoul—a sharp coastal white the restaurant poured without asking. The bouillabaisse was good.

The saffron in the bowl was the saffron she had bought, on a Saturday afternoon nine years before, at a spice merchant on the rue Mouffetard. He held the second glass without drinking it for a moment. The dream of the previous night was still in the wine. He set the glass down.

He waited. Ninety seconds. The bitterness on his tongue did not develop. It was not the precursor bitterness of an organophosphate or the slow bloom of an alkaloid. The wine was wine.

He drank it.

The waiter brought the telephone on a long cord just before two.

The sound was something between an old hotel bell and a fork dropping on a plate.

'A call for Monsieur Dupin.'

Calder took the phone. 'Yes.'

Klaus's voice. 'Eat your soup. Then listen.'

Calder ate three more spoonfuls. 'I am listening.'

'I have your second name. I will be back in the harbor by Friday. We have a problem and we have an opportunity. I cannot tell which is which. Not on a hotel telephone.'

'The problem.'

'The Minox is gone.'

Calder said nothing.

'Yours. The B. The case is empty. The wardrobe was opened. Nothing else missing. The notebook is intact. The FEUERWERK file is intact. The pencil page is intact. Only the camera.'

'When.'

'Between when you left and when I came back. The lock has not been forced.'

Calder thought about this.

'Eat your soup.'

'I am eating it.'

Klaus hung up.

The cat on the windowsill rolled over. The mother at the next table said enough. The father did not respond. The daughter turned a page.

As Calder was paying his bill, the daughter looked up from her book and smiled at him. He did not know he had smiled back until he was on the train to Béziers. It was the only smile he had produced involuntarily since January.

He left the restaurant a little after two.

The Canal Royal was on his left. The afternoon light was the flat winter light of a Mediterranean port in early March. The wind was off the canal. It carried the smell of brine and diesel and the chemical undertone of a fish-meal plant on the southern jetty.

The station was eleven minutes by foot. The next train to Béziers was the afternoon one.

He walked.

He registered the man at the corner of the rue Paul Valéry.

The man was about forty. Mediterranean features. Black canvas jacket of the kind men working at the harbor wore. He stood at the entrance of a marine store on the south side of the street, doing the small fraction of nothing a man did when he was waiting to do something. Calder had marked, at the restaurant, a man of the same description across the canal at the rail of the lower quay reading a newspaper that was not a newspaper.

It was the same man.

The man at the rue Paul Valéry was therefore not a coincidence.

Calder did not change his pace. He registered the alley to his right—a narrow passage between a fishmonger's shuttered for the afternoon and the back wall of a tannery that had not been a tannery in decades. The passage ran sixty meters to the next street over. He had walked it on the morning of his arrival when he had been mapping the narrow streets between the restaurant and the station the way an operative mapped narrow streets when he had been doing this kind of work for some weeks.

He turned into the passage.

The passage was sixty meters. Cobblestones. No side doors. The passage was a decision.

He counted. Three seconds. Four. At five he heard the quick light step of a man who had been waiting for him to take the alley and was now closing the distance.

The Welrod was in the inside left pocket of his coat. The Welrod was the wrong weapon for this. The Welrod was for a man who was standing still and who did not yet know he was about to die. The Welrod was not for a man who was running at his back along sixty meters of cobbled passage at fourteen-minutes-past-two on a Tuesday afternoon. There were also four clean firings left, and at this distance, fired through the case fabric, the report would not stay in the alley.

He did not draw.

He pivoted at the seventh step.

The man was three meters behind him with a knife in his right hand. The knife was a Mercator K55K—a folded rectangle of black-painted steel, thumb-thin, three steel rivets, the leaping cat of the Solingen Katzenmesser stamped into the handle, nine centimeters of carbon-steel blade held open by a spring lock on the spine. It was the working knife half the German tradesmen of two generations had carried in their coat pockets. The blade had been kept. The grip was wrong. The man had been bringing it up from a low carry. The blade was at hip height when Calder turned. The man's eyes were the eyes of a man who had been told the assignment was an old Englishman leaving a restaurant. The man's eyes had not been told what the old Englishman had become in the hours since Marseilles.

Calder stepped inside the knife.

His left forearm went across the man's right wrist, hard, driving the knife arm down and out at a forty-five-degree angle that took the blade off the line of his belly. The forearm carried the work along the scar the chandler's-wall alley had put in it, the line still new enough to pull. He noted, in the half-second the body began the work, that he had not planned this kill, that the body had begun the work before the mind had authorized it, and that the part of him that was watching the part of him doing the work had been a separate part for the eight weeks since Greenwich and was a third part this afternoon. His right elbow came across his body with the weight of the shoulder behind it and met the man under the jaw at the angle where the mandible joined the temporal bone. The blow was the blow Coyle had taught him in a rope-floored gymnasium in Pimlico when the Service had still believed an officer should know the small vocabulary of close work. Coyle had been forty-two. Calder had been twenty-six. Coyle had said: the elbow is the heaviest single thing the body can deliver at the speed of a punch. The mandible is the longest lever the face owns. The point at which the lever meets the skull is the point at which the face stops being a face. He had not used the elbow in twenty-two years. The elbow worked. The trapezius did not. The wound through the right shoulder was eight weeks old and had pulled in the moment of impact—a hot wet line under the bandage that had begun, by the time the man's head went sideways, to make itself known.

The man's head went sideways. Two molars from the lower right jaw came loose in the same instant and fell out of the open mouth onto the stone with the clean sound enamel made on it. The temporomandibular joint on the right side of the man's face gave with a wet click that was the sound the joint made when the joint was no longer the joint. The knife came loose. The blade rang on the stone.

Calder caught the man's right wrist with both hands and turned the shoulder out at the joint. The shoulder did not dislocate. The shoulder gave the faint grinding registration of cartilage that had been asked to do something cartilage was not built to do. The man's left hand came up at Calder's throat.

The fingers found the throat.

Calder had two seconds before the fingers closed.

He drove his forehead into the bridge of the man's nose. The man's nasal bone opened the skin over Calder's left brow in the same instant—the brow taking its own split in the trade—and the blood came down hot into the eye at once, fast and disproportionate to the depth, the way a brow wound bled.

The bridge gave with a wet crack that was the sound a green twig made when it broke. The septum collapsed sideways and the cartilage at the base of the nose folded backward into the nasal cavity. Blood came down out of both nostrils in two unequal rivers and into the man's mouth, mixing with the blood from the loose molars and the wet at the broken jaw. The man's left hand came off Calder's throat and went, by reflex, to his face. Calder caught the loose left hand and bent the wrist back against the joint and felt the small ligament at the base of the thumb separate. The thumb, no longer connected to the muscle that closed it, went limp.

The man made a sound.

It was not a word. It was the sound a body made when the body had begun to understand that the body was not going to win.

Calder went for the knife.

He went down on one knee. His left hand found the haft. He came up inside the man's reach, the blade edge-up against the man's belly. He drove the blade up under the rib cage and across in a short hard stroke that came from the legs. The nine-centimeter blade went in to the hilt. He turned the haft. He pulled the knife out. The man's coat and trousers, in the second after the pull, became dark from sternum to knee in the slow sheeted way wool became dark when wool was being asked to absorb six pints of arterial blood at once. The smell that came up out of the man was the wet copper smell of a body opened from below mixed with the sour saffron-and-garlic smell of the lunch the man had eaten while watching Calder eat his. The man's eyes opened wide and did not close again. His mouth opened. A thin black string of blood came out of the lower lip and down the chin.

The man went down at the knees.

Calder caught him under the arms. The body weighed more than the man had appeared to weigh. The body was sixty kilos, perhaps sixty-two. The body was already the dead weight of a body whose blood was now mostly outside the body.

He lowered the man to the ground against the back wall of the tannery, behind a stack of empty wooden fish crates that had not been moved in some weeks. He wiped the blade on the inside of the man's lapel where the wipe would not show. He folded the blade with his thumb on the spine. The spring lock disengaged with a small clean click. He put the knife in the inside left pocket of his own coat. The black-painted steel went against the wool with the weight of a thing that knew the pocket. He put the man's right hand against the wound at the belly. He stepped back. The arrangement would read, to a Sète police officer on a Tuesday afternoon, as a knife fight between two men who had not finished arguing and that one of them had walked away from with the knife—a thing the alley behind the tannery had seen six times in the past decade.

He went through the man's pockets. A wallet with no identification. Eighteen hundred francs. A folded train ticket from Marseilles to Sète from the previous evening. A pack of Gauloises with two cigarettes left. A key on a leather fob. He kept the train ticket. He kept the key. He left the wallet and the cigarettes and the francs.

He looked at his hands.

There was blood on the left one to the wrist. There was blood on his coat sleeve. There was a fine spray on the right cuff. He took out the pocket handkerchief and wiped the left hand. He turned the cuff up against the cold so that the spray would not show.

His breathing was at thirty per minute.

His breathing was at thirty per minute and his hands had not shaken. The body—his body, the body that had been Calder's body since 1942—had done the work in the alley without consulting him about whether the body was prepared to do the work.

The body had been prepared.

The mind had not yet caught up.

He walked to the end of the alley. He turned left. He walked the four hundred meters to the station at the pace of a man who had nowhere particular to be. He bought the ticket to Béziers in coins. He boarded the afternoon train with three minutes to spare.

In the lavatory of the carriage between Sète and Béziers he washed his hands and the cuff of his coat with the bar of station soap. The water in the basin ran pink for some seconds. He flushed the basin. The water ran clear.

The not-shaking and the running clear were the same thing.

He did not yet have the word for what they were.

He noted, drying his hands on his handkerchief because the lavatory had no towel, that the watch against the inside of his left wrist was warmer than the skin around it. The wrist had been doing work. The watch had done the work with him. The warmth was the mechanical sympathy a man's instrument owed him after the alley.

On the train back, he thought about who had been in the room.

There was an hour he could not account for on the morning of his departure. He walked down to the harbor at 06:00 to make a phone call from the public kiosk by the bell-buoy. The call had been to Klaus, eleven minutes. He had walked back. The room was as he had left it. Or so he had thought.

He took out La Peste, which he had bought at Avignon. He turned to the inside back cover. He wrote, in 2H pencil:

Bakery woman. Saddle-faced fisherman. Bevin. Widow's nephew. Local gendarme. Old Henri at the counter.

Bevin was the Liverpool solicitor's local agent—a man who had handled the lease paperwork, met Calder once over coffee, knew the routine. Klaus had used Bevin for years for administrative cover.

He added two more names:

Old NVA officer in Hamburg bar (per Klaus). Athens contact who arranged the second hire (per Klaus).

He looked at the list. The pattern was now visible to him: he was thinking like Margaret had thought.

He closed the book.

The train passed Béziers.

Lyon-Perrache, late evening

In his wallet, between the operational French banknotes and the ticket stubs of his cover, was a one-thousand franc note with a worn watermark Calder had not, in all his years of carrying French currency, particularly registered. Held to the platform light, the watermark resolved into a sun with eight rays and an eye at the center. He held the note for some seconds. He returned it to the wallet. He had now registered the eight-rayed sun in scores of places across Europe. The count had begun in Marseilles and had been refined through Sète. The places were varied. Banknotes. Brass bank plaques. The corners of certain newspaper mastheads. The spines of particular leather-bound directories at chambers of commerce. The enamel device of a Genevese watchmaker who had supplied a particular kind of pocket watch to a particular kind of customer for the better part of a century. The small embroidered corner of a Lyon silk tie marketed under a particular Faubourg-Saint-Honoré label since before the war. And once, on the small ceramic tile mosaic at the entry of a private chapel attached to a Florentine palazzo whose owner had not visited in years.

The institution did not hide. It stopped needing to hide a long time ago. It registered, by the discipline of an organization that had been operating for sixteen hundred years, that the private set of people who could read the sigil were the private set of people who needed to read it. The reading was the membership. The not-reading was the rest of the world's specific institutional ignorance.

He registered the count. The cars he was not yet able to map were the cars the institution had been planting bombs under. The bombs had been attributed, by the patient institutional discipline of an organization that had been manufacturing political violence for thirty years, to groups that had not planted them. The Birmingham bombs that had killed twenty-one people in November of 1974 had been attributed to Republican paramilitaries. The Piazza della Loggia in May of 1974. The Bologna station in August of 1980. Eighty-five dead on a platform. The institution did not take credit for these. The institution's relationship with the credit it had not taken was the patient administrative fact of an organization that had been sustaining the political conditions it required for sixteen hundred years and had learned not to leave its own name on the work. The map was the subsequent project Klaus had asked him to begin building when Calder was operational again.

The connection to the Atlantic port had been disrupted by a freight strike in the Massif Central. Next train south at 11:40 the following morning.

The hotel was a place above a café that had stopped serving food at 22:00 but whose bar was open until 02:00. He went down at 23:30.

He drank a Pernod at the bar. The room was sparse. A bartender of forty polishing a glass. Two suits at a corner table. A man at the bar three seats down who was drinking the same beer he had been drinking when Calder had come in. The man's left hand never left his lap. The man was, eventually, a man whose discipline at the bar Calder recognized because his father had been the same kind of man.

He went up to the room a little after midnight.

He took the Walther PPK out of the inside pocket of his coat. He set it on the bedside table. He wedged the desk chair under the door handle.

At 04:00 someone tried the door.

The handle turned. The door did not open because the desk chair was wedged against it. Whoever was on the other side did not push. They tried the handle once. They walked away.

Calder did not move. The Walther was chambered and at the

safety. His right hand was on the grip.

He listened to the corridor for forty-five minutes. There was no further sound.

In the morning he walked the corridor before checkout. He saw no one. The night clerk at the front desk was twenty-three, reading a paperback Western, said no one had been in the corridor.

Calder paid in cash. He left.

On the platform at Lyon-Perrache, waiting for the southbound train, he caught something he had not caught the previous afternoon.

At the Avignon station kiosk, when he had bought La Peste and the coffee, a man in a brown raincoat had brushed past him at the kiosk. The brush had been deliberate. The man's right hand had passed across the pocket of Calder's coat where the Welrod's case was riding against his ribs. The brush had been a check. The man had been confirming the presence of a weapon.

Calder had not observed the brush at the time.

He was noting it now.

The man at the door in Lyon at 04:00 had not pushed because the handle had not turned freely. The handle had not turned freely because Calder had wedged the desk chair against it before sleeping—a small paranoid discipline a man developed when he had spent seven weeks in a rented room reading documents that frightened him.

The man at the Avignon kiosk and the man at the Lyon door had been the same man. He followed Calder from the Avignon platform to the southbound train and had been in Lyon before Calder had arrived. The brush at the kiosk had been the confirmation that Calder was armed. The door at 04:00 had been the action: the man had been looking for the Calder who had not yet wedged a chair. The action had failed. The man in the brown raincoat was still operational.

Klaus had not arrived an hour earlier on the overnight ferry. He had arrived eight hours earlier on the previous evening's ferry, which had been the ferry before the one he had told Calder he would take. He arrived at 22:00 the previous night. He had been in the room since.

'You are early,' Calder said.

'I felt something. I came one ferry earlier.'

'Felt what.'

'I do not know. The feeling was three hundred kilometers from here. The feeling was the kind you do not ignore at my age.'

Calder set down his bag. He took off his coat. He looked at the empty Minox B case on the desk.

He reached into the inside left pocket of the coat and took out the Mercator. He set it on the desk beside the empty Minox case. The black-painted steel caught the lamplight in a dull line along the spine. The leaping cat stamped into the handle was the size of his thumbnail. The blade was folded.

Klaus looked at the knife. He was silent for a moment.

Klaus said: 'Where.'

Calder said: 'Sète. The man in the alley brought it. I came back with it.'

Klaus said: 'Yes.' He did not say more. He looked at the knife for some seconds longer. Then he looked at Calder.

Calder, who had carried the knife in his coat pocket for the seventy-two hours since Sète and had felt its weight against his ribs through three trains and a Lyon hotel night and the morning estuary ferry, registered, in the looking, that Klaus had recognized something Klaus was not yet saying. He did not ask. His silence was the form the registration took.

'Lyon. There was a man in a brown raincoat at the Avignon kiosk who brushed my coat. There was a man at my door at 04:00. I think they were the same man. I think the man at the kiosk was confirming I was armed. The man at the door was looking for me to be unarmed.'

Klaus considered this.

'That is the feeling I had at the Sète ferry terminal. The feeling that someone was checking on you. I came one ferry earlier because I have learned, in the weeks of doing this with you, that my feelings about your safety are now operational.'

Calder said: 'Thank you.'

Klaus said: 'I would have come earlier if I had been able to.'

'When.'

'Lyon.'

They sat with that.

Klaus continued: 'When was the room empty.'

'Eleven-minute window when the morning post boat held the harbor's attention. I walked down to the kiosk and called you. The room would have been unwatched.'

'Anyone.'

'Or anyone who had been told the routine. The Athens contact who arranged the second hire is in Athens. The Liverpool solicitor's local agent is in Bordeaux. I have confirmed both.'

'And.'

'I do not know who took it. I have a theory. The theory is that someone has been watching us for several months and decided that the camera would be a useful thing to have. I do not believe they were professional in the conventional sense. A professional would have taken the FEUERWERK file or the pencil list. A professional would have understood that those documents were the operation. The Minox is operationally peripheral. The Minox is sentimental. Someone took the sentimental thing and left the operational things. I find this either reassuring or terrifying.'

'Reassuring how.'

'Reassuring because it suggests we are being watched by someone whose competence is limited. Terrifying because it suggests we are being watched by someone whose competence is unconventional.'

Calder thought about this. 'It also suggests that whoever took it knew it was sentimental. A professional who understood the difference between an operational file and a personal camera is not a professional who broke in by accident. He was looking for the camera specifically. The camera has Margaret's hands on the undeveloped roll. If Margaret is not the geranium woman, the camera is the proof.'

'Yes.'

'I have brought you a Minox C.'

Klaus opened his bag. He took out a leather case slightly larger than the case for the B. He set it on the desk.

'1974 production. Same fifteen-millimeter Complan as the B. Loaded with Agfa Copex Rapid from a stationer in Hamburg who is not on anyone's list because he is fifty-four years old, breeds canaries, and has the political opinions of a canary. I have tested the camera on three frames. The frames are of the curtains.'

Calder picked up the case. The Minox C was in the felt-lined recess. Twenty-two millimeters longer than the B—the battery compartment added at the rear. Body black where the B had been chrome.

'The B was old.'

'I know.'

'I have carried it through everything.'

'I know.'

'There was a roll in it.'

'I assumed.'

'I shot the last roll in the kitchen at Chiswick on a Sunday last November. I had photographed Margaret making bread. The bakery on the King's Road had been closed for the long weekend and she had decided to make her own. She had not made bread in seven years. I had photographed her at the worktop with the dough on her hands. I had photographed the loaf cooling on the rack. I had photographed her hands kneading. I had not developed the roll. The roll was in the camera when I left. The roll is what I have lost. The man in Bordeaux, whoever he is, has my ex-wife's hands kneading bread on the last roll I shot through that camera. The man does not know what he has. I cannot retrieve it without breaking the cover I am operating under. I have been catching for two months that I will not retrieve it. The not-retrieving is the thing I am still trying to file.'

Klaus said: 'I am sorry, James.'

Calder said: 'I know.'

'And now it is in someone's pocket.'

'Yes.'

'And the camera you have brought me is the camera I would have used if I had been a different operative working in the same period. The B was the camera of a Counter-Proliferation officer photographing documents in hotel safes. The C is the camera of a man who has decided to record his own work because he no longer trusts his memory.'

'That is approximately right.'

Calder set the camera down. He took the leather notebook out of the drawer. He took the pencil page. He took the pencil. He drew a single horizontal line through Vernet, Henri. Marseilles. The line was clean. His hand did not shake.

He folded the page. He put it back in the notebook.

'Berlin.'

'Berlin will take time. The Wall has only just fallen. Brückner is in Bonn negotiating a position with a private bank.'

'In the meantime.'

'In the meantime, Brussels. I have a man who has been waiting nineteen years to talk to someone like us about the man Margaret described.'

'Nineteen years.'

'His sister was on a list. She was processed. He has been waiting since.'

Calder thought about this.

'I would like a drink.'

'It is morning.'

'I would like a drink.'

'I will pour.'

They drank in silence. The bell-buoy made its small mournful noise. The light was beginning to change.

Klaus said: 'My grandfather died in Bremen. He was eighty-one. Watchmaker.'

'Did you know him.'

'Someone else's grandfather. A man named Krüger I knew years ago. The grandfather is mine for the duration of the operation. After the operation he goes back to being Krüger's.'

'I have an ex-wife who writes Latin in the margins of pages I do not understand. I have a friend who borrows other men's grandfathers and comes one ferry earlier when his instincts say to. I have a Welrod that I have used once and a Walther I have not used and a new Minox that records its own work. I have eight pages of my ex-wife's I have not yet read and thirty-seven pages of my own and a list of three names with the first crossed out. I have a Mercator from a Sète alley that has been against my ribs through two trains.'

'Yes.'

Klaus did not, in the saying of the yes, look at the knife on the desk. The averted gaze was the way Klaus had decided to say the thing. Then he said, in the flat tone he used for things he was telling Calder for the first time and that he had been deciding whether to tell him for some weeks: 'Elena had one.'

Calder said: 'In her handbag at the Mayflower.'

'Yes. And in the drawer beside the stove in the Kensington flat for the thirteen years before that. She took it from a man named Voss in October of 1977 at Checkpoint Charlie. The Mercator was the only object she carried that she had not been issued. It was the object the institution did not know she had. Voss did not die that October. The architecture kept him. Your ex-wife has known since. I was going to tell you about the knife when we came to the page. We have come to the page another way.'

Calder looked at the black-painted steel on the desk. The leaping cat. The three rivets. The spring lock he had heard click in the alley behind the tannery. He noted, in the looking, that the body had reached for an instrument the mind had not been told was an instrument. The body had been told. The body had been doing the work the mind had not yet authorized for the eight weeks since Greenwich, and the body had reached, in the alley in Sète, for the same kind of knife the woman the body had been failing to grieve had carried for the thirteen years before he had seen her on a hotel-room floor. He did not say any of this. He picked up the knife. He put it back in the inside left pocket of his coat. The pocket received it. The knife was now the knife the pocket knew.

'We are doing better than we were on Tuesday.'

'Yes.'

They finished the drink.

'I am going to sleep.'

'I will be in the chair.'

Calder went to the bed. He took off his shoes. He lay down in his clothes. He closed his eyes.

He slept until the afternoon.

Klaus did not move from the chair the entire time.

5
THE ZURICH BOX

An Atlantic port / Zurich—spring 1990

09:14. Tuesday.

Klaus walked into the Zürcher Kantonalbank, the cantonal bank of Zurich, on the city's main shopping street. He was wearing a wool overcoat that had been pressed in a Lyon hotel the previous afternoon, a tie he had bought new in the station, and black calfskin gloves that did the work of saying he was a man who did not leave fingerprints without saying anything else.

He carried an empty leather attaché case.

He had walked to the bank from the main train station by the longer route he preferred. He passed a bakery on a corner two blocks from the station where a woman of sixty was lifting a tray of croissants from an oven. The smell from the bakery was, for the eleven seconds Klaus was passing it, the smell of his mother's kitchen in postwar Leipzig—yeast and butter and the sharp undertone of yesterday's flour caught in the corners of the floor. He had not eaten his mother's croissants. His mother had not made croissants. The smell had been the smell of someone else's mother's kitchen, but the geometry of the smell had been the same.

On the brass plaque beside the entrance—beneath the bank's discreet name in Helvetica—was a discreet device the size of a thumbnail. A sun with eight rays. An eye at the center. Klaus had walked past similar devices on bank doors in Zurich and Geneva and Liechtenstein for years without seeing them. This one held his eye. He did not yet have a name for it.

He had also walked past it on the lintels of three Zurich insurance buildings, on the iron grate above a private bank in Lugano, and on the bronze plate beside the entrance of the Bank for International Settlements in Basel where he had once attended a funding meeting. The institution had been the printer's mark on European finance for so long that the printer's mark had become indistinguishable from the architectural ornament.

He had walked on. Two streets later a woman walking a white dog had looked at him for too long. He had assessed her while continuing to walk. The woman had been embarrassed. She had been deciding whether to apologize. She decided not to.

Klaus had walked on. The cost of the deciding had been two minutes off his arrival time at the bank.

The bank's marble floor was cold even through the soles of his shoes. The bank smelled of money the way old cathedrals smelled of incense—the smell was not the substance, the smell was the institutional commitment to the substance.

He produced the key. He produced the passport in the name Heinrich Müller, Salzburg, profession architect. The clerk did not look at him with interest.

Klaus was led into a room with two chairs and a steel table. Box 247B was placed on the table. The clerk left.

He opened the box. Inside: a brown leather notebook tied with a black ribbon. He took it out. He placed it in the attaché case. He pressed the button on the wall.

He was back on the main street within the hour.

At the train station a Swiss railway police officer stopped him.

Thirty years old. Standard navy uniform. Working a tip about a pickpocket on the morning IC trains.

'You have visited the bank.'

'I have. Retrieving my grandfather's letters. He died in November.'

'Where did your grandfather die.'

'Bremen.'

'You are Austrian.'

'My grandfather was from Bremen. My mother married my father and they moved to Salzburg. My grandfather refused to move. He stayed in Bremen and died there at eighty-one. The letters in the box are forty years of correspondence with my mother. My family has been retrieving the papers in shifts.'

The officer almost smiled. He handed the papers back.

Klaus walked to platform six. He bought a coffee and an almond pastry. He boarded the next train to Geneva.

On the train, Klaus opened the leather notebook. He read the eight pages. It took him two hours. The handwriting was neat and slightly leftward-slanting—the hand of a primary-school teacher—a hand Klaus had registered, the once he had shaken it across a Hampstead pub table years earlier, as having a faint white scar across the second knuckle of the index finger and the small earth-callused thumb of a woman who staked her own beans. In the margins of pages four and five the neatness had broken. The letters were smaller there, pressed harder into the paper, and on the fifth page she had drawn, in pencil, an eight-rayed sun and then crossed it out.

When he closed the notebook he sat looking out the window for a long time. He had met the woman who wrote the pages a few times—once in a London hallway years earlier, once at a Hampstead pub, once by post when she had written him a single-paragraph letter asking him to retrieve a Zurich notebook in the event her former husband survived an event she did not name. He read the letter four times. He burned it on the fifth reading.

The letter had said: If you read these pages before he does, do not tell him you read them. He will need to find the seventh-and-mine sentence himself. The finding is part of the work.

He folded the pages back. He tied the ribbon. He ate the almond pastry.

In Geneva he changed trains for Lyon. In Lyon, after a fourteen-hour layover, he boarded the overnight ferry. He arrived at the Atlantic harbor before dawn.

Calder was awake at the desk.

Klaus set the attaché case down. He opened it. He took out the brown notebook. He laid it on the desk.

'I have not opened it.'

'I would not have asked.'

'I am telling you because the telling is part of the operation.'

'Thank you.'

Klaus put the kettle on.

That night Klaus put the leather notebook on the kitchen table beside the bottle of Grouse and described, in eight sentences, the mark on the bank plaque.

Calder said: 'I have seen it.'

Klaus said: 'Where.'

Calder said: 'On the 500-franc note in Vernet's wallet. On the Bank of England fifty I paid the kiosk woman with at Charing Cross on the morning after the kill at Webber Street. On the Bundesbank twenty-mark a few weeks later. On the corner of the Le Monde masthead in the Marseilles café. On the watermark of a one-thousand franc note held to the platform light at Lyon-Perrache. The mark has been everywhere I have spent money for nine months. I have been registering it without naming it.'

He paused. His pulse had done a thing it had not done since the morning he had walked into the Greenwich flat and smelled cigarette smoke.

Klaus said: 'I learned about it years ago. I have been collecting instances since. The mark is on every Western banknote whose central bank charter the institution has revised. It is on the IAEA founding seal. It is on the Bretton Woods signature pages. It is on the Treaty of Rome. It is on the SWIFT operating manual. It is on the engraving plate the Federal Reserve uses for the hundred-dollar note. The architecture has been the printer's mark on every instrument the architecture has been operating. The sun is the mark it shows the world. There is a second mark it does not show the world—a small pencil dot, ovoid, pressed into the upper margin of a document the hand wants read by the eyes it has taught to look. The sun is the heraldry. The dot is the tradecraft. Your ex-wife has been reading the dot for nine years. I will tell you the rest in time. Margaret will tell you the part of the rest I do not know.'

Calder said: 'Margaret.'

Klaus said: 'In time.'

Klaus drank. Then he said, in the voice he used when he was being German about something the English had not yet understood: 'You are surprised. I am not. In the East we always assumed the money was a weapon. You in the West assumed it was neutral. That is the difference between a man who grew up behind a wall and a man who grew up believing there was no wall. The wall was the money. It has always been the money.'

They drank. The Grouse went down warm and tasted of peat smoke and the chemical edge of cheap glass.

The first night.

He read the first page on the night Klaus arrived. He did not get past it.

The hand was Margaret's. He had been cataloging that hand on Christmas cards and grocery lists and the back covers of paperbacks she returned to him without remark for nearly thirty years. The hand was also, by the discipline of the pages it had now produced, the hand of a woman who had, for some time, been something other than the woman he had thought he was married to.

The pages were dated November. They were addressed to no one. They began:

If you are reading this, you are alive. If you are alive, the operation went the way I assessed it would go, which is to say, James, that you and I were both lucky and unlucky in approximately the proportions I expected. The lucky part is that you are reading this. The unlucky part is that I will not see you again.

He read the paragraph three times. He set the page down at the third reading.

He sat at the desk with his hands flat on the wood on either side of the notebook for some minutes. His hands did not shake. The shaking had been cleaned out of him in the alley at Sète, the way some kinds of shaking only got cleaned out of a body by the body finding a different argument with itself.

He turned to the second page.

He did not read it. He looked at it. The hand on the second page was the same hand on the first. He looked at the second page until the second page was a thing the eye understood as paper rather than a thing the mind was being asked to absorb. Then he closed the notebook.

He went down to the breakwater.

The bell-buoy was making its small mournful noise. The wind had come up from the southwest at some hour after midnight and was now pulling the buoy hard. Two trawlers at the quay. The saddle-faced fisherman was not on the breakwater. The breakwater was empty.

Calder stood at the end and watched the water against the rocks for a moment. Then he put both hands flat on the cold iron rail, and he leaned his weight onto the rail, and he made a sound that came up out of his chest before his throat had decided to permit it. The sound was not a word. The sound was not a sob either. The sound was the brief involuntary thing the body did when the body had been carrying a registration the body had not been authorized to acknowledge for two months and was now being told to acknowledge it. It lasted, by the count of the bell-buoy, six pulls of the buoy line. Then it stopped.

His hands were not wet. His face was not wet. He had not cried. He made a sound and the sound had been the part of the crying that still found its way out, and the rest of the crying was still in the place his father's grace had been, which was the place his body had decided years ago was the place such things would live, and not the eyes.

The water received the sound and gave it nothing back. The bell-buoy pulled six times. Then a seventh, which was not the wind. He counted the pulls without meaning to count them. The cold of the rail had moved up through his palms into the bones of his wrists. He was forty seven. He had been the man at the desk for more than half his life.

He stood on the breakwater for another twenty minutes. He went back upstairs.

Klaus was in the chair with the loose front leg. He did not look up when Calder came in.

Klaus said: 'I will be in the kitchen if you need me.'

Calder said: 'Thank you.'

Klaus went to the kitchen. He stayed there for the rest of the night.

◆◆◆

The second night.

He read pages two through four.

The pages contained the explanation Margaret had owed him for nine years and that he had not, in any of those nine years, asked for.

She began, in the early eighties, to notice the small architectural irregularities that had begun showing up in the obituaries of senior nuclear engineers across Europe. She had not been working for any service. She had been a Year Six teacher with a Latin master's from Birkbeck, and her noticing was the kind of noticing teachers of a certain age developed on the corners of newspapers in staffrooms during free periods. She began, the year after the noticing, to make a small list. She had made the list because no one else had. The list was the first piece of work she had done in this field that she had not been asked to do.

By 1985 she had identified twenty-three deaths whose obituaries had used the same German construction—*Der Einsatz war operativ gerechtfertigt*, rendered into English as *operationally justified*—translated by the same three press officers across three years.

He set the page down on the table.

He sat for some seconds with the page face-down on the wood. Margaret had been keeping a count that no institution was keeping. She had been doing it alone, in pencil, in margins, in offprints, in a gray notebook in the kitchen of a flat in Ealing while he had been at his desk at Century House signing off on the very files her count would have explained. He registered, in the way he had been registering things in the eight nights at the harbor, that he was reading a woman's dossier of herself.

He turned the page back over.

By 1986 she had identified the Strasbourg, Berlin, and Stockholm cluster.

By the late eighties she had begun to receive small amounts of money from a charitable trust she had been told had been established by an aunt she did not know. The aunt had died long before with thirty-four pounds and a budgerigar. The trust had paid Margaret three hundred pounds every November for fourteen years. She had inquired. The third redirection of the inquiry had been to an address in Vienna. She had not stopped paying attention.

By 1988 she had begun to write Latin papers under her maiden name, Margaret Howell, in the Journal of Medieval Latin on the augural college under Theodosius. She sent the third paper, in March of that year, through the academic exchange to a colleague at the Warburg Institute. The colleague had passed it to a Roman Latinist for correction. The Latinist had returned the paper through the same channel with three small corrections of declension and a single line of pencil in the margin: *si non vis, et hoc*—if you will not, then this also. Margaret had not known the hand. She filed the correction. She had also, for the first time in a year of academic correspondence, begun to suspect that she had been doing the work she had been doing for someone whose presence she had not, in the doing, been able to detect.

She had not stopped writing the papers. She had continued, through 1988 and 1989, in the academic register the Journal favored, and she had watched the margins. The hand had not appeared again. She had begun to assume the hand had been a single small intervention and not a continuing surveillance. She had been wrong about this. The wrongness was the space she was working in.

Calder set the page down at the end of the third entry.

He understood, with a small cold registering, that Margaret had been working the architecture from inside the architecture's own academic corridors for nine years. The architecture was reading her papers. The architecture had not yet decided whether she was an asset or a target, and that the not deciding was the only reason she was still alive.

The Italian hand—the one that had written si non vis, et hoc in pencil in the margin of her March 1988 paper—had been, by the discipline of the academic exchange, the hand of one of the seven men at the top of the institution. The seven men did not write in margins. The seven men ate carbonara in trattorias in Trastevere and authorized things. Except that one of them, in March 1988, had read a Latin paper by a primary-school teacher in Chiswick and had written three words in pencil in the margin and had returned it through the academic channel as if the writing were an academic joke between Latinists.

The three words were the joke. The joke was not a joke. The joke was the institution registering Margaret. The institution had been registering her for two years before the events that had brought Calder to this desk. Margaret had registered the institution registering her. The two of them had been doing a private quadrille across academic correspondence for two years, and Margaret had been keeping the quadrille in pencil in the margins of her own registers, and she had not, in any of those two years, told her former husband.

He banked the Italian hand. He kept the seven men. He held the si non vis, et hoc against the compass rose. The file was the file the eight pages had been opening since the first sentence.

He turned to page four.

Page four contained the names. Three of them. Henri Vernet, Marseilles. Wolfgang Brückner, Berlin. The man at the Brussels phone number. Seventy-three years old. Greek raised in Limassol before 1948. Gold ring on right little finger.

The first two names were the names on his own pencil page. The third was the name his pencil page had been waiting for. The third had been on Margaret's page since November.

He had been killing names from a list a woman in Ealing had been keeping for nine years, and the list had been hers before it had been his, and the operation he was running was the operation she had assessed before he had known an operation existed.

He closed the notebook.

He sat at the desk for some time.

He thought, for the first time in seven weeks, about Andrew Ruskin.

Andrew Ruskin had climbed the stairs to the Greenwich flat at 19:47 on the third of January with a manila envelope and the message that the woman would be delayed. The woman had not arrived. Calder had resigned at 09:32 the following morning. Klaus had shot the second hire at 12:34. The seventeen hours between Ruskin's stair and Klaus's round had been the operational hours during which the substitution had been set in motion. Ruskin had been the messenger. Ruskin had not been at the Mayflower. Ruskin had not been at Webber Street. Ruskin had been the man who had brought the envelope and the message and had then disappeared from the architecture.

Calder had not, in the seven weeks since, allowed himself to wonder why Andrew Ruskin had brought the message at 19:47. The discipline had been the silence around the wondering, since the immediate work had required all the attention he had to give it. The immediate work had not yet permitted the wondering.

He let himself wonder now.

Andrew Ruskin had been a State Department clerk on secondment to Century House. The secondment had been a back-channel arrangement of the kind the Foreign Office maintained with the State Department under a 1972 memorandum, used for the useful work of routing administrative paper between the two services without committing either to a formal exchange. Ruskin had been at Calder's Greenwich flat at 19:47. Andrew Ruskin had also been, at some hour Calder did not yet know, somewhere else with someone else. Andrew Ruskin was the kind of man who carried envelopes for two desks.

Calder banked Ruskin. The file was now the file with Ruskin in it.

He went to the kitchen.

Klaus was at the table with the bottle of Grouse and two enamel mugs and the bakery loaf from the morning. He had been waiting in the kitchen since Calder had gone down to the breakwater the previous evening. He looked up.

Calder said: 'Why now.'

Klaus said: 'Sit.'

Calder sat.

Klaus poured.

Klaus said: 'The Wall came down in November. The Stasi files have been in the hands of citizen committees in Leipzig and the eastern cities since December, and in Berlin since mid-January and will be in the hands of West German civil servants by the spring. Thirty years of the Custodia's small German co-operations are about to be readable by people who can read German and were not in the building when the cooperations were arranged. The Italian services have been preparing for this since October. The Custodia has been preparing for it since June. The November fall accelerated the preparation by approximately eighteen months. The institution planned, for some years, to manage a slow careful exposure across the next decade. The slow careful exposure became, in three days in November, a fast unmanaged one. The Custodia has been making decisions, since the Wall, that it planned to take ten years to make. The decisions have been compressed. The compression is the violence. Vienna in October was the institution telling itself it could still be careful. Webber Street in January was the institution admitting it could not. Margaret began the eight pages in the same week. The eight pages are the work of a woman who had been preparing, also for some years, for an exposure she had not yet known she would be living through. The Wall did to her what the Wall did to the institution. It accelerated her by eighteen months.'

He drank.

'The answer to why now is the Wall. The Wall is what made all of this possible and all of this necessary. The Wall is also what gives us the next four or five years to do the work before the Custodia has rebuilt its discipline. After that, it will be too late. We are doing the work in the only window that will exist for it. That is what your ex-wife caught. That is what she wrote in November. That is why you are reading the eight pages tonight and not in 1995.'

Calder did not respond for some time.

Then he said: 'Margaret has been waiting for the Wall.'

Klaus said: 'Margaret was the only person on this work who knew the Wall would fall in 1989. She wrote it in a paper in Speculum in 1986. The paper was about the patience of late-imperial fortifications. The footnote, in pencil in her own offprint that I read in your study in 1988, named the date. November 1989. Plus or minus six weeks. I have not, in the years since, learned how she knew. She is the most careful reader I have known. I have also stopped trying to learn. She tells what she tells. The silence around what she has not yet told is her discipline.'

Calder ate the bread.

He went back to the desk.

He went to the bed. He lay down in his clothes. He did not sleep until the bakery oven began to warm below him before dawn.

The third night.

He read the seventh page.

He did not read pages five and six. Pages five and six were operational—a list of nodes, a map of European bank addresses, the routine of a man at a Brussels phone number. Pages five and six were for tomorrow. Page seven was for tonight.

Page seven was the sentence.

There are six others. I do not know who runs them. The seventh is mine.

He read it three times. He set the notebook down at the third reading.

He thought of the bracelet.

The bracelet had told him, last November, that Margaret had given the Zurich key to someone who needed it and had replaced it with a key of her own. The new key on the ring had been a quarter-millimeter shorter at the bow than the key he had placed there in 1977. The bow was the upper stem of the key, the throat the groove on its side. A locksmith working from a wax impression rather than the original blank left both measurements slightly off. He registered the difference on a Sunday morning in the Chiswick kitchen as the bracelet had caught the light over the dish beside the sink, and he had not asked. His silence had been the recognition that Margaret was running her own operation. The bracelet had told him, in one Sunday-morning glance at the dish beside the sink, what the eight pages were now naming.

The bracelet had been seven Coordinators.

The bracelet had been Margaret's list.

The bracelet had been Margaret's. She had been the maker of the list. She had been running an operation against an institution that had not yet identified her by name. The key on the fifth ring was the list—the seven regional executives, found one at a time across years of her own quiet work. The making had been hers, and that making was now the work the eight pages were leaving for him.

He sat with that for a long time.

Then he turned to page eight.

The eighth page was, in a smaller hand than the rest:

I have done what I could. The gaps are mine. I am sorry for the gaps. I have loved you, James, in the way the work permitted me to love you, which has not been the way I would have chosen. The work permitted what it permitted. I would have chosen otherwise. I have chosen now what I can choose. Make the list small. Make the list yours. Do not make the list for me. Make it because the work is the work. Margaret.

He folded the eighth page closed.

He went to the kitchen. Klaus was at the table in the corner with the bottle of Grouse and two enamel mugs. Klaus had been waiting for him to come into the kitchen.

Klaus poured.

Calder said: 'She is the seventh.'

Klaus said: 'Yes.'

'You knew.'

'I read the pages on the train from Zurich. I told you I had not. That was the wrong kind of discipline. I read them twice. The reading was operational. The not-reading-again is also operational.'

'I would not have asked.'

'I know. The telling is part of the operation. The withholding would be a different kind of operation.'

'Thank you.'

Klaus drank his tea. Then he said: 'I had a dream on the train back from Zurich. I have not had it since. I am going to tell you because I tell you the things I dream about your ex-wife. There have been four such dreams over the years. This one was the fourth.'

Calder was silent.

'In the dream there was a woman wearing your ex-wife's coat. The coat was the coat she wore in the hallway when I delivered the parcel to her. The woman was older than your ex-wife had been then but younger than your ex-wife was last year. The coat had not aged. The woman in the dream said three sentences I have remembered. The first sentence was: The list does not include all the names. The second sentence was: The names not on the list are the names that are protecting me. The third sentence was: I will not see him again.'

Klaus looked at the wall.

'I am telling you because I dreamed it. I do not know what the dream means. I do not know what your ex-wife meant by the seventh-and-mine sentence or what the woman in the coat meant by the names-not-on-the-list. I am telling you because I have been carrying these dreams alone and you are the only person in the world to whom telling them is operational rather than embarrassing.'

Calder said: 'Thank you.'

Klaus said: 'Your ex-wife was wasted on the geraniums.'

'Yes.'

'Your ex-wife frightens me more than any operative I have known. I will tell you something I have not told you in twenty-one years. I have been afraid of her since the hallway. I did not know I was afraid of her until I read the pages. The fear has not been operationally relevant. I am telling you now because the fear is now operationally relevant. We are working a list she helped to make. And your ex-wife was not on any service's payroll. She has been doing this work outside the structures the rest of us have been doing it inside. The outside is the part that should frighten you also.'

Calder did not respond for a long moment.

'My ex-wife was wasted on the geraniums.'

'Yes.'

They drank.

Klaus said, after some time: 'There is one other thing I have been holding for twenty-one years that I would like to tell you tonight.'

Calder waited.

'The basement. In East Berlin. In 1969.'

'I remember the basement.'

'I have been thinking about it because we are now starting the work and I would like you to have a piece of information about it that I have not, in the years between, given you.'

Calder said: 'Yes.'

Klaus said: 'I had been bleeding from a wound in my left side. The bleeding was slow but persistent. The basement had a concrete drain in the middle of the floor. I had been positioned by the East Germans against the wall opposite the drain. The cellar was the night Bruhn decided I had stopped being his. He decided that morning. He had me brought in at 19:00 and the work began at 21:00. By 03:00 the work had told him most of what he had wanted to confirm. He left the cellar at 03:14. He intended to come back in the morning to finish. He did not get to finish.'

He paused. Then he continued, in the voice he used for things he had been holding for years.

'I spent the first two hours watching my own blood run down the slope of the floor toward the drain. The blood had not reached the drain. The slope had been wrong. The blood had pooled six inches from the drain and stopped, and I had watched the pool widen for the next four hours, and the pool had been the thing I was thinking about when you came down the stairs at 03:42 and cut me loose.'

'I have been thinking about the wrong slope of that basement floor for twenty-one years. The men who built that basement had built it incompetently, and the incompetence was the reason I had been alive when you reached me.'

'The incompetent slope was the operational mistake of the men who built it. The mistake was the thing that gave me the next twenty-one years. The mistake is the reason I am here, in this room, with you, working this list.'

Calder did not speak.

Klaus said: 'There is one other thing I have not, in twenty-one years, made operational sense of. Above the small concrete drain a mark had been scratched into the concrete by some hand, thumbnail-sized, the shape of a small Greek letter. A theta. I registered it in the third hour of my being in the basement when my eyes had become accustomed to the thin light from the high ventilation grille. I filed it as graffiti by some Berlin workman of an earlier construction phase. I had not investigated. I am telling you now because it has, in the past months, been coming back to me at intervals, and I have not been able to file it again the way I had filed it in 1969. I will tell you the one fact about it I am sure of. It was scratched above the drain that had been six inches from finishing me, in the room a man came down a staircase at oh-three-forty-two to take me out of. I do not know what the mark is. I know what the room became.'

Calder said: 'I saw a theta on a doorframe in Marseilles. The back of the Hôtel du Vieux-Port. Inside, chest height. Chalked.'

Klaus looked at him.

'Two thetas.'

'Two thetas,' Calder said. 'Twenty-one years apart. Both at the threshold of an operational space. Neither on any visible surface. The eight-ray sun has been on the visible surfaces—banknotes, lintels, mastheads. The theta has been on the undersides. They are not the same hand.'

Klaus said: 'No. They are not.'

They sat with that.

Klaus said: 'I should have told you about the basement years ago. I should have told you many times. The German in me would like to tell you the delay was operational. It was not. The silence has begun to feel like the kind of debt that compounds. The debt is now the size of the borrowed time. I cannot pay the borrowed time back. I can only spend it.'

Calder said: 'We are spending it.'

Klaus said: 'We are. Yes.'

Klaus went to the bed in the adjoining room. Calder remained at the desk. 1968 and 1969 had been the two years of three rooms. The doorway in Friedrichshain in November of 1968 where a stranger had pulled him in for four hours: his discipline had broken; he had run six blocks through the dark with a forged West German passport in his coat; the Stasi were at the Bahnhof; the failed engineer was not at the rendezvous; the woman had said her name was Natalia, had pressed a finger to her lips, had made him tea on a small electric ring, had not asked who he was, had let him sleep on her sofa, and had not been there to see again. The long polished table at Century House in the autumn where the work had been put to him by a man whose face he could no longer remember. The basement in East Berlin in March of 1969. He went back into the country that had taught him how to fail. He had cut Klaus from the cuffs at 03:42 with the specific intention of a man who had been allowed to live by an unknown woman in November and was repaying the allowance to whichever stranger the work next put him in front of. He had not, in twenty-one years, lined the four rooms up beside one another. The lining-up was an operation that did not produce a feeling. The feeling would come later.

He turned to the eight pages once more.

And he found, on the fourth night of his reading, in a slit in the leather of the back cover, a folded sheet of writing paper. It contained six lines of medieval Latin in Margaret's hand and, beneath them, in pencil, in a different hand he did not recognize—older, smaller, Italian by the cut of the e—a single line of correction: si non vis, et hoc. He did not have the Latin to translate either. He filed the second hand under the file he had begun keeping for the people Margaret had been working with whom Calder had not been told about. The hand was written with a fountain pen of a kind not manufactured since before the war, in an ink the color of dried iris, on a paper Calder did not recognize as English. The pen was the pen of someone who had begun writing Latin under a regime that had since fallen and had not, in the years since, exchanged it for another. The ink was an old ink. The hand was the hand of someone writing Latin in that pen for half a century. The hand of the correction was a hand he would not meet for nine years.

He sat for some time at the desk.

Then he marked, looking at the eight pages, that he had seen

Margaret's primary-school-teacher hand on a notebook before.

The notebook had been spiral-bound. The cover had been cardboard, gray, with a stain at the lower right corner where a cup had been set on it once. Margaret had been writing in it when he had come down to the kitchen early, on a Sunday morning years before. She heard him on the stair. She closed the notebook by the time he had reached the doorway. The closing had been one slow practiced gesture. She had not turned. He had logged the gesture. He had not stopped.

He had crossed to the kettle. He had filled it from the tap. He set it on the gas. He took the blue mug down from the shelf and set out the wooden tray with the marmalade and the honey and the horn-handled butter knife.

While he had done these things, Margaret had not opened the notebook again.

The kettle had boiled. He made the tea. He sat across from her.

She had said, in the voice her voice was on those mornings—the thin one: 'James.'

He had said: 'Margaret.'

She had said: 'I am sorry to be writing on a Sunday.'

He had said: 'You are not sorry. You are working. The work is what it is.'

She had said: 'Yes.'

They had not said anything else. They had drunk the tea. The notebook had stayed closed on the table between them, with Margaret's hand resting flat on its cover. Calder had finished his tea at 06:42. He took the blue mug to the sink. He washed it. He had set it on the rack. He had said, at the kitchen door: 'I am going up to the study for an hour.' Margaret said: 'Yes.' He went up to the study. He had not come back down for two hours.

When he had come back down at 08:42 the notebook had

not been on the table. The marmalade and the honey and the wooden tray had been put away. Margaret had been at the sink, washing the breakfast dishes. The radio had been on, playing the Today program.

The registration he had made on the third Sunday at the harbor—that they had been two operatives in the same kitchen—had one of its sources on this morning. The morning was the morning the registration had been waiting in for ten years.

He had banked the registration.

He had not, in the nine years that had followed, opened the locked drawer of Margaret's writing desk in the front room of the Chiswick house. Margaret had never, in those nine years, asked what was in his locked drawer in the study upstairs.

The two locked drawers had been the marriage.

He sat at the harbor desk now and looked at the eight pages.

The hand was the same hand.

The notebook had been the first list.

Around 03:00 on the fourth night Calder began to laugh.

The laugh was brief. It was something between a cough and a laugh, the laugh of a man who had not laughed in a while and had decided to test whether the equipment still worked.

He had been married, in operational terms, to two women, and one of them he had never met.

He stopped laughing. He sat for another hour.

He sat looking at his hands. Until the laughing the hands had been steady. The hands were now shaking. The laughing had set them off in a way the operation had not. He waited. He set the hands flat on the desk on either side of the notebook, fingers spread, palms down. The shaking stopped at 03:14. The laughing was now the part of him that was harder to control than the killing.

Then he wrote the third name on the page.

3. The man at the Brussels phone number. (Margaret's description.)

He folded the page. He put it in the leather notebook beneath Margaret's eight pages.

He thought, sitting at the desk in the quiet port he could not name to himself, about the inside of Elena's left wrist. The compass rose she had drawn there at eighteen with a needle and shop-bought ink. Four directions. A dot at the center.

He thought of her hands.

He thought of the way her thumb had moved along the inside of his wrist on the morning after the first night, in the Chiswick studio in December 1973, while he had been pretending to sleep and she was deciding, in the long quiet of the room, whether the woman who moved her thumb that way was a woman she was permitted to be. He thought about the small gold Omega he had given her in 1974, which she had worn over the compass rose for sixteen years, the small worn place the watchband had made on the inked dot at the center. He thought of the way she had stood at the Paxton Gallery in October of 1973 in front of the East Berlin window photograph with the curtains and the geranium and the Wall, with the catalog open in her right hand. She had not turned when he had come up beside her. Her voice came out flat and English when she said the title of the photograph aloud, and the way the flatness was the first operational decision she made about him without his knowing she was making it. He thought about her tracing the small faded scar at the corner of his left eyebrow without asking what it was, on a Sunday morning in the Fitzrovia studio, the attention of a woman trained to register everything and who decided, for him alone, that the registering would be in the service of seeing him rather than reporting on him. He thought about the way she had held her hands on the table at the Mayflower, palms down, fingers spread, breathing in the slow measured pattern she managed under every circumstance for twenty-two years. He thought about the way her mouth moved when she said Elena aloud for the first time since 1970.

He thought about the four directions she had inked on her wrist at eighteen.

The four directions were the four directions she planned to walk in. She was eighteen. The directions were the future a girl's wrist permitted itself to imagine, in a Leningrad apartment, with the needle hot from the lamp and the ink from the shop on Vasilevsky Island. He had been the dot at the center of those four directions for sixteen years. The dot was not the future. The dot was the place the four directions agreed to converge for as long as the convergence held. The convergence held for sixteen years. The four directions were not taken. The directions were the future the work did not, in any of those years, allow her.

The compass rose had been the only personal gesture of disobedience her training had ever permitted her. The Akhmatova line on her ribcage was the earlier mark—inked at seventeen by a dissident artist in a Leningrad apartment that no longer existed, six months before he was arrested. *I taught myself to live simply and wisely.* The line of Akhmatova's the institution had not been able to read off her file because the institution did not permit the reading of poets who had outlasted their tyrants. The Akhmatova had been the closing of one self. The compass rose had been the private grammar of the next one—the girl who had been told what the institution would permit and had drawn, in spring 1966 with the needle hot from the lamp, the careful proof that some part of her was not going to fully consent to it. He had been at the center of that grammar without ever being told he was. He had been told, for sixteen years, by the wearing of the watch over the mark.

He banked the four directions.

'All right,' he said, to the empty room.

That was the whole sentence.

In the morning Klaus made tea.

'You read the pages.'

'I read the pages.'

'All of them.'

'All of them.'

'Including the one about the seven.'

'Yes.'

'I do not know what she meant either. I have been thinking about it for some weeks.'

Calder looked at him.

'It came to me on the train from Zurich,' Klaus said. 'I told you the easy reading last night and let it stand. There is a harder reading I want to put on the table this morning. There are six others. I think that means six other regional executives. The seventh is not Margaret. The seventh is the one she has been protecting. There are seven regional executives, and Margaret has been making the list of them. The institution does not know she is making the list. The institution may know she exists. The institution does not know what she is. The unknowing is the room she has been working in.'

'Yes.'

'And we are now working the list she made. And the list she made is the list—the seven the maker could see from where she was standing. The other six Coordinators are running their own lists. The other six lists are not on this paper. We are working one-seventh of the work.'

'Yes.'

'There is one thing I would like to say about Vernet.'

'Yes.'

'Vernet was not a Coordinator. The man at the Brussels phone number—Christofi—is a Coordinator. Brückner in Berlin is a Coordinator. Vernet was the deposition that authorized Elena's killing. He was an old SDECE hand whose name had been kept on a witness retainer by the Custodia for some years and who was used, in October, to give the Vienna board the confirmation that authorized the November order. Your ex-wife put him on her list because he sealed Elena. She did not put him on her list because she thought he was at the top. He was not at the top. The pencil page has two Coordinator names on it. Christofi. Brückner. The other five Coordinators we have not yet named. Vernet was the first kill but he was not a Coordinator. When we close Christofi and Brückner we will have closed two of the seven. Five will still be alive and we will not have their names. The names will come or they will not. The work will be the finding of the names. The names will be the next four years.'

'Yes.'

'I would also like to say one thing about the Italian hand.'

'Yes.'

'The Italian hand is one of the seven men in Rome. The seven men in Rome do not write in margins. They authorize. The fact that one of them has written in pencil in the margin of a Latin paper your ex-wife wrote is the fact that one of the seven men in Rome has registered her. The registration is the most important fact in the eight pages. We do not yet know whether the registration is hostile or sympathetic. The registration is the question we will be working on for some years.'

Calder said: 'And the seventh.'

Klaus said: 'The seventh is alive. I do not know where. I think Margaret may not be in Ealing anymore. I think the address you have for her is one she has not been at since the autumn. I think she has been moving since she gave me the parcel. I think she will continue to move. I think we will not see her again. I am not sure of any of this. I am telling you because the absence is one of the things we should both prepare for.'

Calder said: 'Yes.'

Klaus said: 'Eat your bread.'

Calder ate the bread.

6
LISBON

The Alfama—April 1990

Eddie's place was in the Alfama, on a cobbled street called the Beco do Carneiro that ran down toward the river.

The street was so narrow Calder could touch the wall on either side with his outstretched arms if he had wanted to. The buildings were three and four stories, washed in the faded ochre and pale blue that were the city's defaults. Laundry hung from window-bars on the second floors. The cobbles were uneven and worn smooth by four hundred years of foot traffic.

From halfway down the street one could see the river, a slate-gray ribbon between the buildings, and beyond it the southern bank where ferries were docking and undocking in their slow institutional rhythms. The sound of the ferries reached the street at a delay, which made the docking visible before it was audible.

The marine shop was on the right, halfway down. The shop's window was unwashed. The window display had not changed in nine years—three faded packets of marine rope, a brass compass, a hand-lettered sign in Portuguese advertising winter rates on hull paint that had not been winter for some time.

Klaus and Calder arrived at 11:00 on a Wednesday. They had flown into Lisbon on three separate flights from three different starting points the previous day, with three different passports.

A faint bell rang when they came in. The bell was something between a cat's collar and a teaspoon striking porcelain.

A woman nearing sixty, dressed in widow black, looked up from a ledger.

'Senhora Almeida,' Klaus said, in Portuguese.

She nodded. She did not smile. She pressed a button under her counter.

Klaus said, to Calder, in English: 'Her husband drowned in 1971 in a storm off the Portuguese coast. She was thirty-eight. She had three children at the time. The youngest was four months old. Eddie has paid for her grandson's three years at the Lisbon university. The grandson is in his second year now. Engineering. The grandson does not know who is paying. The grandson believes the money has come from a foundation his late grandfather had set up before the storm.'

Calder said: 'Eddie set up a foundation the year of the storm.'

'Eddie set up the foundation later and backdated the paper-work.'

The door at the back of the shop opened with a mechanical ex-hale, half a refrigerator gasket, half a bus pulling out of a stop.

Eddie Frears, fifty-eight, came through it. Welsh from Bridgend, ex-22 SAS—Britain's special forces regiment—two tours in Borneo and one in Dhofar. Five-foot-eight. Iron-gray hair cut short. The kind of mustache that had stopped being fashionable decades earlier and that Eddie kept because Eddie kept things on his own schedule.

'Klaus.'

'Eddie.'

He looked at Calder.

'You're the dead one.'

Calder did not respond at once.

'Klaus told me. February. I don't mind it. I've worked with dead men before. They keep better hours.'

They followed him through the door. The room beyond was a workshop. Long workbench down one wall, two vises, a small Bridgeport milling machine, a Lyman reloading press. The other wall was racked with weapons.

On the desk, side by side: a telex machine that had been there for years and a brand-new Brother fax that had been there since the previous Thursday. The fax was on, the green light blinking. The telex was off.

'I will give the fax six months. The telex stays.'

The workshop smelled of Hoppe's No. 9 and machine oil and old leather and the subtle sweet undertone of fresh coffee from a percolator on the bench. It also smelled, faintly, of Madeira.

Above the workbench, a framed photograph of Eddie at thirty-three in the Borneo jungle, faded color, four other men beside him. Two of the four were dead by 1968 according to the brass plate underneath.

'Sit. The Madeira's open.'

Henriques and Henriques ten-year. He poured into three glasses that were older than the Madeira.

'You want a Walther.'

Klaus said: 'PPK. 7.65mm. Production date no later than 1975.'

Eddie went to the rack. He came back with three Walthers. He laid them on the bench.

Calder's eye went past Eddie to the wall while the laying was happening. The wall carried what a man like Eddie carried over nineteen years: a Browning Hi-Power that had been taken off a British officer at Suez and had reached the Alfama by way of three previous owners; an SVT-40 from the Eastern Front

Eddie had taken in trade and not sold because the Russian who had brought it had said the rifle had a story and Eddie had agreed not to find out what it was; an Austrian Steyr GB; two Beretta 92s; and a Webley Mk VI service revolver from 1916 in a leather sleeve, given to Eddie in the early seventies by the major who had been his troop commander in Borneo on the day the major had handed in his commission, and that had been oiled twice a year for twenty years and not, in those years, fired. Each weapon was a layer of someone else's war whose work Eddie had been keeping for as long as the marine shop had been the marine shop. Calder did not ask which were for sale and which were not. The asking was not his to do.

'Three Walthers. The oldest is the cleanest. The middle one has the best slide-to-frame fit. The newest has had its barrel replaced last year by a Belgian shop I do not entirely trust. Pick one.'

Calder picked up the middle one. He stripped it without speaking. He reassembled it. The slide cycled cleanly. The trigger broke at four pounds.

'This one.'

Eddie took the Walther back. He cradled it the way he cradled weapons he had been keeping for nineteen years and was now sending out with someone he liked. He stripped it again himself—slide off, recoil spring out, barrel up under the fine inspection lamp he kept on a swing arm at the corner of the bench—and ran a single bronze patch through the bore. The patch came out clean. He passed the patch under his nose by an old armorer's reflex he had stopped explaining to himself in the seventies. He set the Walther on a square of dark green felt at the corner of the bench. The reassembly took him twenty-eight seconds. Calder, who had needed forty-one a moment earlier, logged the difference without comment.

'Geco ammunition. 200 rounds. The lot was made in Germany. The primers are slightly hotter than the current production.

Adjust your point of aim slightly low at twenty meters.'

Klaus added: 'The German lot.'

Eddie looked at him. 'What.'

'Nothing.'

'You also want explosives.'

Klaus answered: '250g of PE-4 with a chemical fuse, six-second delay. Door breaching.'

'I can do PE-4. I am out of Vickers chemical fuses. I have an Italian supplier who has been sending me fuses. I will have a parcel by July.'

Eddie drank his Madeira. 'You don't drink it. You sip it.'

Calder sipped. The Madeira tasted of hazelnuts and burned sugar.

Eddie reached inside his jacket. He took out a worn leather cigarette case, the kind men carried in earlier decades and had stopped carrying years before except for a particular kind of man who had decided his old objects were the old objects he was going to keep. He opened it.

Inside: not cigarettes. A small folded piece of paper, ten years old by the look of it, slightly yellow at the edges.

He unfolded it. He looked at it for a moment. He held it up so Calder and Klaus could see it. A child's drawing in colored pencil. A boy of seven had drawn a stick figure of a man standing next to what appeared to be a tank. The stick figure had a mustache. The tank had a comically oversized gun barrel and a flag on top with a red dragon on it that the boy had been concentrating to draw correctly.

'My brother's son. He's nineteen now. He's studying structural engineering in Cardiff. He doesn't know what I do. He drew this when his teacher asked him to draw what his uncle did for work. He drew me with a tank. I have not corrected him. The drawing is the only piece of paper I carry that has nothing to do with the work.'

Eddie folded the drawing. He put it back in the case. He put the case back in his jacket. He did not show the drawing again.

'I'll need the Walther fitted. I have a leather rig made by a man in Estoril who only does shoulder rigs. He is eighty-one. He is the best man in Iberia for a shoulder rig.'

'Thank you.'

'You don't have to thank me. Klaus is paying me. Klaus has been paying me for years.'

He looked at Calder.

'I will say something to you that I do not say to most people I do work for. I knew your ex-wife.'

Calder did not move.

'I knew her years ago. Eight days. We did not sleep together. She came to Lisbon in November with a question I could not answer at the time. The question was whether I had access to certain ledgers from the period 1962 to 1968 in a particular institutional archive in Vienna. I did not. The question was unanswerable. She accepted the answer. She bought me dinner. She told me she was a primary-school teacher in Chiswick who grew geraniums and had a husband who worked at the Foreign Office and that none of these things were the relevant facts about her. I asked her what was. She said: The relevant fact is that I am paying attention. I have thought about her sentence for years. I have not understood it.'

Eddie poured himself another measure. 'She drank Madeira. She did not finish her glass. She left the unfinished glass on this very bench.' He indicated the workshop bench. 'It sat there until I drank it the next morning. I have not bought another bottle from that vintage. I will not.'

Calder said: 'Neither have I.'

'I am sorry for your loss.'

'Thank you.'

Eddie was quiet for a moment. Then he said: 'I have been alone in this shop for nineteen years. I have had three women in those years. None of the three was your ex-wife. I am telling you because you should know that the woman who came to Lisbon in November of 1981 with a question about Vienna ledgers was the closest thing I had had to a Sunday afternoon since 1968. I did not have the Vienna ledgers. I had wanted to have them. I walked her back to her hotel. I did not go in. The not-going-in was the gift I gave her without telling her I was giving it. The gift was that her husband would not, in any year of the marriage, have a thing he would have to forgive her for that had any of my fingerprints on it. I have kept the gift. I am telling you in this room because the keeping is now the fact you should have on file before you ask me to keep the next thing.'

Calder did not respond for a moment.

He said: 'Thank you, Eddie.'

'Drink the Madeira.'

They drank the Madeira.

Calder left the marine shop at 14:14. The April sun in the Alfama at this hour was the sun that fell at the angle the Alfama had been built around in the eighth century. The cobblestones held the heat. The laundry on the second-floor window-bars moved very slightly in the soft wind off the river.

He walked up the cobbled hill toward the overlook. He did not look back at the marine shop.

On the cobbles ahead a gray cat with a torn ear was sleeping in a square of sun. A boy of eleven was sitting on the third stone step of a doorway with a bowl of soup on his knees. The soup smelled of cabbage and sausage. From a window two doors past came a low Portuguese ballad sung by a woman whose voice had been broken by the weather that lived on the river in October.

He noted that the woman whose husband had drowned in the storm had been a fisherman's wife. The woman who had drunk Madeira at Eddie's bench in November had been a woman whose former husband had been Calder. Both women had given Eddie a piece of paper he had been keeping for some years—the paperwork for the foundation in one case, the unanswered question of the Vienna ledgers in the other. Eddie was the kind of man other people's wives had been giving things to keep, since the foundation, in the back of a marine shop in the Alfama. He looked out over the river. The river at 14:30 in April was the slate-gray ribbon Calder had noted from down at the marine shop at 11:00, only wider, and with a single ferry crossing slowly to the southern bank.

He went down the hill to find the train back to the harbor.

7
THE CLUSTER

Brussels / Lyon / La Spezia / The harbor—May to November 1990

Brussels.

The man Klaus had been waiting nineteen years to put in front of someone like Calder was named Pieter Devos. Sixty-one. He had been a clerk in the Belgian foreign-trade ministry for thirty-four years and had retired in November to a small apartment near the Place du Châtelain whose front window looked onto a green and a war memorial.

Devos's older sister, Mathilde, was a journalist in Antwerp in the early seventies working on a piece about the death of a customs officer at the port. The customs officer stopped a freight transfer that summer that did not, on the manifests, make operational sense. He filed a memorandum. The memorandum was not answered. Two weeks later he drowned in the Schelde, off duty, on a Sunday, during a private sail in a boat he had owned for twelve years and had sailed with the competence of a man for whom the boat was not a hobby. The autopsy raised no concerns. Mathilde Devos was raising them. She filed eight queries with the port authority. The eighth came back with a polite note. She then filed a piece under her own byline questioning the absence of follow-up. The piece appeared on a Tuesday in September. By the following Sunday Mathilde Devos was hit by a tram on the De Keyserlei outside Antwerp's Centraal station in circumstances the Antwerp police had categorized as a probable suicide despite the absence of any prior indication that this was a probable thing. Pieter had been forty-two at the time. He had not, in any of the years that followed, accepted the categorization.

Devos had, since the funeral, been keeping a file. He used the access his ministerial role gave him to ledger entries he had no operational reason to consult. He made photocopies, on foreign-language carbon paper, of documents he had had no professional cause to read. He had been carrying, for nineteen years, the names of the seven men who had been in Antwerp the week Mathilde had filed the eighth query. Three of them were dead. Two of them were on Calder's file. One of them was the man at the Brussels phone number.

They met Devos at the Châtelain market on a Sunday morning in May. He bought a bunch of asparagus. Klaus introduced Calder as a Norwegian cousin. Devos accepted the introduction the way men of a certain age accepted introductions from operatives they had been waiting to meet. They walked together for forty minutes. Devos talked. Klaus listened. Calder listened.

At the end of the forty minutes Devos handed Klaus a brown paper bag. The bag held three asparagus, a wedge of Roquefort, and an envelope. The envelope held seven typewritten pages and a brass key that opened a left-luggage locker at Brussels-Midi.

That afternoon Klaus opened the locker. Inside the locker was a battered leather satchel that had not been emptied in nineteen years. Inside the satchel were forty-one pages of carbon-copy customs records, three photographs of a Dutch coal freighter, and a brown index card on which Devos had written, in his careful clerk's hand, the seven names. The third name on the card was Christofi.

Klaus and Calder went back to the harbor.

On a Tuesday night at the end of May, while Klaus was in

Lisbon to see Eddie about a passport, a man came through the kitchen window.

He came in over the sill and one foot caught the enamel basin on the counter beside the sink and the basin went over and the man swore once in the soft local language of a port-town drunk who had been getting through the back windows of the village's bachelor flats for some years. He was twenty-six. He was thin in the way men who slept rough were thin. He carried a short Opinel from the breast pocket of his coat, open, because the coat was old and the pocket no longer closed and the knife had to be open if he was going to be able to bring it out. He had not come in for a fight. He had come in for the small enamel tin on the dresser where the village's bachelor flats kept their grocery money and the small loose change of a man who came home tired and emptied his pockets without thinking. He did not know there was a man in the flat. He had watched the lane for the better part of an hour and had seen no light. He had not, in any of the months he had been doing the work, met a man.

Calder was on the bed in the front room reading the seventh page for the third time. The basin going over registered through the open door as the specific note of enamel on tile and not as the note any other object in the kitchen would have made falling. The note was followed by the second note, which was the bottom of a man's shoe on the linoleum where the linoleum was loose. The two notes were in the wrong order for a man who had come in through the front and the right order for a man who had come in over the sill. The body had registered this before the mind. The body was already off the bed.

The Welrod was on the chair by the bed in its leather case. Calder did not take it. The case was the wrong instrument for a kitchen door. The Mercator was on the bedside table beside the lamp, folded. He took it. The blade came open without sound in the meat of his right hand. He went barefoot to the kitchen door. He waited at the door for the second footstep that was going to put the man in the middle of the kitchen with his back to the door.

The man took the second footstep. Calder came in behind him. His left hand went over the man's mouth and pulled the head back against his own shoulder and the right hand took the Mercator into the soft notch under the angle of the jaw where the carotid came up close against the skin and the blade went in to the haft and Calder drew it across. The cut opened the right carotid and the right jugular in the same passage. The man's body went rigid for a second and then began the specific slack-becoming the body did when the central pressure dropped. The Opinel fell out of his right hand onto the tile. Calder lowered the body to the floor. The blood went down the front of the man's shirt and across the tile in the slow draining shape blood made when it had been given a tile to spread across. The man's pupils did the dilation. The mouth tried twice to do something the mouth was no longer permitted to do. Then the body did the last thing the body was going to do that night, which was to release the bladder, and Calder registered the warm thin acrid smell of urine on a kitchen tile and registered, in the registering, that the body had done the work without the mind's permission.

He stood for some seconds in the dark with the Mercator in his right hand and the smell on the air and the man at his feet. The seconds were the seconds the mind required to catch up to the hand. The hand had been the hand of an operative. The hand had not asked the mind. The mind had not, until the hand was done, registered that this would be the fact.

The man had nothing on him. A wallet with eleven hundred pesetas and a French driving license in a name that was not, by the unworried way it had been folded and tucked, the name on the license. A second key on a string around his neck for a flat somewhere the harbor did not know about. The Opinel. A small twist of foil with the residue of something the man had been smoking. No papers that connected him to anyone. No instrument heavier than the Opinel. He was a thief. He had been a thief. He had picked the wrong window on the wrong Tuesday.

The saddle-faced fisherman's brother, who had not been to sea in years and who kept eight apple trees and a private opinion about people who came to the bakery woman with the wrong kind of questions, came up the lane an hour before dawn with the truck. He did not ask. He helped Calder lift the body into the bed of the truck under the tarp that smelled of three-day-old hake. He drove out toward the headland. He came back at first light alone. He nodded once at Calder on the doorstep and went on toward the village.

Calder washed the kitchen tile twice with the hot water from the kettle and a hard brush, and a third time with bleach. He took the basin off the floor and set it back on the counter. He closed the kitchen window. He sat at the kitchen table until the bakery oven warmed below him. The Mercator was folded again on the table in front of him. The blade had been wiped on the man's coat and rinsed twice and was clean. The handle held the small dull dark line of where blood had got into the seam of the leaping cat and would not come out.

When Klaus came back from Lisbon two days later, he registered the kitchen at the doorway and the basin on the counter and the table. He did not ask. Calder said: A man came in over the sill. Klaus nodded. He set his bag down. He said: The brother. Calder said: The brother. Klaus said: We will not speak of it again. They did not speak of it again. The Mercator's handle kept the small dull dark line in the seam of the leaping cat through the seven months and the kills that followed and through the Wittenberg barn and into the spring of the second year, and Calder did not, in any of those months, try again to clean it out.

In the second week of June, Klaus was in Lyon for two days.

He came back with a small rectangle of paper which he placed on the desk between them. The rectangle had been cut from a French newspaper. It was a column on the appointment of a new flute teacher at the Lyon conservatory. The column included a photograph. The photograph was small. The young woman in the photograph was twenty-one. She had a flute case in her left hand and her hair was pulled back in a way that exposed the line of the jaw. The jawline was a jawline Klaus had been recognizing in mirrors for as long as he had been old enough to recognize a jawline in a mirror.

'Marianne.'

'You did not introduce yourself.'

'I did not.'

'Why not.'

Klaus did not answer for some seconds. Then he said: 'Because I am working on a list with a man whose ex-wife is on a list and whose lover is dead, and the right time to introduce myself to a daughter who has been told her father died of cancer is not the time when her father is doing the work. The right time is later. The right time may not arrive. I am preserving the option. The preservation is the gift I am giving her until I have decided whether the giving is also a kindness.'

Calder said: 'You will go again.'

'Yes. In the autumn. To listen to her play. From the back of the hall. Not to introduce myself.'

Calder said: 'I will go with you.'

Klaus said: 'You will not. The hall has eight rows. A second man at the back is a second man at the back. I will listen alone. That is the operational discipline.'

Calder said: 'Yes.'

Klaus put the clipping in his wallet behind the photograph of the two children on the Wiesbaden front step. The clippings were now two.

Klaus had brought a second newspaper back from Lyon, four days old, that he had not gone to Lyon to find. A gas explosion had taken the top two floors of an apartment building in a quiet quarter of Turin on a Tuesday evening. Eleven dead. The Italian gas authority had attributed it to a corroded riser in a building that had stood ninety years without the riser corroding. The photograph beside the report showed a stairwell opened to the sky, and in the lower left of the frame, unremarked by the caption, the buckled steel door of a service cabinet that no apartment building kept on its top floor. Klaus held the clipping under the desk lamp at the angle a man holds a thing he is reading rather than looking at. Scored into the cabinet door, and softened by what the grain of the photograph rendered as decades of slow oxidation, was a sun with eight rays around a single eye. Klaus did not say that the building stood four hundred meters from a research siting. He said only that the institution had not corroded the riser that week. The institution had marked the building before the riser was new, and had simply, that Tuesday, come back for the thing it had set aside. The notebook was becoming a record of two kinds of page. The kills were one kind. This was the other—the older one.

In July, Klaus went to La Spezia.

He came back with an envelope of photographs and a Cinzano coaster on which a man named Salvatore had drawn, in blue ballpoint, a diagram of the basement plumbing of a building on the Via Crispi. The diagram showed a service crawl space below the boiler room that did not appear on the building's published plans. The crawl space was fourteen square meters. It contained, by Salvatore's account, a steel cabinet labeled in

German that had been installed decades earlier by a man Salvatore did not name and that had, in the twenty-eight years since, been visited at eighteen-month intervals by two-man teams the building's residents had been told were Italian civil-defense inspectors.

The cabinet held a backpack-sized device. The device was the descendant of an American program from the early sixties—small atomic demolition munitions, the W54 family, sixty-pound tactical units designed to be carried into position by a single operator and detonated to deny terrain to an advancing force. The American program had been documented. The European parallel had not. The European parallel had been the program the Italian and German services had run through the Custodia and that the Custodia had been maintaining, on its eighteen-month rotation, in apartment-block basements across Europe for decades.

The cabinet on the Via Crispi was the eighth Calder had now identified.

Salvatore had been a maintenance contractor for the building for years. He had been waiting nine years to tell someone about the cabinet. He had not chosen Klaus. Klaus had chosen him. The trust had been earned in a Genoa freight yard in 1981, when Klaus had moved Salvatore's nephew off a manifest the Camorra was about to read and onto a Genoese coastal-haulage roster the Camorra did not, and Salvatore had carried, since then, the kind of debt a southern Italian carried for the rest of his working life. The choosing had been Klaus's operational gift to Salvatore, who had been about to tell the wrong person at a parish festival in May.

Calder went to La Spezia in the second week of August. He did not enter the building. He stood across the Via Crispi at twenty-three minutes past nine on a Tuesday morning with a copy of *La Repubblica* folded in his right hand. He held the private discipline of a man who did not wish his hands to register the specific tremor that had been working its way through them. He looked up at the third-floor window of the apartment whose great-grandmother in the kitchen, by Salvatore's nine years of mornings on the staircase, baked a Sicilian honey cake on the second Sunday of every month for a son who had been killed at El Alamein in 1942 and a son who had been killed at Anzio in 1944. Twenty feet beneath the kitchen, in a service crawl space the building's residents had been told held the boiler-feed regulator, was a steel cabinet that contained the specific arithmetic of a half-kilometer radius of an Italian port city becoming uninhabitable for forty thousand years. He had been reading about the cabinet for six years. The cabinet had been beneath the kitchen for twenty-eight. The reading had been the work the file had been doing on him. The standing was the work the cabinet was now doing back. He did not enter. He did not photograph the building. He stood across the Via Crispi. Then he walked north toward the station and did not, in the walking, look back.

At the kitchen window above him a movement registered—the great-grandmother passing the curtain, or the curtain itself in the morning draft. He could not tell which. The kitchen smelled, at this hour and with this window angle, of the second Sunday's cake, baked on the previous Sunday because the second Sunday had fallen on the first of the month. The honey was Sicilian. The honey had been delivered, by the arrangement of a Catania uncle, for decades. The great-grandmother was eighty-one. She had baked the cake every second Sunday for forty-eight years. The kitchen would not register, in any of those months between her first cake and the morning Calder stood across the street, that the building beneath the kitchen contained the device that would, if used by the institution that had placed it there, unmake every second Sunday in northern Italy.

A boy of nine ran past Calder on the cobbles with a small wire-haired terrier on a string. The boy did not look at Calder. The terrier did not look at Calder. A woman in a black dress came out of the building three doors down and shook a small woven mat against the railing twice. She did not look at Calder. A green Fiat Cinquecento went up the Via Crispi too fast and was passed by a Vespa going the other direction. The driver of the Fiat shouted at the driver of the Vespa. The Vespa driver did not respond. Neither of them looked at Calder.

He stood for nine minutes. He counted the minutes by the small watch on his right wrist, which was not the watch Margaret had given him—that watch was now in a drawer at the harbor—but a steel piece he had bought in Marseilles in March because the other had been too specific to wear. At minute eight a small flake of plaster came loose from the third-floor window casing and fell to the cobbles at his feet. He did not pick it up. At minute nine he turned and walked north on the Via Crispi toward the station. He did not look back at the kitchen window. The great-grandmother did not see him go.

The Cinzano coaster went into the leather notebook between pages four and five.

On the morning Calder came back from La Spezia, a left-luggage office in the Genoa station came apart at 07:40. The device was small and shaped; it produced a detonation and not the deflagration a severed gas line produces, and it did to an enclosed room what a detonation does. It took the lockers, the tiled wall, and most of a railway clerk of nineteen who had been four days into the job and had been standing, by the position of what the Carabinieri recovered, with his back to the counter. The afternoon papers carried a separatist communiqué that had reached the papers, by their own account, eleven minutes before the device went off. Klaus read the communiqué twice. Then he read the small item the wire services had not carried: a maintenance foreman clearing the blast wall two days later had found, under the soot, cut deep into the marble and worn glassy at its edges, a sun with eight rays around an eye. The mason who set that marble had been in his grave for the better part of a century. Klaus said the institution had been forging the signatures of other men for thirty years—but that a forger who carves his own mark into the wall a lifetime before the crime is not a forger. He is a priest, and the wall is an altar, and the altar had been cut and consecrated and left to weather until the morning it was wanted. Genoa was ninety kilometers up the coast from the cabinet on the Via Crispi. The sun in the marble was the institution saying: we did not choose this station on Tuesday. We chose it before your grandfather was born. We are only now telling you.

In August Klaus came back from London with a manila folder.

He had been in London for three days. The folder was thin. It contained four photocopies—two obituaries from regional English newspapers, an internal MoD personnel notice Margaret had passed to Klaus before she went dark, and the front page of an internal AWE bulletin that had been left on the desk of a senior physicist in a building Klaus would not name. The physicist had not noticed the absence. Klaus had returned the bulletin before the physicist had returned from his lunch. The photocopy had been made in the back office of a stationer's on Holloway Road that had a key Klaus had been holding for years.

Calder read the four photocopies at the desk in the harbor.

The first obituary was for a man named Dr Peter Morley, fifty-eight, principal scientific officer at the Atomic Weapons Establishment Aldermaston. He had died in March 1989 of a coronary at his home in Tadley. He had been one of the senior physicists working on the Trident warhead program. The obituary in the Reading Evening Post was four paragraphs. It did not mention the work. The phrase that caught Calder's eye was the last line—a phrase, translated from the German institutional pattern Margaret had been cataloguing, that had appeared with different national inflections across twenty-three Continental obituaries in the six years preceding the eight pages. Operationally justified. The same translator. The third press officer. The same hand, now writing in the Reading Evening Post.

The second obituary was for a Dr Ronald Faraday, sixty-one, who had died in May 1989 of a fall on a Sunday walk near the village of Burghfield. Faraday had been a metallurgist at AWE Burghfield, the warhead-assembly facility four miles from Aldermaston. He had been involved with the design tolerances on the secondary stage of a forthcoming British strategic warhead. He had been a widower of eleven months at the time of the walk; the path he had taken that Sunday had been the path he and his wife had walked on the second Sunday of each May since 1962, when he had taught himself the names of the meadow birds for her. The fall had been witnessed by no one. The coroner had ruled accidental death. The obituary, like the first, closed with the same translated formulation—same syntax, same brevity, same absence of personal anecdote—so close in cadence to the Morley notice that the two might have been written by the same English hand under the same German pattern.

The third item was not an obituary at all but an internal AWE personnel notice Margaret had retrieved through an academic contact at Reading University library in the autumn of 1989, and had given to Klaus before going dark. Klaus had been holding it for the right occasion. The notice recorded the death in service of Mr Anthony Wallace, forty-nine, senior procurement officer for warhead-component contracts, on the A303 outside Andover in November 1989. The notice closed with the German formulation in its original—*die Versetzung war dienstlich angemessen*—followed by the standard MoD pension provision. The German had not been translated. The notice had been circulated only to the Procurement Executive.

The fourth document was the AWE internal bulletin from January 1990. The bulletin was a routine staff announcement. On page two, in the small column reserved for personnel changes, was a paragraph noting that the post of senior project liaison for the British–American warhead-design cooperation had been filled by Dr Henry Soames, fifty-three, of the procurement directorate, replacing Dr Dorothy Holcombe, who had retired the previous month. The retirement had not been announced in the same column. The column had not previously included retirements. The column had been altered for this entry. Klaus had circled the alteration in pencil.

Three nuclear engineers and a procurement officer. Three deaths over nine months in 1989. One retirement that had not been a retirement. Four people, all working on adjacent areas of the British strategic warhead program, all gone from their posts in the same nine-month window.

The cluster had a name. The cluster had a shape. The cluster had not, by any institutional standard Calder knew, been registered as a cluster.

Calder set the four photocopies down beside one another on the desk in the order he had read them. He sat looking at the four photocopies for a long time.

He registered, in the looking, that his right hand had begun to shake. He registered the registering. He had been, for forty-eight years, a man whose hand did not shake in the presence of a thing the discipline had not given him a category for. The hand was now shaking. He placed the hand, palm down, against the wood of the desk. The wood received the shake. The shake stayed in the hand against the wood for the better part of two minutes before the wood received it fully.

His father had been at Trinity, on the desert floor, three miles from the tower. Then Calder Hall in 1956, and the charge face for the rest of his working life. The British strategic deterrent had been the public good his father had given himself to making, in the moral architecture he had built around the work. The architecture had assumed the institution that ran the deterrent was the institution that signed the checks and convened the inquiries and published the white papers.

The architecture had been wrong. The institution had been the public face. Behind the public face was the Custodia. The Custodia had decided, in 1989, to clear the cluster of British engineers who had been the public face's best technical talent on a program the Custodia did not approve of. The clearing had been done quietly. The clearing had used three different methods—a coronary, a fall, a road accident. The clearing had been registered, in three regional papers, by the same translator using the same German construction across the same nine months. The Custodia had been operating against the British nuclear deterrent inside the British nuclear establishment. It had been doing so with the same instruments it had used in Germany and Italy and France for thirty years.

His father had said the grace at his table for the dead at Hiroshima and Nagasaki for twenty-three years and had not, in any of those years, named what the grace was for. His father had been a man whose moral architecture had taken those two cities and built itself a shape it could live with. The shape had been the silence at the meal. The silence had been Edward Calder telling himself the work he had done at Trinity had served the country.

The country was not the institution. The institution was the Custodia. The Custodia had been killing the country's engineers since at least March of the previous year, while James Calder had been at Century House compiling a file on hidden munitions in Italian apartment blocks without yet knowing that the country he had been protecting in Italian apartment blocks had been being unprotected in Berkshire by the same hand.

The hand against the wood was steady now.

He turned it palm-up. He looked at it. The hand was the hand of a man whose father had stood on the desert floor at Trinity and walked the charge face at Calder Hall, and whose grandfather had carried a Welrod for the Special Operations Executive, and whose family's work—the bomb and the secret war both—had been used, in the architecture's patient discipline, against the country the family had thought it was serving. The hand had been, for forty-eight years, the wrong hand. The hand was now the right hand. The four photocopies on the desk were the document by which the hand had been given its proper instructions.

He set the photocopies into the notebook beside the Cinzano coaster.

Klaus said: 'I am sorry, James.'

Calder nodded.

Klaus said: 'There is one more thing. Dorothy Holcombe.'

Calder nodded once.

Klaus said: 'I have not, in three days in London, been able to identify any address for her. The retirement was not a retirement. I cannot tell you whether she is alive.'

Calder did not respond.

Klaus said: 'I will continue looking.'

Calder said: 'Thank you.'

He did not tell Klaus about his father. Some registrations were not yet for the operational ledger.

There was, also, a fourth method. He had not named it for Klaus because he did not yet know what to call it. He had read four Continental obituaries across the previous winter in the foreign papers Klaus brought back from Brussels and Hamburg. A metallurgist named Adriano Ferri at Pavia in 1985. A reactor physicist named Lothar Reuss at Karlsruhe in 1987. He held the name beside the marginal note in his own handwriting on page nineteen of the FEUERWERK file—Karlsruhe is not where the file says Karlsruhe is—and registered, in the holding, that the note had been written in the spring of 1988 and that Lothar Reuss had been the institutional knowledge of the location the file's Karlsruhe entries described. He did not yet have the connecting fact. He filed the absence beside the note. A Swedish thorium specialist named Sigurd Lindberg at Studsvik in 1988. All three had died of aggressive leukemia at fourteen to sixteen weeks from the onset of symptoms, and the three obituaries, taken together with the small notice in the AWE newsletter recording seven warhead-assembly technicians lost to marrow failure at Aldermaston between 1986 and 1988, made a fourth shape. A coronary was a method. A fall was a method. A car was a method. The fourth was something the body did to itself over fourteen weeks when an institution had asked it to. Calder did not yet have the institution's word for it. He had begun to wait for the word. He filed the fourth method beside the eight-ray sun and the small folded crane and the theta on the doorframes of three thresholds, in the file of unnamed objects the work had been pressing into his attention since the morning his hand had gone for the tie that Elena had given him in 1981.

In October a car came apart on a wet street in Bayonne. It had been parked outside the marine chandler's the harbor had used for nineteen years, two doors from the box where Eddie's couriers left the diesel chits. The chandler lost his windows. A schoolteacher walking past lost more than her windows: a car bomb is an omnidirectional event, and it did to her the omnidirectional thing. She had been walking the seventeen meters between the chandler's door and the corner of the rue Maubec at the same hour she had walked it on every Tuesday afternoon since 1983, on the route from her infant school to the bus that took her home, and the seventeen meters was the distance an institution that had been reading her for some weeks had decided to make the omnidirectional thing arrive in.

The Pyrénées-Atlantiques préfecture released the cell's name within a day and was not, by any account Klaus could find, wrong about the cell. It was wrong about one detail it had been handed and had not printed. The préfecture's own pathologist had recorded that the fingernails of the woman's right hand had been removed—all five, cleanly, by a single instrument, with the unhurried symmetry of a thing done on a table—and had filed it as avulsion consistent with blast trauma, because a blast does not take five nails and leave the fingers, and the sentence that described what does was not a sentence a French pathologist would write under his own name. When the nails had been taken—before the car, or in the half-minute of smoke and screaming after it, by a hand moving through the wreckage with a purpose no witness would afterward be able to assemble into a memory—Klaus could not say. The not-being-able-to-say was the point. On the chandler's green shutter, at the height of a standing man's eye, a sun with eight rays had been scratched into the paint. The paint was not old. This one the institution had cut fresh. Klaus stood in the harbor kitchen with the clipping and did not put it in the notebook for a day. Bayonne was the town the harbor used. The institution had not struck the harbor. It had struck the room beside it, and had taken five fingernails from a schoolteacher to be read the way an older office had once read a liver, and had knocked once on the wall—to say that it could hear them through it, and that it had begun, again, to practice the oldest part of the work.

In November Klaus came back from Brussels with five pencil fuses, the Italian supplier having delivered through Eddie a small package by courier the previous Thursday.

The package had been wrapped in waxed brown paper and tied with hemp twine of the kind a marine chandler used. Inside had been the five fuses in a wooden cigar box lined with felt, and a single sheet of typed paper folded once with Eddie's small precise hand at the bottom in pencil: *Five. Trieste 8 Oct.*

Tested two on the cliffs at Cabo Espichel on a Sunday with my brother's boy and one of his climbing friends, who think I make fishing buoys. Six-second is six-second. Fourth one stuck for an extra second and I would not trust it for close work. Fifth one is a present. Burn this note.—E. The English was the English of a man who had spent fifty-eight years not writing things down except in this register, and who still wrote them, when he had to, with the discipline of a man not entirely sure the writing did not constitute the leak.

Klaus burned the note in the harbor stove. The wax paper went after it. The hemp twine he kept, on a hook beside the workbench, because hemp twine had been a thing Eddie sent him with packages for years and Klaus had been keeping each piece in a coil that was the small archive of an arrangement he did not yet know how to explain to anyone.

Klaus laid the fuses on the workbench he had built in the corner of the harbor room. The fuses were six-second delay, chemical, manufactured in Trieste by a small firm that had been making detonators for the Italian construction industry since the war. The same firm had been making fuses for the Custodia since 1962.

Klaus said: 'The Italians have been making the fuses for both sides of the work for thirty years. They do not know they have been making them for the work that uses them. They have been told the second buyer is a Belgian quarrying consortium. The story has held since 1962.'

He set the fuses in the leather case. He set the fourth fuse aside.

Calder said: 'Christofi.'

Klaus said: 'February. He is at the phone number on the second Tuesday of every month. I have someone watching the kiosk. The someone is a Belgian woman who runs a flower stand at Place du Châtelain on weekends and a small café across from the kiosk on weekdays. She has been watching the kiosk for me since June. The kiosk has produced its Tuesday call eight times. The man making the call has been the same man each time. He is approximately seventy-three. He wears a gold ring on his right little finger.'

Calder said: 'Margaret's description.'

Klaus replied: 'Yes.'

Calder said: 'February.'

Klaus agreed: 'February.'

8
THE SAUSAGE STAND

The harbor / Brussels / Berlin—February to April 1991

In February of the new year a woman appeared in the harbor.

She was forty-eight. She was wearing a coat that was too good for the harbor, and walking shoes that were too good for the coat, and a leather handbag that was too good for the shoes. She had been at the bakery counter twice in three days. On the second visit she had asked the bakery woman, in French with a German accent, whether the bakery sold the brown loaf the bakery sold. The bakery woman had said yes. The woman had bought the brown loaf. She walked out. She had not returned for two days.

Klaus, who had been watching the bakery from the corner of the rue de la Mer through a coffee-shop window since the first sighting, had photographed her on the second exit through the long lens of a Leica he kept in a leather camera bag for exactly this purpose. He had developed the negatives at the harbor that night.

He set the prints on the desk. 'Frau Engel.'

'Who.'

'A name I have heard from three sources. The name is the operational name of an East German intelligence officer who handled the Stasi's network in Salzburg in the seventies. She retired from the Stasi in 1986. She has been with the Custodia since 1987. The work she does for the Custodia is the work the Custodia uses for advance reconnaissance of locations the Custodia is preparing to act in.'

'Action against me.'

'Possibly. Or possibly action against someone the Custodia thinks is here. The third possibility is that she has been sent to confirm that you are here. The Iowa machinery has been the operational closure for fourteen months. If the Custodia has begun to suspect that the closure was wrong, the suspicion would have begun, in the architecture's procedural rhythm, in late autumn. February is a reasonable interval for the architecture to have moved from suspicion to confirmation. Frau Engel is the confirmation.'

'How long do we have.'

'I think we have until April. I do not know.'

'Then we move.'

'Yes. We finish Christofi in February. We are out of the harbor by the end of February.'

'Brussels first.'

'Brussels first. Then Berlin.'

'And Frau Engel.'

'Frau Engel will not leave the harbor. The saddle-faced fisherman has a brother who has not been to sea in years and who keeps a small stand of apple trees and a private opinion about people who come to ask the bakery woman the wrong questions. The brother has agreed to a piece of work that does not concern us. We will not speak of Frau Engel again. The silence about her will be the brother's discipline.'

The following morning Klaus came in with the bakery bag at oh-seven-twenty. Calder did not ask. Klaus said, setting the bag on the table: 'The brother does the apple work. The brother has done some other work as well. The other work is finished.' Calder said: 'Yes.' Klaus said: 'The bakery woman will not see the same customer twice.' They did not speak of it again.

That night Klaus poured the Grouse. The bottle was nearly empty. He poured the last measure into Calder's mug and set the bottle on the floor beside the chair.

Calder said: 'You are out of Grouse.'

Klaus said: 'I have been drinking Grouse since 1968. I am told the distillery has changed hands. The next bottle will not be the same bottle.'

Calder drank the last measure.

It tasted of peat smoke and the chemical edge of cheap glass and twenty-one years of the man across the kitchen table.

The Brussels man was the third name on the list.

Klaus had been arranging the kill since June.

He had been on the kiosk for eight Tuesdays. The flower-stand woman had been on it for eight more. Calder had been on it for two. The next operational Tuesday was the second Tuesday of February. The man Margaret had named would be there at 11:47, as he had been there at 11:47 on the second Tuesday of every month for some unspecified number of years.

His name, by the registration of three Greek-Cypriot expatriates Klaus had identified through a barber in Limassol, was Konstantinos Christofi, born 1917, raised Greek, naturalized Belgian in 1957. He was the Western Coordinator. He was one of the seven. He was the man Margaret had described in pencil on the fourth page of the eight pages.

Christofi had been the elder son of a Limassol icon-painter who restored the gold leaf on the haloes of the Pantokrators in the village churches above the Akrotiri salt lake, and who taught his sons—from the four years before each boy could read—how to read the small disturbances by which the world signaled in advance: the angle a swallow's flight broke against an east wind; the way the lamp-oil moved in the brass dish when a name was spoken near the icon stand; whether a black crow settled or did not settle on the cemetery wall at the third hour. The boy had grown up inside a Cypriot Orthodoxy that had not yet been disentangled from the older readings the Roman augurs had performed in Latin two thousand years earlier on the Capitoline, and he had carried the habit of the reading—the institutional discipline of treating chance as documentary evidence—out of the village and into the Limassol customs house and out of the customs house and into Antwerp in 1948 and out of Antwerp and into the Saint-Gilles flat from which, by the public arithmetic of the seven men he had administered, he had been quietly reading the European century since 1957. He had been authorized. He had been reading for forty years.

What he had been reading, by the fourth page of Margaret's eight pages, included the freight transfer at Antwerp in the summer of 1971 that a customs officer named Albert Devos had stopped on a manifest discrepancy and had filed a memorandum about, the memorandum having reached, on a Wednesday, the desk of a Greek-Cypriot Belgian-naturalized adviser to the port authority who had read it and had not answered it. The customs officer had drowned eleven days later on a Sunday sail in good weather. The journalist sister had been hit by the tram outside Antwerp Centraal eight weeks after that. Three other names on the seven that Devos's brother Pieter would keep in a Brussels-Midi locker for nineteen years had been authorized by the same hand. The hand had signed nothing. The signing was the not-signing. Christofi had read the omens for the closures and the closures had occurred and the not-signing had been the discipline by which a man trained on the Capitoline grammar of his Limassol boyhood could close an Antwerp port officer at twelve hundred kilometers' distance through a Sunday and a tram and not require, in the long quiet of the Saint-Gilles afternoon, any instrument heavier than the second Tuesday of the month and a public phone.

The kiosk was not at the Place du Châtelain. The kiosk was at the corner of the Rue Berckmans and the Rue Vanderschrick, a quiet residential corner in Saint-Gilles where a man making a monthly call to a retired Coordinator was the kind of man who would not be noticed by neighbors who knew his face.

He went up to the kiosk. He had a folded copy of Le Soir under his right arm. He stepped into the kiosk. He closed the folding glass door.

Calder was in the doorway of a building across the street. He was wearing a postman's coat over his own and was carrying a leather satchel of bills he had spent the previous hour collecting from real letterboxes on the street so that the satchel would be heavy with the right kind of paper.

He waited the three minutes and then he crossed the street.

He walked up to the kiosk. He opened the folding glass door. He stepped inside. The kiosk was the size of a coffin. The man on the phone turned and registered him.

The man's face, in the second of the registration, was the face of a man who had been making this call for so many years that the call had become the rhythm by which the man knew the second Tuesday of the month, and who had not, in those years, prepared his face for the moment another man stepped into the kiosk while the call was in progress.

Calder said, in a Brussels postal worker's French: 'The post for this kiosk, monsieur. They asked me to ring through if you are still on. I will wait.'

The man held the phone. He did not respond. His eyes were on Calder. His right hand on the receiver had a gold ring on the finger. The ring had a small intaglio that Calder did not, at this distance, need to read to recognize.

Calder, in the space of two seconds, took the Welrod out of the satchel. He fired once.

The Welrod made the sound it had been making since the war. The round entered Christofi's chest two inches below the suprasternal notch on the same downward angle Calder had used on Vernet. The kiosk was the size of a coffin. The round had entered the upper chest cavity. It traversed the descending arch of the aorta and the upper lobe of the right lung in the same passage. It exited through the rear scapula at a foot, taking with it a fragment of pulverised rib and a fine wet starburst the diameter of a man's open hand that struck the rear glass of the kiosk and ran in a slow patient draining toward the floor. The aortic transection meant the central blood pressure dropped to zero in approximately one heartbeat; the brain, denied perfusion, would shut down inside fourteen seconds.

Christofi's body went heavy against the rear wall of the kiosk. The phone fell from his hand and swung on its cord. The gold ring on his right small finger struck the receiver as the hand fell, a small clean ringing that was the only sound in the kiosk after the Welrod's quiet cough. Christofi's mouth opened. A dark trickle of blood came over the lower lip and into the white silk handkerchief in the breast pocket. The handkerchief darkened from one corner. His pupils dilated to the limit of the iris. His expression—in the second of the registering, before the hand had decided what to do, before the mouth had decided what to say, before any of the operational alarms a man of his discipline had at his disposal could be activated—was no expression at all. Christofi had not had time for an expression. The kiosk had not been built to permit one.

Calder caught the phone before it struck the wall. He held it. The voice on the other end of the line said, in Italian: Konstantinos. Calder worked the bolt. The casing ejected into his left palm. The casing went into the satchel.

Calder said nothing for a moment.

The voice on the other end said again: Konstantinos.

Calder hung the phone on its cradle.

He stepped out of the kiosk. He closed the folding glass door behind him. On the pavement beside the kiosk, against the aluminium base, was a small folded paper crane. It was the size of a thumbnail. The folds were precise. Calder registered it without stopping. He walked down the Rue Berckmans at the pace of a postman. Klaus was at the corner with the Land Rover.

Calder said: 'It is done.'

Klaus said: 'Three.'

Calder said: 'Three.'

The Welrod was now down to three clean firings.

That night at a roadside Gasthof outside Aachen Calder took the leather notebook from the inside pocket of his coat. He took the pencil page. He took the pencil. He drew a single horizontal line through 3. The man at the Brussels phone number. (Margaret's description.) The line was clean. His hand did not shake.

He folded the page. He put it back in the notebook.

The pencil page now had two names struck through and one to go. Brückner was the one to go. Berlin was where he was. Berlin was the work of the spring.

They drove east from Brussels that afternoon.

Klaus's glass had been pushed across by a barman in a hotel in Hanover the previous summer—a bartender who had recognized Klaus from a Stasi reception in 1984 and had pretended not to. Klaus had drunk the glass. The hotel had been the Maritim. The whisky had been Glenmorangie ten-year. The Glenmorangie ten-year that Klaus drank had a taste he registered at the time and did not, until the autumn, name.

The taste had been metallic. Faint. The kind of taste a man missed if his palate had not been trained in a Stasi facility outside Potsdam in 1965.

Klaus had not died. The compound had been the compound the institution used for slow-induction work over weeks. Klaus had been sick for nine days in October. He told no one. He had recovered. He had, in November, asked Eddie to send him a testing kit that an Italian chemist Eddie knew kept for exactly such cases. The kit had been in the leather case in the harbor since December. Klaus had used it on a sample of the Glenmorangie ten-year he had retained at the bottom of the bottle. The result had confirmed it. The barman in Hanover had been Custodia. The whisky had been the dose.

He had not told Calder until the second week of February.

The telling had happened on a Wednesday evening, in the kitchen of the harbor flat, with the wind off the southwest at the windows and a small fire of sea-coal in the hearth that Klaus had been keeping low for the economy of the coal. Calder had been at the table with a cup of tea. Klaus had set a wooden box on the table between them and had opened it without comment. Inside the box was a leather case. Inside the leather case was a thin cardboard folder. Inside the folder was a single sheet of paper from an Italian laboratory in Genoa, signed by a chemist whose name Calder did not recognize, dated the eleventh of December 1990. The sheet identified, in clinical Italian, a thallium compound at a concentration of seventeen micrograms per milliliter in a sample of Glenmorangie ten-year submitted by a courier on the third of December under the reference number K-887.

Calder had read the sheet twice. He had set it down.

Calder said: 'Why now.'

Klaus said: 'Because we are about to leave the harbor and I am not going to leave the harbor with you not knowing. The silence is now a debt. The debt is paid by the telling.'

Calder said: 'And you are.'

Klaus said: 'I am alive. I will be alive in two years if the architecture has not produced a second dose. The first dose has done what it will do. I have the small ongoing physical fact of it in the inside of my left forearm at the wrist where the skin has been red for some months. He had first noted the red patch in late August, before the October sickness—the skin had registered the compound weeks before the body did. The redness is the dose's small reminder. I have been ignoring it. I will continue to ignore it. The body works.'

He had then unbuttoned the cuff of his left sleeve and pushed the sleeve back to the elbow. Calder looked. The skin on the inside of the forearm had been a pale clinical red at the wrist, in a flat patch the size of a child's palm, with the specific dullness of skin that had absorbed something the body could not reverse. The hair on that patch had not grown back since July. The skin around the patch was the skin Klaus had been carrying since 1939, and the patch was the skin the architecture had given him in the late evening at the bar of the Maritim Hotel in Hanover on a Friday in July of 1990. The two skins had not negotiated their boundary. The boundary was the patch. Klaus had touched it once, with the index finger of his right hand, and had pulled the sleeve back down.

He had also shown Calder the inside of the watchband.

There had been a single ink line on the inside leather, made some weeks earlier with a fountain pen, with the date in his own hand: 27. VIII. The line had been the line of the day Klaus had first registered the redness as a fixed boundary rather than a healing one. He had said: 'When the boundary moves I will mark it. The mark will be the calendar I am keeping. The calendar will be the fact of my own body. I will tell you when the boundary has moved. I will not report the days the boundary holds. The silence is the discipline of the calendar.'

Calder took the watchband from him. He read the date. He handed the watchband back. He had, in the handing-back, registered the specific weight of an instrument a man wore against his pulse to count down what an instrument at a Hanover bar had begun to count down for him in the summer. He had registered also, in the same second, that he was the man who had crossed a Stasi basement floor at 03:42 in March of 1969. He lifted Klaus from a concrete drain that had stopped his blood six inches short of taking it, and that the lifting was now a debt being repaid in the wrong direction—by an instrument that was not a hand and was not a knife and was the patience of a substance the body had been carrying without his knowing it for eight months. He did not say any of this. The silence was the second discipline of the calendar.

He had drunk his tea.

Calder had not spoken for some time.

Klaus said: 'There is also a piece of work I have arranged with Eddie. The work is a contingency. The contingency is not for tonight. I will tell you the shape of it when the shape becomes the shape we need.'

Calder said: 'All right.'

Klaus had said: 'Thank you.'

He had drunk his tea.

◆◆◆

Berlin. April.

The Wall had been down for seventeen months. The city was the city the Wall had ended, which was a city that did not yet understand it was a city.

Klaus walked Calder through Prenzlauer Berg on the second afternoon. The streets had been East Berlin streets until recently and were now the streets of the most rapidly gentrifying neighborhood in Germany. The cafés on the Kollwitzplatz served cappuccinos to West German graduate students. A McDonald's had opened on the Schönhauser Allee the previous month. The McDonald's had a queue at all hours, which was the only specifically post-Wall observation Calder had been able to make, by his own reading, that he believed.

Brückner's apartment was on the fifth floor of a building on the Lychener Strasse. The building had been built in 1908, had been allowed to deteriorate for forty years under the GDR, and had been recently bought by a West German investor who had not yet begun the renovation. The hallways smelled of coal dust and the ammonia of decades of cat urine in the dark stairwell.

They watched the building for three days. Brückner went out at 09:14 and returned at 17:47. He bought a paper at the kiosk on the corner. He stopped at the bakery across from his building. The bakery was run by an East German woman of sixty-two named Annelies, who had also been Stasi—Klaus had recognized her from a 1976 personnel photograph the second day. She was unaware she had been recognized. She continued to sell Brückner his Berliner Pfannkuchen each morning.

On the afternoon of the second day a young woman came out of the building carrying a string bag. Klaus was at the window of the Sredzkistrasse flat with the Leica. He brought the camera up. He took two frames. He did not say anything to Calder, who was at the desk with the building plans. The young woman walked east toward the U-Bahn. Klaus watched her go and then he turned the lens to the bakery. The lens had registered, in the half-second of the second exposure, a mouth Klaus had last seen across a table in a Stasi briefing room outside Potsdam in November of 1965. The mouth was twenty-four years older now and belonged to a face he had not been shown by any photograph and had not, in those twenty-four years, expected to see again. He developed the two frames that night in the bathroom and he laid one of them flat on the kitchen table while Calder slept and he sat with it for some minutes and then he put it inside the cover of the leather notebook against the inside spine and he did not show it to Calder. The not-showing was a discipline he had been doing without instruction since the morning he had read the eight pages on the train from Zurich. There were things a man told his partner before a kill and things a man told his partner after. The mouth, and what the mouth meant, was an after.

At the kiosk on the third day Calder bought a copy of Der Spiegel. He turned to page nine on the corner. There was a half-page article on the previous month's congressional hearings in Washington on intelligence-sharing between the CIA and the Bundesnachrichtendienst, the West German Federal Intelligence Service. The article carried a single photograph. The photograph was of the chief American witness at the hearings, an American intelligence officer named Hannah Doyle, thirty-nine, who had testified in closed session and whose face had been photographed in a corridor afterward by a Spiegel stringer who had not known her name when he had taken the photograph.

The photograph was of a woman of average height with brown hair pulled back in a low knot. She was wearing a dark suit. She was looking past the photographer's shoulder at something Calder could not see.

He recognized the face.

He had seen the face once. In a photograph in the Mayflower dossier, in the section of envelopes Elena had laid out at the corner of the wooden table. The envelope had contained three photographs: a studio portrait of a man in his fifties; a black-and-white eight-by-ten of a tall, dark-haired woman in a Tel

Aviv café, taken from across the room without the woman's knowledge; and a third photograph, smaller, of a different woman in a corridor at what Calder had recognized as the Hart Senate Office Building. The face in the Spiegel was the third woman, the better part of a decade older. The studio portrait had been Thornley—the same face Calder had laid on the Chief's desk in six frames at 09:30 on the fourth of January, the same gold ring on the finger of the same right hand. Elena carried Thornley's face in her envelope for ten weeks before Bermondsey, by an account Klaus had since reconstructed. A woman named Dina Sharabi, who would shoot her on the third of January, had aimed a brooch at the administrator across the courtyard of a Spanish embassy reception in Tel Aviv on the seventeenth of October 1989. The image from the brooch had been the only likeness of the administrator that existed outside the network's own records, and Dina gave it to Elena because Dina decided, at some hour Klaus had not yet placed, that Elena was the operative for whom the photograph was. She did not name either of the women. She did not, at the Mayflower, get to the part of the dossier in which she would have named them. The naming had been one of the gaps. The Tel Aviv woman was a separate gap. Calder registered her, then, as a person Elena planned to name and had not. He filed her without knowing what to file her under.

The face was the face of the woman Margaret had named on the fifth page of the eight pages as the American who is also looking. CIA Counterintelligence. Approach with caution. She is not yet on a list and may be a friend.

The third name was the question mark on the pencil page.

Calder folded the Spiegel and put it in the inside pocket of his coat.

He walked back to the flat Klaus had been using on the Sredzkistrasse. Klaus was at the window with a cup of coffee. He was watching a cat on a window-ledge across the courtyard.

Calder set the Spiegel on the table beside Klaus.

'Page nine.'

Klaus turned the pages. He read the article. He looked at the photograph for a long moment.

'I have heard the name. I have not heard it for a year.'

'Where.'

'In the small Hanover briefing for the Greenwich job. Her name was on a list of names the architecture was watching. The name was at the bottom of the list. The bottom of the list meant the architecture was not yet acting on her. The architecture was watching to see what she did. The architecture has been watching her for two years at minimum.'

Calder looked at it again. The woman in the photograph had been photographed at a wrong moment by a man who had not known her name. The photograph had now appeared in a magazine in a kiosk on a street in Berlin within two hundred meters of the apartment building of the man Calder was about to kill. The architecture had not arranged the photograph. The architecture had only registered it. The registering was the instrument by which the architecture moved a name from the bottom of a list to a position higher on the list. The position higher on the list was the position Margaret had been in by 1986. The position higher on the list was the position Christofi had been in by 1990. By the time the photograph had reached the kiosk, Hannah Doyle was no longer at the bottom of any list she had been at the bottom of.

Calder said: 'She was at the Mayflower. In the dossier.'

Klaus said: 'Then she was in Margaret's pages also.'

'Yes.'

'She is the third name.'

Calder did not respond. He let it sit.

'After Brückner.'

'After Brückner.'

Klaus drank his coffee. He set the cup down. He said: 'I will arrange a meeting for after Berlin. I have a man in Geneva who will set the meeting if I ask him. The man will know where she is. The man owes me a favor from 1979. I will spend the favor.'

Calder nodded.

That night they ate sausages from a stand on the Schönhauser Allee. The sausages were East Berlin sausages. The vendor had been selling them in the same cart at the same corner for over a decade. He had not changed his recipe for the sausages or the mustard or the bread. He changed the West German marks he accepted for D-marks the previous summer and back to D-marks at unification and was now considering, under the recent monetary union, what currency he would accept by Easter.

Calder ate the sausage standing at the cart. The cart was four feet from him. The vendor did not look at him.

He thought about Margaret's hand on the handle of the blue teapot in the Chiswick kitchen in 1979. He thought about Elena's voice at the Paxton Gallery in 1973. He thought about his own father's silence at the long table at Egremont in 1965. He thought about his mother's specific way of folding a napkin in 1953 and the way Klaus had once, in 1973, eaten a bratwurst at an East Berlin platform between trains while pretending not to know Calder was on the same platform.

The sausage was good.

He had not, in fifteen months, eaten standing up at a street cart.

The eating was the thing.

He filed it.

He was still alive.

The being-alive was not the same thing as the being-Calder. The being-Calder was now the work. The work was the sausage. The sausage was the man at the cart. The man at the cart was the city the Wall had ended. The city the Wall had ended was the city in which, the next morning, he was going to step into the ground-floor entrance of an apartment building on the Lychener Strasse and put a single 7.65mm Browning round through the chest of a sixty-eight-year-old former Stasi major named Wolfgang Brückner.

He finished the sausage. He wiped his hands on his coat. He went back upstairs.

He did not sleep.

9

DU BIST JAMES CALDER

Berlin—April 1991

06:58. The Lychener Strasse had not yet begun its day.

It was the hour after a wife had left for her bread and before she had returned. He had stood thirteen months earlier inside another such hour, in another country, with another bakery somewhere on another street. The institution preferred the hour because the household was alone with itself in it. He had registered the preference without yet having a category for it. The category was now the work.

He went into the building behind a postman who had paused at the entrance to consult a list on his clipboard. The postman was East German. He had been delivering mail on this street for nineteen years. He did not look up.

Calder went up the stairwell to the fifth floor. He went up slowly. The Welrod was in the leather case in the inside left pocket of his coat against his ribs. The Walther PPK was in the shoulder rig under his jacket. The third measure he had brought, an item Klaus had pressed on him the previous evening in the kitchen of the Sredzkistrasse flat, was an eighteen-inch length of piano wire with two wooden handles, looped in the leather pouch in his right coat pocket. He had not used the wire. He had not, by his own assessment, decided whether he would. He brought it because Klaus had pressed it into his hand and said: Take it, James. I have not asked you to take an instrument before. I am asking you now.

The trapezius had stopped pulling weeks ago. The right arm did the work without negotiation. The body had become, in the months since Greenwich, the body of a man who did this work. The mind had not yet finished.

He looked at the scar that morning, in the mirror over the cracked sink in the bathroom of the Sredzkistrasse flat, while shaving. The entry was a small puckered moon high on the trapezius the size of his thumbprint. The exit, on the back of the shoulder, was the larger ragged crater the round had made on the way out, raised at the edges where the body had pulled the tissue closed without the help of a surgeon. The scar tissue had taken on, over the months, the dull shine of skin that had decided to be different skin. The skin in front had been Calder's skin since 1942. The skin around the scar was the skin Klaus gave him at twelve thirty-four on the morning of the fourth of January 1990. The two skins had now negotiated their boundary. The boundary was the moon. Lower, on the outside of the left forearm, a thinner line had gone the flat silver of an old scar—the chandler's-wall alley in Sète, the first time the work had asked the body to keep something. Above the left eye was a third mark, a short pale seam an inch above an older faded one. The faded one he had carried since boyhood—a fall against the stone of the yard at Egremont, six stitches from the village doctor, a mark an ordinary life had left and not this one, and the only one of his scars that had never been written into a file. Elena had found it anyway, across a Fitzrovia gallery in another decade, and had wanted its story, and had not lived close enough to the question, in the end, to ask. The shoulder Klaus had given him to keep him alive. The forearm and the brow the work had put there itself, without asking, the way the work put things. He touched the moon with the wet thumb of his right hand. He looked at his own face in the mirror beside the moon. He had noted, in the looking, that the face above the moon had been the face of a man who had been dead for fifteen months and was now the face of a man who was going to put a single 7.65mm Browning round into another man's chest in the next forty minutes. The face had not yet decided what it thought about that.

Brückner's door was at the end of the fifth-floor landing.

The landing had a single window facing the courtyard. The window was open by an inch. The April morning air came in at the inch and held the smell of coal dust and bakery yeast from Annelies's oven across the street.

He knocked.

He decided, on the morning, to knock rather than enter. He was sixty-eight now. He had been Wolfgang Brückner for fifty years. He was the kind of man who answered his own door at 06:58 because his wife was still asleep.

There was a footstep inside. The footstep was the slow careful step of a man who had not yet had his coffee. The lock turned. The door opened.

Wolfgang Brückner was wearing a dressing gown over pajamas. He had a coffee pot in his right hand. He had been on his way to the kitchen.

He looked at Calder.

His face did not register surprise. His face registered, in the third second, the recognition of a man whose work had taught him that a man at his door at 06:58 in April was a man who had come for a particular reason. He had not, in twenty-three years of retirement, prepared his face for the morning the man arrived. The unpreparedness was now visible.

Calder said, in German: Dr. Brückner.

Brückner said: Yes.

Calder said: I would like to speak with you.

Brückner said: Of what.

Calder said: Of Strasbourg. Of Berlin. Of Limassol. Of the seven men and the Coordinator who is now three. Of a primary-school teacher in Chiswick who wrote you a Latin paper in March 1988. Of a Russian woman who was killed in a work-room on Webber Street on the third of January last year.

Brückner did not move for some seconds.

Then he stepped back from the door.

Calder stepped in. He closed the door.

The apartment had three rooms. A living room with a bay window that looked over the Lychener Strasse. A kitchen behind it. A bedroom whose door was closed, behind which Heike Brückner was, by Klaus's calculation, asleep until 07:30.

Brückner walked to the kitchen. He set the coffee pot on the stove. He turned the gas on. He took two cups down from the shelf above the sink. He moved with the deliberate slowness of a man who had decided that the way he was going to die was by drinking a cup of coffee while it happened.

Calder stood in the doorway between the kitchen and the living room.

Brückner said, in German: I have been waiting for you since March.

Calder said: Why March.

Brückner said: Christofi. He has not made his Tuesday call since February. The architecture took six weeks to confirm. The architecture moved in March. By March I knew. The architecture also knows. You are not a single man. You are a man and a man and a third man whose name we do not yet have. The Conclave has decided that the closure was insufficient. The closure has been reopened. The architecture is not going to talk to you. The architecture is going to kill you. The order has been issued. The order has been on three desks for two weeks. The order is now on four. By the end of this calendar year the order will be on the desk of the operative who will execute it. I have decided, in this disagreement, to wait alone. I have not been waiting because I assumed I could survive. I have been waiting because I wanted you to find me before the architecture found you.

Calder did not move.

Brückner said: You are James Calder.

The room went still.

Calder did not respond. He had not, in all his time at the harbor and on the road, heard his own name spoken aloud by anyone outside the room he was in with Klaus. He heard it twice in his own head every morning, in the private way men heard their own names when shaving. He did not hear it from outside. He was not prepared, by any discipline he had been carrying, for the sound of his name coming from a sixty-eight-year-old man in a dressing gown at a stove in Berlin.

The man named him.

The naming was the first.

He waited for the body to do something. The body did not. It had been doing the work long enough to know its part. The mind had now caught up to the body and had been told, by the man at the stove, that the catching-up had not been catching up to the work. The catching-up had been catching up to the name. The name was the man. The man had walked out of Century House on a Thursday morning fifteen months earlier with a face composed into the neutral arrangement of a man who had finished the only thing he had ever needed to finish. The neutral arrangement had not been neutral. The arrangement had been the name. The name was now in the room with Brückner and Calder, and the name was no longer Calder's. The name was the architecture's.

The architecture had been carrying the name since March.

The architecture had been moving slowly. The slow moving had been the architecture's first operational mistake on his account in fifteen months. The mistake was the door he had been working toward without knowing it.

He thought, in the same second, of his father at the long oak table at Egremont, raising the fork after the silence. The silence had been the grace. The grace had been the name his father had not spoken at the table. The name had been Hiroshima. His father had not, in twenty-three years, said the name aloud. The silence was the work it was for.

The name Brückner had just said had been the same kind of name. James Calder. The name had been Calder's silence at his own table for fifteen months. Brückner had spoken it aloud. The speaking had been the work the silence had not been able to do for him.

He let it pass.

He said: Yes.

The word came out at the volume his voice had stopped using since Greenwich. He had not, in all that time, spoken his own name aloud. The not-speaking had been the discipline. The discipline had been the work of being two men. The naming had been the third man. The third man was the man Brückner had named.

Brückner said: I read your file when it crossed my desk in 1979. I read your ex-wife's papers when they crossed mine in 1988. I read the third paper in the journal myself. I returned it to the journal with three corrections of declension and a single line in the margin. The line was the joke. The joke was not for the journal. The joke was for your ex-wife. Your ex-wife caught the joke. She did not write back. She continued to publish the papers. I continued to read them. I have been reading her for nine years. She is the best Latinist on this work.

Calder said: You are the Italian hand.

Brückner said: I write Italian Latin. I have been writing it for fifty years. The hand is German. The Latin is Italian. The two are not the same hand. I am the man who has the Italian Latin and the German hand. There are three of us. The other two will not write to your ex-wife in her lifetime. I have. The writing was the private thing I gave her. I have been giving things to her for nine years. The giving is the fact about me the architecture has not yet caught.

He did not say that the Italian hand Klaus had named was not him. He did not say it was.

Calder said: You are not the man at the Brussels phone number.

Brückner said: No. I am not. I am the man at the Berlin phone number. The Berlin phone number is on a different list. The list is in your ex-wife's pages. The list is after the eight pages. The eight pages were the introduction. There are forty more pages. They are in a second box. I do not know where the second box is. Your ex-wife does not yet know I know about the second box. I am telling you now because the telling is the fact I am giving you.

Calder did not respond.

Brückner said: Christofi was not on my list. Vernet was not on my list. They were on your ex-wife's list. They were not on mine. We have been working different parts of the same Custodia for some years. Your ex-wife and I. I would have told her. I did not have the channel. The lack of the channel has been the fact of my last two years. I have been carrying it.

Calder said: You are saying you are not on her list.

Brückner said: I am on her list. The list is hers to make. I would not have made the list the same way. The list is hers. I have been waiting for her to come for me since March. I assumed it would be her. I am surprised it is you. I am also not surprised. I should have assumed there would be a man.

The coffee pot was beginning to whistle.

Brückner turned the gas off.

He poured the coffee into the two cups.

He set one of the cups on the kitchen table. He set the other cup beside the first. He pulled out the wooden chair on his side of the table. He sat down.

He looked at Calder.

Brückner said: Drink the coffee. Then do what you came to do. I have given you what I could.

Calder did not move.

Brückner said: I would also like you to take a small package from my desk. It is in the second drawer on the left. It is a manila envelope. The envelope contains six photographs of a building in Strasbourg. The photographs were taken by a man who is now dead. The photographs are the only evidence the Custodia has not retrieved. I have been keeping them for nineteen years. I have not been able to use them. I am giving them to you because you are now the man who can use them. The using is the operation. The operation is yours.

Brückner took a sip of the coffee.

The smell of the coffee in the kitchen was the smell of a man's last coffee. Brückner had been a man for sixty-eight years and was now drinking a coffee that he had decided was the last. He drank it the way men drank last things. He drank without comment.

The bedroom door opened.

Heike Brückner was thirty-three. She was wearing a dressing gown over a nightdress. She had brown hair the color of milky tea, cut short to her shoulders. Her face had the soft early-morning quality of a young woman woken by the sound of her father's voice in the kitchen at an unfamiliar hour, and who had not yet, by the quality of the unfamiliarity, registered what the morning was about to become.

She came into the kitchen.

She saw the man in the doorway.

She looked at her father. Her father was holding a coffee cup at the kitchen table. The Welrod was already out of Calder's coat. The Welrod was at the line. The bolt was forward. The chamber was loaded. The kill had been ten seconds away when she opened the bedroom door.

Heike said: Vati.

Calder did not lower the Welrod.

The room had two operatives and a daughter.

Brückner said, without turning: Heike. Go back to the bedroom. Close the door. The man and I are speaking.

Heike said: Vati, who is this man.

Brückner said: He is the man I have been expecting. Go back to the bedroom. Close the door.

Heike did not move.

Calder did not move.

The Welrod was at the line. The line was the line at which the Welrod had been at the moment Heike had opened the bedroom door. The line had been Brückner. The line was now the geometry of a kitchen in which a daughter had walked into the kill her father had been arranging to receive alone.

Calder said, in German, quietly: Frau Brückner. I would ask you to do as your father asks. Please go back to the bedroom. Close the door.

Heike said: No.

She stepped further into the kitchen.

She put her hand on her father's shoulder.

Brückner did not look at her. He looked at his coffee. He said: Heike.

She said: Vati.

She did not move her hand.

The Welrod was still at the line.

Calder thought, in the second the hand was on the shoulder, about Klaus's daughter Marianne in Lyon, who would not know her father was alive and would also not know, when her father died, that he had been alive. He thought about Klaus's son Lukas in Wiesbaden, who caught with his left hand and whose mother had told him his father had died of cancer when his father had been alive in a flat above a bakery in an Atlantic harbor. He thought about Klaus's daughter Ilse, who had carried a recorder in her left hand into the Wiesbaden Christmas card photograph of 1987.

He thought about Margaret. He did not know whose daughter Margaret was. He had never met her parents. He had been married to her for twelve years and had known her for thirty, and he did not know whose daughter she was.

He thought about Heike Brückner, who in the next second was going to watch her father die. He registered, in the same second, that Klaus's three children had been kept from the morning their father was preparing for himself by an architecture of patient discipline that had three forms—the false cancer, the unintroduced visit, the Christmas card photograph—and that Heike, by the small accident of having opened the bedroom door at oh-seven-oh-one, had been given none of the three.

Brückner said, without turning: James Calder. Please do not make her watch.

The naming was now the second. The first naming had been the architecture's acknowledgment that the closure had been wrong; the institution had named him because the institution knew the body in Iowa was not him. The second naming was different. The second naming was a man at a stove asking for the small dignity of a daughter not seeing the morning her father had been preparing himself for since November. The second naming was not the institution's. The second naming was Brückner's.

Calder lowered the Welrod by an inch. By no more.

He said, in German: Frau Brückner. Your father has asked me to do something. He has asked me to allow him to make a decision. I am asking you to permit him to make the decision. I am asking you to step out of the kitchen for three minutes.

Heike said: No.

She said it again: No.

She said, the third time: I am his daughter. If you are going to do this you will do it with me here.

Brückner closed his eyes.

He opened them.

He said: Heike. The man is correct. You will please step out for three minutes.

She did not move.

Brückner said: Heike.

The kitchen held.

She said, looking at her father: Vati, who is the man.

Brückner said: He is a man whose ex-wife was a Latinist who corresponded with me for nine years. He is also a man who has lost a person he cared for in the work I did, and who is now doing the part of his own work that requires him to do this. He is a good man. He has not chosen this. I have chosen it. I have been waiting for him.

Heike looked at Calder.

She said: Whose work.

Brückner said: Mine. The work was mine. The man is the consequence. The consequence is the work I did. The work is now coming to me through the man. The man is not the consequence's author. I am.

Heike said: Vati. You have lied to me my whole life.

Brückner said: I have. I am sorry. I will be sorry in the next three minutes. The being-sorry will be the only honest thing I have ever given you. I am giving it now. Step out.

She did not move for several seconds.

Then she stepped backward, slowly, until her back was against the doorframe of the kitchen. She did not leave the kitchen. She remained at the doorframe.

She said: Do it.

Calder lowered the Welrod by another inch.

He said, in German: Frau Brückner. I will not do it with you in the room.

Heike said: Then you will not do it.

Brückner said: Heike.

Heike said: No, Vati. If you have decided he is the consequence, then I am the witness. I will not permit you to die alone in front of a man who is not your son. I will be your daughter. The being-your-daughter is the last thing I have. You have taken everything else.

Brückner closed his eyes.

He opened them.

He said: James Calder.

Calder said: Yes.

Brückner said: Do not make her watch. Take me to the bedroom. Take me anywhere. But do not make her watch. I am asking you as a man whose ex-wife, by the eight pages, is the woman who has been writing me Latin for nine years. I am asking you as one Latinist to another. I am asking you because I asked her to keep writing the papers and she did, and the papers were the only honest thing in my work for nine years. I am asking you. Do not make her watch.

Calder did not respond.

Then he said: Yes.

Brückner stood. He walked to the kitchen door. Heike stepped aside without looking at him. He passed her. He went into the living room. Calder followed him.

In the living room Brückner went to the bay window. He stood at the window with his back to the room. He said: Here. Please.

Calder raised the Welrod.

In the kitchen, Heike Brückner had her hands flat against the doorframe. She was not looking. She was listening. She was the witness her father had not wanted her to be, and the work Calder had been carrying for fifteen months had now produced a witness. The witness was the daughter. The daughter was the operational mistake he was not able to prevent. The daughter would carry, for the rest of her life, the eight seconds between her father's here, please and the almost-soundless cough of the Welrod.

Calder fired.

The round entered Brückner's back at the eighth thoracic vertebra below the left scapula and traversed the chest cavity in the downward angle Calder had been practicing in Marseilles and Brussels. It severed the descending aorta cleanly between the eighth and ninth ribs and exited the chest two inches above the left nipple, taking with it a small ragged disk of breastbone and a fine spray of pulverized lung tissue. The disk struck the bay window. The glass cracked but did not break. The spray drew a fine red corolla on the inside of the glass at the height of Brückner's heart, a foot of pattern that the morning light through the window would, in the next ten minutes, make legible to the building across the courtyard as a small unmistakable shape that meant something specific had happened in this apartment.

Brückner's legs gave. He sat down at the bay window with his back to the radiator. The dressing gown's lapel was already dark with the wet that was coming up from inside the chest. His face went white in the specific waxen way the face went white when the central blood pressure had dropped to zero in a heartbeat and a half. His hands went up and then came down. The mouth opened. A small red bubble formed at the corner of the lower lip and broke. He did not speak again. He looked at Calder for perhaps two seconds with an expression Calder had now seen four times.

The expression was not the expression of the second hire at Greenwich, which had been the expression of a man whose pupils had told him in the final second of his life that he was the man specified by weight and not by name and that the specification had been the form his death would take. It was not Vernet across the Marseilles tray, who had understood across his coffee that the operation he had signed off on the previous autumn had been the operation that would end him. It was not Christofi in the Brussels kiosk, which was no expression at all, because the round had taken him before he had completed the half-second of registering Calder. The expression was the fourth. It was the expression of a man who had decided, in the final second, that the deciding had been the right decision. Brückner had decided in November. He spent five months waiting to be told whether the deciding would have a cost he was willing to pay. The cost had been the morning. The deciding had been the right decision.

Then the expression went out of the eyes. The body settled against the radiator the way bodies settled when the body had been carrying a man for sixty-eight years and was now no longer carrying him.

Calder worked the bolt. The casing ejected into his left palm. He pocketed it. The Welrod was now down to two clean firings.

He turned.

Heike Brückner was at the kitchen doorframe. Her hands had moved from the doorframe to her face. She was not making a sound.

Calder said, in German: Frau Brückner.

She did not respond.

He said: I am sorry.

She did not respond.

He said: Your father gave me a manila envelope from the second drawer of his desk on the left. He asked me to take it. I am going to take it. Then I am going to leave. I am leaving the door open. The neighbor will come in. You should call your husband.

She did not respond.

He went to the desk. He opened the second drawer on the left. The envelope was where Brückner had said it would be. He took it. He put it inside his coat.

At the doorway he stopped. He looked at Heike Brückner. She had moved from the kitchen doorframe to the floor beside the kitchen doorframe. She was sitting on the floor. Her hands were still on her face. She was making a small sound now, the sound a person made when the sound they were making was the sound that came up before the words.

Calder said: Frau Brückner. Your father said something to me before he died. He said the Latinist who corresponded with him for nine years was the only honest thing in his work in those years. I do not know if that is a comfort. I am telling you because he asked me to make sure someone in his family heard it. I am not the right person to be the one telling you. I am sorry you are.

He left.

He went down the stairwell.

He had not taken three steps from the door of the building when he heard the man on the second floor.

The man was on the landing above him, descending behind. Calder caught the footstep on the eleventh step. He kept descending. He kept walking. He registered, in the rate of the descent and the lightness of the foot and the way the man hesitated at the landing, that the man was not Annelies the bakery woman and not the postman and not a neighbor returning from his morning errand. The man was operational.

Calder stepped sideways onto the second-floor landing. He pressed his back to the wall beside the door of an apartment whose nameplate read Krüger.

The man came down to the second-floor landing and turned toward the next flight.

The man was approximately thirty. Black canvas jacket. Black corduroy trousers. The right hand was inside the jacket. The right hand was at the inside-pocket position of a man drawing a sidearm from a shoulder rig on the right side of the chest.

Calder was three feet to the man's left.

He did not draw the Walther.

He took the piano wire out of his right coat pocket.

He looped the wire over the man's head from behind in the same second the man's hand cleared the rig. He turned his hips. He drove the man forward into the railing of the second-floor landing. The wire bit into the throat at the angle the wire had been designed to bite—just below the hyoid bone, into the soft channel above the trachea where both carotids ran and where a four-pound pull on an eighteen-inch length of music-wire would crush the cricoid cartilage and partially open the right common carotid in the same second. The Beretta 92 in the man's right hand fell at the second. The pistol struck the linoleum with the sound of a metal kettle dropped on a tile floor. The man tried to bring his hands up to the wire. The fingers of his right hand got there. The fingertips slid off the slick metal, finding no purchase. He scrabbled. The fingertips opened on the wire and left small smears of blood from the cuts the wire had immediately made in the pads of three fingers. The man kicked. His left foot struck the railing once. His right foot struck Calder's shin. The shin took the kick. Calder did not let go.

The man's body weight pulled forward against the wire. Calder pulled back. The wire cut. The cut opened the right carotid first and the left carotid a half-second later as the man's head lolled in the loop, the wire tightening as the head fell forward. The blood came up under the chin in a fine pulsed sheet on the man's two open beats of cardiac output before the central pressure dropped and the sheeting became a wet draining. The man's open shirt collar darkened to the navel in a single span of seconds. The blood ran down the man's trousers and into his shoes and over Calder's right hand on the wooden handle and onto the Sredzkistrasse-side stairwell linoleum at the angle the linoleum sloped toward the main door of apartment 2B, where it ran in a thin red line under the door before stopping at the inner threshold. The man's right hand—the hand that had been opening on the wire moments before, the hand that had registered through the fingertips that the wire was going to do what the wire was going to do—made one last attempt at the wire. The fingertips, slippery now with their own blood, caught the metal and slid off it. The hand fell. The man's eyes did the thing eyes did when the brain had stopped being perfused. The pupils dilated to the limit of the iris. The mouth opened. A small clot of blood, the size of a child's marble, came up out of the throat through the open trachea and dropped onto the linoleum beside the dropped Beretta 92. The legs went. The body sagged against the wire.

Calder lowered the body. He had to use both hands. The body was sixty-eight kilos of dead weight. He arranged the man face-up on the linoleum. The throat was open across most of its width. The eyes did not close.

He took the Beretta 92. He took the wallet. He took the leather pouch from the man's left pocket that contained, by the touch of it through the leather, a folded piece of paper and three brass keys.

He went down to the ground floor.

He went out the back of the building into the courtyard. He crossed the courtyard. He went out through the rear gate onto the Sredzkistrasse. Klaus was at the corner with the Land Rover.

Klaus said: 'There is blood on your right cuff.'

Calder looked at his right cuff. There was blood on his right cuff. He had not registered it.

Klaus said: 'Get in the back. Lie down.'

Calder got in the back. He lay down. The dog blanket was over him within four seconds.

They drove west.

In a village outside Wittenberg, Klaus pulled into the yard of a barn that had been part of a Soviet collective farm three years earlier and was now empty. He killed the engine. He turned in his seat. Calder, coming up onto one elbow from under the dog blanket, saw the thing Klaus had not said in the hours of driving. The left hand Klaus laid along the back of the seat was bound—a strip of shirting wound twice around the palm and through the web of the thumb, the cloth dark and gone stiff where it had dried. Klaus had taken a blade somewhere between the courtyard and the corner where the Land Rover had waited, and had driven the dark roads west with the hand closed around the wheel, and had not mentioned it, because the not-mentioning was the older discipline and the daughter had been the more urgent thing. Calder did not ask. The wound was Klaus's to set down when Klaus chose to set it down.

'James.'

'Yes.'

'There was a daughter.'

Calder's hands stayed flat on his knees. He did not turn his head.

'You did not.'

'I did not.'

'Good.'

Klaus did not say anything for some seconds. Then he said: 'There is one thing you should know about Heike Brückner.'

Calder said: 'Yes.'

Klaus said: 'She is not Wolfgang Brückner's daughter.'

'What.'

'She is his stepdaughter. Her mother was Wolfgang's second wife. The mother died of cancer in 1986. Heike was eleven when Wolfgang married her mother. She has been Wolfgang's daughter since 1969. She is not, biologically, his.'

Calder said: 'She is his daughter.'

Klaus said: 'Yes. She is his daughter. I am telling you because the architecture knows the biological fact. The architecture has been keeping it. The architecture may use it. There is also a second fact, and I am going to tell you that I have been carrying this fact since the second afternoon at the window of the Sredzkistrasse flat with the Leica, when I took two frames of a young woman with a string bag and recognized, in the second frame, a mouth I had not seen in twenty-four years. I did not tell you at the window. I did not tell you that night. I did not tell you on the morning of the kill. I was waiting for the after. This is the after. Heike Brückner's birth name was Heike Vollmer. Her mother was Erika Vollmer. Erika Vollmer was, before her marriage to Wolfgang Brückner, the case officer in the Stasi training facility outside Potsdam who handled my own induction into the work in 1965. The same case officer. Werner Bruhn was her supervisor. She trained me for eleven months. I was her best student. She did not know me by my present name. She knew me by an operational name I have not used since 1969.'

Calder said: 'You knew her.'

Klaus said: 'I knew her. She did not know I survived. I am telling you because the woman in the kitchen this morning was the daughter of the woman who taught me the work I have been doing for twenty-six years. The work was hers before it was mine. The mother was the architecture. The daughter was not. The daughter, by the eight pages, was on Margaret's list as a possible. Margaret had registered Heike. Margaret had not yet decided. The undecided question is now the space the daughter is in.'

Calder did not respond.

Klaus said: 'The architecture has been keeping the biological fact about Heike since 1969. The architecture is keeping it as leverage. The leverage may, in the next two years, be applied. It may be applied to Heike. It may be applied to the man Heike is married to. It may be applied to the work Heike does, which I have not yet established. We do not yet know. The unknown is the space we are now in.'

Calder said: 'Margaret had registered Heike.'

Klaus said: 'Yes.'

Calder said: 'Then Heike is the question mark.'

Klaus said: 'Heike may be the question mark. Or the question mark may be the woman in the Spiegel photograph. Or the question mark may be a third person we have not yet identified.'

Calder said: 'Then there are two question marks.'

Klaus said: 'There are two question marks. There may be three. There may be four. The pencil page is going to lengthen. I have been thinking about this since November. I am telling you now because the lengthening has begun.'

Calder said: 'I do not have enough pencil.'

Klaus said: 'I have brought you another. I have brought you several. The pencils are in the bag.'

Klaus said there was one more thing, and that it was not about the daughter. Calder had gone out through the rear gate onto the Sredzkistrasse and had met no one at the gate. There had been a man at the gate. The Berlin desk had set a second operative on the rear of the building from oh-six-forty—a man whose wallet, when Klaus's source reached the body, gave the name Reinhardt—and he had been in position when Calder came down through the courtyard and had not been in position when Calder reached it. He had been in the recessed doorway four meters north of the gate, on his back, with his throat opened in a single transverse cut by an instrument neither Klaus nor Calder could have named from the wound. It had not been a fight. It had been a thing done to a man who had not been permitted to turn around.

A woman two floors up had been at her window for the milk. She had seen a man leave the doorway and walk south, unhurried, before the noise from the fifth floor brought anyone else to the glass. She had given the Volkspolizei a description, because she was the kind of woman who gave descriptions, and the Volkspolizei had written it down and done nothing with it: a light raincoat, the pale kind, not a Berlin coat; and the man, she said, had walked like one of the Americans. Calder said: CIA. Klaus said that was the easy reading, and the reading he would reach for himself, and—he took the Land Rover up through the gears—possibly the reading they were being offered.

Klaus had gone back to the doorway himself before he had come for Calder. On the inside of the doorframe, at the height of a man's eye, chalked, thumbnail-sized, was a theta. Three now. A Stasi basement in 1969. A hotel stair in Marseilles. A Sredzkistrasse doorway in which a man positioned to put a round in Calder had instead been found with his throat open. Three thresholds. Each of the three a threshold a man had walked out of alive—and the man who had walked out, all three times, had been Calder, or had been Klaus.

Klaus said theta was not the Custodia; he was sure of that the way he was sure of very little. The Custodia signed its work in a sun, in public, where the world could fail to read it. This signed its work in a Greek letter, in chalk, under a doorframe, where exactly one tired man going out the back would catch it without meaning to. The Custodia wanted to be obeyed. He did not know what this wanted. He knew only that it had now, three times, wanted him alive, and that he was old enough to be wary of a thing that wanted him alive and would not give him its name. Calder said it had killed a man for them. Klaus said it had removed a man who stood between Calder and a car, and that whether that was the same thing as for them was a question he would like to live long enough to answer.

He drove on.

That night Calder took the pencil page out of the leather notebook. He drew a single horizontal line through Brückner, Wolfgang. Berlin. The line was clean. His hand did not shake.

He wrote, beneath it:

4. Heike Brückner / Heike Vollmer (?). Berlin. (Witness. Possible.)

5. The American woman in the Spiegel. (Hannah Doyle.) Geneva, the man Klaus knows.

6. ?

He folded the page. He put it back in the notebook.

He looked at the third name on the original page—the man at the Brussels phone number, struck through. He looked at the fourth name, just written, with the question mark and the parenthetical Possible.

He kept it.

He held it in the private file that had been, since the Marseilles morning, the file the operation was now writing for him.

He sat for some time at the kitchen table of the safe-house outside Wittenberg, with the pencil in his right hand and the notebook closed on the table beside it, and registered the fact that his name had not been spoken to him in fifteen months. The obituary in the *Times* had been the name's funeral. The architecture had attended the funeral. The architecture had filed the name. Brückner, at the stove on the Lychener Strasse at oh-seven-oh-two, had been the resurrection. The naming had been the institution's acknowledgment that the closure had been wrong. The wrong closure was now an open file. The open file was the work of the next two years.

In the days after Berlin, while Calder and Klaus were still moving west, a tram shelter on the rue Sainte-Catherine in Lyon came apart in the early evening. There were four people under the shelter. The blast killed three of them the way a shaped charge in a confined steel frame kills—fast, total, the bodies doing only what the physics required of them—and it killed the fourth differently, and it was the fourth that the French regional paper described in the language papers use when they have been handed a photograph they cannot print. The small concert hall where Marianne played the second flute stood forty meters up the street. The blast did not reach the hall. It had not been built to reach the hall. It had been built to be reported in a paper that Klaus would read, and to set, on the inside of the shelter's one surviving steel panel, scored fresh and still bright at its edges, a sun with eight rays around an eye —at the exact height, a man paced it out later and found, of a seated flautist's eyeline from the hall's back row. Klaus did not show Calder the paper for two days. When he showed it, he had stopped being able to keep his right hand still, and Calder understood that the hand was not the poison. The hand was the photograph. Klaus said one sentence. The institution has stopped cleaning, James. It has started knocking—and it has learned which wall my daughter is on the other side of.

10

GENEVA

Geneva—October 1991

The café was on the rue de la Confédération, two blocks from the lake. It had been a café for nearly a century. The marble of the bar had a worn place at the elbow, two feet from the till, where a hundred years of right elbows had eroded the stone in a small visible concavity that the waiter never apologized for.

Calder arrived a little before three.

He sat at a table by the window. He ordered an espresso. He had a copy of the Tribune de Genève in his right hand. He did not open it.

The shoulder ached. The cold front coming up the lake had been registering in the entry-wound puckered scar since the previous afternoon, a dull pulse along the trapezius the way the moon ached on the side of the body that had been altered. He noted the ache. He registered, in the registering, that the body had begun to keep weather as a separate ledger from the operational one. The weather ledger was not yet the operational ledger. Some year it would be. He did not roll the shoulder. He held it where it was.

The contact had been the man Klaus had owed a favor to since 1979, a Swiss former federal police officer named Ernst Steiger who had been working in the private space between the Swiss banks and the people who watched them since his retirement. Steiger had taken the favor without comment. He sent the message through a doctor in Basel. The doctor had passed it to a woman in Zurich. The woman in Zurich had passed it to a man in Geneva. The man in Geneva had passed it to Hannah Doyle through a channel Calder did not know and did not need to know. The reply had come back through the same channels four days later. I will be there. Wear nothing red.

He was wearing a dark gray suit. His tie was navy. He was not wearing red. The instruction had been a politeness from a woman who had not asked who he was. By that silence she had told him she already knew.

He waited.

Hannah Doyle came in just before three.

She was thirty-nine. She was wearing a gray wool dress and a leather jacket in a particular shade of brown that had been chosen, in the way a woman chose a leather jacket for a meeting in a Geneva café in October, to be neither memorable nor forgettable. She had brown hair pulled back in a low knot at the base of her neck. She was wearing low brown boots. She was carrying a leather satchel against her left hip.

She walked across the café floor with the deliberate even pace of a woman who had been a person of average height all her life and had decided, in approximately her thirty-fifth year, that the way a person of average height entered a public room mattered. The pace was not assertive. The pace was equally distributed. She had, between the door and his table, looked at four faces and not at him. The four faces were the four working faces in the room. He had registered the same four. The looking-past was the looking.

She sat down across from him. She put the satchel on the floor beside her chair and hooked the strap once around her right boot.

She said, in English, with an accent that was American but had been to Boston for school and to London for work: 'Wear nothing red is a hard instruction in October. The trees are doing the work.'

He said: 'I thought it was an autumn-of-1991 reference.'

She said: 'It was. You read your newspapers. I am pleased.'

She put out her right hand. He took it. The handshake was brief.

He looked at her face. He had seen the face once, in Margaret's eight pages described and in Der Spiegel photographed, and had not yet seen it in front of him. The face in front of him belonged to a woman who had been working the kind of work Hannah Doyle worked for a decade and a half. It had the fine lines at the corners of the eyes that came from squinting at typescript in fluorescent corridors and the careful set at the mouth that came from not being able to comment on what the typescript said. She was not Elena. Calder caught the not Elena in the half-second before the recognition closed. The instant was the cost of looking at a woman of approximately the same age in a café in approximately the same kind of light. He was not prepared for the half-second. He registered it. He let it pass. The face was Hannah's. The face was the face of a person he had not yet met. He set the half-second aside.

She reached into the leather satchel beside her chair, without looking down, and took out a photograph. She set it face-down on the table between them. She did not turn it over.

After a moment she said: 'You are James Calder.'

She turned it over. Personnel-card stock, four-by-five, slightly soft at the corners from being carried in a satchel for some time. Calder, 1986, Century House—the kind of photograph Century House took every three years and the kind a CIA Counter-Intelligence officer would have a copy of through a channel her superiors would not interrogate. She held it on her side of the table for a count of three. Then she placed it back in the satchel.

'I have been carrying that since March of last year. I have looked at it most days. I am pleased to put it back.'

He said: 'I am.'

She said: 'You are also a man who is dead.'

He said: 'I am that too.'

She said: 'I have been hoping to meet you for eighteen months. Most of the people who hope to meet a man of your description hope to meet him in his living room with his wife in the kitchen. I have been hoping to meet you in approximately this configuration. I am sorry for the configuration.'

He said: 'I am also.'

She said: 'I would like to talk for an hour. Then I would like you to leave first. I will leave fifteen minutes after you. I will not turn my head when I leave. You will not turn your head when I am leaving. We will not contact each other again until I send the message to the channel through which I sent the first message. The message will arrive when it arrives. You will not solicit it. You will not send a return channel of any kind. The discipline is the discipline. Do you understand the discipline.'

He said: 'I understand the discipline.'

She said: 'Good.'

She drank from a glass of water the waiter had brought her without being asked.

She set the glass down. She folded her hands on the table. The hands were small. They were the hands of a woman of average height who had been a swimmer in college and who had the particular small-boned wrist of a woman whose arms had been, at twenty, a different kind of instrument than the arms had become. The watch on her left wrist was a steel Rolex Air-King in 34mm, a size Rolex had been manufacturing for decades and that women in her line of work had been buying secondhand since the early eighties. The watch was older than the woman wearing it. The crystal had a hairline crack at the eight o'clock that she had not, at any point in the last several years, had repaired.

She caught him looking at the crack. She did not move her wrist. She did not cover it. She turned the face of the watch a quarter-turn so the crack was visible to him in better light, and she said, in a register one degree below operational: 'My brother gave it to me. He was twenty-four. The crack is from a doorframe in our parents' house in 1985. I have not had it repaired because the man who would have had it repaired is not here to be told that I had it repaired. The not-repairing is the private fact about me that the architecture has not been able to read off any of my files. I am telling you because you have already read it off my wrist.'

She said: 'I am Hannah Doyle. I am thirty-nine. I am from Boston. I have been with the agency since 1979.'

She drew breath, with the specific care of a person who had rehearsed the breath as well as the words.

She said: 'The training is what you would expect. Soviet history from Tufts. Russian from Middlebury. A year of fieldwork at the Hoover Institution. Beirut from 1979 to 1981 on a junior cover, learning the work in the city it could only be learned in. Langley Soviet desk for two years. The East European cell from 1983—Prague, Warsaw, the work the agency had been doing on the Eastern bloc's nuclear scientists.'

She turned the white coffee cup a quarter-turn on its saucer. The action was not done for him. The action was done for her.

She said: 'I was at the cell when your ex-wife was at the Anglican charitable trust. I have read her papers. I have not, at any point in those years, been at the same conferences. The non-overlapping was an institutional accident that I have come, in the last two years, to register as not entirely accidental. Berlin from 1989, on a small temporary detail that I would like to say was my own idea but that I now suspect was the agency's.'

She said: 'I was a Soviet desk analyst until 1986. I moved to counterintelligence in the autumn of 1988 after my brother was killed. He was thirty-one. He was a fast-breeder physicist at the Atomic Weapons Establishment at Aldermaston. He had been seconded to a Devon municipality for the summer of 1988 to consult on a civilian reactor cooling protocol. He was identified by the people who killed him as a person who had made an inquiry he was not supposed to make. He was killed in a manner that was not investigated. I made the inquiry that was not investigated. I was given a closed-session hearing on the matter eight months ago. The closed-session hearing did not produce a finding. The closed-session hearing produced a transfer for me to a desk in Berlin where I am now, by my employer's discipline, no longer permitted to investigate the death of my own brother.'

He said: 'Yes.'

Then she said: 'The Berlin desk is the desk a counterintelligence officer is given when the institutional answer to her competence is to relocate her. The desk has access to the cable traffic of the Eastern-bloc residual stations. The desk does not have access to the cable traffic of the German station.'

She paused for the count of two.

She said: 'I have been at the desk for fourteen months. I have been writing my own reports on the Eastern cables. The reports go to a senior officer who is not the senior officer they should go to. I have not raised the question.'

She said: 'I have come to assume that someone not on the formal distribution list has been reading them. I have not yet identified the someone. Whoever it is has been working in that space for fourteen months. I have been working in it too.'

She said: 'I am telling you because the fact that someone outside the formal channel is reading my reports may, in due course, become a fact that affects you. That uncertainty is something I am asking you to carry.'

She paused.

She said: 'I am still investigating.'

She paused.

She said: 'I have been on this work for two years. I have identified a thing I do not yet have a name for. I have identified, separately, the woman who was your ex-wife's correspondent at the Journal of Medieval Latin under the maiden name Margaret Howell. I have read the four papers. I have read the marginal correction in the third paper. I have identified the hand. The hand is a man named Wolfgang Brückner. I have read this morning's wire copy. I am pleased to see Brückner is no longer in a position to write in the margins of journals. I am also concerned that you appear to have left a witness.'

He said: 'I left a witness because the alternative was making a daughter watch her father die.'

She said: 'The witness's name is Heike Vollmer. The architecture has been keeping the biological fact about her since 1969. The architecture is going to make her an offer in the next eighteen months. The offer is going to involve the work her stepfather did. The offer is going to involve revealing the biological fact to her in a way that is operationally specific. The architecture is going to spend the leverage. We will not get to her before the architecture does. That is the fact you produced this morning. I am not faulting you. I am noting the fact.'

He said: 'Yes.'

She said: 'Now I will tell you what I have come here to tell you.'

He said: 'Yes.'

◆◆◆

She said: 'My brother was Michael Doyle.'

The room did not move.

His hands on the edge of the table did not move.

He waited for the breath to do something. It did not.

She said: 'I am sorry. I had been going to find a slow way to say it. I am thirty-nine years old and I have not yet learned a slow way to say things that need to be said quickly. I am also going to give you twenty seconds.'

She did not look away.

He took the twenty seconds.

He thought, in the twenty seconds, about a small notice in the *Times* he had seen and not filed in the autumn of 1988. It had been the obituary of a young Aldermaston physicist whose death had been classified as an atypical cardiac event in a Devon municipality. The obituary had said, in two lines beside a photograph of a young man at thirty-one, that the father had been at Trinity in 1945, on the desert floor, three miles from the tower. The father was an American physicist who had returned to Massachusetts and had raised two children in Boston. He had not, in his lifetime, eaten a meal at his table that he had not first held a private silence over. He thought about the quality of the deliberate non-filing. He thought about the fact that the not-filing had been a discipline he had been mistaking, for fourteen months, for an absence of pattern. He thought about Andrew Ruskin at the door of the Greenwich flat at 19:47 on the third of January 1990 with a manila envelope and a polite young man's tired face. He registered, in the same twenty seconds, that Ruskin had been a courier for one architecture and Michael Doyle had been a researcher for another. The two architectures had been the same architecture. The same architecture was the one that had killed the Russian woman in the workroom on Webber Street and was now sitting across from him in the form of a thirty-nine-year-old American who had been carrying her brother's death in a leather satchel since the autumn of 1988.

He registered, also, in the same twenty seconds, that her father had been at Trinity in 1945. His own father had been at Trinity in 1945. The two men had stood three miles from the tower with welding glass against their faces and had registered, between them, the half-second in which the desert had become brighter than the sun. They had not known each other. They had not, in any of the years that followed, met. They had each returned to a different country and had each held a private silence over a meal three times a day for twenty-three years. The two children at the table across from him now—he, forty-nine; she, thirty-nine—had been raised by men who had stood on the same desert floor in the same half-second in 1945. The private silence had carried, by the architecture's patient discipline, into the morning the two children were sitting across from each other in a Geneva café preparing to take the architecture apart.

He said: 'How.'

Hannah said: 'Devon, August 1988. He was killed for asking a question about the published cardiac mortality figures of three British research stations over the prior eighteen months. The figures had not been possible. He had run them in a small notebook in his Aldermaston office on a Sunday in May. He took the notebook to a friend at Imperial College in June. The friend had taken the figures to a man at the BMA who was the editor of an epidemiological journal years before. The man at the BMA had been retired the previous autumn. The retirement had been the reason my brother had picked him. He had not been retired for the reason my brother had thought. He had been retired by the architecture in advance of his contingency, against the small kind of inquiry my brother made. Within seventy-two hours of my brother handing him the figures, the architecture knew. Within fourteen weeks, my brother was dead. The mechanism was an instrument I have spent two years not yet identifying. The instrument leaves no forensic trace. The deaths are recorded as atypical cardiac events. There have been forty-one of them since 1962. My brother is the most recent I have located. The number, by my reading, is not the real number. The real number is some multiple of forty-one I have not yet seen the dossiers to set.'

He said: 'And the Brussels affair.'

She said: 'The Brussels affair was the cover. The papers reported it as a robbery; the State Department classified it as an accidental death of an unrelated American on a European business trip. He had been in Brussels for forty-eight hours that summer, asking the same question of a Belgian colleague. The architecture used the Brussels timing to attach his death, in the public record, to a place that was not Devon and a category that was not the figures he had been asking about. The architecture has been doing this since 1962. The Brussels affair was the one I followed first because Brussels was where the inquiry had been visible. Devon was where the death had been arranged.'

He said: 'And Andrew Ruskin.'

She said: 'Andrew Ruskin is alive. He is a State Department clerk on secondment to Century House—exactly what his clearance says he is. He delivered the envelope to your Greenwich door at 19:47 because he had been asked to deliver it by his desk officer, and because the envelope had your name on it, and because the request was consistent with the work he did. He did not know what was in the envelope. He has not, in all the time since, been told. He is by my reading the only fully innocent man in the entire chain of the third of January, and the architecture has been using his innocence as the operational bandwidth across which it ran the substitution. Mr Ruskin is in this work the way the postman is in a kidnapping. His ignorance was what made the using possible.'

He was quiet for some time.

She did not interrupt.

He said: 'I have been carrying your brother's name since the harbor without knowing it was his name. I have been carrying the *Times* obituary I did not file. I have been carrying the discipline of not-filing it. I should have asked the question in November. I have been not asking. The silence has been my failure of discipline.'

She said: 'You were not failing. You were waiting for the architecture to put the missing piece in your hands. The architecture has not, until tonight, been willing. I am the architecture's discontinuity. I am the missing piece walking into the café.'

He said: 'I am sorry about your brother.'

She said: 'I am sorry about your ex-wife.'

He said: 'My wife is not dead.'

She said: 'No.'

She paused.

She said: 'She is in Birnam.'

The room held for a second.

He said: 'Birnam.'

She said: 'Perthshire. A village near Dunkeld. She has been there since November of last year. She is renting a cottage from a widow named MacIntyre who has been running a small B&B for years. The widow does not know who Margaret is. Margaret has been writing under another name. The writing is academic. The papers are no longer in the Journal of Medieval Latin. The papers are now appearing in Speculum. The papers are under a different name and have a different set of footnotes and an entirely different set of marginalia, which the architecture has not yet, by my reading, identified as hers. I do not know how long the architecture will fail to identify them.'

She said: 'I am telling you because I have been keeping the address for you for two months. The keeping has been the operational fact about me you needed to know first. I am not going to give you the address tonight. I am going to give it to you when we are ready. The architecture is hunting you. The order has been issued. The order does not name Margaret. If you go to Birnam, you bring the order to her. The architecture will then close her ledger as well as yours, and the closure of her ledger will be the closure of the second box of pages, which I do not yet have and which I do not yet know where to find. I have a list of the villages the architecture is watching. Birnam is on the list. The list has thirteen villages on it. Margaret is in one of them. I know which. The architecture does not. The architecture will identify the village by the end of the calendar year if it has not already. After that, our window closes.'

She said: 'I am telling you Birnam because withholding Birnam was a discipline I was no longer able to keep. The discipline has been failing for some weeks. I would rather you have the name than not have it. I am asking you, in exchange, not to go.'

He said: 'I will not go.'

She said: 'Thank you.'

She took a piece of paper from the pocket of her jacket. She placed it on the table beside her empty espresso cup. She did not push it across.

She said: 'This is a Geneva phone number. The phone is at a particular bar in the Pâquis neighborhood. The phone is answered by a particular bartender. The bartender will ask you for the name of the woman who took the photograph of the curtains at the gallery. You will say Elena. The bartender will ask the second question. The second question is: Which curtains. The answer is: The ones with the geranium on the sill. He will give you a phone number. The phone number is the number you will use to reach me from now on. The number is not in any registry. The number is not on any list. The number changes every six weeks. The bartender always has the current number. He does not know what he is keeping. He knows that the questions are the questions and that the answers are the answers. He has been doing this small bit of work for me since 1985. The bartender's name is Pascal. He is a man whose name you should not learn beyond Pascal. He has a son. The son is twenty-three. The son works in computers. The son does not know what his father does on the side. The keeping is the bartender's private operation against his own family. I respect it. So should you.'

He said: 'Yes.'

She said: 'I am also going to tell you what I am.'

He said: 'Yes.'

She said: 'I am still CIA. I have not resigned. I am working inside. The work I am doing now is not all of it authorized. The agency knows. The agency has decided not to investigate. I am exploiting that. The reason I am exploiting it is my brother. I do not yet know whether the agency was unable to protect him or was involved in the failure to protect. The day I have evidence one way or the other will be the day I decide whether to remain. I do not have evidence yet. I expect to take six more years.'

She said: 'You are now part of my evidence-gathering. You are a man whose name the architecture has used on a clearance the architecture should not have had. I am a woman whose brother's clearance has been used on the same architecture. We are working the same problem. We are not, however, the same operation. You are running the list your ex-wife began. I am running the inquiry my brother started. The two operations overlap. They do not coincide. I will help you when I can. You will help me when you can. We will not formalize the help. We will not codify it. The codifying would produce a record. The record would produce the leverage the architecture needs. We are doing this as two operatives who are not in the same service and not in the same architecture and not, by any institutional definition, on the same side.'

She said: 'I am not your colleague.'

He said: 'I understand.'

She said: 'I am not your friend.'

He said: 'I understand.'

She paused.

He said: 'Yes.'

She said: 'There is one more thing. I have spent two years investigating my brother's death. I have spent two years not investigating one specific thing. The one specific thing is the woman my brother was sleeping with at the time of his death. He had a girlfriend in Brussels. She was a Belgian woman of his own age. She was a journalist for Le Soir. She was not, by my reading, involved with the architecture. She was a Belgian journalist who had been sleeping with my brother for nine months. I have not investigated her. I will not. I am telling you because I want you to know I am the kind of person who has a thing she will not investigate. The thing is a woman my brother loved. The woman has the right to be left alone. I am leaving her alone.'

He said: 'I am also.'

She said: 'I assumed.'

She drank the last of her water.

She stood. She picked up her satchel. She did not extend her hand again.

She said: 'You are going to leave first. I will leave fifteen minutes after you. Do not turn around. Do not look at the window when you walk past it. The bar I have indicated is two streets north of here. The bartender will be there until 18:00. The bartender will not be there tomorrow. I will be in Berlin by tomorrow night. I will not, in the next eighteen months, be in Geneva. I will be reachable through Pascal. Be well, Mr Calder.'

He said: 'Be well, Miss Doyle.'

He did not say her first name. Neither did she say his. The silence was the discipline.

He left the café first. He paid in cash. He took his coat. He walked out.

He walked north.

He did not turn his head.

At the corner of the rue de la Confédération and the rue du Mont-Blanc, before he turned, he caught—in the small reflective field of the corner shop's plate-glass window—a man at the news kiosk on the opposite side of the rue de Coutance who had been at the kiosk since before Calder had arrived for the meeting at fourteen-thirty. The man was approximately fifty. He was wearing a cream raincoat of a cut Calder did not associate with a Geneva shop. The cut was American. The coat was not the architecture's coat. The man had not looked at Calder. The man was looking, in the small unhurried way a man looked at a kiosk's display when the man was waiting for someone, at the magazines.

He registered the man.

He filed the man.

He did not file what to do with him.

The cream raincoat would not speak to Calder. It would not explain itself. The agency's relationship with Hannah Doyle's off-book work was, in his reading, neither a sanction nor a license but the institutional courtesy of a service that had decided not to interfere with what one of its officers was doing in the space between the Berlin desk and the brother she was no longer permitted to investigate. Not interfering was not the same as not watching. The watching had its own weight. The weight was a man at a kiosk on the rue de Coutance at fourteen-fifty-eight on the second of October 1991. Calder would not, in the years he carried the question, decide whether the watching had been a kindness or a leash. He carried it as a kindness on the days the work permitted the assumption and as a leash on the days the work did not. But the cream raincoat carried, under the reading he had filed it beneath, a second reading he could not make it release. He had stood in a barn outside Wittenberg in April and heard Klaus describe a pale coat that had walked, unhurried, away from a Sredzkistrasse doorway—away from a dead man and a theta chalked at eye height—and a woman at a window who had said the walk was the walk of one of the Americans. Two pale coats. Two unhurried American walks. One had cleared a gate for him in Berlin; one had watched him leave a café in Geneva. He had filed the cream raincoat under the agency because the agency was a category he possessed. He was not certain the cream raincoat belonged to it. He kept it, after that afternoon, in both files.

He had walked four blocks before he saw the postman.

The postman was thirty-five. Brown raincoat. He was carrying a leather satchel of bills the way Calder had carried a leather satchel of bills in Brussels in February. He was on the opposite side of the rue de la Confédération. He was walking parallel to Calder at the pace Calder was walking. He had been there since the second block. Calder registered him at the third. The registration had been a quarter-second behind the registration he would have made in Marseilles. The quarter-second was the cost of the half-hour with Hannah Doyle.

He took the next side street. The postman did not turn.

He walked two more blocks. He turned left. He turned left again. He had now made three lefts, which was a square, which would put a tail in the same place a tail would not be if the tail were any good.

The postman was at the corner.

The postman had not made the same three lefts. The postman had made one. The postman had been on a parallel street. The postman had been competent enough to predict the route, and incompetent enough not to vary it himself.

The postman was looking at Calder across an intersection.

The postman's right hand was inside the leather satchel. The hand was not on bills. The hand was at the angle a hand was at when it was on the grip of a pistol oriented forward through the opening of a satchel for a quick clean draw at twelve meters.

The intent was not capture. The intent was the thing Calder had been preparing for in twenty-one months and now had a half-second to deliver against. He assumed a kill from the morning at Greenwich. The architecture was delivering one, slowly, in the form of three desks and the patient discipline of an institution that had been not-counting its bodies for thirty-four years. The Conclave had decided, by the operative across the intersection in Geneva at 16:18 on a Thursday afternoon in October, that the two-stone margin in the Iowa ledger was now to be closed. The closure was to be done in a Geneva alley by a man with a leather satchel and a Walther PP with a Swiss can and a cleaning crew in a panel van two streets over.

Calder turned right into the narrow rue Diday.

The rue Diday ran sixty meters between two stone buildings of the kind Geneva had been building since the eighteenth century. There was a recessed doorway at the thirty-meter mark on the left, set back twenty inches from the line of the wall. He had registered the recess on his way to the café. He had registered everything on his way to the café. The registering had been the discipline.

He went into the recess. He pressed his back against the stone. He took the piano wire out of the leather pouch in his right coat pocket. He worked the wooden handles into his palms. He held them at his sides.

Eleven seconds.

The postman's footsteps came down the rue Diday at the pace of a man who was confirming a corner. Brisk. Not a run. The pace of a man who had a kill arranged and was closing without alarming the street. The pace of an operative who had been told the target was fifty-five years old, walked with a slight favoring of the right shoulder from an old wound, and would be turning at the second left.

Calder waited until the footstep was at the doorway.

He came out of the recess.

His left hand caught the postman's right wrist as the satchel swung past the doorway. His right hand looped the wire over the man's head from behind. He turned his hips. He drove the man forward into the opposite wall. The wire bit. The man's right hand on the satchel opened. The Walther PP—threaded barrel, Swiss aluminum can, .32 ACP, eight-round magazine—dropped onto the cobbles with the small heavy metallic sound a suppressed pistol made on stone.

The man got his left hand under the wire at the second second. The fingers were strong. He had been doing this work for some unspecified number of years. He was the operative the architecture had assigned to a senior man because the architecture had assessed the assignment as a clean piece of professional work that did not warrant a more expensive operative. The assessment had been the architecture's third operational mistake on Calder's account in twenty-one months.

Calder rolled the man face-down. He pulled the wire backward across the throat from above. The wire cut. The body went still at perhaps the eleventh second.

Calder got the wire off. He sat back on his heels. His breathing was at fifty per minute. His right shoulder was wet inside the bandage from the trapezius having pulled. His hands to the wrists were wet on the outside from the man's blood.

He went through the man's pockets. He took the wallet, which contained no identification and three thousand Swiss francs in fresh notes. He took the spare magazine for the Walther PP from the inside coat pocket, plus a leather case containing a Geneva apartment key on a brass tag with the address of a building on the Rue de Berne handwritten in pencil. He took a folded slip of paper from the breast pocket. The paper had three lines on it in a competent typewriter hand.

The first line was Calder, James. 13 stone. 55. Right shoulder old wound. Slight limp on left.

The second line was Café Confédération 14:00. Rue Diday alternative.

The third line was Closure to be confirmed. 17:00 Pâquis pickup. Schauer.

Schauer was the cleaning crew's signal. Schauer was the man at the panel van on the Rue de Berne. Schauer was the man who would be wondering, by 17:30, why the operative had not arrived at the rendezvous with the body in a sailmaker's bag for transport to a marine launch on the lake.

They had his age wrong by six years. He was forty-nine. The brief had him at fifty-five. They had the limp wrong too. There was no limp; there had never been a limp. The line that read slight limp on left was what a true thing became after a file had carried it too long—a man once watched favoring the side that carried an old shoulder wound, the observation copied forward by hands that never saw him again until the shoulder had migrated to the leg and the right side had drifted to the left. The shoulder itself they had right. Right shoulder old wound was the one true line on the slip—the one fact written on his body rather than in a file, and so the one fact that could not drift. The six years was the operational margin of whoever had built the brief. The six years had been on his account in three previous files Hannah had named in the half-hour at the café and that he had not, in the half-hour, registered as a pattern. He registered it now. The architecture had been running him at a constructed age since 1985. The constructed age was older than he was. The constructed age was the age of a man closer to retirement, less likely to act, less likely to be the kind of man who had held discipline in a harbor for fifteen months. The constructed age was the institutional comfort of an architecture that had built its closure on a man it had decided, before the deciding, was already nearly done.

Calder folded the slip. He put it in the inside left pocket of his coat.

He stood up.

He picked up the Walther PP from the cobbles. The slide-cover had a small chip in the chrome at the rear sight from where the suppressor had absorbed the impact of the drop. The chip was the kind a Swiss armorer would replace at the next service. The Swiss armorer would not get to the next service. The Walther went into the inside right pocket of his coat. The piano wire went back into the leather pouch on the wet handles. The leather pouch went back into his right coat pocket.

He pulled the man's body the four feet into the recessed doorway. He arranged the body in the posture of a drunk who had decided to sleep, the way he had arranged the man in Sète. He pulled the brown raincoat closed over the throat. The blood would soak through the coat; by then he would be on the lake.

He looked at his hands. He took the pocket handkerchief out of his left coat pocket. He wiped his hands. He wiped the wet handles of the wire through the leather pouch. He turned his cuffs up against the cold. The cuffs were not visibly stained from the doorway angle. They would be stained at the inner seam. The inner seam would be a problem for tomorrow.

He went out of the rue Diday at the southern end. He turned left onto the quai. He walked the four blocks to the Quai du Mont-Blanc at the pace of a man who had nowhere particular to be. He bought a ticket on the small ferry that ran from the Quai du Mont-Blanc to the southern shore. He boarded the ferry at the bow. He stood at the rail. He did not turn his head.

The ferry left in the late afternoon.

He did not see the postman on the boat.

He stood at the rail for the twenty-minute crossing.

When the ferry reached the southern shore he disembarked. He walked four blocks east to the Cornavin railway station. He bought a ticket to Lyon under the third of his cover names. He waited on the platform for twenty-three minutes. The platform held the small ordinary traffic of a Geneva railway station at 17:00 on a Thursday in October. There was no postman on the platform. There was no operative on the platform. There was a woman with two small children who was buying biscuits at a kiosk, and a businessman with a briefcase who was reading a copy of Le Temps and not turning the pages, and a railway official in a navy uniform who was looking at the timetable above the kiosk.

He boarded the evening train to Lyon.

He sat by the window. The train pulled out.

He did not sleep on the train.

He thought, instead, about Hannah Doyle's hands on the table. About the fine bones of her wrist. About the hairline crack in the crystal of the steel Rolex Air-King at the eight o'clock that she had not had repaired. About the satchel she had set on the floor beside her chair with the strap looped once around her right boot, and the way she had not, at any point in the half-hour, looked at the satchel. About the Boston in her vowels. About the woman she had, in the first ten seconds of seeing him, looked past him and chosen not to look at again. The looking-past had been her discipline. The choice never to look at it again had been her gift. The gift had been the specific kindness of a woman who had decided, in her own work, that there were things she would not investigate.

He thought, also, about the second line on the slip. The operative had known the café. The operative had known the alternative. The channel had been Steiger to the doctor in Basel to the woman in Zurich to the man in Geneva to Hannah. The channel was compromised at one of its links. He had six possibilities and would not arrive at the seventh tonight. He filed the six. He moved.

He thought, also, about Andrew Ruskin at the door at 19:47.

He thought about the arrangement by which the architecture had, in the autumn of 1989, recruited a State Department clerk on innocent secondment to be the carrier of an envelope to Greenwich on a January evening. About the small boy with the brown jumper Klaus had not killed at the bookseller's shop in Greenwich on the morning of the fourth of January 1990 because the brown jumper had been a brown jumper Klaus could not bring himself to kill a man wearing. The brown jumper had been a small accidental kindness. The use of Ruskin had been the long deliberate cruelty—the architecture's habit of running its operational instructions through men whose innocence was the bandwidth across which the cruelty traveled. Hannah's list of forty-three intercepted envelopes was the small forensic record of the bandwidth. Calder's envelope had been one of them. Michael Doyle's death had been an earlier one. The architecture had not invented the practice. The architecture had only kept the books.

The two were the work.

He filed Andrew Ruskin's name beside the third name on the pencil page.

He thought about Margaret in Birnam.

He had not, in all his time at the harbor and on the road, thought of Margaret in any specific place. Margaret was the woman in Ealing he believed to be in Ealing because he had been told in November 1989 she was in Ealing. Margaret had then become the woman in Ealing he no longer believed to be in Ealing because Klaus told him in the harbor she might not be. Margaret was now the woman in Birnam, in a cottage rented from a widow named MacIntyre, writing papers under a third name in Speculum whose marginalia the architecture had not yet identified as hers.

Birnam. Perthshire. A village near Dunkeld. He had been to Dunkeld once with his father in the summer of 1963. They had walked along the Tay. His father had pointed at a beech tree above the river and had said: the wood for the butt of a Lee-Enfield. Calder had been twenty-one, the summer before his first Cambridge term. He filed the comment. He had not understood it for years. He understood it eventually. His father had been pointing at a tree the way other men pointed at women in other men's company.

The morning train would carry him north from Geneva to Paris. The afternoon train would carry him further north. The evening train would carry him to Edinburgh by the hour the fog came down the Pentlands. The next morning a small two-carriage line would take him through Pitlochry to Dunkeld and a cottage rented from a widow named MacIntyre would be at the end of a lane near a beech tree he had passed through with his father in 1963. He mapped the route. He registered, in the mapping, that this was a route he was not going to take. The not-taking was the discipline. The discipline was the cost. The cost was the shape of the morning he was choosing to spend on the operation rather than on his ex-wife. He held the cost where it was.

Margaret was, by Hannah's reading, four hundred yards from

that tree.

He would hold the discipline. He would hold it because the order was now on a desk and the desk would deliver an operative and the operative was already delivered once today and a second one would be delivered before December and a third in the new year and there would not be a year in which the next one was not coming. The architecture would close his ledger. The architecture would close hers if he reached her. Her ledger stayed open at the price of the distance between the train carriage and the cottage. He would hold the discipline because Hannah had asked, and because the asking had been the price of the address she had given him in trade.

He held it.

He looked out at the dark of the French countryside through the window of the train.

He thought about the four directions of the compass rose on the inside of Elena's left wrist, and the sixteen years he had been the dot at the center, and the four directions she had not been permitted to walk in. He thought about the bracelet on Margaret's wrist, the four charms and the silver key that had not been his silver key for two years and that pointed, by the fact of its replacement, to a lock Margaret had been holding the key to without telling him. Two women. Two wrists. Two private architectures of marking. They had not, in any of the years, met each other in any room except the Kensington bookshop in December 1973. They had met him.

The list, when he took the pencil page from the leather notebook in the lavatory of the train carriage between Geneva and Lyon, had now to be amended.

He took the pencil from the leather pouch. He drew, beneath 5. Hannah Doyle:

She knows about the list. She is not on it. She will not be on it.

She is the third operative in this work.

He folded the page.

He put it back in the notebook.

He went back to his seat.

In the morning the train arrived in Lyon. He took the connecting train to Marseilles. He took a connecting train to the Atlantic harbor.

Klaus was at the kitchen table when he came in.

Klaus said: 'She is alive.'

Calder said: 'She is alive.'

Klaus said: 'She is in Perthshire.'

Calder said: 'She is in Perthshire.'

Klaus said: 'You are not going.'

Calder said: 'I am not going.'

Klaus said: 'Good.'

Klaus poured the tea.

There was a new bottle on the shelf. Klaus had been to Bayonne while Calder had been in Geneva. The bottle was Glenmorangie ten-year. He bought it from a wine merchant on the rue Pannecau. The merchant had not been on any list.

Klaus opened the bottle. He poured a small measure into each of the enamel mugs beside the tea. Calder watched the pouring without comment. Klaus saw him watching.

Klaus said: 'I tested the seal on the way back from Bayonne. The seal was the seal. I tested the contents in the harbor before I poured. The contents are the contents. The mark on my left wrist is unchanged. It will not change. I am drinking again. The drinking is mine.'

Calder said: 'Yes.'

He drank. The whisky tasted of the clean things Glenmorangie had always tasted of. There was no metallic undertone. There was the small bright fact, in his throat, that the institution had not, in this bottle, reached him. The bottle was a kindness Klaus's testing had provided.

Klaus said: 'I have been thinking.'

Calder said: 'Yes.'

Klaus said: 'The architecture has reopened the closure. The order has been issued. Brückner told you. The Geneva operative was the first delivery against the order. There will be more. The work is now a hunt and the work is now run.'

Calder said: 'Yes.'

Klaus said: 'The list is the answer to the hunt. We finish the list before they finish us.'

Calder said: 'Yes.'

Klaus said: 'We will need a fourth.'

Calder said: 'We will. Hannah.'

Klaus said: 'And a fifth. I have someone in mind. I will tell you in a week.'

Calder said: 'In a week.'

They drank the tea.

Outside, the bell-buoy at the breakwater made the small mournful noise it had been making since January of the previous year. The buoy was the same buoy. The buoy was the buoy.

Calder thought, with his hands around the warm enamel mug: I am still alive.

The thought was the thought.

The work was the work.

The list was six entries. Three names struck through. One name with a question mark beside it and the parenthetical Possible. One name annotated, in pencil beneath, as not on the list and not going onto it. A sixth line that was a question mark and nothing else.

The architecture's list, by Brückner's count, had one name on it.

The two lists were the same work.

The list was the list.

It would lengthen.

The lengthening was the work.

He drank the tea.

ACT II

1991–1992

11

BIRNAM

Perthshire—October 1991

She wakes at six.

The room is cold. The Aga in the kitchen below has been kept low overnight and the heat does not climb the staircase the way the heat climbs in a properly insulated cottage. This cottage was not properly insulated when it was built in 1841 and no one has corrected the matter since. She got it at a low rent because the widow MacIntyre was not certain she could let it for a higher one. The windows whistle in the wind off the Tay. Her bedroom faces south, which is a small mercy on mornings the wind is from the east.

She sits up.

She puts her feet on the boards. The boards are cold. She finds her slippers. She takes her dressing gown from the back of the chair by the window. The dressing gown was bought at the Dunkeld charity shop for one pound forty. The label is cut out. It is a man's dressing gown. She bought it because the man's dressing gown had pockets and the woman's did not.

She goes downstairs.

In the kitchen she lifts the Aga lid and feeds it three small pieces of birch from the basket beside the door. She puts the kettle on the warm plate. She takes a brown earthenware mug from the shelf and the tin of Brodie's loose-leaf from the cupboard and a white china pot from the dresser. She measures the tea into the pot. She measures it the way she has measured tea for fifty years. The measuring is a fact. The fact is that the tea is sufficient.

The kettle whistles.

She makes the tea. She lets it sit. She sits at the table with her hands flat on the wood and looks at the private array of objects she keeps on the kitchen windowsill.

The objects are: a small clay pot with a single shoot of geranium that the Dunkeld florist sold her for a pound; a brown wren's egg she found on the path in July, perfect, unbroken; a smooth gray pebble from the Tay; a pencil stub of the kind a primary-school teacher kept in her left pocket between 1956 and 1989; a folded square of paper that has been folded for thirty years; a silver thimble that was her grandmother's; and a Latin tag on a slip in her own hand that reads Tu si non vis, et hoc. If you do not wish it, then this also.

She looks at them. She does not move them.

The tea is the tea.

At seven she eats the porridge she has made on the warm plate —oats, water, salt, no sugar. She reads two pages of Tacitus while she eats. The book is Annales in the Loeb edition, with the English on the right page. She does not need the English. She uses it the way a swimmer uses the lane line: to know where she is in the water.

At seven-forty she goes upstairs to dress.

She wears the brown wool skirt and the gray cardigan and the cream blouse that has been with her since the Easter of 1979. Stockings. The thick-soled walking shoes. The silver bracelet on her left wrist with the small charms—a book, a silver cat, a heart, the letter M, and a fifth charm that is a silver key on a ring. She has worn the key on the bracelet for fourteen years. She has been wearing the key on the bracelet, since November of 1989, in the knowledge that the key is no longer the key her husband placed there in 1977. She has replaced it with a key of her own. She wears the new key on the same ring her husband used. The wearing is the private continuation of the silence their years together used to say the things neither of them could bring themselves to say.

She fastens the bracelet. The clasp is stiff. She fastens it.

She goes downstairs.

She puts on the navy raincoat at the back door and the green wool scarf that has the white scar across one corner from the ironing she did badly in 1968. She takes the leather satchel from the hook beside the door. She walks out of the cottage into the October morning.

The wind is from the southwest. The leaves on the beech at the gate have begun to turn. The Tay is half a mile to the west, behind the line of pines.

She walks down the lane to the road.

The post is at the village shop.

The shop is a single room. The shopkeeper is a woman of seventy-one named Iris Beith who has been keeping the shop for three decades and does not ask after anybody whose business is not her own. The post box is a wooden cubby behind the counter. Iris hands her three pieces.

The first is a gas bill.

The second is a circular from the John Lewis department store in Edinburgh.

The third is a brown paper envelope, A4, with a Vienna postmark and a typewritten address in the hand of an academic editorial assistant. The return address is the Schriftenreihe der Wiener Klassischen Studien. She does not subscribe to this journal. She has not, in any of the eleven months she has been in Birnam, received anything from this journal.

She puts the three pieces in the leather satchel.

She buys a tin of sardines and a half-pound of butter and a brown loaf and pays in coins. Iris gives her the change without comment. Iris does not look at the satchel.

She walks back up the lane.

In the kitchen she sets the satchel on the table. She does not open it.

She makes a second pot of tea.

She takes the brown paper envelope from the satchel. She holds it for some seconds. She does not open it.

She goes upstairs to the front room she uses as a study. The room has a small desk facing the lane and a single bookshelf and a chair with a green cushion she had made herself some years earlier. The desk has a fountain pen, a brass inkwell with Quink Permanent Black, a stack of writing paper from Smythson she has been using for nine years, a brass paper-knife, and a notebook of the cheaper sort, hard-covered, ruled, that she bought in Dunkeld.

She sits at the desk.

She opens the envelope with the paper-knife.

Inside the envelope is a single offprint. The offprint is sixteen pages. The title at the top of the first page is Augural Procedure in the Late Codex Theodosianus: A Reading of CTh 16.10.20, by M. Howell, B.A., M.A. (Birkbeck). The paper is hers. She submitted it under that name to Speculum in March. The paper appeared in the September issue. The offprint is her own offprint, sent to her by Speculum in September. She has fifty offprints of this paper. Forty-eight are in a wooden box in the cupboard upstairs. One is on her desk. One was the offprint she sent to the Warburg Institute through the academic exchange in late September.

This is the one she sent to the Warburg.

It has come back to her.

The marginalia.

She turns to page five. The page contains the central argument of her paper—a reading of the rescript of Theodosius the First that abolished the public consultation of the auspices in 391 AD. She has argued, against the consensus reading, that the rescript was not the dismantlement of an obsolete state ritual but the privatization of a state function—that the augural college had been moved, by 391, into the private custody of an aristocratic clerisy who continued to perform it for the imperial inner circle for a further forty years. She has argued this on the basis of three sentences in three letters of Symmachus. She has argued it carefully. She has not used the word Custodia anywhere in the paper, although the word is the word the paper is about.

In the margin of page five, in pencil, in a hand she knows, are written four Latin words.

The four words are: Et qui custodit eos?

And who guards them?

The hand is the hand that wrote Tu si non vis, et hoc in the margin of her Journal of Medieval Latin paper in March of 1988.

She has been waiting for this hand for three years.

She sits at the desk and looks at the page and breathes.

She breathes the way she has been breathing for forty years

on the mornings something has happened. Slow. From the diaphragm. Counting. She breathes for two minutes. Then she sets the offprint down on the desk and folds her hands on the wood on either side of it and looks at the page again.

The hand is the hand. The hand has reached her again. The hand has registered her paper. The hand has read the paper as the paper she wrote, and the hand has answered the paper with the question the paper was asking.

The question is the question.

The question is the question her former husband has been asking since 1990 and the question she has been asking since 1981 and the question one of the seven men in Rome has now asked her in the margin of her own offprint in pencil through the academic exchange.

Et qui custodit eos?

Who guards the guards?

She does not know who has written it.

She does not yet know what the writing means.

She does know that the writing means that the hand has decided, for the second time in three years, to register a small unauthorized contact with her. The registering is an operational fact that is now going to require her to make a decision for which she has been preparing for nine years. She has not, in any of those years, been ready to make it.

She picks up the fountain pen.

She turns the offprint over.

On the back of the last page, beside her own pencilled note from September—off to the Warburg, vol. 67 no. 4, ML's reply if any?—she writes, in her careful left-leaning hand:

23 October 1991. Returned through the Warburg. Pencil hand, page 5. Same hand as 1988.

She closes the offprint.

She slides it into the second drawer of the desk on the left, the drawer she has been keeping for material that needs to be looked at again in twenty-four hours by a woman whose pulse has come back to its proper rate.

She closes the drawer.

She goes downstairs.

In the kitchen she finishes the tea.

She washes the mug. She washes the porridge bowl. She wipes the table. She does these things in the order she does them every morning. The order is the order. The order is the private discipline a woman uses to keep the morning that has now happened from rearranging the order of the things that have not.

At ten-fifteen she puts on the navy raincoat again.

She walks out of the cottage and down the lane and across the road and through the kissing-gate at the corner of the field. The field is the lower pasture of the MacIntyre farm. The widow has not kept cattle since her husband had died some years before. The pasture has gone to nettle and dock and the white-flowered weeds Margaret has not learned the local names for.

She crosses the pasture diagonally.

She comes to the line of pines at the western edge.

She enters the pines.

The path through the pines is a path she has walked once a week for eleven months. The path goes down to the Tay through a small wood of mixed pine and birch, with one beech tree at the southern bend that is older than the planting around it. At the foot of the beech, in the angle between the trunk and the largest of the surface roots, is a shallow depression about the size of a child's footstool. The depression has, since November of last year, been covered by a piece of mossy rotten plank from a fence she found on the bank of the river in her second week.

She kneels at the foot of the beech.

She lifts the plank.

In the depression is a small zinc box of the kind a mid-Victorian gardener used for keeping seed. The box is eight inches by ten by four. The box is wrapped in two layers of waxed canvas. Margaret has wrapped it. The canvas is dry. The zinc beneath the canvas is dry. The depression has been engineered, by the angles of the root and the slope of the ground, to drain water away from the box on three sides.

She has not opened the box in eleven months.

She does not open it now.

She lays her left hand flat on the canvas. She holds the hand there for the count of three. The bracelet on her wrist catches a fragment of the morning light through the pines. The silver key on the ring catches it.

She lifts her hand.

She replaces the plank.

She stands.

She walks back through the wood and across the pasture and up the lane and into the cottage by the back door, and she takes off the navy raincoat and hangs it on the hook beside the door, and she goes back upstairs to the front room and sits at the desk.

She does not open the second drawer.

She picks up the fountain pen and a clean sheet of writing paper and writes, in her careful hand, a single Latin sentence at the top of the page, in the way a Latinist set out the working of a problem before allowing herself to consider the problem.

The sentence is: Custos custodum custos est.

The guard of the guards is itself a guard.

She sets the pen down.

She looks at the sentence for some seconds.

Then she takes the pen up again and adds, in English in pencil beneath the Latin:

Cf. Juv. Sat. 6.347–8—but the Juvenalian guard is also a man. Custos here is institutional. Read with Symmachus, Ep. 1.13. The Custodia answers to itself in the same grammar.

She sets the pen down again.

She closes the notebook.

She goes downstairs.

At noon she eats a piece of the brown loaf with butter and three of the sardines on a plate at the kitchen table. She drinks a glass of water from the tap. She does not have a radio. She has chosen not to have a radio. The choice was one of the operational decisions she made when she came to Birnam.

She does not know, on the twenty-third of October 1991 at a kitchen table in Perthshire, that her former husband is at this hour walking out of a Geneva railway carriage onto a Lyon platform. He is also alive, also reading, also keeping a notebook, also using a desk facing a road in a small foreign place. He has, in his coat pocket, a folded slip of paper containing the typewritten brief of an operative who tried to kill him in an alley five days earlier. In the slow careful order he has been doing things in for twenty-one months, he is on his way back to a harbor that is also her harbor. Neither of them will say so.

She does know that the hand has reached her.

She does know that the reaching has begun the next phase of the work.

She does not know what the next phase will require of her.

She finishes the bread.

She washes the plate.

She goes back upstairs.

At three-thirty she walks to the Tay.

The walk to the Tay does not pass through the wood with the beech. The walk to the Tay goes north along the lane past the church and down the hill to the small footbridge and across the footbridge to the bench at the southern bank where the river bends west.

She has walked this walk most afternoons since November.

The bench faces upstream. From the bench you can see the river running clear and brown and fast over the gravel beds. Beyond the gravel beds, the line of trees on the northern bank. Beyond the trees, the rounded hills toward Birnam Hill itself. On a clear afternoon in October the hills hold the soft red-brown light the late afternoon gives a Perthshire valley in which most of the trees are bare.

She sits on the bench.

She watches the water.

There is a man fishing in waders forty yards downstream. He is sixty-five. He is a retired schoolmaster from Crieff who fishes the Tay every Tuesday and Thursday. He has nodded at her once in October last year and once in March of this year. The nodding has been the entire register of their acquaintance. He has not spoken to her. He has not asked her name. He keeps the silence the river keeps for any man who fishes it alone.

She sits on the bench for forty minutes.

She thinks, in the forty minutes, about the four words on page five.

Et qui custodit eos?

The hand had decided to reach her. The hand had read the paper. The hand had used Latin because Latin was the channel they had been sharing for three years without speaking. The hand was not asking the question rhetorically. The hand was asking the question because the hand was, by the discipline of the asking, in the position of a man who had been one of the guards and had begun to want a guard for himself. The hand was looking for an interlocutor. The hand had decided that the interlocutor was Margaret Howell.

She had been waiting for the hand to ask.

She did not know whether the hand would ever ask.

The hand had asked.

She would have to answer.

She does not yet know what the answer will be.

She sits and watches the water and lets the four words sit in her until the body has registered them and the body has decided what to do with them, which is the way she has been making decisions for nine years and the way her grandmother in Aberystwyth had made decisions before her.

The light begins to go at four-fifteen.

She stands.

She walks back across the footbridge and up the hill and along the lane to the cottage.

At the gate she stops.

The beech at the gate has, in the time she has been at the river, dropped two more leaves onto the path. She picks them up. She holds them for a second. She lets them fall.

She goes inside.

That evening she lights the lamp at her desk and sits with the offprint open at page five and a clean sheet of writing paper to her right and the fountain pen in her hand.

She writes for forty minutes.

She writes a paper.

The paper is two pages. It is in Latin. The paper is for Speculum but it is also the answer to the four pencilled words. The paper is on the institutional grammar of custodia. In the late imperial period, the word came to denote not the protector but the protectorate, not the act of guarding but the body that did the guarding. The institution's own self-naming, Margaret has noted in the margin, is precise: custos ignis novi, occulte vigilans, semper. Guardian of the new fire. Secretly watchful. Always. With the particular grammatical wrinkle that the protectorate, once instituted, was its own protector and could not be guarded by an external authority because the external authority had already, by the act of instituting it, become its subordinate. The paper argues that the grammar is the architecture and that the architecture has, in the fifteen hundred years since the rescript, repeated itself in a number of European institutions whose modern names she does not, in the paper, mention.

The last sentence of the paper is: Sed custodes ipsos quis custodiet? Hoc enim quaerimus, et hoc quaerere debemus, etiam si non novimus an respondebitur.

But who shall guard the guards themselves? For this we ask, and this we must ask, even if we do not know whether it shall be answered.

She sets the pen down.

She reads the paper through.

She does not change a word.

She takes a fresh envelope from the top drawer of the desk. She addresses it to the editor of Speculum in Cambridge, Massachusetts, in the careful left-leaning hand that her former husband has been registering on Christmas cards and grocery lists and the back covers of paperbacks she returned to him without remark for thirty years. She seals the envelope. She places a stamp.

She takes the offprint that has come back to her from the Warburg, with the four pencilled words on page five, and she folds it in three. She places it inside a second envelope. She does not address the second envelope.

She sets both envelopes on the corner of the desk.

She turns off the lamp.

She goes downstairs.

In the kitchen she banks the Aga for the night. She washes the cup she has had her supper tea in. She wipes the table. She closes the door of the larder. She turns off the light.

She stands at the kitchen window for a minute in the dark, looking at the lane.

The lane is empty. The wind has gone down. The moon is half. The moon is, she registers, the same moon her former husband is somewhere under, on whatever lane in whatever country he has reached by the night of the twenty-third of October. He had been at the harbor, in February. Klaus told her in November of last year. He had been at the harbor. He had been alive. He had been reading.

He would not come to Birnam.

She had asked Klaus to ensure that he would not come.

Klaus had agreed. He had not said how he would arrange the

not coming. Klaus had told her, the morning he had come up the steps of her Cumbrian doorway in December of 1989 and had said the sentence that had folded a Hamburg hydrologist into the architecture in fourteen seconds, that he would do whatever the work required. The work had required, by November of 1990, that her former husband not know where she was. He arranged it. Klaus had been arranging things for twenty-one years. Klaus would continue.

She does not pray. She has, however, written seven letters to seven women in four countries whose names she will not say aloud in this kitchen. She has not yet received a reply from any of them. The not-replying is the discipline she asked of them. The discipline is holding. Seven women. The same number as the men in Rome. The same number as the Coordinators. The number had not been her choosing. The number was the architecture's own grammar, and she had, in the building of the counter-architecture, adopted it without deciding to.

She does, however, send a specific thought, as she stands at the dark kitchen window with her hands flat on the cold sink, to a man whose face she has not seen in fourteen months and whose body she has not touched in four years.

The thought is: I am still here.

She stands at the window for one minute more.

Then she goes upstairs to bed.

She is fifty-six years old.

She sleeps.

In the morning she will burn the offprint with the four pencilled words in the Aga. She will keep the new paper for Speculum. She will post the new paper from the village on the Friday afternoon train. She will return to the cottage. She will eat. She will read. She will walk to the Tay.

On the night of the twenty-third of October 1991, with the half moon on the lane and the wind down and the Tay running brown and clear over the gravel beds half a mile to the west, she has begun the answer.

The answer is the answer.

The answer will be the work of the next two years.

She sleeps.

12

THE HARBOR RETURNS

An Atlantic port—November 1991

Calder reached the harbor at dawn on the second of November.

He came up the road from the village in the back of the saddle-faced fisherman's truck, lying under a tarp that smelled of three-day-old hake. The leather satchel containing the Geneva slip and the postman's wallet and the Walther PP was against his ribs. The right shoulder was doing again what it had begun to do in the cold at Geneva: aching without the prompting of an immediate exertion. The truck stopped at the end of the lane. He came out from under the tarp. He thanked the fisherman in the French of a man who has lived twenty-one months in a harbor village and learned its tongue. The fisherman nodded once and drove on.

Klaus was at the window of the second-floor flat, watching. He came down to open the door.

The room was the way Calder left it. The desk was the desk. The leather notebook was on the desk. The cleaning kit was in its tin under the bed. The kettle was on the warm plate. The dried lavender was new—Klaus bought a fresh bunch from the Bayonne market the previous Wednesday, and in Calder's six-week absence the room took on a green cleanness it had not carried since the spring.

He opened the leather notebook to the pencil page. He read the entries. Beside each struck name he had begun, at some hour he could not now place, to write a small marginal note in pencil—a date, a detail, the private annotation the killing had asked of him. The writing had become its own discipline.

Klaus did not embrace him. The not-embracing was the discipline.

He said: 'Sit. Eat. The coffee is hot. The bread came up an hour ago.'

Calder sat. He ate. The bread was the brown bread the bakery woman baked on Tuesdays, the same loaf she had been setting out each week since before either of them arrived. The butter was the salted Bayonne butter Eddie began sending up by courier in October. The coffee was the hot coffee Klaus made when he knew a man was coming up the road.

After eating Calder said: 'I have things.'

Klaus said: 'Show me when the hands are clean.'

He went to the basin. He washed his hands. The right shoulder pulled at the lifting of the arm to the basin and he noted the pull without comment. The shoulder had been reminding him, since the train back from Lyon, that a wound nearly two years old was now the wound a fight in a Geneva alley asked it to be again. The body carried a memory. The memory was a wound that stayed quiet for some months and was now going to be quiet for fewer.

He came back to the table. He laid out the things.

The Walther PP with the threaded barrel and the Swiss aluminum can. The eight-round magazine and the spare magazine. The Geneva apartment key on the brass tag. The wallet with three thousand Swiss francs in fresh notes and no identification. The folded slip of paper with the typewritten brief on Calder's appearance and the operational rendezvous and the cleaning-crew signal Schauer. The piano wire in its leather pouch—Klaus pressed it on him in April and he used it twice.

The small leather pouch from the Berlin staircase operative containing a folded paper and three brass keys. He did not open the Berlin pouch. He set it on the desk.

He said: 'I have not opened it.'

Klaus said: 'You will not need to. I know what is in it. I have known for some weeks.'

He said: 'How.'

Klaus said: 'Eddie. Through a man in Lisbon who keeps a list of brass key signatures by their cut-pattern. The three keys are a flat in Charlottenburg, a safety-deposit box in Liechtensteinische Landesbank in Vaduz, and a private library in the first district of Vienna. The library is a name. The name is the fourth.'

Calder said: 'The fourth Coordinator.'

Klaus said: 'The fourth.'

Klaus poured the second coffee. The left hand that held the pot still carried, across the palm, the healed seam of the Berlin staircase—half a year on now, gone the dull color of the scar it was going to be, the hand having long since learned to work around it the way a body learned to work around the things the work left in it.

'I have been waiting to tell you. I did not want to tell you in Berlin. I did not want to tell you in Geneva. I wanted to tell you here.'

Calder said: 'Tell me.'

Klaus said: 'The library is the Bibliothek der Wiener Klassischen Studien on the Bäckerstrasse. The name on the door is Klassische Studien e.V., a private learned society. The library has eleven members. The members are senior academics and senior bureaucrats and one cardinal. The library is governed by a board of three. The chair of the board is a man named Friedrich Adler. He is seventy-four. He was born in Győr in 1917. He was a junior officer in the Hungarian foreign ministry before and during the war and was on the staff of the Hungarian delegation that signed the armistice with the Soviet Union in January 1945. He spent eight years in Moscow as the deputy of an attaché whose name I do not have. He returned to Austria after the war. He has held a chair in late-imperial Roman law at the University of Vienna for three decades and has been the editor of the Schriftenreihe der Wiener Klassischen Studien since 1969. He is not a Latinist. He is a Romanist of the legal tradition. He is the man your ex-wife's papers have been read against by the Custodia for nine years. He is the institutional Latinist of the Conclave's Vienna desk. He is one of the seven Coordinators. He has been Coordinator for the eastern Habsburg arc—Austria, Bohemia, Hungary, the Balkans—since 1965.'

Calder did not move.

Klaus said: 'There is one further fact about Adler. The Schriftenreihe under his editorship has, in two issues out of every three for twenty-two years, printed the word *auspex* in the body of an article without an editorial note and without any explanation by the contributing scholar. Eleven different contributors have used the word. The contributors do not know each other. The word has not been the subject of any review essay. The word has been the signature by which Adler has been identifying, to whomever has been reading the journal for the same purpose, that the issue carries an institutional cargo. I have been reading the issues for the cargo since 1989. I have not yet found the cargo. I have found the word.'

Calder said: 'The word Klaus had named at the harbor.'

Klaus said: 'The word I had named at the harbor. It is a Latin word. It is the word for the diviner who reads the auspices. It is also, in the institution's use, a thing. We do not yet know what the thing is. Adler may know. Adler will not be alive long enough to be asked.'

Klaus said: 'I would have told you in Berlin. I did not have the name then. I had the name two weeks ago. The name came through Eddie, through a Lisbon notary, through a Liechtenstein deposit-box clerk who has been on Eddie's running list for years. The clerk reported, in early October, that the box at Vaduz had been entered on the second of October by a man traveling under the name Adler. The passport photograph matched the photograph of a Vienna academic named Friedrich Adler. The man at Vaduz had been carrying a flat parcel which he had placed in the box. He noticed the parcel because Eddie had instructed him, twelve years ago, to notice any parcel placed in any of seven specific boxes by a man whose passport photograph matched any of seventeen specific faces Eddie supplied through a courier. Adler's photograph had been the fourteenth face on Eddie's list. He did not see it operationally activated until the ninth of October. He then activated it. Eddie told me later that month.'

Calder said: 'And you did not tell me.'

Klaus said: 'I did not tell you because Hannah told me on the eleventh that the institution had assigned Geneva to a man we now know was Schauer's operative. I did not want you in Vienna with a Vienna name in your head while you were also in Geneva with a Geneva man on your trail. The compartmentation was the discipline. I have been keeping things compartmentalized from you for six weeks. I am undoing the compartmentation now.'

Calder said: 'And the parcel.'

Klaus said: 'The parcel is a flat object the size and weight of a half-bound book. The clerk does not know what is inside. Eddie believes, on the basis of the size and the weight and the fact that the parcel has been deposited and not retrieved, that the parcel is one of two things. The first is a registry. The second is a manuscript. The Vaduz box is the private library of the Conclave's Vienna desk. The Conclave's Vienna desk has been depositing items in that box for thirty years. The box has not been emptied since 1962. It is, by Eddie's reading, the best single physical record of the Custodia's operational paper that exists anywhere outside Trastevere.'

Calder said: 'And we have a key.'

Klaus said: 'We have one of three. The other two are with Adler and with the chair of the Liechtenstein bank. We have the key the institution's Berlin operative was carrying when you killed him on the Sredzkistrasse stairwell. The key was on his person because he had been instructed, in the operative briefing for the Berlin kill, that if the kill went the wrong way and he survived, he was to make for Vaduz to retrieve the parcel for the architecture before the institution's secondary cleaners would arrive. The key was the operative's contingency. The contingency did not survive the contingency.'

Calder did not respond for some seconds.

Then he said: 'Adler is the fourth.'

Klaus said: 'Adler is the fourth.'

That evening, after Calder had gone to the basin and Klaus had poured the second coffee, Klaus took the two Minox cassettes Calder had been carrying since Geneva. He took them to the small room behind the bathroom where he had built, in the first week at the harbor, a darkroom from a plywood partition and a red bicycle lamp and three enamel trays he bought at the Bayonne Tuesday market. The room smelled of acetic acid and sodium thiosulfate—fixer and stop bath, the same two chemicals that had been developing secrets in small rooms since before either of them had been born. Klaus worked in the red light with the economy of a man who had been bringing images out of silver halide since 1971. He processed the two rolls. He hung the negatives on a wire with small wooden clips.

He made a contact sheet on a single strip of Ilford paper. He brought the contact sheet to the kitchen table and pinned it to the cork board beside the map.

The contact sheet held eleven frames. Nine were operational: the Geneva approach, the postman's route, the alley where the wire had been used, the wallet contents, the key. Two were from an earlier roll—the Brussels approach to Christofi's phone kiosk, taken on the morning of the reconnaissance three days before the kill.

Klaus circled one of the Brussels frames with a red china-pencil.

Calder looked.

In the lower right of the frame, on the inside of the kiosk's aluminium doorframe at ankle height, was a small mark. The mark was a Greek letter. The letter was theta. It was approximately four millimetres tall in the print. Calder had walked past the kiosk three times on the reconnaissance. He had not seen the mark. The fifteen-millimetre Complan at f/3.5 had seen it. The lens had been the honest witness the eye had not.

Klaus said: 'The same mark as Marseilles.'

Calder said: 'The same mark as the cellar in 1969.'

Klaus said: 'Yes.'

He did not say more. The not-saying was the discipline of a man who had been filing the mark since oh-three-forty-two on a morning in March of 1969 and who had not yet decided what the filing was the filing of. The mark went into the private file beside the eight-ray sun and the cranes and the other small unnamed objects Calder had been carrying since the work began. The contact sheet stayed on the cork board. The red circle stayed on the frame. The theta, four millimetres tall in the grain of the Complan's silver halide, was patient and unexplained.

◆◆◆

That afternoon Calder slept for four hours.

He woke at sixteen-twenty. The light through the window had gone the soft gray-pink the light went above the harbor in the November late afternoons. Klaus was at the kitchen table with a paring knife and three small apples and a glass of wine. The bottle of Glenmorangie ten-year was on the shelf above the sink. The bottle had not been touched since the night Calder had come back. Klaus had been keeping it untouched as a small fact about the new bottle.

Klaus said: 'I am pouring the wine. The whisky I am taking once a week. The discipline is the discipline.'

Calder said: 'How is the wrist.'

Klaus said: 'The redness has spread half an inch in the last ten weeks. The half inch is the half inch. I will tell you when the half inch becomes an inch. I am keeping a calibrated mark on the inside of the watchband.'

He showed Calder the watchband. The original ink line was there on the inside leather in his own hand, the date dry as the leather around it: 27. VIII. Beside it, a second ink line a sixteenth of an inch outboard of the first, made some weeks earlier with a fountain pen, with the date: 2. XI.

The second line was the line that morning.

Calder said: 'And the other signs.'

Klaus said: 'The hair on the inside of the left forearm has not grown back since July. The skin in the same area is one shade lighter than the skin on the right. The fatigue I noted in October was a fatigue I now understand. The body has been doing the work it does on a body that has had the dose. I have not yet had the second dose. If I have the second dose I will know within forty-eight hours. I have arranged with Eddie for a sample of every bottle of every spirit I drink to be tested. The arrangement is functional. The arrangement is not the same as not getting the second dose. The arrangement is the comfort a man takes when there is no other comfort.'

Calder said: 'Yes.'

Klaus was quiet for some seconds.

Then he said: 'I told you in February that I had arranged a contingency with Eddie. I have not, between February and now, told you the shape of it. The shape is now the shape we may need. The contingency is the form the work will take, with Eddie's help, if the work I am doing by my own hand stops being possible by my own hand. I will not describe the contingency further to you tonight. The silence around it is the discipline. You will register it, if it ever becomes operational, by means of small things Eddie will do in your presence that you will not understand. You will not ask Eddie what he is doing. He will not tell you. The two of us have agreed.'

Calder did not respond for some seconds.

Then he said: 'Klaus.'

Klaus said: 'I am asking you to leave the second arrangement alone, James. I am asking you because I do not yet know what shape it will take. The shape will be Eddie's shape and mine. The shape will not be a shape we will ask you to approve. The shape will be the shape the work will need on the morning the work needs it. The morning may not come. If the morning comes, you will know it has come by the form of the things Eddie does. You will not be told. The not-being-told is the gift.'

Calder sat with this for some time.

Then he said: 'All right.'

Klaus said: 'Thank you.'

He sat at the table. He ate one of the apples.

The apple was the apple from the orchard at the back of the

saddle-faced fisherman's brother's house. The brother was a wiry man of seventy who had not been to sea in over twenty years and who kept eight apple trees on a quarter-hectare and would not sell to anyone he had not seen at his brother's boat. Klaus had been buying apples from him through the brother for fourteen months. Calder ate the apple slowly. He watched, through the window, a gull settle on the breakwater post and sit there doing nothing in particular. He watched it for longer than the watching required.

Calder ate three of them.

After the third he said: 'Tell me about the Hannah message.'

Klaus said: 'It came through Pascal on the fifth, while you were on the train. The message was four lines on a single sheet of paper that came up through a courier from Geneva to a man in Bordeaux to a fisherman in our village to me, in the order I have specified. The four lines are at the desk. Read them when you are ready.'

Calder went to the desk.

The sheet was on the leather notebook. Hannah's hand was a slightly-leaned-right American hand that had been trained on a typewriter for fourteen years and had gone back to longhand in 1989 for the work she was doing now. The four lines read:

Adler is in the Schriftenreihe. He has been editing it under his own name since 1969. He has accepted, this week, an offprint by Howell, M. (Birkbeck) on the augural college and the Custodia of the late codex. He has not yet replied. He intends to. The reply is the operation. The reply will produce, by my reading, a contact within four weeks.

Calder read it three times.

He set it down.

He said: 'The Italian hand is reaching her again.'

Klaus said: 'The Italian hand is not Adler. Adler is the Vienna desk. The Italian hand is a Conclave member in Rome. The two have been operating on her for three years through the same correspondence channel without, by Hannah's reading, knowing about each other. Margaret has been running, for nine years, a private quadrille against two distinct Custodia hands who have each thought they were the only one. The mutual ignorance is the operational space she has been working in.'

Calder registered the distinction. The three corrections of declension and the single tag on the 1988 offprint had been two hands on the same piece of paper. He had been carrying them as one for twenty months.

Calder said: 'And Hannah believes the reply is the operation.'

Klaus said: 'Hannah believes Adler will reply through the Schriftenreihe. Hannah believes the reply will be a public correction in print, in the next issue, that will be the institution's first public registration of Margaret as an interlocutor. The registration will be the fact the institution can no longer pretend not to have made. After the registration, the institution will move. Hannah does not yet know how. Hannah is asking us to be in Vienna by January. Hannah is asking us to be at the Bäckerstrasse library when the issue goes to press.'

Calder said: 'And Adler is also the kill.'

Klaus said: 'Adler is also the kill.'

That night Calder took the leather notebook from the desk.

He opened the pencil page. He read it through.

1. ~~Vernet, Henri. Marseilles.~~

2. ~~Brückner, Wolfgang. Berlin.~~

3. ~~The man at the Brussels phone number.~~

4. Heike Brückner / Heike Vollmer (?). Berlin. (Witness. Possible.)

5. The American woman in the Spiegel. (Hannah Doyle.) Geneva, the man Klaus knows.

↳ She knows about the list. She is not on it. She will not be on it. She is the third operative in this work.

6. ?

He took the pencil from the leather pouch. He wrote, beside the question mark on the sixth line:

Adler, Friedrich. Vienna. Bäckerstrasse. Late-imperial Romanist. The chair of the Klassische Studien. The one your ex-wife has been writing to without knowing the name.

He folded the page.

He went to bed.

He did not sleep until the bakery oven warmed below him before dawn.

In the morning Klaus made tea.

Klaus said: 'There is a parcel from Eddie.'

The parcel was on the table. It was wrapped in brown paper and tied with the fine cotton string Eddie used because the cotton would not show up on a customs scanner. Calder cut the string. He unwrapped the parcel.

Inside the parcel was a single object. The object was a Welrod.

It was not the Welrod Calder had been carrying since February. It was a different Welrod—newer, the bluing slightly fresher, the bolt action slightly tighter, the wipes inside the can clean and unfired. With it was a small slip of paper in Eddie's careful pencil hand:

The wipes you were using were the originals. They are now in Lisbon for replacement. They were good for two more rounds. This is your second instrument until I have refurbished the first. Five clean firings, perhaps six. Eddie.

Calder set the new Welrod on the desk beside the old leather case. He took the old Welrod out of the old case. He laid the two side by side. The two Welrods looked, on the wood of the desk, like two versions of the same idea forty-nine years apart.

He picked up the new one. He worked the bolt. The action was clean. The action was the small tight clean action of an instrument that had not yet been fired at a person.

He set it down.

He picked up the old one. He worked the bolt. The action was the action of the instrument that had killed Henri Vernet in a Marseilles hotel on a Tuesday morning in March of 1990. The same instrument had killed Konstantinos Christofi in a Brussels phone kiosk on a Tuesday morning in February of 1991. The same instrument had killed Wolfgang Brückner at the bay window of a Berlin apartment at oh-seven-oh-two on a Tuesday morning in April of the same year. The bolt was looser now than the bolt of the new instrument. The wipes were burned. The instrument had become, in twenty-one months, the instrument that knew his hand. Three men. Three Tuesdays. Three different cities. The same bolt, in the same hand, on three Tuesday mornings in the ninety-one weeks the instrument had been in his coat.

He set it down.

He said: 'I will use the new one in Vienna.'

Klaus said: 'Yes.'

Calder said: 'The old one I will keep. It is the instrument that has done the work. It will not be used again. It will be the instrument of the work that is finished.'

Klaus said: 'Yes.'

That afternoon Calder walked down to the breakwater.

The wind was off the southwest. The bell-buoy was making its small mournful noise. The saddle-faced fisherman was on the breakwater with a bucket of cockles he had picked at the low tide that morning. The fisherman did not say anything. He handed Calder the bucket. The bucket was the bucket. The cockles were not the fish on a Wednesday morning. The fisherman had registered, by some specific reading of the harbor that did not require him to be told, that the bucket was the last bucket. He nodded once. He went back to his boat.

Calder stood at the end of the breakwater with the bucket in his right hand and the wind on his face and the right shoulder aching the clean ache it had been aching since the Geneva alley.

He thought about Vienna.

He thought about the library on the Bäckerstrasse.

He thought about Friedrich Adler—the seventy-four-year-old chair of the Klassische Studien, a man who was the editor of his journal for twenty-two years, a man who had published Latin papers under his own name for six decades, a man who had been the institutional reader of his ex-wife's papers for nine years.

He thought, also, about Margaret.

He stood at the breakwater for some minutes.

Then he turned and walked back up the lane to the second-floor flat. The bucket of cockles was in his right hand. The right shoulder ached. His mind moved through the careful arithmetic of how a man got from a harbor on the Atlantic to a library on the Bäckerstrasse with a Welrod in his coat and an ex-wife in a Perthshire cottage neither of them was permitted to admit they were thinking about.

The arithmetic was the work.

The work was the list.

The question mark had a name.

That night Calder did the careful packing he had been doing on the eves of operations since Bonn. The Welrod in its case. The Walther in the inside right pocket of the coat. The Minox C in the leather sleeve. Two boxes of subsonic. The leather notebook. The pencil pouch. The pencil. The pages.

He took the Mercator out of the inside left pocket of his coat and laid it on the desk.

The black-painted steel had been against his ribs for twenty-three months. The leaping cat. The three rivets. The spring lock he had opened twice and closed twice in those months and not, in either of the openings, used the blade for. The knife had been in his coat through Sète and Lyon and Lisbon and the Cumbrian doorstep he had not crossed and the Geneva box and the Birnam morning. It had not, in the months since the alley, asked anything of him. It had been the other thing the knife was. It had been the specific weight of the woman he had come back with from a hotel-room floor.

He looked at it on the desk for some seconds.

Klaus, at the kitchen table, did not turn his head.

Calder stood. He went to the small painted cabinet in the corner of the room, beside the stove, where Klaus kept the operational gear from the start—the cleaning kit, the spare wipes, the boxes of rounds, the small tin of gun oil, the felt pads, the brass rod. The cabinet had a wooden door that did not close flush with the frame. Calder had not, in all his time at the harbor, asked Klaus to fix it. The small gap had been the cabinet's way of telling them, by the thin draft that came out of it on cold mornings, that it was the cabinet that was holding the work.

He opened the door.

He set the Mercator on the second shelf from the top, behind the tin of gun oil, on the folded square of dark green felt Klaus had been keeping there for instruments waiting between operations. The black-painted steel went onto the felt with the dull sound a thing made when it was being set down by a hand that had decided to set it down.

He closed the door.

The cabinet was the cabinet again.

Klaus, at the kitchen table, said: 'Yes.'

Calder said: 'It is not for Vienna.'

Klaus said: 'It is for whatever the next thing is. Or it is for nothing. The cabinet will hold it either way.'

Calder said: 'Yes.'

He went to bed.

He slept for some hours.

The next morning at oh-five-forty Klaus brought the Land Rover up the lane. Calder put the leather case in the back. He closed the door of the second-floor flat for the last time. The bell-buoy was on the wind. The saddle-faced fisherman was on the breakwater coiling a line. He did not turn his head as the Land Rover passed. He raised his right hand once, palm flat, at the height of his shoulder, and he held it there until the Land Rover had cleared the corner of the rue de la Mer. Calder watched the rail in the wing mirror until it dropped out of sight. The hand had not moved. The hand was the harbor's farewell.

13

DIE BÄCKERSTRASSE

Vienna—February to April 1992

They arrived in Vienna on the eleventh of February.

Calder came up by train from Munich in the early afternoon. Klaus came down from Hamburg the same day on a different train and met him at a café on the Schottenring at sixteen-thirty. They drank coffee. They did not embrace. Klaus had been in Hamburg for ten days arranging a set of provisions through a man Eddie had identified years earlier and whom Klaus had met for the first time in early February. The man was a Hamburg ship-chandler whose backroom doubled, for a small clientele, as the only competent armorer between Bremen and Lübeck. He supplied Klaus with two service pistols—a Hungarian Tokarev TT-33 and a Czech CZ-75 in 9mm—three Italian suppressors of the kind a man bought when going to a country where the import of suppressors was serious, and a black-leather case containing a single instrument Klaus had not asked for and the chandler had insisted he take.

The instrument was a folded straight razor with a horn handle, made by Friedrich Herder of Solingen.

The chandler had said: Take it. It is for the kind of work you have not yet decided you are going to be doing. The Solingen blade is a Solingen blade. The handle is the kind of horn you cannot now buy. Take it.

Klaus had taken it.

He did not show the razor to Calder.

It was in the leather case in the inside left pocket of Klaus's overcoat for the entire seven weeks of the Vienna operation, and he did not, in those seven weeks, take it out of the case.

They had taken two flats.

The first was on the Wipplingerstrasse in the first district, one street north of the library on the Bäckerstrasse. The flat was on the fourth floor of a building that had been built at the end of the previous century and re-roofed after the war and not significantly changed since. The flat had two rooms and a kitchen and a bath. The window of the front room looked across an internal courtyard at the back wall of the library. The view from the window was the view a man wanted when he was running a surveillance on a Vienna academic library that had eleven members and one cardinal on its roll.

The second flat was on the Lerchenfelder Strasse in the seventh district, twenty-two minutes by tram from the library. The flat was the operational fall-back. The flat held the weapons, the notebooks, the photographs, the pieces of laminated paper Klaus had been making with the new identity documents, and a tin of biscuits Klaus had bought because Klaus could not be in any flat for more than twenty-four hours without a tin of biscuits.

Hannah Doyle was at neither flat.

Hannah Doyle was in Berlin.

Hannah was running, in parallel, the Heike Vollmer thread the architecture had told her in October it would be opening in eighteen months. The architecture had moved, in the second week of January, three months ahead of Hannah's projection. Heike had received, in January, a letter on the letterhead of a private trust that had agreed to fund her late stepfather's archive. The letter had asked for a meeting. Heike had asked for time. The architecture had given her four weeks. Heike was now, by Hannah's reading, two weeks from having to make the decision the architecture had been keeping her biological mother's identity in reserve to extort. Hannah was in Berlin to be near the decision.

Calder and Klaus would not, in the seven weeks of the Vienna operation, see Hannah.

They would communicate with her once a week through Pascal in Geneva. The messages were three lines on flimsy paper. The paper came up by courier through the Swiss-Austrian border in the inside lining of a series of suitcases belonging to a Bordeaux wine merchant who had been moving a sequence of consignments to a Vienna restaurant for years.

The first such message arrived on the fourteenth of February.

It read: Adler reply in print 1 March. Margaret response 18 March. Italian Latinist second contact 20 March direct mail Birnam. Margaret moves second box 22 March—location unknown to me—she has not used courier since November 1990 and is using none now. Decision window narrows. Adler must come down before April Conclave meeting Trastevere 10 April. Heike pre-decision day 16 days. Wear nothing red.

Klaus read the message. He passed it to Calder. Calder read it.

Calder said: 'The Italian Latinist is reaching her at her cottage.'

Klaus said: 'Yes. The architecture has identified Birnam. Hannah's window is closing.'

Calder said: 'And Margaret moves the second box.'

Klaus said: 'And Margaret moves the second box. She does not yet know whether the Italian hand is hostile or sympathetic. She is preparing for both.'

Calder said: 'And Adler comes down before the tenth of April.'

Klaus said: 'Adler comes down before the tenth of April. Or

Adler is at Trastevere on the tenth and Margaret has lost the only inside reading the Conclave will produce in this calendar year.'

He folded the message. He held it over the gas ring on the kitchen stove of the Wipplingerstrasse flat. The flimsy caught. He let it burn down to his fingertip. He dropped the ash in the sink. He ran the tap.

He said: 'We have six weeks.'

For the first three weeks they watched the library.

The library had an entrance door of polished oak under a stone lintel on which was carved, in careful late-baroque epigraphy, the words USQUE AD FINEM CUSTODIENDA. To be guarded to the end. The carving was 1683. The library had been the private collection of a counter-Reformation cardinal who had bequeathed it to a learned society at his death and whose successors had added to it across three centuries. The eight-rayed sun, in a small wreath around the lintel inscription, was the cardinal's personal device. The Custodia had not invented the symbol. The Custodia had inherited it.

The library had two other entrances. The first was a service door at the rear of the building that opened onto a small inner courtyard with a single elm. The second was a door from the library's interior reading room into the back kitchen of the small Hungarian restaurant at number twelve Bäckerstrasse, which had been, in the mid-nineteenth century, the residence of the librarian and which had been, since the postwar years, leased to a series of restaurateurs whose discretion had been vetted.

The current restaurateur was a woman of fifty-three named Erzsébet Várady whose father had died in the 1956 uprising and whose mother had been on the staff of the library for over two decades. She had been keeping the restaurant for years. The library's eleven members ate at the restaurant on alternating Tuesdays. Adler ate there on the second and fourth Tuesdays of every month, at a table at the back, alone.

Klaus had identified the alternating Tuesday pattern in the second week.

The third week he confirmed it.

In the third week he also confirmed that on the fourth Tuesday of every month—the Tuesday before the first Tuesday of the new month—Adler did not return directly to his apartment after dinner. He instead walked the four blocks down the Bäckerstrasse to the church of the Jesuiten on the Dr.-Ignaz-Seipel-Platz. He sat in the third pew from the rear on the left side for forty minutes. Then he walked the further three blocks to a small apartment building at number eight Sonnenfelsgasse where he climbed the stairs to a third-floor flat and let himself in with a key he kept in the inside pocket of his overcoat.

The flat was not Adler's flat.

The flat was registered to a woman of sixty-one named Ilona Zsigmond, a retired secretary of the Hungarian State Bank who had worked at the Klassische Studien in a clerical capacity for years. She had been Adler's lover for over twenty years. Klaus had identified the relationship within days. The relationship had not been previously documented in any operational paper Eddie sent.

Klaus said, when he confirmed the Sonnenfelsgasse flat: 'The Sonnenfelsgasse is the kill.'

Calder said: 'Why.'

Klaus said: 'Because the Bäckerstrasse library is the institution and the Sonnenfelsgasse is the man. The library is the place an operative would expect a Coordinator to be killed. The flat is the place a Coordinator is most permitted to be himself. Adler is, on the Sonnenfelsgasse, not the editor of the Schriftenreihe and not the chair of the Klassische Studien and not a Coordinator. He is a man who has been visiting a woman for twenty-three years on the fourth Tuesday of every month. He is sixty-one minutes of unprotected operational time. He is the man who has the parcel in the inner pocket of his overcoat for the four blocks between the church and the flat. The parcel is the parcel he carries every fourth Tuesday because the parcel is what he gives Ilona Zsigmond at the door of her flat for her to keep until he returns the following month.'

Calder said: 'A book.'

Klaus said: 'A book. Adler's monthly entry into the running account he has been keeping, against his own retirement, of the institution's operational dispositions in the Habsburg arc since 1965. The account is a hedge. He has been writing it in his own hand for twenty-six years. He has been giving the most recent volume to Ilona Zsigmond on the fourth Tuesday of every month for safekeeping for the next four weeks because his own apartment is, by his own assessment, no longer the safest place to keep it.'

Calder said: 'And we know this.'

Klaus said: 'Eddie's man at Vaduz also handles a small bookbinding operation in Bregenz that has been receiving, for years, a single bound volume by registered mail every six months from a clerical address in Vienna whose return address has shifted twice and is currently a post box at the Wien-Zentrum sorting station rented to a Frau Zsigmond. The Bregenz binder rebinds the volume in the same gray buckram he has rebound it in twenty-four times and returns it to the post box. The pattern is the pattern. The book is the running account.'

Calder said: 'And Ilona Zsigmond.'

Klaus said: 'Ilona Zsigmond is sixty-one. She has emphysema. She is a woman of considerable private dignity who has been keeping her Tuesday for twenty-three years and is not, by my reading, an operational person. She is a woman who loves a man who is the Conclave's Vienna Coordinator and who has been keeping the man's private hedge against his own institution because the man asked her to. She is not on the list.'

Calder said: 'No.'

Klaus replied: 'No.'

In the fourth week the Schriftenreihe came out.

The issue was 67/4. Adler's editorial was three pages. The third page contained a single short notice under the heading Korrespondenz und Korrekturen. The notice read, in Latin:

Domina Howell, Latinistarum optima, in commentariolo recente de Codice Theodosiano 16.10.20 lectionem proposuit quae nostram rectiorem reddere posse videtur. Custodia enim, ut illa scripsit, custodes nullos extra se admittit. Hoc grammaticale est, sed et institutionale; recte vidit. Nos in mense septembri ad eam de his iterum scribere intendimus.

Calder, who had been keeping his Latin in good order for forty years on a discipline of Tacitus before bed, translated it for Klaus over the kitchen table at the Wipplingerstrasse flat that evening. Klaus had three lines of Latin from his hydrology degree and was content to be read to.

The notice said: Mrs. Howell, finest of Latinists, has proposed in a recent essay on Theodosian Code 16.10.20 a reading which seems to me capable of correcting our own. The Custody, as she has written, admits no guards outside itself. This is grammatical, but also institutional; she has seen rightly. We intend to write to her further on this matter in September.

Klaus said: 'September.'

Calder said: 'September is the public timeline. The private timeline is the second contact through the academic exchange.

The second contact has already happened.'

Klaus said: 'On the twentieth of March.'

Calder nodded.

Klaus said: 'In the meantime Adler has decided to register her in print. The registration is the public fact the institution is now committed to. The architecture will read the notice on the morning of the second of March in seven different Conclave residences in Trastevere and one in Tuscany, and the architecture will decide, by the end of the day, whether to permit the public registration to stand or to have Adler retract it in the next issue. The deciding will take a week. The week is the operational space we have to take Adler before the architecture's deciding becomes Adler's instruction.'

Calder said: 'The fourth Tuesday is the twenty-fourth of March.'

Klaus said: 'The fourth Tuesday is the twenty-fourth.'

Calder said: 'That is when we take him.'

Klaus agreed: 'That is when we take him.'

He poured the tea. The mark on the inside of his watchband was now three small lines apart, with the dates 27. VIII., 2. XI., and 18. II. The third line was an additional sixteenth of an inch outboard of the second. Klaus showed Calder. Calder did not comment.

Klaus said: 'I am still alive. I will be alive on the twenty-fourth of March.'

Calder said: 'Yes.'

Klaus said: 'I would like to take him myself. I have not asked you for an instrument since Greenwich. I am asking now.'

Calder did not respond for some seconds.

Then he said: 'No.'

Klaus said: 'James.'

Calder said: 'No. The Welrod is mine. The kills have been mine. I will not be the man who lets you take a kill on the fourth Tuesday of a month in which the wrist mark is moving outboard at three sixteenths of an inch a quarter. The work was mine when Greenwich was the price of my being alive. The work has been mine since. The work will be mine on the twenty-fourth.'

Klaus was quiet.

Then he said: 'Yes.'

He drank the tea.

He said: 'Then I will be the second. I will be on the Sonnenfelsgasse at the corner of the Bäckerstrasse with the Land Rover. I will be the cleaning. I will be the man who carries you out of the building when the work is finished.'

Calder said: 'Yes.'

The fifth week was the week of preparations.

Calder walked the Sonnenfelsgasse three times at the hour the kill would happen, on a Friday and a Sunday and a Monday. His right hand stayed in the right pocket of his coat in the position it would be in on the night. The body learned the specific weight of the new Welrod against the case fabric on the inside of his left pocket, and the right shoulder's clean ache becoming, in the rhythm of the walking, the reliable companion the wound had been promising it would become since the November aching had started.

Klaus walked the route Calder would take coming out: through the courtyard of number eight Sonnenfelsgasse; across the cobbled yard; out the rear gate onto the Schönlaterngasse; the four blocks down the Schönlaterngasse to the corner of the Bäckerstrasse, where the Land Rover Klaus had bought from a man in the Burgenland in the second week would be parked at twenty-three forty-two with the engine running and the rear door unlocked.

They tested the timing. They tested it three times.

In the sixth week Calder bought, from a small Trafik on the Stephansplatz, a Vienna street map of the kind a tourist bought, and he drew on the map, in pencil, the route. He drew it on the map because the pencil page in the leather notebook was the work and the map was an operational instrument that could be discarded and was discarded, that night, in the gas ring of the Wipplingerstrasse stove.

In the seventh week Klaus tested the engine of the Land Rover at three different temperatures. The Burgenland man had given him a winter additive Klaus did not entirely trust. The engine started, all three times, on the first turn.

On the morning of the twenty-fourth Calder shaved at the cracked sink in the bathroom of the Wipplingerstrasse flat and looked at the scar on the right shoulder in the mirror over the sink the way he had looked at it in Berlin in April. The puckered moon was the puckered moon. The skin around the moon was the skin Klaus gave him at twelve thirty-four on the fourth of January 1990, twenty-six months earlier, in a flat in Greenwich whose address he had not, in the time since, allowed himself to write down.

He looked at the moon. He touched it with the wet thumb of his right hand. He looked at his own face beside the moon.

The face had decided, since Berlin, what it thought.

The face had decided that the work was the work and that Adler was the work and that the four-blocks walk between the church and the flat was the operational space the work had been preparing for him since November.

The face had also decided, since Berlin, that it was going to look at the scar one more time, on the morning of the day Margaret would learn from a courier in Birnam—through a channel none of them had yet established—that the work had taken the man who had been writing in the margins of her offprints for nine years.

The face had decided that the looking would be the form of the saying-to-her that the work was now hers and his together.

He set the razor down.

He dressed.

He went into the kitchen.

Klaus had the coffee. Klaus had the bread. Klaus had the new Welrod in its leather case on the table with the bolt cleaned and the seven Belgian rounds in the magazine and the can checked.

Calder ate the bread.

He took the Welrod.

They drove to the Bäckerstrasse at sixteen-thirty.

The fourth Tuesday of March 1992 had begun at midnight. The operation had begun in the late afternoon. The kill itself would happen at twenty-three forty-one at the door of an apartment on the third floor of number eight Sonnenfelsgasse. The Land Rover would leave the corner of the Schönlaterngasse and the Bäckerstrasse at twenty-three forty-eight. The architecture would learn of the kill the following morning. Ilona Zsigmond, who had heard the almost-soundless cough through her own front door at the moment it had happened, had not opened the door—she had been told, twenty-three years earlier by the man she loved, that if she ever heard such a sound at her door she was not to open the door. The woman had, in the intervening twenty-three years, prepared herself for the sound by a set of breathing exercises that she had practiced on the night of the second of December 1969 while the man she loved was at the Klassische Studien and a Hungarian friend of his had been killed in the basement of the institute. She would lift the receiver of the telephone in her kitchen and dial the Klassische Studien at the moment the library opened.

By that hour Calder and Klaus would be on a road in the Burgenland, eighty kilometers south-east of Vienna, with the Welrod in its case in the inside left pocket of Calder's coat and a flat parcel the size and weight of a half-bound book, wrapped in gray buckram, in the inside right pocket.

The parcel was the running account.

The running account was the answer.

The answer was the work.

14

DIE SONNENFELSGASSE

Vienna—24 March 1992

At twenty-two forty Adler left the Jesuiten church.

He came out the south door, past the bronze plaque that named the seven cardinals who had been buried in the church between 1623 and 1841. He stood for a moment on the steps. He did the small measured breathing of a man of seventy-four who had just spent forty minutes on a hard pew with his hands folded in his lap not praying. He buttoned his overcoat. He lifted the brim of his hat. He walked east on the Dr.-Ignaz-Seipel-Platz at the unhurried pace of a man for whom the walk was the part of the evening he had been looking forward to since the morning.

Calder was in the doorway of the small bookshop opposite the church. He had been there for forty-five minutes. The bookshop was closed. The doorway was set back from the line of the pavement by twenty inches. He had been still for the entire forty-five minutes. The right shoulder had begun, somewhere in the second half-hour, to perform the slow steady ache it had been performing in March for some weeks. He had registered the ache and let it be the clean companion it was now going to be on the evenings of his life that required the body to stand still in doorways for half an hour at a time.

He let Adler get to the corner.

He came out of the doorway.

He followed Adler at thirty paces along the Bäckerstrasse, past the closed shutters of the wine-merchant at number sixteen and the lit window of the bookbinder's at number nine and the dark front of the Klassische Studien at number twelve. Adler did not turn. Adler had not, in the seven weeks of Klaus's surveillance, ever turned on a fourth-Tuesday walk to the Sonnenfelsgasse. The unbroken discipline of those walks had been the vanity of a man who had been doing a thing for twenty-three years on a discipline that had not, in those years, required him to vary it.

The vanity was the operational space.

At the corner of the Schönlaterngasse Adler turned left. Calder kept going straight along the Bäckerstrasse for ten meters, then turned left at the next corner onto the Sonnenfelsgasse and approached number eight from the opposite end of the short street. The two of them converged at the door of the building from opposite directions. Adler was three paces ahead.

Adler took the key out of the inside pocket of his overcoat.

He did not see Calder.

He turned the key in the lock of the street door. The door opened. He went in. He held the door for the man behind him without looking.

Calder came in behind him.

The hall was dim. A single bulb at the foot of the staircase. The stairs were stone, worn in the center of each step by two centuries of footwear. The wallpaper was a faded green damask of the kind a Vienna apartment building had on its stairwells and never replaced. There was the smell of cabbage and laundry and the faint underlying smell of mineral coal that Vienna apartment buildings still had in the corners they had not been able to clean of it after sixty years.

At the half-landing on his way up, in the half-second between the second step and the third, Calder looked at the inside of the door-frame at chest height. Marseilles had taught him to look. The frame was clean. The Sonnenfelsgasse had no theta. He looked at the windowsill on the half-landing. No crane. No ashtray. Clean sill. He registered the absences and went on. The thetas had been at Marseilles and in the Berlin cellar of 1969—thresholds, both, that a man had walked out of. He had begun, without deciding to, to read the mark as a thing that belonged to the doorways the work let a man back out of. The Sonnenfelsgasse carried no mark. He did not yet have a category for the presence of the theta. He had less of one for the absence. He went up.

Adler began climbing the stairs.

Calder followed at five paces.

On the second-floor landing Adler stopped to catch his breath. He was seventy-four. He had been climbing this staircase on the fourth Tuesday of every month for twenty-three years. The staircase had become, in recent years, an operational fact about his Tuesdays.

Calder waited at the half-landing below.

Adler resumed.

At the third-floor landing Adler stopped at the door on the right. The door was painted a slightly darker green than the doors on the second floor, with a small enamel plate at eye-height that read, in a careful hand, I. Zsigmond.

Adler took a second key from the inside pocket of his overcoat.

He inserted the key in the lock.

He turned the key.

The lock clicked.

He set his hand on the door handle.

He paused.

He paused because there had been, in the last second of his climbing, a small registration that he had not made operationally explicit but that the seventy-four years of his trained Romanist's reading of operational texts had registered as a small change in the texture of the staircase below him. The change in the texture was a footfall that had been three paces back through the second-floor landing and was now not three paces back. The footfall was on the third-floor landing.

He turned his head a quarter to the right.

He saw Calder.

He registered Calder.

He understood Calder.

His expression—in the second of the registering, before his hand had decided what to do, before his mouth had decided what to say, before any of the operational alarms a man of his training had at his disposal could be activated—his expression was the expression Calder had now seen five times.

It was not the expression of the second hire at Greenwich, who had been told by his pupils' dilation that he had been the man specified by weight and not by name. It was not the expression of Henri Vernet across his coffee. It was not the expression of Konstantinos Christofi in the kiosk, who had not had time for an expression. It was not the expression of Wolfgang Brückner, who had decided, in the last second, that the deciding had been the right decision.

It was the fifth expression. It was the expression of a man who had decided, in the last second, that the deciding had not been the right decision—but who had also decided, in the same second, that he would not say so.

Adler said, in German, very quietly: Ah. Heute also.

Calder said: Yes.

Adler said: I have a letter in my pocket that I would have liked to post in the morning.

Calder said: Yes.

Adler said: May I—

He did not finish the sentence.

Calder did not let him finish it.

The Welrod was already in his right hand at low ready. He brought the Welrod up. He fired once.

The Welrod made the sound it had been making since the war —something between a magazine drawer closing and a man clearing his throat. The new Welrod, the second instrument Eddie sent up from Lisbon in November, had a slightly tighter action than the old. The bolt rotated. The casing did not yet eject.

The round entered Adler's chest at the level of the second intercostal space, two inches below the clavicle on the left, on a downward angle Calder had been practicing in mirrors and at distances since the first morning at the harbor in February of 1990. The round traversed the upper lobe of the left lung at an angle that took it through the descending arch of the aorta and the principal pulmonary artery in the same passage. It did not exit. It lodged in the body of the seventh thoracic vertebra at the back, the spent round stopping against the dense bone with a dull tap that was, by the acoustics of the staircase, audible only to Calder and not to the woman on the other side of the green door.

Adler did not slump.

Adler stood for a moment with his right hand still on the door handle and his left hand inside the front of his overcoat near the breast pocket, where the parcel and the letter and the leather case of fountain pens had been riding for the four blocks from the church.

He looked at Calder.

His pupils dilated to the limit of the iris.

His mouth opened. A small dark trickle of blood came over the lower lip and down the chin and into the white scarf at the throat. The scarf was a Sulka silk, cream-colored with a faint pearl-gray pattern, a gift his daughter Margit had given him. The scarf darkened from the corner the trickle reached at the rate the silk had been built to absorb such things.

His knees gave.

He did not fall sideways. He did not fall forward. He lowered himself, in the slow boneless way bodies lowered themselves when the central blood pressure had dropped to zero and the body had decided to use its last six seconds of cerebral oxygenation to sit down with as little disturbance as possible, onto the stone of the third-floor landing. His right hand left the door handle. His left hand stayed inside the overcoat. His back came against the wall beside the door of I. Zsigmond. The hat tipped forward over his brow.

The eyes did not close.

Calder caught the hat as it tipped further and set it on the floor beside the body.

He worked the bolt. The casing ejected into his left palm. He pocketed it.

The Welrod was now down, after its first firing, to four clean firings, perhaps five.

He went through the inside pockets of the overcoat.

The breast pocket on the left contained the flat parcel wrapped in gray buckram, tied with two careful ribbon-cuts of black cotton string, addressed in Adler's own hand on a folded slip of paper to Frau I. Zsigmond, Sonnenfelsgasse 8/3, Wien I. The parcel was the running account. He took it.

The breast pocket on the right contained a single envelope of heavy cream paper of the kind a senior academic kept for personal correspondence, sealed with a disc of red wax that had been impressed with the device of a sun with eight rays around an eye at the center. The envelope was addressed in Adler's hand, in pencil, to Mrs. Margaret Howell, c/o the Editor, Speculum, Cambridge, Massachusetts USA—forwarding through Hofbibliothek Vienna academic exchange, Box 14B.

Calder held the envelope for some seconds.

Then he placed it inside the parcel of buckram. He put both inside the inside left pocket of his coat against his ribs.

He stood up.

He looked at Adler.

Adler had not moved. The hat was on the floor. The white scarf was now black-red from collar to mid-chest. The eyes were the eyes of a man who had decided, in the last second, that the decision was not the right decision. The expression was still on the face. The expression would still be on the face when the cleaning crew arrived sometime before dawn. The expression would not be there by the time the body reached whatever back room the architecture used for the documentation of its own dead.

Calder took out the Vienna handkerchief he had bought from the Trafik the previous week. He wiped the door handle. He wiped the section of green paint where Adler's right shoulder had brushed the wall. He pocketed the handkerchief.

He listened.

Inside the flat, behind the door, there had been no sound after the small almost-soundless cough. There was no sound now. The not-sound was, by Klaus's reading, the sound a woman of sixty-one made when she had been told twenty-three years earlier that if she ever heard such a sound at her door she was not to open the door.

She had set a book face-down on the hall table when she had heard his key in the downstairs lock at twenty-three thirty-seven—the Rilke she had been reading since August. She had not picked it up after the sound. In the morning, when the library secretary came to check on her at oh-eight-ten, the book would still be face-down on the hall table where she had put it.

She would not open the door.

She would stay in the kitchen with her hands flat on the table for the rest of the night.

In the morning she would dial the number she had been told to dial.

By that hour the work would be in the Burgenland.

Calder turned.

He went down the stairs.

He came out of number eight Sonnenfelsgasse at twenty-three forty-three. He turned right. He walked down the Schönlaterngasse at the pace of a man who had nowhere particular to be.

At the corner of the Bäckerstrasse the Land Rover was running with its headlights off. Klaus was at the wheel.

Calder got in the back. He lay down. The dog blanket was over him within four seconds. The Land Rover pulled out into the Bäckerstrasse and turned south.

They cleared the first district at twenty-three forty-nine.

They cleared the city before midnight had aged into the small hours.

They cleared the Lower Austrian border into the Burgenland in the second hour after midnight.

Klaus pulled into a small clearing in a beech wood three kilometers south of Mattersburg some forty minutes later. He killed the engine. The night was cold. The wood was silent. There was a thin sliver of moon over the tops of the beeches, and the wind had gone down at some hour during the drive.

Calder came up out of the back.

He sat in the front seat beside Klaus.

He took the leather notebook out of the inside left pocket of his coat. He turned to the pencil page. He took the pencil from the leather pouch. He drew a single horizontal line through Adler, Friedrich. Vienna. Bäckerstrasse. Late-imperial Romanist. The chair of the Klassische Studien. The one your ex-wife has been writing to without knowing the name. The line was clean. His hand did not shake.

He sat looking at the strike-through for some seconds.

The strike-through was the fourth he had made in the leather notebook since the harbor. The hand that had drawn it had not shaken since the morning of the Vernet kill in March of 1990. The shaking had started at oh-six-eighteen and stopped at oh-six-twenty-one. It had been cleaned out of him in the alley at Sète in the second week his body had been doing the work, the way some kinds of shaking only got cleaned out by a body finding a different argument with itself. The argument had finished in the alley. The mind had not. The mind was still not finished. The mind was, on the dashboard of a Land Rover in a Burgenland beech wood at oh-two-fourteen on the twenty-fifth of March, holding the fact that the man whose name he had just struck had been writing in the margins of his ex-wife's papers for nine years. The man had decided, on the night of his writing, to come out. He had not had the time to come out. The work the mind had not finished had required the body to take him before the coming-out could become an action.

He closed the notebook.

He put it back in the inside left pocket of his coat against his ribs. He felt the small ache in the right shoulder under the coat, the clean companion ache that had been there since the third week of November, and the puckered moon of the scar that the ache reported to. The scar was the scar Klaus had given him on the morning of the fourth of January 1990 to keep him alive for the work. The work was, in the Burgenland beech wood, the fourth man on the pencil page.

He took the parcel out of the inside left pocket of his coat. He laid it on the dashboard. He took the Adler letter to Margaret out of the parcel. He held it in his hands for some seconds. Then he handed it to Klaus.

Klaus said: 'What is it.'

Calder said: 'A letter from Adler to Margaret. He had been going to post it in the morning. The seal is the eight-rayed sun. The address is to Speculum in Cambridge for forwarding through the Hofbibliothek to her.'

Klaus held the letter under the small map-light Klaus had clipped to the dashboard before they had left Vienna.

He said: 'You have not opened it.'

Calder said: 'I have not opened it.'

Klaus said: 'Open it.'

Calder said: 'It is for Margaret.'

Klaus said: 'It is for Margaret in due course. Now it is for the work. Open it.'

Calder broke the seal.

He took out the single sheet of cream paper. The paper was folded once. He unfolded it. The letter was in Latin. He read it. He read it twice.

Klaus waited.

Calder set the letter on his knee.

He said: 'It is two paragraphs. The first paragraph thanks her for her papers. He says that for nine years he has been reading her work the way a man reads the letters of a friend he has not been permitted to meet. Her reading of the custodia grammar is the reading he has been waiting to find for forty years, because he had not been permitted to write it himself. The second paragraph says he has decided, on the night of the writing—which is three nights ago, the twenty-first of March—to make an operational decision. He says he has decided to come out. He says the next issue of the Schriftenreihe, which he is finalizing this week, will contain his last contribution as editor. He has already prepared a successor. He wishes to meet Margaret in person at a place of her choosing in May. He has, against this meeting, kept a private ledger for twenty-six years that he proposes to bring with him. He gives an address in Trieste where he can be reached after the fourth of April, when he will be in Italy on academic business and will not be returning to Vienna.'

Klaus did not respond for some seconds.

Then he said: 'I am sorry, James.'

Calder said: 'Yes.'

Calder was silent for a moment. He registered, in the private way he registered such things, the shape of the three days. The calendar had been the calendar. The calendar had said the tenth of April. The calendar had been correct by every operational metric the architecture issued and every operational metric the network had been able to read. The calendar had been wrong by three days. The three days had been the man. The letter had arrived because the architecture had killed the man three days before the man would have sent it himself. There was no grief in the registering. The cold was the cold of a shape. The shape was the shape of a calendar with a three-day gap and a man inside it.

Klaus said: 'We did not have his letter. We had his calendar. His calendar said he was on the Conclave roster for the meeting on the tenth of April in Trastevere. The calendar said the architecture would have him in Trastevere by the tenth. The institution does not allow a Coordinator to leave its meeting rooms without the architecture's permission. The work required him to come down before the calendar. The letter was the operational fact we did not have. The work was the work we did have. The work has cost.'

Calder did not respond.

He folded the letter.

He held it in his hands for some seconds.

Then he said: 'Margaret will receive this letter.'

Klaus said: 'She will.'

Calder said: 'Through what channel.'

Klaus said: 'Hannah will arrange it. Through a courier we have not yet used. The letter will reach her at Birnam in May, in the time frame Adler proposed, with a note in my hand explaining that the writer had been killed before the letter could be sent and that the sender of the letter is the man who killed him. The note will not say who I am. The note will say that Margaret should burn the note after reading it. I will arrange that the writing is done in a hand that is not mine. I will arrange that the letter goes to her at the address she does not know we have. The address she does not know we have is the cottage. She does not know we know the cottage. She will know after she reads.'

Calder nodded once.

He set the letter on the dashboard beside the buckram parcel.

He sat looking at it for some seconds.

Then he opened the parcel.

◆◆◆

Inside the buckram was a single small bound book.

The book was the size and weight of a half-bound prayer book. Gray buckram boards. No title. A small bookplate on the inside front cover bearing the eight-rayed sun and the words F.A.—Custodiae Auspiciorum—Vol. XXVI—1992.

The pages were lined. The hand was Adler's. The pages had been written in a left-leaning Latin of the sort a Romanist of his generation wrote when he was writing for himself. The book was the running account.

Calder turned to the first page.

The first page was dated Januarii 1992. The page contained a list of seventeen names. The names were the names of seventeen men. Six of the names had a marginal annotation Calder could not, at first reading, decipher.

Then, in the clean light of the dashboard map-lamp, with the Burgenland night silent around them, Klaus waited with his hands on the wheel. The Welrod was in its case in the inside left pocket of Calder's coat against his ribs. The Adler letter to Margaret was on the dashboard. The fourth Tuesday of March 1992 was ending around them in a small beech wood three kilometers south of Mattersburg. Calder understood what he was looking at.

The seventeen names on page one were the seventeen senior operational members of the Custodia Auspiciorum as of January 1992. The seven men in Rome. The seven Coordinators. Three operational deputies whose existence had not been recorded in any document Eddie or Klaus or Hannah had been able to identify in seven years of looking.

The six marginal annotations were six dates. Three of the dates were dates of deaths Calder had been part of producing. Vernet, Brückner, Christofi. The fourth date was tonight—Adler's date. The fifth date was for a man Calder did not know. The sixth date was for the woman Adler had thought was making the list.

The sixth date read 3. Januarii 1990.

The third of January 1990.

The maker's date, by Adler's reckoning, was the date Elena had been killed.

Calder read the name beside the sixth date.

The name was Marsh, A.

He held still for a moment.

Then he closed the book.

He held the book on his knee.

He thought of the hand that had fired the round in the workroom on Webber Street. Klaus had named the hand to him on the third day at the harbor. The leather page had not, in the twenty-six months since, taken the name. The not-taking had been a decision the body had made before the mind had given itself the instruction. The hand was not the architecture. The architecture had been using the hand. He had registered the distinction at some hour at the harbor he could not now name, and had filed it in the same private drawer in which he kept the small unnamed objects he had been carrying since Marseilles.

He said, very quietly: 'Klaus.'

Klaus said: 'Yes.'

Calder said: 'Adler thought Elena was the woman who was making the list.'

Klaus said: 'He thought that.'

Calder said: 'Margaret has been making the list since 1985. Adler had thought, on the third of January 1990, that he was killing the maker. He had been killing Elena. He had been wrong. The architecture had been wrong. Margaret had been working in a position the architecture did not know existed, because the architecture had thought it had eliminated her.'

Klaus said: 'Yes.'

Calder said: 'And the architecture is now going to find out, in some weeks, that Adler was wrong.'

Klaus said: 'In some weeks. Or by the tenth of April. The Conclave will, in the absence of Adler at the meeting, audit the third of January 1990. The audit will require them to revisit what Adler did and did not do that night. The architecture's records of the third of January will be re-examined. The re-examination will identify—'

Calder said: 'Margaret.'

Klaus replied: 'Margaret.'

Calder did not respond for some time.

Then he said: 'How many weeks.'

Klaus said: 'Eight, perhaps. Six if the audit is good. The audit will be good. The audit is the kind of audit the institution does well.'

Calder said: 'Then we have six weeks to get Margaret out of Birnam.'

Klaus said: 'We have six weeks to get Margaret out of Birnam.'

He started the engine.

The Land Rover came out of the beech wood at oh-three-oh-eight and turned south on a road that would, by mid-morning, take them to the Slovenian border and from there, on a different set of papers, by a different route, back to the Atlantic harbor.

Calder did not sleep.

He held the buckram book on his knee for the entire drive.

The book was the running account.

The running account was the answer.

The answer had become, in the small beech wood south of Mattersburg, a question.

The question was Margaret.

The question had six weeks.

15

ADVENIAM AD TE

Birnam, Perthshire, and elsewhere—April–May 1992

The letter arrives on the twenty-ninth of April.

She is at the kitchen table when she hears the post van on the lane. It is a Wednesday. The post van does not normally come on Wednesdays. The Wednesday post is the Edinburgh and Aberdeen post, the post that comes in the early afternoon on Thursdays. The Wednesday van is operational.

She does not get up.

She finishes the cup of tea.

She washes the cup.

She walks to the post-box at the gate at her usual eleven o'clock pace.

The post-box has three pieces. A bill. A circular. A flat parcel wrapped in brown paper, addressed to her at the cottage in a hand she does not know.

The hand is a slightly forward-leaning Continental hand of the sort a Mitteleuropean had been taught at a German school between 1948 and 1960. The postmark is Edinburgh. The stamp is a second-class British stamp. The parcel has been posted from inside the country.

She takes the three pieces back to the cottage.

She sets them on the kitchen table.

She does not open the parcel for ten minutes.

In the ten minutes she puts the kettle on the warm plate. She makes a fresh pot of tea. She sets out the white plate with the two oat biscuits she has been allowing herself in the late morning since February. She sits at the table with her hands flat on the wood on either side of the parcel.

The breathing she does in the ten minutes is the breathing she has been doing since 1981.

At the end of the ten minutes she opens the parcel.

Inside the parcel is a smaller envelope of heavy cream paper, sealed with a disc of red wax that has been impressed with the device of a sun with eight rays around an eye at the center. Beside the envelope is a single sheet of unmarked typing paper folded in three.

She unfolds the typing paper first.

The note on it is in a careful unfamiliar hand—not the slightly forward-leaning Continental hand of the wrapping but a third hand, a man's hand of the kind taught in a German Gymnasium in the late nineteen-forties to a boy who would later have, at some point in his life, learned to keep his identity off his correspondence:

Madam,

The enclosed letter was carried, on the fourth Tuesday of March, in the inside pocket of a man you have not met but have been writing to in the margins of journals for nine years. The man had been intending to post it to you in the morning. He reached, on the night of the writing, a decision he had been deferring for some years. The decision did not have time to become an action. I am the man who prevented the action. I am, also, the man who has been arranging that you not be reached by the architecture for the seventeen months you have been at this address. I am known to you only by name. The name is not on the letter. The letter is, in the operational sense, the final thing the writer accomplished. I have read the letter. The reading was the price of my making sure it reached you. Burn this note and the wrapping paper after reading. The letter is yours.

An audit has begun. The architecture is by my reading six weeks from identifying you. We are coming for you in not more than seven days. Be ready.—K.

She holds the note for some seconds.

Then she sets it down.

She picks up the cream envelope.

The seal is the seal she has been seeing on banknotes and lintels and corners of mastheads for the better part of a decade. She has not, in the eleven months at the cottage, held the seal in her hand. She holds it now. The wax is fresh. The impression is clean.

She breaks the seal.

The letter inside is a single sheet, folded once.

The hand is the hand whose writer she has, for nine years, been waiting for. The Latin is the Latin of a man trained at a Vienna Gymnasium between 1928 and 1935.

She reads it once.

She reads it twice.

She sets it down on the kitchen table.

She places her left hand flat on the table beside it.

The bracelet on her left wrist catches the gray morning light from the kitchen window. The book. The silver cat. The heart. The letter M. The silver key on the ring.

She looks at the key.

She does not move.

The letter is not from the man she had been waiting to be written to by.

The letter is from a man who has been reading her papers for nine years. He has decided, in the third week of March, to leave the institution he has served since 1965. He will bring with him the private ledger of his service he has been keeping against this hour for twenty-six years. He asks whether she might consider meeting him in May at a place of her choosing. The work she has been doing alone across the academic exchange had been the work he had been waiting his whole career to find a colleague for. He decided that he would rather make the journey to her than expect her to make it to him.

The letter is signed F. Adler.

She has not heard the name from anyone. She has not, in the academic correspondence she has had with this man for nine years, ever been told a name.

The note from K. has told her the writer is dead.

The note from K. has told her the writer was killed by the operative who has been doing the work she has been pointing toward for nine years.

The note from K. has told her that the operative who killed the writer is the man who has been arranging her safety since November of 1989.

The note from K. has told her, by the careful absence of any third name on either the note or the wrapping, that the operative who killed the writer is also the man whose smile across a doorway in Cumbria in December of 1989 had folded a Hamburg hydrologist into the architecture in fourteen seconds.

She sits at the table.

She reads the Adler letter a third time.

She does not cry. She had known, for some time, that she would not.

She has been preparing, for nine years, for the possibility that a man who had been writing in the margins of her papers in pencil would one day either come to her or be killed before he could come to her. She has been preparing herself to receive the news of the second possibility in a kitchen in some country she has not yet been told she would be in. The preparing had been the work she had been doing alongside the other work, and the preparing had not equipped her against the specific quality of his Latin in the second paragraph.

She thinks, also, of Brückner.

She has not allowed herself to think of Brückner often. Klaus told her, in a single line in a mail drop she collected from the box at the gate on the second of June of 1991, that the German correspondent who corrected her papers in the Journal of Medieval Latin for nine years was dead, killed in Berlin on a Tuesday morning in April. Klaus did not say by whom. Klaus did not need to say by whom. The sentence was four words: The German has gone. She read the four words at the kitchen table on the morning of the fourth of June. She laid the slip of paper face-down on the wood. She finished her tea. She washed the cup. She went upstairs to the front room and had sat at the desk with her hands flat on the wood on either side of the closed notebook for the count of forty. Then she had stood, and she had gone downstairs, and she had walked to the Tay, and she had sat on the bench facing upstream, and she had watched the water for an hour, and the watching of the water had been the form of the registering. She has not written the German's name in any document since. The not-writing has been the private discipline she brought back from the bench.

The German had been Wolfgang Brückner. She named him, by his correspondence pattern and by his Latin and by the careful operational reading of his three earlier institutional papers, on page six of the eight pages. She typed those pages in the spring of 1986 in a kitchen in Chiswick on the Olivetti her former husband had given her in 1979. The eight pages had been the document her former husband had read in October of 1991 in a flat above a bakery on the French Atlantic coast and had used, between February and April of that year, as the working list of his first three operational kills. She named Brückner. Brückner had died. She also named Vernet, although in a different way, and the man at the Brussels phone number, by description rather than by name. She has been carrying the eight pages' arithmetic for fifteen months. The arithmetic does not become easier by the addition of a fourth name on a fifth April afternoon at a Perthshire kitchen table.

The arithmetic is the work. The work had been accumulating cost since the morning of the fourth of January 1990.

The second paragraph contains a sentence she will carry, in the years to come, the way her former husband has been carrying the geranium and the saffron and the four directions on a Russian woman's wrist.

The sentence is: Latinitatem nostram non aliam vidi inter viventes per quattuor decennia.

I have not seen our Latin in any other living writer in forty years.

She sits at the table.

She breathes.

At eleven-thirty she stands.

She goes to the front room.

She opens the second drawer of the desk on the left. She takes out the sixteen items she has been keeping there, in the order she has been keeping them in for eleven months, against the day she would have to leave the cottage.

The sixteen items are: a passport in the name of Mary Howell she has had in a deposit-box at Drummonds in Edinburgh and that her brother Iain, who works at the bank, retrieved for her in November 1990 without telling anyone he had done so; a second passport in the name of Marigold Cathcart-Ross she had had a man in Bayonne make for her through Klaus in March of 1990 against this contingency; eleven hundred pounds in cash; eight hundred Deutsche Marks; six hundred Swiss francs; the silver Zurich key from a deposit-box in the Zürcher Kantonalbank that her former husband had placed on her bracelet in November of 1977 and that she had removed and replaced with a different key in November of 1989 (the original key has been in this drawer since); a small Schubert Lieder score her mother had given her in 1948 for which she has not, in forty-four years, found a substitute; a notebook of her own from 1986 containing the first draft of the eight pages; a sealed envelope addressed in her own hand to her brother Iain, to be opened only on the news of her death; a leather pouch with a pair of nail scissors that had been her grandmother's; a silver locket she has not worn in twenty years; a folded square of paper that has been folded for thirty years; a single half-sovereign from her father's collection; a brass paper-knife; a small blue glass bottle of lavender water; and a folded clean cotton handkerchief.

She takes everything.

She puts the items in the leather satchel.

She goes upstairs.

She packs the canvas grip she has kept under the bed for eleven months. Two changes of clothing. One pair of walking shoes. The dressing gown. A bar of Pears soap. A towel. A toothbrush. A bottle of glycerine for her hands. The Tacitus.

She comes downstairs.

She puts on the navy raincoat and the green wool scarf and the walking shoes.

She takes the leather satchel and the canvas grip.

She goes out the back door.

She crosses the pasture diagonally.

She enters the pines.

She comes to the beech.

She kneels at the foot of the beech. She lifts the plank. She takes out the zinc box. She unwraps the two layers of waxed canvas. She holds the zinc box for a moment, in the gray light through the pines, the way a woman held a thing she had been keeping for a long time and had not been able to hold openly until the hour required it.

She puts the zinc box in the canvas grip.

She replaces the canvas. She replaces the plank.

She walks back across the pasture and up the lane and into the cottage by the back door.

She places the canvas grip and the leather satchel beside the kitchen table.

She sits at the table.

She makes a fresh pot of tea.

She waits.

At one-forty in the afternoon there is a second envelope in the post-box at the gate.

The post van has not come back. No van has come up the lane. The envelope has been hand-delivered by someone who has come up the lane on foot at some hour between her morning visit to the box and now, and who has gone back down the lane on foot, and whom she has not seen.

The envelope is small. It is of the same heavy cream paper as the Adler envelope but the seal is different. The seal is a small disc of black wax, impressed with a different device—a small circle the size of a wedding ring with nothing inside it.

The address is to M.H., this address, in a hand of which she has been keeping the only known specimen in pencil in the margin of her own offprint since the twenty-third of October of last year.

She takes the envelope back to the kitchen.

She does not break the seal at once.

She holds it for a minute.

The Italian hand has reached her.

The Italian hand has reached her at the cottage, by hand, in person, on the same day a courier of K.'s has reached her with the letter from a Vienna Romanist who has been killed five weeks earlier by K.'s operative.

The two hands have, on the twenty-ninth of April, both made physical contact with her at the same address on the same day.

The two hands are not the same hand. The seals confirm it. The Adler seal was the institutional sun. The Italian seal is the empty circle, which is not the institution's mark and is not the resistance's mark and is, by her reading, a mark the writer has made for himself out of an old shared private vocabulary.

She had known, since December, that the 1988 paper had carried two hands. Brückner had corrected the declensions. The Italian had written the tag. Her October pencil note—Same hand as 1988—had been a Latinist's haste. The April afternoon was the confirmation.

She breaks the seal.

The note inside is two lines, in pencil, in the same hand:

Adveniam ad te. Maius non extremum est.

I shall come to you. May is not the last month.

She sets the note on the table.

She places her left hand flat on the table beside it.

She closes her eyes.

She holds them closed for the count of nine.

When she opens them she is the woman who has decided.

At nine in the evening she hears the truck on the lane.

She has been at the kitchen table since six. She has eaten a piece of bread with butter. She has drunk three cups of tea. She has read four pages of Tacitus. She has not opened either of the two notes on the table again. The notes are on the table because she has decided to take them with her, and she has not yet placed them in the satchel because the placing-them-in-the-satchel will be the last thing she does before she stands.

The truck is not the post van. It is a heavier engine. Diesel. The engine has the knock a Land Rover developed in its eighth year that the Land Rover then never lost.

The truck stops at the gate.

The engine is not turned off.

There is a footstep on the path.

There is a footstep on the stone steps.

There is a knock on the door.

Three knocks. Light. The first two close together, the third half a second later. A small private rhythm. Klaus had taught her the rhythm in the kitchen in Cumbria in December of 1989, the only time he had been in any kitchen of hers, when he had said that if a day came when he needed to come for her, the knock would be the rhythm.

She stands.

She walks to the door.

She opens it.

Klaus is on the step.

He is wearing a Barbour over a wool jumper, with a tweed cap pulled low. He has aged since he was last on a stone step belonging to her. The hair at the temples is grayer. The skin around the eyes is the skin of a man who has not been sleeping well. The left hand he holds slightly bent at the wrist in a way she registers without comment. The right hand is in the right pocket of the Barbour at the angle a hand sat at when the hand was on a sidearm.

He says: 'Margaret.'

She says: 'Klaus.'

He says: 'I have a Land Rover at the gate. I have papers for you in the name of Mary Howell. I have a flat in Edinburgh we will be at by oh-four-hundred. I have a courier on a ferry to Bilbao tomorrow evening that you and I will be on. James is at the harbor. He will meet us at a different harbor in the second week of May. The harbor is not the harbor he and I have been at. The new harbor is one I have arranged through Eddie. The new harbor is in the north of Spain. I am sorry to come up your steps a second time on an evening when you would have preferred not to see me on them.'

She says: 'Come in. The bag is by the table. I will put on the coat.'

He comes in.

He sees the canvas grip and the leather satchel.

He sees the two notes on the kitchen table.

He sees the seal of the Italian on the second envelope.

He says: 'When did this come.'

She says: 'This afternoon. By hand.'

He says: 'He was here.'

She says: 'He was here. I did not see him.'

Klaus looks at the two notes for a long moment.

Then he says: 'We are going to need to think about that. We will think about it on the way to Edinburgh. I am sorry he was here. I am sorry I had not arranged to be here before he was. The architecture I have not been able to read is the Italian one. The six-week clock is on the Conclave's formal audit. Vinciguerra did not come through the audit. He came through the academic exchange he has been using since 1985. The two channels do not communicate. The hand of the first man arrived at four in the afternoon, and the institution that would have arrived behind him is still six weeks away. He will be a problem in some way I do not yet understand. We will not know what kind of problem until later. For now we leave.'

She says: 'Yes.'

She puts on the navy raincoat.

She picks up the leather satchel.

Klaus picks up the canvas grip.

She turns out the kitchen lamp.

At the back door she stops for a single second. She looks at the kitchen the way a woman looks at a kitchen she has occupied for eleven months and is now leaving without expectation of return. She looks at the windowsill with the geranium and the wren's egg and the gray pebble and the pencil stub and the folded square of paper and the silver thimble and the Latin tag in her own hand.

She does not take any of the windowsill.

She closes the back door behind her.

She locks it. She puts the key under the third stone of the path, where the widow MacIntyre had told her to put it on the morning she had taken the cottage, in case Margaret was ever locked out.

She walks down the path.

She walks down the lane to the gate.

The Land Rover is at the gate. The engine is running. The headlights are off.

Klaus opens the rear door for her. She gets in. He puts the canvas grip on the floor beside her. She sets the leather satchel on her lap. She places her left hand flat on the satchel. The bracelet catches the small dashboard light. The silver key is the key.

Klaus gets in the front. He takes the cap off. He puts it on the seat beside him. He puts the Land Rover in gear.

The truck pulls away from the cottage.

She does not turn her head.

At eleven-thirty in the evening Calder is on the breakwater of an Atlantic harbor in the south-west of France with a bell-buoy ringing a hundred meters out and a wind off the southwest and the right shoulder aching the clean ache it has been aching since November.

He knows that Klaus left the harbor on the morning of the twenty-fifth and that Klaus has not yet sent the message that he has reached her.

He stands on the breakwater for some minutes.

He thinks about Adler and the buckram book and the seventeen names on page one and the sixth date.

He thinks about Margaret.

He thinks about the private fact Klaus had told him on the morning after the Burgenland—that Margaret had been making the list against the architecture for nine years without the architecture knowing it. The architecture would in the next six weeks find out, and that the architecture would then move with the speed of an institution that had been carrying a wrong assumption for nine years and had been required, all at once, to correct it.

He thinks about the three names that have come off the list since Greenwich. The one name that is still on it. The fifth name that is Hannah Doyle. The sixth that is now Adler-struck-through. The seventh that is Margaret. The four that are not yet on the page because their names have not yet come.

He thinks, also, about the Italian hand—the man whom Klaus had told him on the morning after the Burgenland that he, Klaus, did not yet know how to read. The Italian hand had been one of the seven men in Rome for some unspecified number of years. The Italian hand had decided, in March of 1988, to register Margaret with a single pencil tag in the margin of her paper. The Italian hand had decided, on the twentieth of March of 1992, to register her again with a different tag and a different ink and a hand-delivered envelope to a Perthshire post-box. The Italian hand had decided, on the thirty-first of March, to write three further words in pencil that would reach her—Hannah had told them on the evening of the second of April—at some hour in the next several weeks.

The three words were Adveniam ad te.

I shall come to you.

He stands on the breakwater for some more minutes.

The wind goes down at twenty-three forty-eight.

The bell-buoy keeps its rhythm.

The Atlantic is the Atlantic.

He thinks: Klaus has reached her.

He does not yet have the message.

He thinks: Klaus has reached her.

He will have the message in the morning.

He turns. He walks back up the breakwater. He goes up the lane to the second-floor flat above the bakery whose oven will, at oh-four-fourteen, begin to warm the ceiling beneath his bed in the specific way it has been warming the ceiling since the second week of February of 1990. He sits at the desk. He opens the leather notebook. He turns to the pencil page.

He looks at it.

He does not write anything.

He closes the notebook.

He goes to the bed.

He lies down in his clothes.

He does not sleep until oh-four-fourteen.

When he sleeps he dreams, for the first time in twenty-eight months, of a kitchen at Chiswick with Margaret at the table pouring tea from the blue pot into the blue mug and a window above the sink with the early morning light coming through it onto the bracelet on her wrist.

He cannot, in the dream, see whether the silver key on the ring is the silver key he placed there in 1977 or the different key she replaced it with in November of 1989.

In the dream, it does not matter.

He sleeps until seven-twenty.

In the morning, the message will be at the bakery counter, folded inside the brown loaf, in a hand he will know, with three words.

The three words will be: She is with me.

16
PASAIA SAN PEDRO

A Basque harbor—May 1992

Calder left the French harbor on the morning of the fifth of May.

He took nothing he was not able to wrap in oilcloth. The leather notebook in the inside left pocket of his coat. The Mercator beside it, against the inside of the same pocket—Eddie had sent it down from the harbor in April through Joxe Mari's nephew, and Calder had placed it back against his ribs on the morning the coat came south. The new Welrod in its case at his ribs. The Adler ledger wrapped twice in waxed canvas inside a brown leather portfolio of the kind an academic publisher's representative carried. The Walther PPK in the shoulder rig. A change of clothing in a canvas bag. The eight pages, in their original brown envelope, in the bottom of the bag beneath the clothing. The pencil page from the leather notebook, removed and folded twice and slid into the inside spine of a paperback copy of Tacitus he had bought in Bayonne the previous Tuesday.

He left the bottle of Glenmorangie ten-year on the shelf above the sink.

Klaus would be in Lyon in September. He would not introduce himself. He would sit in the back of the small concert hall on the rue Sainte-Catherine while Marianne played the second flute in the chamber group. The watchband marks would be at four when he went. They would be at five before the year was out.

Klaus had drunk three glasses of it in the seventy hours since he had returned from Birnam. Klaus had drunk no more than one glass a week of any spirit since the Hanover testing kit had returned its result in November of 1990. The three glasses in seventy hours had been a private permission Klaus had granted himself, by his own statement, on the basis of having brought Margaret as far as Hendaye without the architecture having intercepted them on any of the eleven points along the route at which the architecture might have. Calder did not begrudge him the three glasses. He left the bottle.

He took the eleven-fourteen train from Bayonne.

He went through Hendaye and Irún at the border without incident, on the Mary Howell passport's husband's-equivalent—a passport in the name of John Howell, retired schoolmaster, Edinburgh, that Eddie had had made for him the previous year against precisely this contingency. He carried no other identification. The Howell papers were a clean set. He had not used them before.

He reached Pasaia San Pedro on the seventeen-twenty bus from San Sebastián.

Pasaia San Pedro was the western village of a small Basque port that was, by the geography of the land, two villages and one harbor.

The harbor opened to the sea through a narrow channel between two cliff-faces a hundred and twenty meters apart, and inside the channel the water broadened into a small protected bay around which the villages had been built. San Pedro was on the western shore. San Juan was on the eastern. The two villages were connected only by a small launch that crossed the channel every twenty minutes from oh-six-hundred to twenty-three-hundred. Each village had its own square, its own frontón for pelota, its own small parish church, and its own particular dialect of the Basque that the children spoke in the streets and the older men spoke in the bars and that the priests had still been, until recently, not permitted to use in confession.

Eddie's man, a wiry Basque of seventy-one named Joxe Mari Arrese who had been a courier for the maquis during the war and had been on Eddie's running register for decades, had taken the lease on a first-floor flat above a fishmonger's on the Calle Donibane two streets back from the western quay. The flat had two rooms and a kitchen with a window facing the bay. The fishmonger was Joxe Mari's nephew. The nephew did not ask questions. The flat had been ready for Calder since the eleventh of April.

Eddie had arranged it through a phone call placed from a public telephone in the Alfama to a number Joxe Mari had answered with a single syllable in Basque. Eddie said, in the Spanish he kept for matters that traveled across phones: *Joxe, I have a man. He needs a kitchen with a window over the bay. He needs the kind of quiet your village does well. He is a friend. He has been alone for a year. The man is named Edinburgh. Edinburgh will arrive when Edinburgh arrives.* Joxe Mari had said, also in Spanish: *I have a kitchen. The kitchen has a window. Edinburgh is welcome.* The conversation had ended. Eddie had walked back up the cobbles. He had not, in the four weeks since, called the number again. He had not needed to. The arrangement had been the arrangement. The discipline was the discipline. The man was named Edinburgh and the kitchen had a window over the bay.

Calder reached the flat at eighteen-oh-five.

He set the canvas bag on the kitchen table.

He stood at the window for some minutes looking at the bay.

He waited at the flat for six days.

He kept the routines he had kept at the French harbor. He woke before dawn. He did the breathing exercises a Bonn instructor had taught him in 1969 for nights when sleep had not done its work. He shaved at the cracked sink in the bathroom. He looked at the puckered moon of the scar on the right shoulder. He touched it. He registered, in the touching, the clean ache it had been carrying since the third week of November. He shaved. He dressed.

He walked, at oh-six-thirty each morning, the half-mile down the western quay to the small fonda on the harbor wall where Joxe Mari had a standing arrangement for his breakfast. The breakfast was a coffee, two slices of pan tostado with olive oil and a smear of fresh tomato, and a glass of fresh-squeezed orange juice. The proprietress was a woman of fifty-two named Mari Carmen. She did not address her customers in Castilian unless they addressed her in Castilian first. She treated Calder, on the basis of his Edinburgh passport and his careful Basque-accented Castilian, with the grave courtesy a Basque shopkeeper extended to a foreigner who had had the discipline to learn the language of the place at which he was a guest.

He read the morning paper at the fonda for forty minutes.

He walked back along the quay.

He climbed the stairs to the flat.

He sat at the kitchen table with the Adler ledger and read.

The ledger was the work. The ledger was twenty-six years of operational dispositions. The ledger was, at one or two pages a day at the pace Calder was reading it, the slow careful unfolding of an institutional memory the institution had not believed any of its members had been keeping.

He read the ledger for four to five hours each morning.

In the afternoons he walked.

He walked the western quay end-to-end, then the eastern path through the small terraced gardens of lemon and fig. He came back.

He cooked his own dinner. Boiled vegetables, a portion of fish from his landlord, a piece of the rough country bread the western village's two bakeries produced. He ate at the kitchen table.

He read until twenty-two-thirty.

He slept.

He did not, in the six days, see anyone he knew.

The waiting was the work.

On the morning of the eleventh he walked down to the bus stop at oh-eight-forty.

The eleven-oh-five bus from San Sebastián was the bus Klaus had said he would be on. Klaus was driving south through France for two days and had abandoned the Land Rover in a village outside Bayonne. He had taken Margaret across the border on foot through a small unmonitored shepherd's path Eddie's man had identified years earlier against this kind of contingency. The two of them had slept the night of the tenth in a farmhouse outside Hendaye that belonged to a cousin of Joxe Mari's. They had taken the morning train to San Sebastián and the bus from there.

The bus came a little after eleven.

Calder was on the bench across the road.

The doors opened.

A small group of women came down—four, with shopping bags, returning from the morning market in San Sebastián. Two old men in caps. A young couple with a baby. Then Klaus. Then Margaret.

Klaus had a canvas grip in his right hand and Margaret's

leather satchel over his left shoulder. Klaus came down first. He did not look at Calder. He turned and offered his hand to Margaret. Margaret took the hand. She came down the steps of the bus carefully. She came down them in the way a woman of fifty-six came down bus steps. She had been preparing herself, since the morning of the eleventh, for the moment she was going to be on the steps of a Basque country bus in the village of her former husband's first sight of her in twenty-eight months.

She straightened on the pavement.

She looked across the road.

Calder stood up from the bench.

He did not move toward her.

She did not move toward him.

The two of them stood, sixteen feet apart, on opposite sides of the road that ran along the western quay of Pasaia San Pedro. The bus pulled away behind them. The water of the harbor was flat in the morning light to her left and his right. Klaus stood two paces back from her with both bags and the grave attention of a man who had been carrying a marriage between his hands for twenty-eight months and was now about to set it down.

Calder said: 'Margaret.'

Margaret said: 'James.'

Klaus said: 'I will take the bags up. Joxe Mari is at the bottom of the calle. He will give me the second key. I will be at his nephew's flat above the bar. I will not come back until tomorrow morning at oh-nine-hundred. The two of you will eat. The two of you will sleep. The two of you will not talk about the work tonight. The work will keep until the morning.'

He picked up the second bag.

He walked across the road.

He went up the calle without looking back.

Calder crossed the road.

He stood in front of her.

He did not embrace her. He did not, by the rigor he had been keeping for twenty-eight months and that she had been keeping for the same twenty-eight months, take her hand. He looked at her face. He took it in. The hair was the hair, slightly more gray at the temples than he had remembered. The skin around the eyes was the skin of a woman who had been spending eleven months in a Perthshire cottage with a kitchen window facing south and a bench at the river half a mile to the west. The mouth was the mouth he had been seeing in the mirror of the kitchen at Chiswick on Sunday mornings for thirty years. The small white scar across the second knuckle of her left index finger was where it had been since the August of 1969 when she had sliced the finger on a tin of cat-food and had bled into the sink and had said, of her own bleeding, that she had always wanted a scar she could remember the kitchen by.

Then she looked at his face the way he had looked at hers, and he let her, because the cataloguing hand was the hand he had just used on her. He watched her find the careful set of the right shoulder. He watched her find the thin pale seam on the left brow, an inch above the older faded scar that had been on his face every day of the years she had known him. The old one she knew. The new one she did not, because she had not been there for it. That was the shape of the twenty-eight months, and it was on his face now in a line an inch long above a line she had known for thirty years, and she read it and set it down and did not ask.

He said: 'Welcome.'

She said: 'Thank you.'

He said: 'There is a flat. It is up the street. Joxe Mari took the lease in April. The fishmonger downstairs is his nephew. The nephew does not ask. There is a kitchen with a window over the bay. There is bread. There is fish. There is tea. There is a small Spanish tomato that is the best I have eaten in fifteen years. I have been keeping the kitchen for you.'

She said: 'Then we will go to the kitchen.'

She walked beside him, along the calle, up the stone steps, into the flat.

In the kitchen she set the satchel on the table. She unbuttoned the navy raincoat. She hung it over the back of the chair. She sat at the table.

He put the kettle on.

He took down the brown earthenware pot from the shelf and the tin of tea from the cupboard. He measured the tea. He measured it the way he had measured tea for thirty years.

She watched the measuring.

She said, after a moment: 'You measure it the way I do.'

He said: 'I have been measuring it the way you do since 1962.'

She said: 'I had not registered.'

He said: 'No. You were the one teaching me to measure.'

The kettle whistled.

He made the tea.

He sat down across from her.

For some minutes neither of them spoke.

Then she said: 'Tell me about the shoulder.'

He said: 'It is sound. It aches. It aches every night since November. It is the clean companion ache of a wound the body has decided to keep as a record. It pulled in Sète in March of 1990 and again in Geneva in October. It does not pull at rest. It will be with me for the rest of my life. Klaus put the round through it in Greenwich on the morning of the fourth of January.'

She said: 'I had registered the date.'

He said: 'You had registered the date how.'

She said: 'Klaus came to me on the fifteenth of December. He came up the steps of the Cumbrian house before first light. He said the sentence. The sentence was: He is at the harbor. He is reading. He is alive. The wound was not the wound that was meant for him. I had been preparing for the news of your death since June. The not-news was the news. I sat at the table for a long while. I made tea. I drank it. I went to Drummonds the following Monday and asked Iain for the Mary Howell papers. I left for Birnam the third week of December.'

He said: 'And in the eighteen months.'

She said: 'I have been writing. I have been waiting. I have been keeping the bracelet on. I have been registering the facts the world has produced in my direction, in the order it has produced them, and I have been holding them against the morning I would be either at this kitchen table with you or at a different kitchen table I had not been told yet I would be at. The kitchen table tonight is the kitchen table.'

He said: 'Yes.'

She said: 'The shoulder is the shoulder.'

He agreed: 'The shoulder is the shoulder.'

She drank the tea.

In the early afternoon they walked to the chapel above the harbor.

They did not speak on the climb. The path was steep. She was fifty-six. He was fifty. Neither of them was the person they had been on a Saturday afternoon in November of 1981 when she had brought a paper twist of saffron from the rue Mouffetard into the kitchen at Fitzrovia and had unwrapped it on the counter and held a single thread up to the light and named it after a crocus that knew a thing.

They sat at the chapel for forty minutes.

The chapel was a whitewashed cell with a wooden door that did not lock and a bench inside on which two people could sit without being touching. They sat on the bench.

She said: 'Adler.'

He said: 'Yes.'

She said: 'The letter you brought.'

He said: 'Yes.'

She said: 'He had decided to come out.'

He said: 'He had decided to come out three nights before the morning we took him. I did not know on the morning. I read the letter in the Burgenland four hours after. Klaus and I made the decision to bring you the letter despite the cost of bringing it. The bringing was the work. The cost was the work. I am sorry.'

She said: 'I had been preparing for him to be killed before he could come to me. I had not prepared for him to have decided to come to me. The not-preparing is what I will be carrying. The preparing I had done for nine years. The not-preparing is new.'

He said: 'Yes.'

She said: 'And Brückner.'

He said: 'Yes.'

She said: 'Brückner had not decided.'

He said: 'Brückner had decided in November of 1989 to wait. He had been waiting since then. He had decided not to flee. He had decided to be the man at the door when I came. He had been waiting because he wanted me to find him before the architecture found me. He told me as much on the fifth-floor landing. He had a daughter in the kitchen. Heike. She was the witness. Klaus did not want me to leave a witness. I left a witness because the alternative was to make a daughter watch her father die and then to make her not watch.'

She said: 'You did the right thing.'

He said: 'I do not know whether I did the right thing. I did the thing I could live with. That discipline is the one I have been working out for myself for twenty-eight months in a flat above a bakery on the French Atlantic coast. The discipline has not been entirely successful. The not-being-successful is the form the work takes for me.'

She said: 'That is the discipline I have been working out for myself in a cottage in Birnam.'

He said: 'Yes.'

They sat for some minutes more without speaking.

She said, after a while: 'There is a thing I have been carrying for some years that I would like to say to you in the chapel rather than at the kitchen table.'

He said: 'Yes.'

She said: 'The afternoon at the Paxton Gallery. October of 1973. The geranium photograph. The Russian woman at your right shoulder reading the curtains.'

He did not move.

She said: 'I had filed her.'

He said: 'Filed her how.'

She said: 'In the way a woman files a thing she has not been told to file. I had been to the gallery to collect a frame I had asked the Paxton woman to hold for me. The frame was for a print I had bought that Tuesday in Cecil Court. I had not been planning to be at the Paxton on the afternoon you were. I was at the desk at the back. I saw you come in. I saw her come in three minutes later. I saw the quality of the arrangement between you. I saw the half-second she gave you on the way to the curtains and the half-second you gave her on the way to the geranium and the third half-second between the two half-seconds in which you each registered the other and decided not to register it. The three half-seconds were the half-seconds I filed. I did not name what I had filed. I went home with my frame. I did not say anything at supper. I said nothing on the Sunday. I have not, in the eighteen and a half years since, said anything. The silence was the form of the filing. The filing was the form of the marriage. The marriage has been carrying, as a result, the specific weight of one woman's seeing of another woman's seeing of her own husband from October of 1973 onward.'

He was quiet for some time.

Then he said: 'Margaret.'

She said: 'James.'

He said: 'I did not know that you had seen.'

She said: 'No.'

He said: 'And in the eighteen and a half years.'

She said: 'In the eighteen and a half years I watched the file fold itself out, in the way a file folded itself out when it had been opened by an interested woman who was paying attention and not closing the file again. I read the set of byproducts your work produced at home. The faintly disordered shoes on the rack on Tuesday mornings when you said you had been at the office on Monday nights. The post-office receipts in your jacket pockets that did not match the postage you had told me you had used. The November weekend in 1974 when you said you were at a small Whitehall conference and the conference, by the discreet inquiry I made of the Foreign Office switchboard, was not a conference. The specific quality of your sleep on the nights you came home from the seeing. I watched. I did not act. The not-acting was the discipline. By 1979 I had concluded that the woman at the gallery was not Western—the timing of her movements and the specific quality of her English in the half-sentences I had heard from across the room at the Paxton had told me, without my naming it then, what I had named to myself by 1979. By 1981 I had concluded that she was Soviet. By 1986 I had decided that the small architecture I had begun to read on the side of the work I was doing as a Latinist was the architecture that had been running her against you and against the state. The eight pages were the form of the deciding. The deciding had begun, by an arithmetic I have only recently become able to articulate, in the half-second at the Paxton Gallery in which I had decided, without being told to, that the woman who was looking at my husband was a woman whose looking I would myself, eventually, have to read.'

He did not speak.

She said: 'I am telling you this in the chapel because I had decided, at the kitchen table that January in Chiswick, that I would tell you in person if I were ever to see you again. Klaus had come to me through the back gate before dawn and had said: Madam, your former husband requires the discretion of a different kind of arrangement. I have been carrying it as the debt they had been carrying that they could not carry forever. I am setting it down. I am setting it down in a chapel in a Basque village above a small bay because the chapel is a place a person sets things down. The setting-down is the setting-down. You may, as the private discipline of receiving the news, take whatever time you need before you respond.'

He took some time.

He looked, in the time he took, at the whitewashed wall opposite the bench, at the wooden door that did not lock, at the small square of afternoon light that had crossed a quarter of the stone floor between the moment they had sat down and the moment she had begun to say what she had now finished saying.

He said, finally: 'You have been the seeing one.'

She said: 'I have been the seeing one.'

The chapel was quiet. The afternoon light had crossed another inch of the stone floor.

He said: 'And Elena had registered your seeing.'

She said: 'I do not know.'

He said: 'I do. I had not understood it until you said it. She had been quieter at the gallery for the second half of the afternoon than the first. She registered your seeing. She registered it the way a Soviet asset registered a kind of seeing that did not appear in the operational manuals. She had not, in the sixteen years that followed, told me she had noted. I had not, in the same years, registered that she had. Our two refusals to register were our version of your silence. The marriage was therefore not the only silence the three of us were keeping.'

She said: 'No. The marriage was the third silence. There were always three.'

He said: 'There were always three.'

He said, after a further moment: 'I am sorry, Margaret.'

She said: 'I am not asking for an apology. I am laying down the file. The file has been heavy. The laying-down is the discipline. The discipline is the marriage.'

He said: 'Yes.'

They sat for a further period in the chapel without speaking.

The light moved a further three inches across the stone floor.

When she stood, the file had been laid down.

She said: 'Let us go down.'

They went down.

That evening he cooked the fish.

She set the table. She had set their table at Chiswick for thirty years. The motions were the motions. He did not see the motions in twenty-eight months. He registered, as she set out the two plates and the two glasses and the two of the Basque earthenware tumblers Joxe Mari had laid in for them, that not having seen the motions for twenty-eight months had been one of the specific lacks his body had been carrying without naming it.

He thought, briefly, of another kitchen. Elena had set a table for him too, at the Fitzrovia studio, in the autumn of 1985—two plates placed with the economy of a woman who had been trained to treat every table as a temporary thing. Margaret set a table as if it would be there in the morning. The two settings had been the two women.

He said: 'You set the table the way you set it.'

She said: 'How else would I set it.'

He said: 'No other way.'

They ate.

She drank the small Basque red Joxe Mari had laid in. He drank the same. They ate the fish and the rice and the small tomatoes with olive oil and salt. The meal took fifty minutes. They spoke about the food. She said, at one point, that the tomatoes were better than anything she had grown at Chiswick in four years of trying, and that the Spanish had done in a morning what she could not do in four summers, and that she found this humbling. He had not, in thirty years of knowing her, heard Margaret use the word humbling about a tomato.

After the meal she helped him wash up.

The washing-up was a precise operation she had been doing at the Chiswick sink for thirty years and that he had been doing for sixteen years on the alternate nights. They did the operation now without negotiation. She washed. He dried. He put the plates back in the cupboard. The order was the order.

When the operation was finished she stood at the kitchen window with her hands on the sill and looked at the bay.

The water was black. The lights on the eastern shore were the steady lights of San Juan. The bell-buoy at the harbor mouth was making its small mournful noise. She stood at the window for some minutes.

He did not come up behind her.

He did not put his hand on her hip.

He stood in the doorway and looked at her standing at the window.

She said, after a while, without turning: 'I am too tired to be the wife tonight.'

He said: 'I am too tired to be the husband tonight.'

She said: 'Tomorrow.'

He agreed: 'Tomorrow.'

She said: 'There is a bed.'

He said: 'There is a bed. It is in the second room. I have been sleeping in it for a week. The sheets are clean. The pillow on the left is the harder one. The pillow on the right is the softer. You should take the right.'

She turned from the window. She walked past him into the second room. She did not touch him on the way past. He watched her go.

He sat at the kitchen table in the dark with the kettle still warm on the warm plate and the lights of San Juan across the water and the bell-buoy doing its work.

He sat there for an hour.

Then he stood. He went to the second room.

She was asleep on the right side of the bed. The pillow on the right was the softer one.

He took off his jacket and his shoes. He laid down on the left side, on the harder pillow, in his shirtsleeves and his trousers, on top of the coverlet, with his hands folded on his chest the way a man slept when he had not yet decided he was permitted to sleep in the bed in which his ex-wife was already sleeping.

He listened to her breathing.

The breathing was the breathing he had been listening to in the dark of the Chiswick bedroom for thirty years.

He fell asleep at some hour before the bakery oven below him would have warmed his ceiling, in a different country in a different bed beside his ex-wife.

At oh-three-forty-two her left hand came across the small distance between them on top of the coverlet and found his right hand. The bracelet on her wrist made the specific quiet metallic sound the silver charms made when they shifted against one another, the sound he had been hearing in the dark of the Chiswick bedroom for thirty years and had not heard for the twenty-eight months he had been at the harbor. The hand was warm. The hand had not, by the careful discipline of its movement, woken her. The hand had moved in sleep. He took it. He registered, in the taking, that the hour was the hour at which he had come down the stairs of a Stasi cellar in East Berlin in March of 1969 and lifted Klaus from the concrete floor. Twenty-three years and two months. The same hour. A different room. A different hand. The same man.

He held her hand for the remainder of the night.

He did not wake her by holding it.

In the morning, when the gray first light of a Basque dawn came through the kitchen window into the second room, her hand was still in his.

But the night of the eleventh of May was not the night of the work. The night of the eleventh was the night the two of them had decided, by the careful protocol of two people who had been carrying it in absent margins for ten years, to take one shared breath in one room before resuming.

He slept.

She slept.

Joxe Mari, on the bench at the corner of the calle, kept watch through the small hours. He was relieved by his nephew before dawn, and took up his post again at first light, and kept it until Klaus came up the calle in the morning.

The work would resume at nine.

17

THE SECOND BOX

Pasaia San Pedro—12 May 1992

Klaus came up the calle in the morning.

He did not knock. He came up the stairs at a measured pace and let himself in with the second key Joxe Mari had given him. He stood in the doorway of the kitchen for a moment without speaking. Calder was at the kitchen table with the kettle on the warm plate and the brown earthenware pot ready. Margaret was at the window with her left hand on the sill and her right hand at the corner of her mouth in the habitual gesture she had made for thirty years when she was thinking about a thing she had not yet committed to speaking about.

She turned. She nodded at Klaus.

Klaus said: 'Good morning, Margaret.'

She said: 'Good morning, Klaus.'

He set a canvas bag on the kitchen table beside the canvas grip from Birnam. He took off his Barbour. He hung it on the hook beside the door. He sat down at the table.

He said: 'I have brought the eight pages. They were in the inside breast pocket of my coat for the journey south. They are with the originals James kept in the harbor. Eddie sent them down in his portfolio yesterday. I have brought also the pencil page from the leather notebook, which James asked me to keep separately for the night.'

He set the brown envelope on the table. He set the pencil page beside it.

He said: 'I will make tea while you do the rest.'

Margaret looked at the pencil page first.

She had not, since the eight pages had been delivered to Calder at the harbor through Klaus's hand, seen the pencil page. The pencil page was the document her former husband had been keeping. She had been keeping the green notebook. The two documents were the two halves. She had been carrying the half he had not seen and he had been carrying the half she had not seen, and the pencil page was, on the kitchen table at Pasaia on the morning of the twelfth of May 1992, the first time the half he had been carrying had become visible to her.

She read it.

She read it twice.

She held still for a moment.

The page was not what she had expected. The page was a single sheet of cheap-grade ruled lined paper that had been folded twice. The paper had aged to the slight cream color cheap paper took on in an inside coat pocket against a man's ribs. The hand was her former husband's careful right-leaning hand, the hand she had been registering on Christmas cards and grocery lists and the back covers of paperbacks for thirty years. The numbered entries were six. Beside three of them—Vernet, Brückner, and the man at the Brussels phone number—were single horizontal lines drawn in the same pencil that had written the entries, the lines slightly different in their pressure and angle. The fourth entry—Heike—had a small annotation in the same hand: Witness. Possible. The fifth entry was Hannah Doyle's name with the annotation third operative. not on list. The sixth entry was the question mark her former husband had been carrying for fifteen months. Into the margin he had written a name, a city, and a description. She recognized the description as the man she corresponded with through the Schriftenreihe for nine years. The marginal description had been struck through, in the same pencil, on the morning of the twenty-fifth of March at oh-two-fourteen in a Land Rover in a Burgenland beech wood by the same hand that had drawn the three earlier lines.

She set the page down beside the brown envelope of the eight pages.

She placed her left hand on the table between the two documents.

She said, after some seconds: 'You have been carrying the page for as many days as I have been carrying the notebook.'

Calder said: 'Yes.'

She said: 'The page is shorter than the notebook.'

He said: 'The page is the kills. The notebook is the work that pointed at the kills. The two documents are the same document divided by the discipline of the man writing one and the woman writing the other. The two documents are the marriage.'

She said: 'The marriage is the marriage.'

He said: 'Yes.'

She turned the pencil page face-down on the table beside the brown envelope. She did not touch it again that morning.

She carried the canvas grip to the table. She sat down. She unbuckled the grip. She took out the zinc box.

The zinc box was eight inches by ten by four. It had been wrapped in two layers of waxed canvas. She unwound the canvas. The zinc beneath was clean and dry. She laid the canvas to the side. She set the zinc box at the center of the table.

Calder watched her hands.

Her hands did not shake.

She lifted the lid.

Inside the box were three things.

The first was a hard-covered notebook of the cheaper sort, ruled, a hundred and ninety-six pages, the cover the dull green of a Smythson business diary. The notebook had been bought in Dunkeld for sixty pence in November of 1990. It was three-quarters full. The hand inside was Margaret's careful left-leaning hand. The notebook was, by the marginal date marks at the head of each entry, the running journal of her research between November 1990 and April 1992. It contained, by her own marginal numbering, three hundred and eighty-one numbered observations, two hundred and four cross-references to scholarly publications across nine European languages, and a small index at the back keyed by surname. Beside seventeen of the index entries were tiny pencilled crosses she had not, even to herself, explained. One of those crosses was beside the name *Hatch, Thomas*—an English journalist who had been writing on the NATO stay-behind networks since the early 1970s, and whom the institution had tried and failed to silence in a Geneva hotel room in March of 1976.

The second was a folder of cardboard tied with twine. The folder contained forty-three single sheets of typing paper. The sheets were the typed continuation of the eight pages of 1986—pages nine through fifty-one, typed in Birnam between January of 1991 and February of 1992, on a portable Olivetti Lettera 32 she had bought in Perth secondhand in December of 1990 against this contingency. The pages were keyed to the index at the back of the green notebook.

The third was a single sealed envelope of heavy cream paper of the sort she had been keeping in the top drawer of the desk at Birnam. The envelope was unaddressed. The seal was of plain red wax with no device. The envelope was thin. By the touch of it through the paper, it contained a single folded sheet.

Margaret laid the three things on the table.

She said: 'The notebook is the working file. The folder is the typed report through the end of February. The envelope is the conclusion I drew on the eighteenth of April that I have not, in the three weeks since, been able to bring myself to type into the report. I will read the envelope first. The notebook and the folder we will work through after.'

She broke the seal.

She unfolded the sheet inside.

She read it once.

She set it on the table between the three of them.

She said: 'I am going to tell you the contents in my own words. The contents are the conclusions of nine years of work, four of which I have been doing alone in Birnam after a spell of doing it alone in Cumbria after the Ealing years and the Chiswick years before them. The contents are not, by any standard of academic confidence I have ever held, fully proved. The contents are the most defensible best reading I have been able to produce on the available evidence. I have been preparing to give them to either the two of you or to the proper authorities at MI6 for nine years. I am giving them to the two of you because the proper authorities at MI6 have, by Klaus's reading and my own, been, for at least the last six years, not unaffected by the architecture under discussion. I am asking you to accept the contents on the basis of my own forty years of training in textual interpretation and on the basis of the operational record the four of us have produced together since January of 1990. The asking is, by my discipline, the request a Latinist makes of her three best readers.'

Klaus said: 'Margaret, you are the colleague we have. We are not asking you to ask. We are asking you to tell.'

She said: 'Then I will tell.'

She told them four things.

The first thing was the identity of the Italian Latinist.

She said: 'The Italian hand that wrote Tu si non vis, et hoc in the margin of my paper in March of 1988 and that wrote Et qui custodit eos? in the margin of my returned offprint in October of 1991 and that wrote Adveniam ad te. Maius non extremum est. on a slip of cream paper that was hand-delivered to a post-box at the gate of my cottage on the afternoon of the twenty-ninth of April is, by my reading, Augusto Vinciguerra. Brückner had corrected the declensions. Vinciguerra had written the tag. The two men had used the same academic-exchange paper without knowing the other had reached it. I identified the distinction in December of last year and have not, since then, been able to find a reason it should not be so. Vinciguerra was born in Bari in 1916. He has held the chair of late-imperial Roman law at La Sapienza since 1968. He has been editor of Studi e Documenti per il Diritto Romano since 1971. He has been a corresponding member of the Pontifical Academy for Latin since 1955. He resides in a flat on the Via Giulia in Rome, where he has been living for decades. He is the only Romanist of his generation in the Italian academy whose published Latin uses the particular elliptical construction that appears in all three of his pencilled corrections to me. The construction is Quid enim ni sic? = idem facio. What else would one do? = I do the same. It appears in three of his published papers between 1958 and 1979. It appears in no other Italian Romanist's writing in the same period. The match is, by the discipline of the philological reading, conclusive at a level of probability I would put at ninety-three percent.'

She paused.

She said: 'Vinciguerra is one of the seven men in Rome.'

Klaus said: 'You are confident of that.'

She said: 'I am confident on the basis of three independent observations. The first is that the operational dispositions of the Custodia in Italy between 1971 and 1989, as reconstructed from the small public traces I have been able to identify, follow a calendar that matches Vinciguerra's known travel itinerary at thirty-one out of thirty-three calendar points. The second is that Vinciguerra was the dedicatee of a Festschrift decades earlier to which contributions were made by Wolfgang Brückner, Friedrich Adler, Eñaut Iturbe, Olaf Hjorth, Theodoros Akritas, and three other men whose biographical patterns match the patterns we have been identifying for Coordinators. The 1976 Festschrift was, by my reading, the Custodia's institutional acknowledgment of Vinciguerra's seniority within the Conclave. The third is that the Latin of his pencil corrections is the Latin of a man who is not asking a question. The Latin is the Latin of a man who has been deciding, slowly, across nine years, that he is going to come out of the institution. The man who has been deciding to come out of the institution has been one of its senior members. That is Vinciguerra.'

Calder said: 'And he is going to come to Birnam.'

Margaret said: 'He has already come to the gate.'

Calder said: 'And the Adveniam ad te is his commitment.'

Margaret said: 'The Adveniam ad te is his commitment. The Maius non extremum est—May is not the last month—is his timing. He is telling me he will not come in May, but in some month after May, and that the not-coming-in-May is itself a discipline he has imposed on himself to make sure his coming, when it happens, is the coming of a man who is no longer of the institution.'

Klaus said: 'Margaret. He is sixteen Conclave years older than the rest of them. He has the seniority. He has the will. He has the Latin. He has the address. He is the most dangerous man at the table for us. He is also the only man at the table who is not, by your reading, hostile to us.'

She said: 'I have been working that argument out for three years. I have not yet, in the three years, found the form of words that would let me put him on the list. He has not, in any of the corrections he has made on my papers, given me a reason to put him on the list. He has, in the specific Latin choices he has made, given me reasons not to. He is the seventh man at the table for us. Whether the seventh man is friend or enemy is the question the work of the next twelve months will answer.'

She held still for a moment.

Then she said: 'That is the first thing.'

The second thing was the three remaining living Coordinators.

She said: 'You have killed three. You have killed Brückner, who was the Northern Coordinator for the German-speaking and East European arc. You have killed Christofi, who was the Western Coordinator for the Benelux and Western European arc. You have killed Adler, who was the Habsburg Coordinator for Austria, Bohemia, Hungary, and the Balkans. There are three remaining living Coordinators who are not me. They are, in the order you should consider them: Eñaut Iturbe of Bilbao for the Iberian arc; Olaf Hjorth of Lillehammer for the Scandinavian and Baltic arc; and Theodoros Akritas of Athens for the Greek and Eastern Mediterranean arc. I have been keeping a dossier on each in the green notebook. The notebook is on the table. Each dossier contains the operational pattern, the personal habits, the known weak points, the family circumstances, and a small calendar of where each man has been on each fourth Tuesday of the year for the last twelve calendar years. I have not been able to identify their kill points. I have been able to identify each man's predictable monthly walk, of the kind Adler had been taking on the fourth Tuesday in Vienna, that gave you the kill point for him. I will leave the identification of the kill points to the three of you. I have done my part of the work.'

Calder said: 'Iturbe is a hundred kilometers west.'

Margaret said: 'Iturbe is a hundred kilometers west. He is seventy-one. He has been keeping an apartment in Algorta on the bluff above the river and a country house in Mungia. He visits the Mungia house on alternate Sundays. He visits a small concert series at the Sociedad Bilbaína in the center of Bilbao on the second Wednesday of every month at twenty-hundred and walks back to his Algorta flat from the Sociedad Bilbaína by way of the Plaza Nueva at twenty-two-thirty. He is not, in his Wednesday walks, accompanied. He has been doing that walk on the second Wednesday for fourteen years. The next second Wednesday is the tenth of June.'

Klaus said: 'The tenth of June.'

Margaret said: 'The tenth of June. I would not, by my reading, do it on the tenth of June. I would do it on the second Wednesday of July, when the Sociedad Bilbaína performs the Brahms quintet that Iturbe has not missed in years and that he will leave the building at twenty-two-fourteen with the quality of attention a man has when he has just heard the third movement of the Brahms quintet for the eighteenth time. The second Wednesday of July is the eighth.'

Calder said: 'The eighth of July.'

Margaret said: 'The eighth of July is the day. The kill point is on the Calle Carnicería Vieja between the Sociedad Bilbaína and the Plaza Nueva. The kill point is the back doorway of the Café Iruña, where the Wednesday-evening waitress has a smoking break between twenty-two-twenty and twenty-two-twenty-eight in which the doorway is unwatched. James can take Iturbe at the doorway at twenty-two-twenty-six. Klaus will be at the corner of the Plaza Nueva with the Land Rover. The extraction will be along the Calle Bidebarrieta to the river and out of Bilbao on the BI-636. By the time the architecture's cleaning crew arrives at the doorway you will be on the Mungia road with the Land Rover and the second body of work you have produced in 1992.'

Klaus said: 'Margaret. You have been planning the kill of Eñaut Iturbe for some weeks.'

Margaret said: 'I have been planning the kill of Eñaut Iturbe since the third week of February of last year. I have been, in fact, planning the kills of all three remaining Coordinators since November of 1990, on the assumption that the architecture would force the matter and that the three of you would, by some hour, need a piece of paper that gave you the operational room. I have produced the piece of paper. The piece of paper is the green notebook. The notebook is on the table.'

She lifted her teacup. It was empty. She set it down with the grave precision a primary-school teacher set down a teacup in a kitchen at the end of a sentence. Klaus, without speaking, took the kettle from the stove and refilled the cup. He refilled his own. He did not refill Calder's. Calder had not finished his. The morning light through the window above the bay had moved an inch on the table since she had begun. Out on the water the small launch from San Pedro to San Juan had completed two crossings.

Calder said: 'And Hjorth and Akritas.'

Margaret said: 'Hjorth and Akritas are also in the notebook. Hjorth has a fortnightly walk in the cathedral park at Lillehammer that I have, by my reading, identified as the kill point. The walk is on alternate Sundays. The next walk you should consider is the twentieth of September. Akritas has a Tuesday lunch on Plaka at a small taverna he has been frequenting for forty-two years and that has, by the architectural geometry of its rear courtyard, the operational space for the kill. The next Tuesday you should consider is the seventeenth of November. The seventeenth of November is, by my reading, the latest date the architecture will permit you any of the three to be on the open ground after the Conclave's audit identifies me as the maker of the list. After that date, the three remaining Coordinators will be, by the institution's protective discipline, in the protected interior of the institution's apartment buildings in Bilbao, Lillehammer, and Athens, and you will not be able to take them on the open ground.'

She paused.

She said: 'I have been pacing the work for eighteen months. The work has a calendar. The calendar requires, on the figures, an Iberian kill in July, a Scandinavian kill in September, a Greek kill in November, and a Roman conversation in December. After December, the Custodia will be either in three Coordinators with no executive arc or in seven Conclave members and one Coordinator with no executive arc, depending on whether Vinciguerra is friend or not. By the third week of December the institution will be functionally crippled at the operational level for the first time in thirty years. The crippling will be the work of the four of us. The crippling is the answer to the work that began with a body swap in Greenwich on the morning of the fourth of January 1990.'

She was silent for a moment.

Then she said: 'That is the second thing.'

The two-and-a-half thing was Margaret making the list.

Calder said: 'And the maker of the list.'

Margaret was quiet for some seconds.

Then she said: 'The seventh seat is the architecture's confusion. The architecture has me in it. The architecture is wrong. The seventh is not me. The seventh is alive. The list has been mine, by the careful protocol of three Latin papers I sent in the autumn of 1985. I will not name the seventh in this kitchen. Leaving him unnamed is the discipline of it. The seventh will become operationally visible to the rest of you in some year between the third remaining Coordinator and the last Roman conversation. The morning of that visibility is not this morning. We will use the architecture's wrong assumption about me for as long as the architecture continues to make it. The architecture's wrong assumption is the operational latitude I have been spending for seven years.'

She paused.

She said: 'The seventh is the part of the work I am keeping for myself.'

Klaus said: 'Margaret.'

She said: 'Klaus. You will not ask. You will not ask because you understand why I cannot tell you. The seventh has been keeping a Coordinator's chair on the architecture's table for twenty years and the architecture has not registered, at any point in those twenty years, that the chair was mine before it was the architecture's. I am not keeping it from you because I do not trust you. I am keeping it because the architecture cannot take what the architecture cannot name, and the architecture can name everything I tell to three other people. The not-knowing is the leverage. The leverage will hold for as long as the not-naming holds. I am not naming.'

Klaus did not respond.

Calder said: 'All right.'

Margaret said: 'Thank you, James.'

She said: 'That is the two-and-a-half thing.'

◆◆◆

The third thing was the Heike Vollmer leverage.

She said: 'You both know that Heike Brückner is the biological daughter of Erika Vollmer. Erika Vollmer was a Stasi officer who recruited and trained Klaus in 1965 and who died of cancer in 1986 in Magdeburg. Erika Vollmer had, by the operational record I have reconstructed from her published papers between 1958 and 1972, been the primary intelligence asset of the Custodia inside the Stasi between 1962 and her death. The Custodia ran her, not the other way around. The architecture's Berlin desk inherited her operational files in 1973 when the architecture moved her into a retirement that was the first stage of its eventual use of her, and has been keeping the Heike-as-Erika's-biological-daughter fact in a sealed archive at Marzahn since 1973 against precisely the kind of leverage operation the architecture activated in January of this year. The leverage is therefore not Heike's accident of paternity. The leverage is the piece of paper Erika kept in 1973 in which she identified, by name, the three Custodia operatives who controlled her in the early 1960s, against the contingency of her being herself activated against the institution. The piece of paper is in the Marzahn archive. The piece of paper is the asset Hannah will be using to acquire Heike. Hannah does not yet know the piece of paper exists. I am giving Hannah, through the green notebook, the location of the file and the access protocol Erika established in 1972 for retrieving it. Hannah will be in Berlin by the end of May. Hannah will, by my reading, have Heike out of the architecture's reach by the third week of June. Heike will then become the team's fourth operative.'

Klaus said: 'Margaret.'

She said: 'Yes, Klaus.'

Klaus said: 'You have been working out the Vollmer file for some time.'

She said: 'I have been working it out since 1985. I had the working out by 1989. I had not, in 1989, been able to find the operational way to deliver it. I have, since November of 1990, been able to deliver it through Hannah. The delivery has, in fact, been the principal reason I asked you, in November of 1989, to keep me alive. The asking was the asking. I have been keeping the file for this hour.'

Klaus did not respond for some time.

Then he said, in German: Du bist eine andere Frau, als ich gedacht habe.

You are a different woman than I had thought.

She said: 'I am the woman I have always been. I have been the woman quietly while the three of you have been the men loudly. The arithmetic is the arithmetic.'

She said: 'That is the third thing.'

The fourth thing was the folded paper she took, last, out of the bottom of the zinc box.

It was a hand-drawn map. Eight inches by ten. The map was a map of Europe at the scale of the Times Atlas of 1985. There were, on the map, fifty-seven small black dots. Each dot was numbered. Each number had, on a single sheet of paper she also took out of the bottom of the box, a corresponding entry of one or two lines.

The fifty-seven dots were the locations of fifty-seven W54-family atomic demolition munitions emplaced in the basements of fifty-seven civilian apartment buildings across Europe by the Custodia across two decades. The map was the operational geography of the architecture's principal physical asset. The map was the answer to the question Calder had been carrying since the morning Klaus had read the FEUERWERK file at the kitchen table at the harbor in February of 1990 and had said the words the bomb that does not look like a bomb.

Calder did not speak.

Klaus did not speak.

Margaret said: 'I have not given this map to Hannah. I have not given it to Eddie. I have not given it to anyone. I have been holding it for the morning the four of us would be in one room together with the work. The morning is the morning. The map is the map. Whatever we do with the architecture in the next twelve months, the map is the document that has the institution physically. The institution is a paper architecture. The map is the architecture's body. A paper architecture cannot live without its body. The body is fifty-seven cellars in fifty-seven cities. Fifty-seven cellars are, by the right protocol and the right courier and the right hour, fifty-seven empty cellars. After they are emptied, the institution will have one weapon left. The weapon will be its Latin. We have, between the four of us, more Latin than the institution.'

She set the map on the table.

She said: 'That is the fourth thing.'

She did not move for some seconds.

Then she said: 'There is a fifth thing that is not for tonight. The fifth thing is the answer to the question of why the architecture has been maintaining fifty-seven civilian apartment buildings in seven countries on an eighteen-month rotation for three decades. The architecture has been maintaining them because they are the cover. The cover has held for thirty-nine years because the cover is correct: the basements contain the munitions. The architecture has not, in any of those years, planned to detonate one. The munitions are not the work. The munitions are the public face of the work. The architecture has another face. The other face was registered, in the institution's ledger I will name to the four of us in some year between the third Iberian kill and the last Roman conversation, on the eighth of December 1953. The registering was the institution's response to a speech given that morning at the United Nations in New York by an American president. The speech proposed to share the new fire with the world. The world would come to call it Atoms for Peace. The institution decided, in the eleven days following the speech, that the speech would not become the American president's policy. The decision held for forty years. The work the architecture has been doing in those forty years is the work the deciding has been protecting. The fifty-seven cellars are the public arithmetic of the protecting. The actual work is in nine other places, of which I have, by the green notebook, identified six.'

Klaus did not respond.

Calder said: 'Margaret.'

She said: 'James. The fifth thing is for after. I am telling you tonight only that there is a fifth thing, because the four of you should know, on the kill nights you are about to be on, that the kills are not the whole work. The kills are the operational fact. The fifth thing is the work the kills are clearing the room for. We will name the fifth thing when the room has been cleared. The kills come first.'

She paused.

She said: 'That is what is not the fourth thing.'

For some time after she had finished none of them spoke.

Then Calder said: 'Margaret.'

She said: 'James.'

He said: 'You have been carrying this for nine years.'

She said: 'I have been carrying this for nine years.'

He said: 'I am sorry I have not been carrying it with you.'

She said: 'You have been carrying the half of it I could not have carried. The doing-of-the-work has been your half. The mapping-of-the-work has been mine. The two halves only become the work when the four of us are in a room with the table between us. We are in the room. The table is between us. The work is now the work.'

She closed the zinc box.

She set the green notebook in the center of the table.

She said: 'I will make a fresh pot of tea.'

She stood. She went to the warm plate. She lifted the kettle.

Klaus and Calder sat at the table looking at the green notebook and the typed pages and the unfolded map of Europe with its fifty-seven small numbered black dots.

Klaus said, without looking up: 'James.'

Calder looked at him.

Klaus said: 'The eighth of July.'

Calder said: 'The eighth of July.'

Klaus said: 'We have eight weeks.'

Calder said: 'We have eight weeks.'

The four of them—three in the room and the fourth in Berlin—were now, on the morning of the twelfth of May 1992, the four people in the world who knew what the Custodia Auspiciorum was, where its body was, and what it would take to bring the body down.

The work would take twelve months.

The work was now the work.

They had twelve months.

18

LA CALLE CARNICERÍA VIEJA

Bilbao—June to July 1992

For three weeks at Pasaia they were the four of them at one table—the three in the room and Hannah at the other end of a slip of paper through Pascal twice a week.

Then on the second of June Calder and Klaus took the small fishing launch east along the coast to the small Basque fishing port of Mutriku. From Mutriku they took the bus south through the mountains to Eibar. From Eibar they took the train west to Bilbao. There they took a flat in a building behind the Mercado de la Ribera in the Casco Viejo on a one-month lease that Joxe Mari's wife's brother had arranged with a landlord who kept three flats in the city for whatever purpose his brother-in-law's old maquis network occasionally required.

Margaret stayed at Pasaia.

She was, by the unanimous reading of the three of them and by her own quiet acknowledgement at the kitchen table on the morning of the second of June, the asset the institution had now spent two and a half years thinking it had killed. She would, in the eight to ten weeks before its audit corrected the error, be identified as the maker of the list. After the identification she would have, by the architecture's protocol, a kill order on her of the kind it had had on her former husband for two and a half years and was still attempting to execute. Until the identification she had operational latitude. The latitude was the latitude. The latitude did not extend, by Klaus's reading and Calder's, to her presence in Bilbao on a kill night.

She accepted the reading.

She said, at the kitchen table on the morning of the second: 'I will read in Pasaia. I will keep the maps. I will write the letters. I will be at this kitchen window when you come back. I will not, in your absence, leave the calle. I am, as you have noticed, capable of discipline.'

Calder said: 'Yes.'

She said: 'Go.'

They went.

Bilbao in June was a city of two weathers and one river.

The two weathers were the morning and the afternoon. The mornings were gray and damp and warm; the afternoons turned in the second hour after lunch to the sustained heat the basin between the green mountains took on in early summer. The wind from the sea died at the river's mouth. The heat sat on the streets of the Casco Viejo until the late evening, when the wind came up again and the city rinsed itself of the day's heat in the slow current of air that came down the Nervión from the bay.

The river was the river. The river had been the city. The Casco Viejo had been built on its right bank in the fourteenth century around the seven streets that came down to the river in seven parallel lines. The seven streets were the Siete Calles. The Sociedad Bilbaína was on the Plaza Nueva, two streets back from the river. The Café Iruña was on the Calle Carnicería Vieja, one street up from the Plaza Nueva, on the corner of the Calle del Correo. The walk Iturbe took on the second Wednesday from the Sociedad Bilbaína to the Plaza Nueva was the walk of two and a half blocks at the pace of a seventy-one-year-old Basque lawyer who had been keeping his Wednesday for fourteen years and was not going to vary the pace for a wet evening or a dry one.

They walked the route on the tenth of June, as a rehearsal.

Iturbe was on the route that night.

They watched him from the doorway of a small shoe shop on the Calle Bidebarrieta. Iturbe came out of the Sociedad Bilbaína at twenty-two-fourteen, exactly the hour Margaret said he would. He was walking with the slight forward lean of a man who had been listening, for the seventeenth time that decade, to the Brahms quintet, and whose head was still half-inside the third movement when he had stepped out onto the cobbles. He was wearing a charcoal-gray summer suit, no overcoat, a Panama hat of the older style, and a white silk handkerchief in the breast pocket. He was carrying a black leather portfolio of the kind a senior Basque lawyer of his generation had been carrying for over four decades.

He turned right out of the Sociedad. He walked north on the Calle Bidebarrieta to the corner of the Calle Carnicería Vieja. He turned right again. He walked east on the Carnicería Vieja toward the Plaza Nueva. He passed the back doorway of the Café Iruña at twenty-two-twenty-six.

The doorway was a small recessed service door painted the dark green of a Bilbao back doorway in the rainy season. The doorway was set back from the line of the street by approximately twenty inches. The waitress on her smoking break—a brown-haired woman of forty-one named Itziar Etxeberria—was at the corner of the next street smoking the second of her three cigarettes. Her night-shift schedule was the same Wednesday smoking break Margaret had identified from the internal staff roster of the Hostelería de Bizkaia of January 1990. By the established pattern, she would not return to the doorway until twenty-two-twenty-eight.

Iturbe was at the doorway for one and a third seconds.

The seven-street geometry of the Casco Viejo carried the small block-section of the Calle Carnicería Vieja in a pocket of stone-amplified silence at that hour, with the next nearest pedestrian movement seven seconds back at the Calle del Correo and four seconds forward at the Plaza Nueva, and the doorway itself was, by Klaus's measurement, in a pocket of operational space that would close again at twenty-two-twenty-seven. The pocket was thirty-eight seconds long. The kill required no more than four. Iturbe, on the tenth of June, walked through the pocket without registering it.

Calder did not move.

Klaus did not move.

Iturbe walked on. He turned left into the Plaza Nueva at twenty-two-twenty-eight. He crossed the plaza on the diagonal. He went out the northeast arch of the plaza onto the Calle Sombrerería and from there back to the river embankment and along the embankment to the Puente del Arenal, where he caught the eleven-fifteen tram across the river to Algorta. The tram was the same tram he had been catching at twenty-three-fifteen on the second Wednesday of every month for years.

The rehearsal was the rehearsal.

The next second Wednesday was the eighth of July. Iturbe would, by the published program of the Sociedad Bilbaína concert series—which Margaret had been receiving by post through an academic subscription since 1990—hear the Brahms quintet that night for the eighteenth time in his life.

He would not, after twenty-two-twenty-six on the eighth of July, hear it again.

For the remainder of June and the first week of July Calder kept the flat behind the Mercado de la Ribera the way he had kept the second-floor flat above the bakery on the French Atlantic coast.

He woke at oh-five-forty.

He shaved at the cracked sink in the bathroom. He looked at the puckered moon of the scar on the right shoulder. He touched it. The shoulder registered the morning with its clean ache. The shoulder ached the clean companion ache it had been aching since November. The ache had become, in the eight months since the postman in the Geneva alley had elbowed the trapezius back into a recollection of itself, the small reliable companion the wound had promised it would become. The companion was the companion.

He read the green notebook.

Margaret had marked, in the back index of the green notebook, a section of forty-three pages dedicated to the operational and personal records of Eñaut Iturbe. Calder read the section three times. The second time through he made small marginal notes in pencil in his own hand. The third time through he transferred the notes to a single sheet of paper that became the operational brief for the eighth of July. The brief was four pages. He memorized the four pages over the second week of June. He burned the brief in the kitchen sink on the morning of the twentieth.

Klaus, in the same period, made the provisions. He acquired a Land Rover from a man in Ondarroa who had been on Eddie's running register for years and who delivered the vehicle, with two registrations and three sets of plates, to a garage in the Erandio district of Bilbao in late June. He confirmed the engine on a long drive south to the Cantabrian coast and back. He laid in two changes of clothing for Calder and one for himself and a small bottle of distilled water and a tin of biscuits and a surgical kit of the kind he had laid in at the French harbor before Marseilles and that he had not, in the twenty-eight months since, had to use beyond the changing of a single bandage.

On the night of the seventh of July they went to bed at twenty-two-thirty.

They did not speak about the eighth.

They slept.

On the afternoon of the eighth Calder shaved a second time at sixteen-thirty.

He looked, in the small mirror above the sink, at the puckered moon for the third time that day. He looked at it on the morning of the kill in Berlin in April of 1991 and on the morning of the kill in Vienna in March of 1992 and now, on a Wednesday afternoon in July of 1992 in a flat in the Casco Viejo of Bilbao, the looking had become a private discipline of its own. The scar had changed. Not in shape—the shape had been the shape since the healing—but in the skin around it, which had begun, in the months since Vienna, to age at a different rate from the rest of the shoulder. The skin around the moon was the skin of a man of fifty. The moon itself was the skin of a man of two and a half. The two ages sat beside each other on the same shoulder. He touched the moon with the wet thumb of his right hand. The two ages were the two men.

He dressed.

Charcoal-gray summer suit. No overcoat in the July evening. A small straw hat of the kind a Basque pensioner wore in summer. A white shirt. A dark blue tie. The new Welrod in the leather case at his ribs. The Walther PPK in the shoulder rig under the jacket. The small length of piano wire in the leather pouch in his right coat pocket—he had not used the wire since Geneva and would not, by his assessment, use it tonight, but the wire was the wire and the wire was at hand.

Klaus dressed in workman's clothing—a blue boilersuit over a white singlet, with a flat cap and rope-soled shoes, in the disguise of a Bilbao garage mechanic on his evening break.

They left the flat at nineteen-forty.

At twenty-one-forty-nine Iturbe came out of the side entrance of the Sociedad Bilbaína, on the Plaza Nueva side. He wore his Panama hat. His black leather portfolio was in his right hand. He carried the quality of attention a man had when he had just heard the third movement of the Brahms quintet for the eighteenth time and had decided, in the small pause between the third and fourth movements, that this had been the eighteenth-best of his eighteen hearings of the third movement.

He stood at the door of the Sociedad for a moment. He looked at the Plaza Nueva. The plaza was almost empty. Two men at a café table on the south side. A young couple at the central fountain. A small boy with a kite that was not flying.

Iturbe turned right.

He walked north on the Calle Bidebarrieta.

He passed the doorway of the small shoe shop in which Calder and Klaus had stood on the tenth of June. Calder was no longer in the doorway. Calder was three doorways further north, in the small recess of a closed glove-maker's, with the Welrod already in his right hand at low ready and the small straw hat tipped slightly forward to obscure the line of his eyes.

Iturbe passed Calder's doorway at twenty-two-twenty-three.

He did not see Calder.

He turned right at the corner of the Calle Carnicería Vieja.

Calder gave him eleven seconds.

Then Calder came out of the doorway and turned the same corner.

Iturbe was twenty meters ahead. The Carnicería Vieja was, at twenty-two-twenty-five on a Wednesday in July, the pocket of stone-amplified silence Klaus had measured. The waitress

Itziar Etxeberria was at the corner of the next street smoking the second of her three cigarettes. The back doorway of the Café Iruña was empty. The kill point was the kill point.

Calder closed the distance to four meters.

Iturbe, somewhere in the careful late-evening attention of his Wednesday, did not register the closing. He had been listening to the Brahms quintet in his head since he had stepped out of the Sociedad. He had been listening, specifically, to the second movement, which was the movement that had been, for over forty years, the movement he had listened to on the second Wednesday walk back to the tram. The second movement had a long sustained passage in the strings that Iturbe had been carrying in his head, on second Wednesdays, for forty-three years. He was carrying it in his head now.

The carrying was the operational space.

At the back doorway of the Café Iruña, with Iturbe two meters ahead and the recess of the doorway twenty inches deep on his left, Calder said, quietly, in Basque: Jauna.

Sir.

Iturbe stopped.

He turned.

He looked at Calder.

He registered Calder.

He understood Calder.

His expression—in the second of the registering, before his hand had decided what to do, before his mouth had decided what to say, before any of the operational alarms that a man of his discipline had at his disposal could be activated—his expression was the expression Calder had now seen six times.

It was the sixth expression. It was not the first or the second or the third or the fourth or the fifth. It was the expression of a man who had decided, fifty years earlier, that he would meet the moment of his own death by paying attention to whatever music had been in his head when the moment arrived; and who therefore was, in the second of the registering, deciding, with the determined neatness of his life's longest discipline, to keep listening to the second movement of the Brahms quintet rather than pay attention to the man who had spoken to him on the corner. The expression was the expression of a man whose last attention had decided to be the music and not the killer.

Calder fired once.

The new Welrod made its second firing in three months. The bolt rotated. The casing did not yet eject.

The round entered Iturbe's chest at the second intercostal space slightly left of the sternum, on a downward angle of the sort Calder had been practicing in mirrors for two years. The round transected the descending arch of the aorta on the upper left quadrant of the chest cavity and lodged, in the same passage, in the body of the sixth thoracic vertebra at the back. The round did not exit. The aortic transection meant the central blood pressure dropped to zero in approximately one heartbeat. The brain, denied perfusion, would shut down inside fourteen seconds.

Iturbe did not slump.

He stood for a moment with the Panama hat still on his head and the black leather portfolio still in his right hand and his eyes still on Calder.

The eyes did not change. The eyes were still on the second movement.

His legs gave at the count of three. He sat down at the foot of the recessed doorway in the slow boneless way bodies sat down when the central blood pressure had dropped to zero and the body had decided to use its last six seconds of cerebral oxygenation to lower itself onto stone. The Panama hat tipped forward over his brow. The portfolio fell to the cobbles beside his right hand. A small dark trickle of blood came over the lower lip and into the white silk handkerchief in the breast pocket. The handkerchief darkened from one corner.

The eyes were still on the second movement.

The second movement finished in his head at the count of nine. The eyes went out at the count of ten.

Calder stepped into the doorway. He worked the bolt. The casing ejected into his left palm. He pocketed it. The new Welrod was now down to three firings, perhaps four.

He took the Panama hat off and laid it on the cobbles beside the body.

He took the portfolio. He set it inside the recess against the wall, in the position a man's portfolio would be in if he had set it down deliberately to enter the doorway for some reason of his own. He arranged the body in the posture of a man who had sat down in the doorway because he had felt unwell. He set the small handkerchief in the body's right hand. He stepped back. The arrangement would read, to the first passer-by who came along the Carnicería Vieja, as an elderly Basque gentleman who had felt the small attack of his own age in a doorway and had decided to sit. The reading would last, by Klaus's calculation, eleven minutes. After eleven minutes the attending passer-by would notice that the gentleman had not moved and would summon assistance. By that hour Calder and Klaus would be on the BI-636 north of Mungia.

Calder stepped out of the doorway.

He walked east along the Carnicería Vieja to the Plaza Nueva at the unhurried pace of a Bilbao pensioner returning from a small evening errand. He crossed the plaza on the diagonal. He went out the northeast arch onto the Calle Sombrerería. He turned right on the Calle Sombrerería. He turned left on the Calle Tendería. He came down to the river. The Land Rover was at the corner of the Plaza del Arenal with the engine running and the rear door unlocked.

He got in the back. He lay down. The dog blanket was over him within four seconds.

The Land Rover pulled out into the embankment and turned north along the Calle Bailén.

They cleared Bilbao at twenty-two-fifty-eight.

They cleared Mungia at twenty-three-fifty-one.

They were on the small coastal road that ran east from Mungia to Lekeitio a little after midnight, with the Bay of Biscay on their left and the dark mass of the Pyrenees foothills on their right and the moon a thin sliver over the water.

In the back of the Land Rover Calder took the leather notebook from the inside left pocket of his coat. He opened the pencil page. He took the pencil from the leather pouch. He drew a single horizontal line through 7. Iturbe, Eñaut. Bilbao. Iberian Coordinator. Brahms Wednesdays. The line was clean. His hand did not shake.

He folded the page. He put the notebook away.

He thought, as the Land Rover took the small bend at the top of the Lekeitio escarpment and the headlights swept the white wall of a farmhouse on the inland side of the road, about Eñaut Iturbe's last expression. The last expression had been the sixth. The last expression had been the expression of a man whose last attention had been the music. The man had decided fifty years earlier that this would be his discipline. He kept the discipline. The keeping had been the only honest thing in his work in the years since 1965, by Calder's reading, in the same way Margaret's correspondence had been the only honest thing in Brückner's. The architecture had been incapable, by the discipline of its own institution, of producing any other kind of honesty in any of its members. The honesty its members could keep was the private discipline of their own attention at the moment of their dying.

Five men. Six expressions. The same architecture.

The architecture was the work.

The work was the list.

The list now had five men struck through.

They reached Pasaia in the small hours.

Joxe Mari was at the corner of the calle. He took the Land Rover for the night.

Calder went up the stone steps to the flat.

Margaret was at the kitchen table with a lamp on and a cup of tea half-drunk in front of her and the green notebook open at page eighty-one.

She looked up as he came in.

She said: 'Eight of July.'

He said: 'Eight of July.'

She said: 'Bilbao.'

He said: 'Bilbao.'

She said: 'The Brahms.'

He said: 'The Brahms.'

She said: 'Was it the second movement.'

He said: 'It was the second movement.'

She said: 'I had thought it would be the second.'

He said: 'Yes.'

He sat down at the table.

She set the green notebook to the side. She poured him a cup of tea from the brown earthenware pot on the warm plate. She set the cup in front of him.

He drank.

She did not ask any further question.

They sat at the table for some time in the lamp-lit silence of a Basque summer night. The bay of San Pedro was outside the window. The bell-buoy at the harbor mouth was doing its work. The Brahms quintet was finished, in another country in another decade, in a doorway on the Calle Carnicería Vieja in the head of a seventy-one-year-old man whose name had now been struck through on a pencil page in a leather notebook in the inside left pocket of her former husband's coat.

Klaus came up before dawn with the second cup of tea on the small Basque tray.

The three of them sat at the table until the eastern sky began to lighten over the rooftops of San Juan across the bay.

Then they went to bed.

In Berlin, at the same hour, Hannah Doyle was standing in the underground archive room of the Stasi records facility in Marzahn. She had a thin cardboard file in her hands. The access protocol Margaret had identified in the green notebook was in her coat pocket. A second operative stood two paces back from her, watching the door—Heike Brückner-Vollmer, thirty-four, who had decided in a kitchen on the Lychener Strasse on the morning of the seventh of July that the work the man at her father's bay window had done in April of last year was the work she would now consent to be the fourth operative of.

The work was now the work of five.

The list now had five men struck through.

The list still had two.

The list still had Vinciguerra.

19

DAS MARZAHNER ARCHIV

Berlin—June to July 1992

Hannah Doyle had been in Berlin since the end of October 1991.

She took a small one-bedroom on the Crellestrasse in Schöneberg, a third-floor flat in a building whose ground floor was a Turkish bakery. The stairs smelled of cardamom and yeast at all hours of the day and night.

The cardamom was the difficulty. Michael had baked with cardamom once, at fourteen, in a cake for their mother's birthday in the kitchen on Beacon Street. The cake had burned. Their mother had eaten it. Michael had said, with the certainty of a boy who would become a physicist: the oven is wrong, not the recipe. Hannah had not, in the four years since his death, been able to pass a bakery that used cardamom without hearing the sentence.

She had been keeping the flat in the manner of a CIA officer who was, by her employer's official discipline, on a closed-station rotation that did not require her to do operational work and did not, by the same official discipline, prevent her from doing it. The cover was the cover. The cover was the useful operational space the agency's discomfort with her brother's death had given her since the closed-session hearing in February of 1991. She had been operating, since the morning she had walked out of the closed session, in the useful space between her employer's decision not to fire her and her employer's decision not to ask.

She identified Heike Brückner-Vollmer in Berlin in November.

She had not approached Heike in November.

The not-approaching had been Klaus's instruction. Klaus had said, in the message that had come up through Pascal in the second week of November, that Heike was a young woman who had watched her stepfather killed at oh-seven-oh-two on a Tuesday morning at the bay window of an apartment on the Lychener Strasse in April of 1991. She spent the eleven weeks between April and the early summer in the work of arranging the archive and the burial and the unwinding of the small estate of a sixty-eight-year-old former Stasi major whose institutional pension had stopped being paid on the seventeenth of April. The architecture would, by Klaus's reading, attempt to activate her against her stepfather's surviving institutional record sometime between January and April of the next year. The activation had come in January. It had come, by Hannah's confirmed observation, in the form of a letter on the letterhead of a private trust called the Stiftung für mitteleuropäische Studien, registered in Liechtenstein. The letter offered to fund the cataloging of Wolfgang Brückner's academic and operational papers under a research arrangement. The arrangement would require Heike to accept a small advisory role and a small honorarium and to grant the trust access to the Lychener Strasse apartment at agreed times.

Heike had asked for time.

The trust had given her four weeks.

Heike, in February, had asked for four further weeks.

The trust had given her two.

Heike had then begun, quietly, to do the specific things a woman of thirty-four did when she had begun to understand that the institution she had assumed she was unaffected by was, in fact, in the second hour of a process of activating her. She had moved her own small cardboard file of her stepfather's most personal papers from the apartment on the Lychener Strasse to the apartment of a school friend on the Rykestrasse three streets away. She stopped going to her university lectures at the Humboldt. She had stopped using her bank card. She had cut the cord of the apartment's telephone line at the wall socket and replaced it, the same evening, with a length of cord she had not cut from the wall socket. She had begun, in early March, to walk a different route to the small Bäckerei on the corner of Annelies Schmidt's bakery for the bread she had been buying on Tuesday mornings for over a year.

Hannah had observed each of these operational improvisations from the doorway of the closed Polish-pierogi shop opposite the entrance to the Lychener Strasse building.

She had not approached.

Klaus had said, in the message of the second of February: Wait until she has decided to want a colleague. The deciding will produce a physical sign. The sign will be the morning she stops walking the new route to the bakery and resumes the old one. The resumption will be her decision that the architecture's surveillance is no longer the surveillance she fears. She will then be open to a colleague. Approach in that week.

The resumption had come on a June morning.

Hannah approached two days later.

Heike was at the corner table of Annelies Schmidt's bakery at oh-seven-thirty-five, drinking a cup of coffee and reading a paperback edition of Christa Wolf's Kassandra, with a canvas bag of bread on the chair beside her. She was wearing a brown wool jumper and a darker brown corduroy skirt and small round wire-rimmed reading glasses she had bought, by the habitual mark of the lens-cleaning cloth at the corner of the table, in the past month. Her hair was the dark blond of her stepfather's hair as a younger man and the green eyes were the green eyes Hannah had seen, once, in the black-and-white photograph of Erika Vollmer's official Stasi personnel file that Eddie's man at Marzahn had quietly photocopied for Hannah in February.

Hannah sat down at the next table.

She ordered a coffee.

She ordered it in the careful North-Boston-accented German she had been keeping at the level of a passing fluent for fourteen years.

She unfolded the International Herald Tribune she had bought at the Friedrichstrasse station on her way over.

After a minute Heike turned a page in Kassandra.

After a further minute Hannah said, in German, without looking up from the Tribune: Frau Brückner.

Heike did not move. She did not look up. She did not turn the next page. The hand that had been about to turn the page held still on the corner.

She said, after some seconds, also without looking up: Wer.

Who.

Hannah said: Hannah Doyle. CIA Berlin. Designated closed-station rotation since February 1991. Sister of Michael Doyle who was killed in Devon in August 1988 by an instrument I have spent two years not yet identifying. Colleague of two men you have not met. The two men sent the operative to your father's bay window in April of last year. The two men have asked me, after eight months of waiting at the closed Polish-pierogi shop opposite your building, to come and talk to you on a morning of your choosing. You appear to have chosen this morning.

Heike, after a further moment, turned the page of Kassandra. She set the book down on the table, spine flat, the page held open with the back of her left hand. The hand was steady. The hand of a woman who had taught herself, at thirty-two, how to wait.

She said, still without looking up: Why does the talking happen now and not in November.

Hannah said: Because Klaus instructed me to wait until you had decided to want a colleague. The deciding produced, on Monday morning, a physical sign you had not produced for fourteen weeks. I observed the sign. I am here on the basis of your sign.

Heike said: Klaus.

Hannah said: Klaus.

Heike said: That is the name my father said before he died. He said it three times in three months at the kitchen table. He had been writing it on the back of envelopes and crossing it out. I had not understood that he had been writing the name of an actual person. The actual person killed him.

Hannah said: No. The actual person did not kill him. The actual person was at the corner of the Lychener Strasse with a Land Rover. The man at the door was named James Calder. Klaus is the man who has been arranging your safety since the morning of the seventeenth of April of last year, when he and Calder concluded that the architecture would activate you between January and April of this year and that the activation would be designed around the operational fact of who your biological mother was. The architecture has activated you. You have, by the set of operational improvisations of the last four months, begun to refuse the activation. I am here to help you finish the refusal. I am here because the three of us—Klaus, Calder, and I—will need a fourth operative to finish the work that began with my brother's death and your father's death and a number of other deaths between. You are the fourth operative. The deciding is yours.

Heike, finally, looked up from Kassandra.

She looked at Hannah.

She said: My biological mother.

Hannah said: Erika Vollmer. Stasi officer. Recruited by the Custodia in 1958. Her original handler was a man named Werner Bruhn, who was the same man who tortured Klaus in the cellar at oh-three-fourteen on a morning in March of 1969 from which he was extracted by Calder at oh-three-forty-two. Erika was not the architecture's instrument. Erika was the architecture's asset. The difference is the difference. Erika gave you to your stepfather to raise in 1969 because she had, by that month, registered that the architecture had begun to use her against the Stasi, and she had decided that her child would not become an instrument of the same institution. She kept a single piece of paper in 1973 against the contingency of her being herself activated. The paper is at Marzahn. The paper has been at Marzahn since 1973. The architecture knows where the paper is. The architecture has not been able to retrieve the paper because the access protocol Erika established in 1972 requires the agreement of three institutional signatories and at least one of those signatories has been outside the architecture's reach since 1989. The paper is therefore the leverage. The leverage is yours.

Heike was silent for some seconds. She lifted the white cup of coffee in front of her. She did not drink. She set the cup back on the saucer at a different angle from the one it had occupied. The new angle had been her mother's habit at the kitchen table in the Friedrichshain flat in 1958. Heike did not know that. The hand had decided.

Heike said: And the leverage is what.

Hannah said: The leverage is the names of three men who were operationally responsible for your biological mother in the early 1960s, and whose names will, when they are made public in the right form, be the institutional registration of the Custodia's penetration of the Stasi between 1958 and 1989. The registration will be the thing that converts the Custodia from an institution that does not exist to an institution that does. Once the institution exists, in the public record, it can be opposed. While it does not exist, it cannot.

Heike was quiet for some time.

Then she said: And what does the deciding require of me.

Hannah said: It requires you, this morning, to walk back to the apartment with me. It requires you to make me a cup of tea. It requires you to sit at your father's kitchen table and tell me, in the order I will lay out for you, the pieces of operational paper your father kept at the apartment that you have not yet shown to anyone. It requires you, on a date we will set together in the next forty-eight hours, to walk into the Marzahn records facility on the basis of an access pass I will provide. You will retrieve a particular small thin cardboard file from a particular shelf in the basement. The file will not be retrieved by me. The file's access protocol requires the retriever to be a biological descendant of the original signatory. I am not. You are.

Heike, after a further moment, closed Kassandra.

She set it on the table.

She placed her left hand on top of the book.

She said: Yes.

Hannah said: Yes.

Heike said: Pay for my coffee.

Hannah said: I will pay for it.

She stood. She paid at the counter. She came back. Heike picked up her bread bag and her book and her canvas shoulder bag.

The two of them walked out of the bakery onto the Sredzkistrasse. They passed the closed Polish-pierogi shop opposite the Lychener Strasse building where Hannah had stood for eight months on a series of intermittent observations. They went along the Lychener Strasse to the entrance of number twenty-three. They climbed the stairwell to the fifth floor where Heike's stepfather had answered his own door at oh-six-fifty-eight on a Tuesday morning in April of 1991 to a man who had said his name was James Calder and who had then, four minutes later, sat the same man at the bay window of the front room with a single 7.65mm Browning round in his chest.

Heike unlocked the door of the apartment.

She held the door for Hannah.

Hannah went in.

Heike closed the door behind her.

For three weeks they worked at the kitchen table.

Heike showed Hannah, in the order Hannah had laid out for her, the operational papers her stepfather had kept at the apartment. The papers were not, by the architecture's measure, operational. They were the private notes and marginal corrections of a senior Coordinator who had decided in November of 1989 to wait, and who had spent the seventeen months of his waiting in the slow steady discipline of writing, by hand, a series of careful notes on the institution he had served for forty-three years. The notes were in German. The notes were the small interpretive apparatus a man left behind for a daughter he had decided would, at some hour, need it.

Heike had not, in all the time since, read the notes.

She read them now, with Hannah at the table beside her, in the careful nine-hour days she had been keeping since the morning of the tenth of June.

The notes contained, among other things, the names of seventeen senior members of the Custodia Auspiciorum as of November 1989. Seven Conclave members in Rome. Seven Coordinators across Europe. Three operational deputies. The seventeen were the same seventeen Adler had been keeping in the buckram book that Calder and Klaus had taken out of the Sonnenfelsgasse on the night of the twenty-fourth of March. The small revision was that Brückner's seventeen included two names that were not in Adler's January 1992 list. Adler's list included two names that were not in Brückner's November 1989 list. The cross-reference between the two lists, when Hannah laid them side by side at the kitchen table on the night of the eighteenth of June, produced a master list of nineteen names that was the most comprehensive operational map of the Custodia's senior membership that anyone outside the institution had been able to assemble in three decades.

Both names on Brückner's list that were not on Adler's were the names of two further Conclave members in Rome.

The names were: Augusto Vinciguerra. And Cardinal Umberto Caracciolo, age seventy-nine, retired Curial cardinal, resident at the Domus Sanctae Marthae in the Vatican City since 1988.

Hannah had registered the Vinciguerra name as confirmation of Margaret's identification.

She had registered the Caracciolo name as a new fact for the team. Margaret said: 'Caracciolo is seventy-nine. He has held three Roman chairs since 1962 and edited the Pontifical Academy's classical history journal for sixteen years. He is the philological mind of the Conclave. He is also the only member of it who has, by anything I have read in his published work, treated the older texts as if they still contained something he was hoping to find. He may be the most dangerous man at the table for us. He may also be the only man at the table I would have wanted to argue with.'

She had registered them both at the kitchen table at twenty-three-eleven on the eighteenth of June, with Heike at the table opposite her and the lamp on and Brückner's notebook open between them, and she had sent the registration up to Pasaia by Pascal's courier the following morning.

The Marzahn operation took place on the night of the seventh of July.

The access pass Hannah had provided had been arranged through a handful of small specific bureaucratic transactions Eddie's man at Marzahn had been arranging for Hannah since February. The pass was authentic. The signatory protocol was the protocol Margaret had identified in the green notebook. Heike, as the biological daughter of the original signatory, was the only person living who could lawfully retrieve the file.

Heike walked into the Marzahn records facility at twenty-two-forty-eight.

She walked out in the dark on the morning of the eighth.

In her left hand she carried a thin cardboard file four inches by six by half an inch thick, sealed with a strip of paper that bore Erika Vollmer's signature in green ink, dated 17. Mai 1973.

In her right hand she carried a canvas bag. The bag contained her own ID, her copy of the access protocol, and a folded piece of paper Hannah had written for her in case the operation went wrong. The paper had the address of a safe house in Magdeburg and the name of a man who would, on the basis of the paper, get her to the German-Austrian border within twelve hours.

The operation did not go wrong.

She walked out of the facility into the parking lot.

Hannah was at the wheel of a gray Trabant she had bought from a man on the Karl-Marx-Allee the previous afternoon. The engine was running. The lights were off.

Heike got in.

Hannah pulled out of the parking lot in the dark before dawn.

The two of them drove west across the city in the slow gray first light of a Berlin July morning. The file was on Heike's lap. The small canvas bag was at her feet. Hannah's hands were on the wheel at the position the hands of a careful driver were on the wheel in the dark hour before dawn, when the careful driver had a piece of paper next to her that the institution had been waiting twenty-six years to keep from anyone outside itself.

They crossed the Oberbaumbrücke as the sky began to gray.

By the time the Crellestrasse bakery had begun to warm its first ovens beneath them, they were in the safe-house flat in Schöneberg.

Hannah opened the file.

The file contained four sheets of typing paper.

The first sheet was Erika Vollmer's own statement, dated 17. Mai 1973, on the institutional letterhead of her Stasi department. The statement was a single paragraph. It read, in the careful institutional German of a senior Stasi officer who had decided to leave a piece of paper for her daughter against the contingency of being herself silenced:

This file is the registration of three names. The three names are the operational handlers who controlled the Custodia Auspiciorum's penetration of the State Security Service of the German Democratic Republic between 1958 and the present date. I, Erika Vollmer, served as the principal asset of that penetration without my knowledge between 1958 and 1962 and with my knowledge between 1962 and the present. I am leaving this file for the institutional record because I have, in the past month, registered that the architecture has begun to use me against the Stasi in ways that will, in time, terminate my biological life by means I will not be permitted to record. The file is therefore the small protection I am leaving against the architecture's continuing use of me after my death. The reading of the file is restricted to my biological daughter, who is at this date fifteen years old and who is in the care of an arrangement with which the architecture has not, to my knowledge, become operationally involved. The reading is therefore deferred to the daughter's majority. I sign this on the seventeenth of May 1973 in Magdeburg.

The second, third, and fourth sheets were each a single typed page. Each page contained one name and an operational annotation.

The three names were:

Augusto Vinciguerra. Roma, Via Giulia 142. Conclave.

Friedrich Adler. Wien, Bäckerstrasse. Coordinator, Habsburg arc.

Wolfgang Brückner. Berlin, Prenzlauer Berg. Coordinator, Northern arc, primary contact 1965–.

Heike read the three pages.

She read them once.

She read them twice.

Then she set them down on the kitchen table of the Crellestrasse flat, and she put her hands flat on the table on either side of them, and she did not, for some minutes, speak.

Hannah did not interrupt the silence.

After some time Heike said: Mein Stiefvater hat ihren Tod arrangiert.

My stepfather arranged her death.

Hannah said: Yes. He signed the closure himself, by Coordinator authority, on the eleventh of June 1973. The signing is on the second sheet of the file you have just read. Wolfgang Brückner had been her primary contact for eight years and the man who decided when an asset had become a liability. The deciding was his.

Heike said: And then he raised me.

Hannah said: Yes.

Heike said: And he died waiting for the man your friend sent.

Hannah said: Yes.

Heike said: And the man your friend sent was the man who had the right to send him.

Hannah said: Yes.

Heike said: Then we work.

Hannah said: Then we work.

Heike picked up the three pages.

She put them back in the cardboard file. She sealed the file with a fresh strip of paper torn from the kitchen pad on which the bakery downstairs took its weekly orders, and she signed the new strip in green ink in her own hand, dated 8. Juli 1992, Berlin.

She set the file on the table.

She said, in English, for the first time in the four weeks Hannah had been working with her: 'When do I meet the others.'

Hannah said: 'When the kill in Bilbao is finished. We expect a confirmation in the next twenty-four hours. After that we go south.'

Heike said: 'Bilbao.'

Hannah said: 'Bilbao. The Iberian Coordinator. His name is Eñaut Iturbe. The kill is tonight. The kill is at twenty-two-twenty-six on the Calle Carnicería Vieja in the Casco Viejo. The man taking the kill is the man who was at your stepfather's door. The driver is Klaus.'

Heike said: 'And the fourth.'

Hannah said: 'The fourth is the woman you have not met. Her name is Margaret Howell. She is fifty-six. She is a Latinist. She has been keeping the running file on the Custodia for nine years. She is the ex-wife of the man at your stepfather's door. They divorced in 1984. They are at a Basque port in the Spanish north. We will be at the same port within the week.'

Heike said: 'Howell. She wrote the Speculum paper on Theodosian 16.10.20.'

Hannah said: 'Yes.'

Heike said: Mein Stiefvater hat das Papier auf seinem Schreibtisch zwei Wochen lang gehabt.

My stepfather kept the paper on his desk for two weeks.

Hannah said: I do not know whether he registered her by name. He registered her work.

Heike said: 'I have read the paper. I have read it three times. I had not known the writer was the ex-wife of the man who would come to my father's bay window.'

Hannah said: 'No.'

Heike said: 'Then I will be at the Basque port in a week.'

Hannah said: 'A week.'

Heike's left hand, which had been flat on the table, came up and closed around the spine of the book. Heike said: 'Yes.'

She stood.

She went to the small window of the kitchen.

She looked out at the Crellestrasse in the early-morning gray light, with the yeast and cardamom of the Turkish bakery below beginning to come up the stairwell.

She said, without turning: 'I am very tired.'

Hannah said: 'There is a room. The bed is the bed on the right.'

Heike walked into the second room without speaking further. She closed the door.

Hannah sat at the kitchen table for some hours alone. She drank two cups of coffee and read, twice, the three sheets of typing paper from Erika Vollmer's file. She thought, in the second reading, about her brother Michael Doyle and a man named Christofi in a phone kiosk in Brussels in February of 1991 and a primary-school teacher in Birnam who had been keeping a green notebook for eighteen months, and the specific arithmetic that had made each of those three facts the consequence of one of the other two.

The sky lightened over the rooftops opposite.

The bakery below began to warm the ovens.

Early in the morning the courier brought the first message of the day.

It was a folded slip of flimsy paper inside the loaf of brown bread the bakery delivered to her door each morning. The slip was in Klaus's hand.

The slip read: Bilbao confirmed. 22:26. The Brahms second movement. We are at the harbor. Come.

Hannah folded the slip.

She put it in the inside pocket of her jacket.

She went into the second room.

Heike was already awake. Heike was sitting on the edge of the bed in the same brown wool jumper and the same brown corduroy skirt of the bakery. The wire-rimmed glasses were folded on the bedside table.

Hannah said: 'Bilbao is confirmed.'

Heike said: 'Then we go.'

Hannah said: 'We go.'

The two of them packed the canvas bags they had each been keeping for the eventuality. Hannah took the green file. Hannah took the Stiftung letter. Hannah took the small cardboard from Marzahn. Heike took two changes of clothing and the paperback Kassandra and a framed photograph of her stepfather she had taken from the Lychener Strasse apartment in May, in which he was standing on a beach in Rügen in the summer of 1971 with his right hand on the small two-year-old shoulder of a brown-haired girl in a yellow dress.

They left the Crellestrasse flat in the morning.

By the evening they were in Frankfurt.

By the morning of the tenth they were in Bayonne.

By the afternoon of the eleventh they were on the bench at the corner of the western quay in Pasaia San Pedro, with Joxe Mari on the bench beside them and Calder coming down the calle to meet them and Klaus three paces back in the doorway of the fishmonger's and Margaret at the kitchen window above with her hand on the sill.

The team was now five.

The list still had two.

The list still had Vinciguerra.

The list still had the seven men in Rome.

But the team that was going to take the list was now five. The five were, on the afternoon of the eleventh of July 1992, in one Basque village on one Atlantic bay. The green notebook was on the table. The maps were on the floor. The work of the next twelve months was in the lamp-lit kitchen of a first-floor flat above a fishmonger's that smelled of salt and fish-oil and the specific pine-rosin of a Basque country wine.

The work was now the work of five.

20
THE CLOCK

Lausanne—July 1992

On the fourth night of reading the Adler ledger at the kitchen table in Pasaia, Calder found the name.

It was not on the seventeen-name list on page one. It was on page forty-three, in a marginal annotation beside an entry dated November 1974. The entry recorded an institutional disbursement—a quarterly pension, drawn on a Liechtenstein trust, paid to a numbered account at the Banque Cantonale Vaudoise in Lausanne. The annotation, in Adler's careful hand, read: Thornley, L.H.—admin. dormant since '74. BCV Lsne. Hôtel du Théâtre, r. permanente.

Calder had been carrying the name since Greenwich. He had been carrying it in the half-second between the manila envelope Andrew Ruskin delivered at 19:47 on the third of January and the six photographs he had spread across the Chief's desk at oh-nine-thirty-two on the morning of the fourth. The six photographs had shown the face of a man whose administrative signature had been on every operational directive the Custodia had issued through the NATO counter-proliferation desk since 1967. The man had been officially dead since September of 1974. A faked motor accident on the A21 in Kent—a car driven off the road by a man who had himself died four months later, a death certificate signed by a coroner who retired six weeks after signing it, a cremation ordered by a cousin who did not exist in British civil records. The man had been, by the careful institutional discipline of four intelligence services across three decades, the one asset whose existence none of them would acknowledge. The man was Laurence Henry Thornley. The man was the clock.

He showed Klaus the annotation.

Klaus said: 'Lausanne.'

Calder said: 'Lausanne. The Hôtel du Théâtre. A permanent resident.'

Klaus said: 'He has been there for eighteen years.'

Calder said: 'He has been there because the clock needs a quiet room. The man is process. He does not hide in the manner of a man who is hiding. He hides in the manner of a permanent guest at a small Swiss hotel who pays in cash from a Liechtenstein pension and reads the Neue Zürcher Zeitung in the morning and walks to the lake in the afternoon and eats alone at the corner table in the evening. The hiding is the process. The process is the clock.'

Klaus said: 'And the clock is not on the list.'

Calder said: 'The clock is not on the list because the list is Margaret's list and Margaret's list is the Coordinators and the Conclave. Thornley is neither. Thornley is the administration. Thornley is the man who signed the directives. Thornley is the man whose signature is on the order that killed Elena on the third of January 1990.'

Klaus was quiet for some seconds.

Then he said: 'I will drive you to Bayonne on Thursday.'

Calder said: 'Thursday.'

On Wednesday the fifteenth of July Klaus drove Calder to Bayonne in the Land Rover. Calder took the afternoon train to Geneva. He changed at Geneva for the lakeside train to Lausanne.

He arrived at twenty-one-forty.

The Hôtel du Théâtre was on a small street behind the Place de la Riponne, a four-storey building of the kind Lausanne had been keeping since the previous century. Cream stucco. Green shutters. A glass door with brass fittings that had been polished every morning since before the war. The hotel had eleven rooms and a small dining room and a library of dark oak and leather that the proprietor kept for his long-term guests.

Calder took a room on the second floor under the name John Howell. He paid in cash. He did not request a room number. He was given Room 14.

He watched Thornley for three days.

Thornley's routine was the routine of a man who had been providing consistency for forty years and had, in the eighteen years of his administrative death, continued to provide it to himself. The routine was a clock. The clock did not vary. The clock did not need to vary. The clock had been set, at some hour in the autumn of 1974, to the rhythm of a small Swiss hotel, and the clock had not, in the eighteen years since, lost a minute.

Breakfast at oh-seven-thirty in the hotel dining room. The corner table by the window. A pot of English tea and two slices of toast with honey. The Neue Zürcher Zeitung, read front to back, folded in quarters. The reading took forty minutes.

At oh-eight-fifteen he returned to his room on the third floor. Room 17. He stayed in the room until oh-nine-forty-five.

At oh-nine-forty-five he walked—always walked, never took a tram—down the rue du Théâtre to the Ouchy promenade along the lake. The walk took eighteen minutes. He walked the promenade east for twenty-two minutes. He turned at the small marina beside the Château d'Ouchy. He walked back. He stopped at a bench above the water—the same bench, third from the eastern end, facing the Savoy shore—and sat for twelve minutes. He did not feed the birds. He did not read. He sat with his hands on his knees and his back straight and his eyes on the water the way a man sat when the sitting was not rest but process. The process was the twelve minutes. The twelve minutes were the clock.

At eleven he walked back up the hill to the hotel.

Lunch at twelve-thirty. The plat du jour. A glass of mineral water. No conversation with the staff beyond the placing of the order.

At fourteen he retired to his room.

At sixteen he came down to the library and read for two hours. On the first day he read the Financial Times. On the second and third he read a slim institutional history of the Bank for International Settlements. The reading was the reading of a man who had been administering the financial architecture of a European institution for three decades and who continued, in his administrative death, to keep his institutional literacy at the level the institution had trained him to keep it.

Dinner at nineteen-thirty. The corner table. A half-carafe of white wine. The plat du jour. The meal took fifty minutes. He ate with the specific deliberation of a man who had decided that the meal was not nourishment but schedule.

At twenty-one he retired.

The clock was the clock. The clock did not deviate. The clock was, in its eighteen years of ticking in a small Swiss hotel, the purest expression of the institutional discipline Calder had encountered since he had begun the work.

In the three days of watching, Calder registered three additional facts.

The first was the ring. It was on the right hand's little finger, where it had been in the photographs Dina had taken at the

Spanish embassy reception in Tel Aviv and in the six photographs Calder had carried into Century House. A gold signet ring with the worn intaglio of a sun with an eye at its center—eight rays, slightly uneven from the wear of generations. It was the same device he had seen on Vernet's right hand in Marseilles and on Christofi's right in Brussels. The ring was the uniform. The uniform was worn by the man who did not require cruelty.

The second was the face. Calder had seen the face six times in the six photographs. The face in the photographs had been the unremarkable face of a man in his late fifties with a receding hairline and the eyes of a man looking left at something out of frame. The face was now sixty-one. The hairline had receded further. The jaw had loosened in the way a jaw loosened on a man who ate alone. The eyes still looked left when the man was thinking. The man was always thinking. The thinking was the administration.

The third was Thornley's left hand. On the second morning, at breakfast, as Thornley lifted the teapot, Calder registered a small tremor in the left hand that had not been present in the right. The tremor was not the tremor of age. The tremor was the tremor of a man whose left hand had been carrying, for some unspecified number of years, a private neurological fact the right hand had not yet been told about. The tremor lasted for two seconds. The teapot did not spill. The hand corrected itself. The correction was the process.

On the evening of the third day—Friday the seventeenth of July—Calder went to his room and took from the inside lining of the leather notebook a single photograph he had been carrying since the morning of the fourth of January 1990.

The photograph was the sixth of the six. It was the photograph that showed Thornley's face at the Bermondsey meeting—three-quarter profile, the gold ring visible on the right hand, the eyes looking left at something out of frame. It was the photograph Calder had held in his hand at oh-nine-thirty-two on the morning of the fourth of January when he had set it on the Chief's desk and said the word that had begun the work. The word had been: I resign. He had been carrying the photograph for thirty months. He had been carrying it in the same leather notebook that held the pencil page. The photograph was not on the pencil page. The photograph was the page before the page.

He turned the photograph over. On the back, in pencil, in his careful right-leaning hand, he wrote three lines:

Room 14. 20:00. 2 January.

The room number was the room at the Mayflower in which Calder had been summoned on the second of January 1990 at twenty-hundred—the summons that had begun the architecture's forty-hour sequence ending in the body swap at Greenwich. The time was the time of that summons. The date was the date. The three together were the institutional grammar of the Custodia's own operational discipline—a summons in the format only a man who had been inside the architecture would recognize.

He sealed the photograph in a plain white envelope. He addressed the envelope, in pencil, to L. Hargreaves, Room 17.

At oh-six-fifteen on Saturday morning he went down to the lobby. The night porter was in the office behind the counter. The desk was unmanned. Calder placed the envelope in the wooden mail-slot marked 17. He went back upstairs. He shaved. He looked at the puckered moon of the scar on the right shoulder. He touched it.

He waited.

◆◆◆

At oh-seven-thirty-five Thornley came down to breakfast. He collected his post from the wooden slot—the envelope and a

Swiss telephone bill—and took them to his corner table.

Calder was at a table across the dining room with a copy of the Tribune de Genève. He did not look up.

Thornley opened the telephone bill first. He set it to the side. He opened the white envelope.

Calder, from behind the Tribune, watched Thornley's hands.

The hands were steady. They were the hands of a man who had been opening envelopes for forty years and had decided, approximately thirty years earlier, that no envelope would change the set of his fingers. The right hand drew the photograph from the envelope. The right hand turned the photograph face-up on the table beside the toast rack. The gold ring caught the morning light through the window.

Thornley looked at the photograph for fifteen seconds. He did not move. He did not set down the teacup he was holding in his left hand. The left hand did not tremble. The clock had received its information. The clock was processing it.

He turned the photograph over. He read the three lines on the back. He read them once. He set the photograph face-down on the table. He placed his right hand flat on the photograph—the gold ring against the photographic paper—and held the hand there for the count of three.

Then he resumed his breakfast. He drank his tea. He ate his toast. He folded the Neue Zürcher Zeitung in quarters. He collected the telephone bill and the photograph and went upstairs at the usual oh-eight-fifteen.

The clock had received its instruction. The clock would respond. The clock would respond because the clock was process, and the process required response. The machine did not require courage. The machine required consistency.

At nineteen-forty Calder set the room.

He placed the five remaining Bermondsey photographs—the five that did not show Thornley's face—in a row on the narrow desk beneath the window. He drew the curtain three-quarters closed. He turned the desk lamp on. He turned the overhead light off. The room was dim. The photographs were visible.

He took the new Welrod from the leather case. He checked the magazine. He worked the bolt. The action was tighter than it had been at Bilbao—a small increase in the resistance of the slide that was, by the mechanical discipline of a suppressed bolt-action pistol whose wipes had been fired twice, the first sign that the instrument was entering the third quarter of its operational life. Eddie had estimated five clean firings, perhaps six. This would be the third. The third was the firing at which a prudent man checked the action twice. Calder checked it twice. The bolt seated. The round chambered. The action was tight but functional.

He stood behind the door. He held the Welrod at low ready against his right thigh. He waited.

At nineteen-fifty-eight he heard footsteps on the corridor carpet. The footsteps were the footsteps of a man of sixty-one who walked at the pace of a man whose administrative discipline had taught him that haste was the signature of an operation that had not been properly filed. The footsteps stopped outside Room 14.

There was a pause of four seconds.

Then a single knock. Firm. The knock of a man who had been knocking on institutional doors for forty years and had decided, approximately thirty years earlier, that one knock was sufficient.

Calder did not respond.

After three seconds Thornley tried the handle. The door was unlocked. Calder had left it unlocked.

The door opened.

Thornley came in.

He was wearing the dark-gray suit he wore to dinner. The gold ring was on his right hand. His hands were empty. He had left everything in his own room—wallet, keys, the photograph Calder had sent him. The emptiness was the process. The process was the administrative discipline of a man who had been attending institutional summoned for forty years and who understood, by the grammar of the three lines on the back of the photograph, that the summons required him to arrive without personal effects. The clock had read the instruction. The clock had complied.

He saw the five photographs on the desk.

He walked to the desk. He stood looking at the photographs for five seconds. He registered the five faces that were not his. He registered the absence of the sixth—his own face, the face he had received that morning.

He said, without turning, in the English of a man who had been born in Vienna to an Austrian mother and raised at an English school and had been speaking the language for fifty years with the faint residual Habsburg vowel the English had never quite burned out of him: 'The filing is incomplete.'

Calder stepped from behind the door.

Thornley turned.

He saw Calder. He saw the Welrod.

He registered Calder the way a man of process registered an operational fact—without alarm, without the dilation of the pupils that had been the first physiological response of Vernet and Brückner and Adler and Iturbe in the seconds before Calder had fired. The pupils did not dilate. The pupils of a man of process did not dilate because the man of process had decided, at some administrative hour decades earlier, that the dilation of the pupils was not a response the institution required.

He said: 'You are the man from the photographs.'

Calder said: 'I am.'

Thornley said: 'The Bermondsey photographs. The operation in January of 1990. The resignation.'

Calder said: 'Yes.'

Thornley said: 'You have been a long time coming.'

Calder said: 'I have been doing the other work first.'

Thornley looked at the Welrod. He looked at it the way a man who had been signing operational directives for thirty years looked at the instrument those directives had been designed to deploy—with the specific administrative recognition of a man who had approved the purchase order for the suppressed 7.65mm bolt-action pistol program in 1968 and had initialled, in the same careful hand, the quarterly ammunition requisitions ever since.

He said: 'That is one of ours.'

Calder said: 'It was.'

Calder brought the Welrod up. He fired.

The bolt rotated. The firing pin struck the primer.

The round did not discharge.

The sound the Welrod made was the sound of a bolt striking a dead primer—a dry metallic click, precise, definitive, that filled the hotel room the way a misfire filled any room in which a man had committed his body to the specific set of muscular contractions that a killing required and the killing had not come. The click was the loudest sound in the room. The click was louder than the cough the Welrod would have made if the round had fired. The click was the sound of a Belgian primer that had been manufactured in a batch of seven at a munitions works outside Liège in the autumn of 1991 and had been, by the small statistical incidence of all primer manufacture, the one round in the batch whose mercury fulminate charge had not been seated to the depth the firing pin required.

Calder worked the bolt. The unfired round ejected into his left palm. He cycled the next round. He brought the Welrod up.

In the one and a half seconds the cycling had taken, Thornley moved.

Thornley was sixty-one. Thornley was not a field operative. Thornley had not been a field operative since 1967. But Thornley had been an MI6 officer for fourteen years between 1953 and 1967, and the training the Fort had given him in 1953 included a set of close-quarters responses the body retained long after the man had stopped using them. The body retained them the way a clock retained the memory of the hour it had been wound to. Thornley's body used one. He lunged for the door.

Calder did not fire the second round. Thornley was between him and the door. The angle was wrong. The subsonic 7.65mm Browning round required a stationary or near-stationary target at close range for the aortic placement Calder had been practising in mirrors for two and a half years. The placement required the chest to be facing him. The chest was not facing him. The chest was moving.

Thornley reached the door. His right hand found the handle. He pulled the door inward.

Calder dropped the Welrod on the bed.

He took the piano wire from the leather pouch in his right coat pocket. He worked the wooden handles into his palms in the quarter-second Klaus had drilled into him at the harbor—left handle seated against the heel of the left palm, right handle against the heel of the right, the wire taut between them at eighteen inches, the killing length.

Thornley had the door open six inches. The corridor light fell across his right shoe and the hem of his dark-gray trousers.

Calder's left hand caught the door above Thornley's hand and drove it shut. His right hand looped the wire over Thornley's head from behind in the motion Klaus had taught him in the basement of the harbor flat in the third month—the same motion he had used on the postman in the Geneva alley, the same motion Klaus had said was for the moment the instrument failed. The wire dropped to the level of the throat. Calder pulled backward and crossed his wrists.

The wire bit.

The first thing the wire cut was the external jugular vein on the left side of the neck, two centimetres below the angle of the jaw. The vein opened at the pressure a nineteen-gauge steel wire produced when drawn across living tissue by a man whose arms were pulling at full extension. The blood came—venous, dark, at moderate pressure—in a sheet that went forward across the inside of the door and onto the cream-painted wood and the brass chain-lock and the brass number plate that read 14. The spray pattern on the door was the pattern a lateral laceration of the external jugular produced at a distance of four inches from the substrate—a fan, twelve inches across at the widest point, darkening from the edges inward as the initial arterial mist gave way to the heavier venous flow.

Thornley's hands came up to the wire. Both hands. The fingers of both hands got under the wire on the right side, where the crossing of Calder's wrists had produced a fraction less pressure than the left. The gold ring on the little finger of the right hand pressed against the wire. The wire, impartial, cut into the adjacent ring finger to the depth of the proximal phalanx. Blood came from the finger—bright arterial blood now, from the proper digital artery, a different color and a different pressure from the venous blood on the door. The blood from the finger ran down the wire to Calder's right handle and made the handle wet.

Calder drove his right knee into the small of Thornley's back. He pulled the wire backward and upward at the forty-five-degree angle Klaus had demonstrated—backward and up, so that the wire moved across the anterior surface of the throat toward the carotid sheath rather than the trachea. The carotid sheath contained the common carotid artery, the internal jugular vein, and the vagus nerve in a fascial envelope at the lateral border of the thyroid cartilage. The wire reached the sheath at the second second.

The common carotid artery opened.

The blood that came from the carotid was arterial—bright, oxygenated, at the systolic pressure of a man whose heart was still beating at approximately a hundred and forty beats per minute from the adrenaline of the lunge for the door. The blood came in a pulsed jet that followed the rhythm of the heartbeat. The first pulse hit the door at the level of the chain-lock. The second hit the wall beside the door at the height of Thornley's right shoulder. The third hit the carpet at the base of the door in a dark fan-shaped spread that would, by the time the morning staff found it, have soaked through the weave of the carpet to the floorboards beneath and through the floorboards to the plaster of the ceiling of the room below.

Thornley's legs gave at the fourth second. His knees went. He dropped. The weight of his body—thirteen stone, the weight of a man who had eaten the plat du jour at a corner table for eighteen years—came down against the wire at the full hanging weight of a man whose legs had ceased to function. The wire held. Calder held. The wire cut deeper. The trachea opened at the fifth second—a small wet sound, not a gasp, because the lungs behind the trachea had already lost the air pressure to produce a gasp. The sound was the sound of a structure failing. The structure was the throat.

The hands fell from the wire at the sixth second.

The body went still at the seventh.

Calder held for three seconds more. He counted them. The counting was the discipline.

He got the wire off.

He stepped back.

He let the body settle forward against the door. Thornley came to rest with his forehead against the brass plate marked 14 and his right hand at his side. The gold ring on the little finger was wet and dark. The ring finger beside it was cut to the bone. The throat was open from the external jugular on the left to the carotid sheath on the right in a single transverse laceration eight inches across that had, in the seven seconds of the wire's work, opened every major vessel and structure in the anterior triangle of the neck. The dark-gray suit at the collar and the chest were black with blood. The carpet beneath the body was wet in a radius of two feet. The door was painted in the arterial spray from the chain-lock to the floor in the specific fan pattern Calder had not seen before and would, in the years that followed, not be able to stop seeing.

He stood for three seconds. His breathing was at fifty-five per minute. His right shoulder was performing the clean ache. His hands to the wrists were wet. The wire handles were wet. The wire itself, in the eighteen-inch length Klaus had cut for him, had a small concavity in the fifth inch from the left handle where the wire had pressed against the anterior surface of the cervical vertebrae and had found, in the bone, the limit of what nineteen-gauge steel could do to a living man in seven seconds.

The room was quiet.

He wiped his hands on the hotel towel from the bathroom. He wiped the wire handles. He placed the wire back in the leather pouch. He put the pouch in his right coat pocket.

He retrieved the Welrod from the bed. He ejected the chambered round—the round that would have fired—and examined the mechanism. The bolt cycled cleanly. The action was tight but functional. The misfire had been the primer. A single defective round from a batch of seven. The Welrod itself was sound. The instrument had not failed. The ammunition had. The distinction was the distinction of a man who had been trusting instruments for thirty months and had, on the third firing, been taught by a Belgian primer that trust was a discipline and not a guarantee.

He placed the Welrod back in its case. He placed the case in the inside left pocket of his coat.

He went through Thornley's pockets. The pockets were empty. Thornley had come to the summons with nothing. The nothing was the final administrative act.

Calder took the gold ring from the little finger of the right hand. The ring came off with the small wet resistance a ring made when the finger beneath it was slick with blood. He held the ring for a moment. He turned it in the lamplight. The intaglio—the sun with the eye at the center, the eight rays—was the intaglio he had seen on the hands of dead men in four countries across two and a half years. He placed the ring in the inside left pocket of his coat, beside the leather notebook.

He picked up the five photographs from the desk. He laid them beside the body, face-up, in a row on the wet carpet. He took the sixth photograph—the one showing Thornley's face—from the inside pocket of his coat, where he had been keeping a duplicate since Pasaia, and set it at the end of the row. Six photographs. Six faces. The filing was now complete.

He looked at Thornley.

Thornley's expression—in the seven seconds between the wire and the stillness—had not been the expression of a man who was afraid. It had not been the expression of a man who was angry. It had been the expression of a man who had understood, in the administrative discipline of his entire career, that the clock he had been providing for forty years had been, by a man with a length of piano wire in a hotel room in Lausanne, stopped. The expression was the expression of a clock at the moment of its stopping—not grief, not resistance, but the specific quality of a mechanism that had run its course and was now, by the application of an external force, no longer running. The face was the face of a man who had not complained. The face was the face of a man who had marked the hour.

The expression was the seventh.

The room held its breath for a moment longer than the room had reason to. Calder stood at the foot of the bed in the silence the wire had left. The door at his back held its pattern.

Calder opened the window. The alley below was dark. He climbed out onto the narrow stone ledge. He dropped the six feet to the cobbles below. The right shoulder registered the landing with the clean protest the wound had been lodging since November.

He walked out of the alley onto the street behind the hotel. On the low stone wall beside the alley mouth, in the yellow of the streetlamp, was a small folded paper crane. It was the size of a thumbnail. The folds were precise. The paper was dry. It had been placed there within the hour. Calder registered it without stopping. He filed it in the place where he had been filing the cranes since Brussels. His shirt cuffs were wet inside his coat sleeves. He turned the cuffs up against the dark of the fabric. The stains were not visible at the angle of a man walking under streetlights. They would be visible in daylight. Daylight was eleven hours away. He would not be in Lausanne in eleven hours.

He walked four blocks to the Lausanne railway station. He bought a ticket to Geneva under the Howell name. He waited on the platform. He boarded the twenty-one-fourteen.

On the train he went to the lavatory. He washed his hands. He washed them twice. The blood came off the backs of the hands on the first washing. It came off the cuticles and the creases of the knuckles on the second. The water in the basin was pink. He let it drain. He dried his hands on the paper towels. He folded the cuffs of his shirt back to their proper position. The cuffs were stained at the inner seam. The inner seam was the problem for tomorrow. Tomorrow was Bayonne. Bayonne would have a laundry.

He went back to his seat.

He took the leather notebook from the inside left pocket of his coat. He opened the pencil page. He took the pencil from the leather pouch.

Thornley was not on the list. Thornley was the man who had administered the list that had produced the list. The man was not a Coordinator. The man was not Conclave. The man was the process by which the Coordinators and the Conclave had been permitted to do the work the Custodia did. He was the institutional ligature. He was the thing that held the other things together in the filing cabinet of the architecture's operational life.

He wrote, below the entry for Iturbe:

8. Thornley, L.H. Lausanne. The administrator. The clock. Off list. The wire.

He drew a single horizontal line through the entry. The line was clean. His hand did not shake.

He folded the page. He put the notebook away.

The clock had stopped.

The work was the work.

He reached Bayonne at oh-three-forty on the morning of the twentieth. Klaus was at the station with the Land Rover. They drove south to Pasaia. They reached the flat at oh-six-twenty. Margaret was at the kitchen window with the lamp on and the green notebook open. She did not ask where he had been. She handed him a cup of tea. He drank it.

He set the gold ring on the kitchen table between her cup and his. He set the ejected round beside the ring. Eddie would collect it on Friday. Eddie would hold the round to the light of the chandler's bench lamp and turn it once and say, in the flat voice he kept for mechanical failures: The primer seat is shallow. Belgian batch. I will test twice from now on. The testing-twice would become, in the years that followed, the operational discipline by which no round Calder carried would fail again.

She looked at the ring. She looked at the intaglio. She looked at the eight rays and the eye.

She said: 'The administrator.'

He said: 'The administrator.'

She said: 'The clock.'

He said: 'The clock has stopped.'

She picked up the ring. She held it for a moment. She set it back on the table. She did not ask about the wire. She did not ask about the blood. She did not ask about the filing. The not-asking was the discipline of a woman who had sent her former husband to Lausanne with a pencil page and a photograph and had received him back with a gold ring and a tea. The not-asking was the marriage.

He went to bed. He lay in the dark and listened to the tide-mill below the flat. The tide-mill had been turning since before either of them had been born. It turned now.

In the morning they would begin the preparations for Vila Praia.

21

VIANA DO CASTELO

Pasaia / Bayonne / Northern Portugal—
Late July to early September 1992

The five of them were at the table in the Pasaia flat for ten days.

They were not, in those ten days, five operational agents in a working safe-house. They were five people who had not been five people in one room together at any point in the previous five years and who were not, by the careful protocols a successful operational cell had to observe, going to be five people in one room together again at any unscheduled hour. The ten days at Pasaia were therefore the hour before the dispersal. Calder and Klaus understood this. Margaret understood it. Hannah, who had been the operational planner for fifteen months at the level of slips of paper through Pascal, understood it most of all. Heike, who was the youngest by a margin of fifteen years and who was the newest by a margin of seventeen months, understood it because she had been told, in the way Hannah told a young person an operational reality, that this would be the only ten days.

They worked at the table.

They ate at the table.

They mapped the Hjorth kill in Lillehammer for the twentieth of September. They mapped the Akritas kill in Athens for the seventeenth of November. They mapped, less precisely, the set of coordinated approaches that would, after the seventeenth of November, be available to them against the seven Conclave members and their three deputies in Rome.

They mapped, on an additional sheet of typing paper Margaret produced on the following morning, the seven possible meetings with Augusto Vinciguerra at seven possible locations, with the specific reasoning for each, ranked by the operational risk to the team and by the symbolic clarity of the choice for Vinciguerra.

The seven possible meeting locations were:

Birnam, the cottage (highest symbolic clarity for V., highest operational risk for us);

A small Italian academic library in a city of his choosing (low risk, low clarity, would permit him to come in the careful institutional discipline of his own life);

The chapel at the Trastevere monastery of Sant'Egidio (medium risk, high clarity, would require a Roman setting for the meeting);

A small Latin philological conference in Krakow scheduled for early October (low risk, low clarity, would permit V. cover);

A bench on the Pont des Arts in Paris on a Sunday afternoon (medium risk, medium clarity, would require V. to travel without institutional cover);

A small Latinists' working group at the British School at Rome in early November (medium risk, medium clarity, would permit V. cover);

A garden chair on the Piazzetta on Capri at sunset on a date of his choosing (low risk, high clarity, would permit V. the small theatricality of the offering).

Margaret had ranked them, on a separate small sheet, in the order in which she would, if she were Vinciguerra, find them acceptable as offers. Her ranking placed Capri at one and Birnam at seven.

She offered the rankings to the table.

The table considered.

Klaus said: Capri.

Hannah said: Capri.

Heike said: I do not know him. I cannot rank him. But the woman who has been writing to him for nine years has put Capri at one. I will follow the writer.

Calder said, after some seconds: Capri. With one revision. The date should be the third Sunday of October. The third Sunday of October falls after the Conclave's regular monthly meeting on the second Friday of October in Trastevere, the meeting at which Vinciguerra will have the operational opportunity to register his decision to leave the institution, ahead of the Capri conversation, in such a way that the institution will not be able to prevent the leaving. The third Sunday is the eighteenth. We will have, by that hour, taken Hjorth and have not yet taken Akritas. We will be in the operational pocket that exists between two of the three remaining kills. The pocket is the operational space we offer V. The offering is the offering.

Margaret said: The eighteenth of October.

Calder said: The eighteenth.

Margaret took the small additional sheet of typing paper. She wrote, at the top of it, in her careful left-leaning Latin hand:

Octobris die XVIII, hora decima nona, in Capri Piazzetta, ad sedile angulare ante Caffè Senafine. Verba: 'Adveniam ad te, et tu venies ad me.'

She folded the paper.

She handed it to Hannah.

She said: 'You have the channel. I do not. The channel is the channel I asked you for in May. The Pascal courier has, since June, had the running arrangement with a small bookseller's clerk in Trastevere who has, in his turn, the running arrangement with the Vatican Librarian's secretary, who has the small Tuesday-morning protocol with one of the four Latin doctors of the Pontifical Academy, of whom Vinciguerra is the most senior. The paper will reach Vinciguerra's reading desk by next Tuesday. He will register. He will come or he will not. The reading is the reading.'

Hannah took the paper.

She said: 'Margaret.'

Margaret said: 'Yes.'

Hannah said: 'If he comes.'

Margaret said: 'If he comes, then we are six, and the architecture is, by the public arithmetic of the nineteen names on the master list, one Conclave member short of operational quorum, and the institution will, by the discipline of its own grammar, have begun the small slow process of being unable to function. If he does not come, we are five, and the institution remains seven, and the work that began with a body swap in Greenwich on the morning of the fourth of January 1990 will require, for its completion, that we take the seven Conclave members in Rome at a pace and with a discipline we have not yet established. The two outcomes are the two outcomes. We will, on the eighteenth of October, find out which.'

Hannah folded the paper into the inside lining of the leather case in which she had been keeping the operational papers for sixteen months.

She did not speak again that morning.

On the last morning, on the table, Hannah laid out the small dispersal.

The dispersal went as follows.

Hannah would return to Berlin. She would resume the careful CIA closed-station discipline her cover had provided since 1991. She would be the team's Northern operational planner for the Hjorth kill and the seventeen-November Athens approach. She would communicate with the rest of the team through Pascal in Geneva and through a new courier she had identified in Vienna on the night of the second of June, a wiry archivist of the Hofbibliothek named Dr. Agnes Fuchs, who had been on Eddie's running register for years and who had agreed, on the basis of an operational demonstration Hannah had conducted in early June, to handle two pieces of paper a week between Vienna and Geneva.

Heike would go with Hannah to Berlin. She would, by Hannah's discipline, be the operational asset that Hannah's CIA cover did not register, and she would be Hannah's principal field hand for the Hjorth approach. She had, by her stepfather's papers, an institutional reading of the Custodia's Northern operations that no one outside the institution had been able to assemble in three decades, and she had, by her own measure of the previous fifteen months, the specific operational temperament a senior agent acquired in the field. She would not return to the Lychener Strasse apartment. The apartment had, by Hannah's reading of the institutional documents she had seen in late June, been registered by the architecture as a possible target since the second week of July, and it would, by the eighth, be a confirmed target. Heike would not be there to be a confirmed target. She would be at Hannah's Crellestrasse flat under a different name on a different lease.

Calder, Klaus, and Margaret would leave Pasaia at the end of July.

The leaving was not because the architecture had identified Pasaia as a location. The architecture had not, by Hannah's small specific reading of the institutional traffic at the end of June, identified Pasaia. The leaving was because, on the discipline a successful operational cell had to observe, the location at which a successful operation had been conducted on the eighth of July could not be the location at which the next operation was planned. The hygiene required relocation. The relocation had been arranged by Eddie in the second week of June.

The relocation was to a first-floor flat above a tide-mill in the village of Vila Praia de Âncora on the northern Atlantic coast of Portugal, twelve kilometers south of the Spanish border at the mouth of the Minho river. The flat had been the private summer house of a Portuguese widow whose husband had been on Eddie's running register for decades.

The widow had agreed to the arrangement on the basis of three considerations. The first was that Eddie's man in Lisbon was the same man her husband had served with in Mozambique. The second was that the lease had been paid in advance for nine months in escudos drawn from a Lisbon bank by a man whose passport she had not been required to inspect. The third was that the wooden statue of São Bento on the lintel of the flat's front door had been there for ninety years and would not be moved. The third had been Eddie's small private joke. The widow had not registered the joke. She had agreed to the lease.

Calder and Klaus and Margaret would arrive at the Vila Praia flat on the twenty-fourth.

They would be there until the morning of the fourteenth of October, when they would leave for Capri by way of a private launch from Bayonne to a Spanish freighter at Vigo to a Maltese cargo vessel at Lisbon to the Sicilian port of Palermo, from which the small inter-island ferry would put them on Capri on the morning of the seventeenth.

Margaret would, on the eighteenth of October, sit at a corner table at the Caffè Senafine on the Piazzetta of Capri at nineteen-hundred and wait.

Vinciguerra would arrive or he would not arrive.

The work of the next two months was the work of arriving at the seventeenth of October in operational fitness.

On the morning of the twenty-second they left.

Klaus drove the Land Rover.

Margaret sat in the front passenger seat with the green notebook on her lap and the leather satchel at her feet.

Calder rode in the back, lying down, with the dog blanket over him. The discipline was the discipline of a man whose face had been registered by the architecture on a passport at the Hendaye border in the first week of May. By the paranoia of a successful cell, he was not going to use the same border on the same passport on the same engine for the same direction.

They came south through Madrid, west through Salamanca, west again through the Portuguese border at Fuentes de Oñoro, and northwest through Porto to the coast.

They reached Vila Praia de Âncora two days later.

The widow met them at the gate. She handed Klaus the keys without speaking. She nodded at Margaret. She did not look at Calder. She walked back across the cobbled courtyard to her own house behind the tide-mill. She did not, while the three of them were in residence, speak to any of them again.

The flat had two rooms and a kitchen and a small balcony facing the Atlantic.

The view from the balcony was the view Margaret had not had at any kitchen window in any house she had occupied since the spring of 1981.

She stood at the balcony for a quarter of an hour on the morning of the twenty-fourth.

She did not speak.

She did not need to speak.

The Atlantic was doing what the Atlantic did.

He thought, briefly, of the operational coincidence: that the name on the valley in Cumbria was the same name as the name on his passport, and that the architecture had been patient with that coincidence for sixty years. He set the thought aside.

He thought of Elena's wrist, of the four directions inked on the inside of it, of the small dot at the center. He had been the dot, for sixteen years of his life. He was no longer the dot.

They did the work.

They mapped Hjorth.

They mapped Akritas.

They drafted, between them, the specific protocol Margaret would observe at the Caffè Senafine on the Piazzetta on the eighteenth of October.

They received, through Pascal's courier and through Hannah's new Vienna channel, the careful run of operational papers a successful cell received in the weeks before a major action.

In early August Hannah's CIA contact in Berlin confirmed, on the basis of a specific intelligence pickup at the Bundesnachrichtendienst, that the Conclave's audit of the third of January 1990 had been completed. The completion had occurred at the regular Trastevere meeting on the second Friday of August. The audit had identified Margaret Howell of Birkbeck College as the maker of the list, alive—the woman the architecture had thought it had eliminated on the third of January 1990 by killing Elena Vasilieva. The architecture had issued a kill order on her on the same day. The kill order had been allocated to a Portuguese contractor whose name was on Eddie's running register for years. By Eddie's small careful reading, the contractor's small private operational habits included a preference for the eight-millimeter bolt-action rifle and an aversion to coastal terrain. Both, by Eddie's reading, would be the useful pieces of information the team needed at Vila Praia.

The contractor would not, by Eddie's reading, attempt the kill in those weeks.

He would attempt it after the third Sunday of October on the assumption that the team had emerged from operational cover for the Capri meeting. He would, by Eddie's reading, position himself in Naples by the first week of October and would attempt, on a date and at a location the architecture would identify by intelligence pickup of the team's Capri travel papers, the kill on Margaret on the return journey.

Eddie would, by mid-September, have an operational counter-arrangement that would address the Portuguese contractor before the third Sunday.

The team would, in the meantime, do the work.

22
VIGO

Vigo / Vila Praia—Second week of September 1992

In the second week of September Calder went, alone, by ferry across the Minho to a small Galician village on the Spanish side, and he took the train south to Vigo, and he met Eddie Frears at a small taberna on the harbor wall for the first time since November of 1989.

Eddie had been in Lisbon for thirty months. He had aged in those months. The hair at the temples was now white. The hand he placed flat on the table when he sat down was the hand of a man who had been carrying, since the summer of 1990, the responsibility for keeping six adults alive across nine countries, and the hand had developed, in the weight of the carrying, a specific tremor that had not been there in 1989. He registered the tremor. He set the hand under the table and did not lift it back to the surface for the duration of the meeting.

He said: 'James.'

Calder said: 'Eddie.'

Eddie said: 'Hjorth.'

Calder replied: 'Hjorth.'

Eddie said: 'I have been reading the green notebook through Hannah's channel for eleven weeks. The Lillehammer approach is sound. The cathedral park is the right kill point. The twentieth of September is the right date. The walk after the eight-fifteen mass on the Sunday is the habitual walk Hjorth has been keeping for the last seven years and that is the operational space he has not registered as the operational space. He will be at the third bench from the eastern gate at oh-nine-fourteen. He will sit on the bench for eight minutes feeding the small cluster of pigeons that has been receiving him on the second and fourth Sundays since 1985. The kill point is the bench. The instrument is the new Welrod. The driver is Klaus. The route out is the route Margaret has identified through the southern gate, along Storgata to the rented car at Stortorget, and out of Lillehammer on the E6 toward Hamar.'

Calder said: 'Yes.'

Eddie said: 'I have arranged the cars.'

Calder said: 'And Margaret.'

Eddie said: 'Margaret stays at Vila Praia for the Hjorth operation. She will not leave the flat. She will not, in the four days you and Klaus are in Norway, register on any document. The widow has agreed to take the canvas bag of flour and the small basket of eggs to her three times a week so the lights in the flat are not the only lights at the tide-mill in those four days.'

Calder said: 'Good.'

Eddie said: 'And Capri.'

Calder said: 'Capri is the seventeenth.'

Eddie said: 'I have been arranging the route for ten weeks. The route is the route. The Maltese vessel is the specific consideration. The captain is the brother of the man at the Lisbon bookbinder who has been receiving Adler's running account at Vaduz for years. The captain has been told, by his brother, that the cargo is two pieces of paper and three people, and that the cargo is to be on Capri by oh-six-hundred on the morning of the seventeenth, and that the cargo will reembark, if it reembarks at all, on the night of the eighteenth. He has agreed.

He has not been told the names. He will not ask.'

Calder said: 'And the contractor in Naples.'

Eddie said: 'The contractor is a Portuguese named Jorge Cabral. He will be at the Naples station on the morning of the eighth of October. He will not be at the Naples station on the morning of the ninth. The arrangement for the eighth I have made. The arrangement is the arrangement. You will not need to register it. Margaret will not need to register it. Klaus will not need to register it. The contractor will be the small residual administrative matter the institution will be asked to clean up at its meeting on the second Friday of October.'

Calder nodded.

Eddie did not speak for some seconds.

Then he said: 'James.'

Calder said: 'Eddie.'

Eddie said: 'I am sixty.'

Calder said: 'I know.'

Eddie said: 'I have been at this for forty years. I have been at this with you for twenty-six. I have not, in the twenty-six, registered a piece of work the magnitude of the work the four of you and the German woman have been doing in the last three years. I want to say to you, before the eighteenth of October, that the work has been the work I have been waiting my career to be at the useful end of. I am sorry I did not say it in November of 1989 when you came to me in Lisbon and asked me, in Klaus's kitchen on the Beco do Carneiro, whether I would be at the useful end of a piece of work whose shape I had not yet seen. I am saying it now.'

Calder did not respond for some time.

Then he said: 'Eddie. The work has been the work because of the useful end you have been at. I have not, in all the months at the harbor, written a piece of paper that did not pass through a Lisbon postman who did not exist outside of your discipline of him. I have not, in the same months, fired a Welrod that did not have wipes you replaced. I have not, at Vila Praia, slept on a bed whose sheets were not laundered by a widow whose husband you knew. I will not, on the eighteenth of October, sit at a corner table on the Piazzetta of Capri with a Latinist whose Latin no living writer has matched in forty years if you have not, in the meantime, arranged the boat. The work is the work because of the man who arranges. You are the man who arranges.'

Eddie nodded once.

He did not lift the hand from under the table.

He said: 'On the eighteenth I will be in Lisbon. I will be at the second-floor flat above the bookshop on the rua do Alecrim. The flat is the flat I will be at when the message comes. The message will be either Vinciguerra has come or Vinciguerra has not come. I will be at the flat for either message.'

Calder said: 'Yes.'

They drank the glass of white vinho verde the proprietor had set down between them.

They did not speak again.

Eddie left the taberna at sixteen-eleven.

Calder caught the ferry back across the Minho at sixteen-forty.

He was at the flat at Vila Praia by eighteen-twenty.

23
LILLEHAMMER

Vila Praia / Lillehammer—19–27 September 1992

On the night of the nineteenth of September Calder stood on the cobbled jetty below the tide-mill at Vila Praia.

The Atlantic was the Atlantic. The wind was off the southwest. The bell-buoy at the harbor mouth was a different bell-buoy with the same small mournful note.

He had been at the small jetty for forty minutes.

Klaus had said, at the table at twenty-two-fifteen, that he should walk down to the jetty before sleeping if he had not yet decided whether he was prepared, on the morning, to begin the eighteen-hour journey to Lillehammer. Calder had not been certain whether he was prepared. He had walked down to the jetty.

The jetty had not, in the forty minutes, decided for him.

He thought about Margaret upstairs in the flat with the green notebook open on the kitchen table and the lamp on and the silver bracelet on her left wrist. The bracelet had, on the small key on its ring, the silver Zurich key she had switched in November of 1989. The original silver key—the one he had placed on the empty ring on the bracelet on the night of the third of November 1977 in the kitchen of the Chiswick house—was now in the canvas grip in the kitchen of the Vila Praia flat.

He had not, in all the time since the eleventh of May, asked her why she was no longer keeping the original key on the ring. She had not, in the same period, asked him why he had been carrying the second key in the inside lining of the leather notebook in the inside left pocket of his coat. The silence was the silence. It was the private discipline of two people who had decided, after their long separation, that what they had would resume by the careful protocol of accumulating un-asked questions, in the manner of the bracelet's original empty ring, for some unspecified hour in the future at which the questions would either be asked or be the answer.

He thought about Klaus upstairs with the small calibrated mark on the inside of the watchband. The mark had now four ink lines on it, with the dates 27. VIII. 1990, 2. XI. 1991, 18. II. 1992, and 14. VIII. 1992. The fourth line was an eighth of an inch outboard of the third. The third had been a sixteenth outboard of the second. The second had been a sixteenth outboard of the first. The intervals were the intervals: fourteen months between the first and the second, three between the second and the third, six between the third and the fourth, and the boundary moving twice as far across the last gap as it had across either of the prior two. The redness on the inside of Klaus's left forearm at the wrist had spread from a coin the diameter of a dime when the bartender at the Maritim had pushed the glass across the bar in the summer of 1990, to a coin the diameter of a quarter by July of 1992, to something approaching a small saucer at the inner edge of the cuff by the morning Calder had stood across the kitchen from him at Vila Praia three weeks earlier. The body was doing, slowly and then less slowly, what the dose at Hanover in the summer of 1990 had instructed it to do.

He had not looked at the inside of the watchband since the fourteenth of August. He would look in the morning. He suspected the suspicion was the looking. The contingency Klaus had described to Eddie in October had been the work of some months away then. By the morning Calder stood on the jetty it was the work of some weeks. The weeks were getting shorter.

He thought about Hannah and Heike in Berlin with the small green file from Marzahn in the safe of a flat on the Crellestrasse and the further file Hannah had been compiling, in her quiet discipline, on the specific question of who had given the order for her brother's death in Devon in August of 1988.

He thought about Eddie in Lisbon with the private tremor in his right hand that he had set under the table at the Vigo taberna.

He thought about Ilona Zsigmond, who had been interviewed three times by the architecture since April—once by a man calling himself a colleague of Adler's from the Klassische Studien, once by a Vienna police inspector who had not given a name, and once, in July, by a woman in a beige raincoat who had stood in the doorway and not been invited in. Ilona had been consistent across the three. She had heard nothing on the night of the kill. She had been in her kitchen with the radio on. The radio had been a Hungarian-language broadcast from Budapest. She had not opened her door. By Klaus's reading through a Hungarian contact at the embassy, she had moved in July to live with her sister in Eger. The architecture had not, by August, sent a fourth visitor. The architecture's silence was, by Klaus's discipline, not the same as its absence. He filed her, also, in the place where he filed the things the work was not yet finished with.

He thought about Dina Sharabi. She was alive. She was not on the list. The list was the architecture. Dina Sharabi was the instrument the architecture had used on the third of January 1990 at eighteen-fourteen in a workroom on Webber Street, and the work did not yet have a category for instruments. Calder did not know where Dina was. He had not asked. The not-asking was a discipline he suspected would not hold for the full term of the work. He filed her, for the moment, where he had been filing her since the kitchen of the Bermondsey flat. He went on.

He thought about Vinciguerra in Rome at his desk on the Via Giulia, with the green-leather inkwell that had been his father's. He was, by Margaret's reading, finalizing the careful Latin paper for the Studi e Documenti of the autumn issue. A single pencil correction in the margin of a paper sent to him from a small Portuguese address through the Pontifical Academy's correspondence channel would, by the third Sunday of October, have given him the operational fact of where Margaret was and where Margaret was going to be on the eighteenth.

He thought about the nineteen names on the master list, of which six were now struck through.

He thought about the fifty-seven dots on Margaret's hand-drawn map of Europe.

He thought, also, about something he had not let himself name. He was keeping a catalog he never intended to keep. The entries were expressions. He had no name for it. It was the file of last faces. He kept the file in the discipline of not naming it. He had seven. The second hire at Greenwich, whose pupils had told him at the last second that he had been specified by weight and not by name. Vernet across the Marseilles tray, who had understood across his coffee that the operation he had signed off on the previous autumn had been the operation that would end him. Christofi in the Brussels kiosk, which had been no expression at all, because the round had taken him before he had completed the half-second of registering Calder. Brückner at the stove on the Lychener Strasse, who had decided, in the last second, that the deciding had been the right decision. Adler on the Sonnenfelsgasse landing, who had decided that the deciding had not been the right decision and had decided, in the same second, not to say so. Iturbe in the Bilbao doorway, whose last attention had chosen the second movement of the Brahms over the man who had spoken his name. Thornley in

Room 14 at the Hôtel du Théâtre, whose expression had been the expression of a clock at the moment of its stopping—not resistance but the specific quality of a mechanism that had run its course and been stopped. The catalog had seven entries. The catalog carried a cover Calder never intended to give it. The cover was that he opened the file each morning when shaving. He opened it again at Pasaia in May when Margaret handed him the second box. He opened it again on the jetty at Vila Praia tonight. He expected the catalog, by the end of the work, to stand at nine when Hjorth and Akritas had been added to it, and to stand higher than nine if the men at the corner table on the Piazzetta of Capri on the eighteenth of October required it. He held the catalog where it was. He went on.

The bell-buoy did its work.

The Atlantic was the Atlantic.

After fifty minutes he walked back up the cobbled path to the tide-mill. He climbed the small wooden stairs to the flat. He came in. Margaret was at the kitchen table with the green notebook and a cup of tea half-drunk and the lamp on. Klaus was at the second chair with the small testing kit Eddie had sent and a sample of the local vinho verde he had not yet drunk.

Calder said: 'Lillehammer.'

Klaus said: 'Lillehammer.'

Margaret looked up from the notebook. She did not speak. She nodded once.

Calder sat down at the third chair. He took the leather notebook from the inside left pocket of his coat. He opened it to the pencil page. He read it through.

The page had been a single sheet of cheap-grade ruled paper since the eleventh of February 1990, when Calder had taken it from the second leaf of the leather notebook and had committed the first two names to it on the morning he had begun the work. The paper had aged twenty months in his coat pocket against his ribs and a further nine months against the inside lining of the leather notebook, and it had taken on, by the weight of the carrying, the specific cream color cheap paper took on when it had been carried by a man who had been the man carrying it. The hand was the same hand throughout. Each strike-through bore, in pencil also, in his careful right-leaning hand, a small dated annotation in the margin opposite the entry.

The page read:

1. ~~Vernet, Henri. Marseilles.~~—13 III 1990. The first. The Welrod's first. Hands shook for three minutes.

2. ~~Brückner, Wolfgang. Berlin.~~—2 IV 1991. Daughter at the kitchen door. Witness. Brückner's last expression: the deciding had been the right decision.

3. ~~Christofi. Brussels.~~—12 II 1991. Phone kiosk. The kill of the second. He had not finished his second of registering me.

4. Heike Brückner-Vollmer. Berlin. Witness.—not on list. now operational. fourth. by H.D.'s discipline since 7 VII 1992.

5. Hannah Doyle. Geneva, Berlin. Third operative.—not on list. Pascal channel since 14 X 1991.

6. ~~Adler, Friedrich. Vienna.~~—24 III 1992. The Sonnenfelsgasse landing. Had decided to come out three nights earlier. Letter to Margaret in inside pocket. Buckram running account in breast pocket. The calendar was correct. The calendar was wrong by three days. The cost is the work.

7. ~~Iturbe, Eñaut. Bilbao.~~—8 VII 1992. Café Iruña doorway, Car-

nicería Vieja. Brahms second movement in his head at the moment of the round. The sixth expression.

8. ~~Thornley, L.H. Lausanne.~~—18 VII 1992. The wire. The Belgian primer. The filing. The administrator. The clock.

9. Hjorth, Olaf. Lillehammer.—20 IX 1992 confirmed. Cathedral park, third bench, eastern gate. Pigeons since 1985.

10. Akritas, Theodoros. Athens.—17 XI 1992 estimated. Plaka taverna courtyard. Tuesday lunch.

11. Vinciguerra, Augusto. Rome—off list.—18 X 1992 Capri Piazzetta, Caffè Senafine. The conversation, not the kill. M's reading is sound. Adveniam ad te.

12–17. The remaining six in Trastevere.—names: pending. timeline: 1993–1994. method: t.b.d.

He read it through.

He read it through a second time.

He registered, in the second reading, that the page was no longer the operational document it had been in February of 1990 when it had begun with a question mark. The page had become, over twenty-nine months, a private record of the work: each entry annotated with the date of its closure and the specific physical or moral fact that had attended the closing. The page was therefore not only the operational record of the men who had been killed and the men who would be. The page was the small accumulated moral arithmetic of a single man's twenty-nine months in the discipline of doing the killing. Each strike-through was a date. Each annotation was a fact about the man at the moment of his dying. The list was, by the discipline of the man writing it, a private liturgy of the dead.

He closed the notebook on the page.

He did not write anything new.

He folded the cover closed.

He set it on the table between his cup and Margaret's.

He said: 'In the morning.'

Margaret agreed: 'In the morning.'

Klaus said: 'In the morning.'

The three of them sat at the table for an hour. The lamp was on. The bell-buoy did its small mournful work. The Atlantic was on the other side of the wall. The work of the twentieth of September was one operational sleep away. The work of the eighteenth of October was twenty-nine days away. The work of the next twelve weeks was the work of the team of five on three continents in seven cities in pursuit of an institution that had, by the public arithmetic of the nineteen names on the master list, been required, on the morning of the eighth of July 1992, to stop being an institution that did not exist.

They did not speak further.

At twenty-three-forty-eight Klaus poured the testing-kit sample of vinho verde into the sink.

The wine was clean.

They went to bed.

In the morning Calder and Klaus would leave Vila Praia for Bayonne, for Paris, for Oslo, for Lillehammer.

Margaret would be at the kitchen window when they left.

She would still be at the kitchen window, by the discipline that had been her discipline since November of 1990, when they returned.

The work continued.

The list now had six men struck through and two to come. The Roman conversation, off list, was to be had on the third Sunday of October at a corner table at the Caffè Senafine on the Piazzetta of Capri at nineteen-hundred, with a single sentence agreed between the woman at the table and the man approaching it across the lamp-lit square in the autumn dusk:

Adveniam ad te, et tu venies ad me.

I shall come to you, and you shall come to me.

In the morning, when he stood at the gate of the Vila Praia flat with his coat on and Klaus at the wheel of the Land Rover and the leather notebook in the inside left pocket against his ribs, his ex-wife came down from the kitchen with an enamel mug of tea and stood at the gate without speaking. She held the mug out to him. He took it. He drank. He handed it back. She took it. The silver bracelet at her left wrist made the specific quiet metallic sound the silver charms made when the wrist moved —the sound he had been hearing in the dark of the Chiswick bedroom for thirty years. He heard it at oh-three-forty-two in the dark of the Pasaia bedroom in May. He would carry it, in his head, on the road to Bayonne and on the train to Paris and on the morning at oh-eight-fifteen at the third bench of the Lillehammer cathedral park where Olaf Hjorth would sit down with a bag of stale bread for the pigeons that had been receiving him on second and fourth Sundays since 1985.

He set his right hand for a single second against the wood of the gate, against the wood her hand had passed through that morning on her way down with the tea.

In his inside left pocket, beside the leather notebook, was a small Pascal note Eddie had laid there in early September. The note read: *Bayonne to Vigo to Lisbon to Palermo to Capri. The cars are at every gate. The boats are at every harbor. Walk on.*

He turned.

He got into the Land Rover.

The list was the list.

The work was the work.

The work would continue.

Margaret stood at the gate until the Land Rover was out of sight at the bend in the lane. The wind was from the south-west. She closed the gate behind her, walked back up the path to the kitchen door, and went inside. She stood at the kitchen window for one minute by the small clock on the dresser. Then she made the tea.

Six days later, on the third bench from the eastern gate of the Lillehammer cathedral park, on a Sunday morning in late September, Olaf Hjorth sat down with a bag of stale bread for the pigeons that had been receiving him on second and fourth Sundays for years.

He fed them. He watched them. He did not look at the man who had come up the gravel path behind him.

The Welrod's quiet cough, when it came, did not disturb the pigeons. The 7.65mm Browning round entered Hjorth's back at the eighth thoracic vertebra below the left scapula, traversed the chest cavity in the downward angle Calder had been using since Marseilles, severed the descending aorta cleanly, and exited two inches above the left collarbone, taking with it a fine wet mist of pulverised lung that the September wind blew east toward the cathedral. The bag of stale bread tipped from Hjorth's right hand. Crumbs spilled across the gravel between his shoes. The pigeons did not stop eating.

Hjorth's body settled forward against the back of the bench. The expression on his face, in the second of the registering, was the expression of a man who had come to the bench that morning in the same spirit in which he had come on every alternate Sunday since 1985. He did not expect the morning to be different from the morning before it. It was the expression he had been wearing on alternate Sundays for seven years. It was the expression of a man on the bench he was always on. It was, in the second of the registering, the first time the face knew it was the last time. The dressing-gown blue of the September Norwegian sky behind his head darkened in the specific way the sky darkened when a man stopped seeing it. The blood began to come up from the chest into the collar of his coat in a slow patient seep that would, by the time the cathedral bell rang nine, have darkened the wool to the third button.

The expression was the eighth.

Calder caught the casing in his left palm as the bolt ejected. He pocketed it. The Welrod was now down to two clean firings. The instrument was entering its last operational phase. The next work, when it came, would ask for a different weapon.

He walked east through the cathedral park. The cathedral clock read oh-nine-fourteen. He had been registering the number for some time without registering it. The number was the architecture's. The work had taken it.

The pigeons continued to eat the bread.

At the southern gate Klaus had the window down. Calder registered, in the getting in, the watchband on Klaus's left wrist at the wheel. He had not looked at the inside since September. He looked now. He did not ask. Klaus said: 'Drive or not drive.' Calder said: 'Drive.' Klaus drove.

The list now had seven men struck through and one to come. The Roman conversation, off list, was also to come.

EPILOGUE
PASAIA SAN JUAN

22 September 1992

The post on the calle came up the lane in the early afternoon, on the Tuesday after the third bench at Lillehammer. The postman handed Margaret three pieces—the gas bill, the parish newsletter, and an envelope she had not been expecting.

The envelope was small, heavy, cream. The hand on the front was the careful late-imperial Latin script of a man trained by the same Roman discipline she had been trained by—a man named Caracciolo whom she had cited twice in 1986 and once in 1988 without his knowing she had been the citing hand. She had read this hand twice before in the Schriftenreihe, both times unsigned, both times unmistakable by the specific lateral curve of the lowercase r—a Roman discipline of a generation now mostly gone. The hand had not changed in six years. The envelope had no return. The seal on the back was a small wax disk the color of dried blood.

She thanked the postman in Spanish. She closed the gate. She walked to the kitchen and set the envelope on the table beside the geraniums.

She made tea. She drank half of it. She did not look at the envelope. The clock on the dresser moved through nine minutes she did not register.

Then she lifted the envelope. She broke the seal. She read the lines inside.

The lines were in Latin. The hand was Caracciolo's careful unhurried late-imperial. The lines read:

Margareta, sedes septima tibi vacat.

Pacem offerimus.

Roma exspectat. Quid enim ni sic?

She read the four lines twice. She read them a third time. Margaret, the seventh seat awaits you. We offer peace. Rome awaits. What else would one do? The Latin was the Latin of a man who expected her to read it without assistance. She could. She had been reading it for nine years.

She did not move from the table for several minutes.

Then she folded the paper along its three creases. She placed it inside the envelope. She placed the envelope inside the leather notebook beside the small pencil entry that read 12. She closed the notebook.

She stood at the kitchen window. The wind was from the southwest. She watched it move the small gray light across the stone of the breakwater.

She did not write back. She stood at the window and registered, in the small cold light of the breakwater, that the woman who had built a network of seven to destroy the institution's seven was now being offered the seventh chair at the institution's own table. The arithmetic was the architecture's. The arithmetic had always been the architecture's. She had been working inside it for nine years without seeing that the number she had chosen was the number they would offer her.

She did not, that evening, mention the envelope at the kitchen table where Calder and Klaus were marking the small map of the Capri harbor with the four points of the Roman conversation. Calder looked at her once across the table—the long slow look of a man who had been reading her face for thirty years—and did not ask. She did not offer.

The envelope stayed in the leather notebook.

It was still there on the morning of the seventeenth of November.

Pax in tutela

ABOUT THE AUTHOR

STEN SVEHN was born in Oslo and has lived and worked across Northern Europe, the United Kingdom, and the United States. He spent two decades in roles that required him to understand how institutions communicate, how information moves, and what makes it into the official record.

His nonfiction book, *Survival Over Service*, examined the documented history of institutional self-preservation across the major intelligence agencies.

The Line Between Lies, *The List*, *The New Fire*, and *Auspex* are his first novels.

www.ingramcontent.com/pod-product-compliance
Lightning Source LLC
LaVergne TN
LVHW100504110826
845146LV00002B/510

9798995166795